P9-BZI-984

WINDY CITY BLUES

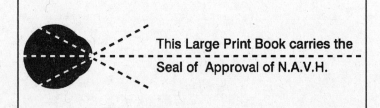

This Large Print Book carries the
Seal of Approval of N.A.V.H.

WINDY CITY BLUES

RENÉE ROSEN

THORNDIKE PRESS
A part of Gale, Cengage Learning

GALE
CENGAGE Learning·

Farmington Hills, Mich • San Francisco • New York • Waterville, Maine
Meriden, Conn • Mason, Ohio • Chicago

GALE
CENGAGE Learning®

Copyright © 2017 by Renée Rosen.
Thorndike Press, a part of Gale, Cengage Learning.

ALL RIGHTS RESERVED
This is a work of fiction. Names, characters, places, and incidents either are the products of the author's imagination or used fictitiously and any resemblance to actual persons, living or dead, business establishments, events, or locales is entirely coincidental.
Thorndike Press® Large Print Historical Fiction.
The text of this Large Print edition is unabridged.
Other aspects of the book may vary from the original edition.
Set in 16 pt. Plantin.

LIBRARY OF CONGRESS CATALOGING-IN-PUBLICATION DATA

Names: Rosen, Renée, author.
Title: Windy city blues / by Renée Rosen.
Description: Large print edition. | Waterville, Maine : Thorndike Press, a part of Gale, Cengage Learning, 2017. | Series: Thorndike Press large print historical fiction
Identifiers: LCCN 2017012451| ISBN 9781432840587 (hardcover) | ISBN 1432840584 (hardcover)
Subjects: LCSH: Jewish women—Fiction. | Blues musicians—Fiction. | Interracial dating—Fiction. | Race relations—Illinois—Chicago—Fiction. | Chicago (Ill.)—History—20th century—Fiction. | Large type books. | BISAC: FICTION / Historical. | FICTION / African American / Historical. | FICTION / Literary. | GSAFD: Historical fiction.
Classification: LCC PS3618.O83156 W56 2017b | DDC 813/.6—dc23
LC record available at https://lccn.loc.gov/2017012451

Published in 2017 by arrangement with The Berkley Publishing Group, an imprint of Penguin Publishing Group, a division of Penguin Random House, LLC

Printed in the United States of America
1 2 3 4 5 6 7 21 20 19 18 17

*To John Dul for sharing your love of music
with me as well as your heart.*

ACKNOWLEDGMENTS

When it comes to writing a novel, it takes a village. At least for me it does, so here is my heartfelt thanks to all those who helped make this book possible.

In terms of my research for *Windy City Blues,* you'll see a complete list of sources in my author's note, but I am also very grateful to Lorra Rudman, who asked, "Do you know Pam Chess?" From there I had the great pleasure of speaking with Pam, who in turn put me in touch with her brother, Terry Chess, and his wife, Roberta. The Chess family graciously shared many stories about growing up with their father, Phil Chess, and their uncle Leonard Chess. Terry was also kind enough to provide me with a copy of *Who Do You Love,* a movie about Chess Records. Without the support of the Chess family and their willingness to trust me with their memories, I could not have written this book with the kind of authenticity I tried to convey.

Special thanks as well to Keith Dixon, who was a tremendous help and shared many stories with me about his late grandfather, Willie Dixon, the famous blues musician, songwriter and producer. His contributions to the Chicago blues, as well as rock 'n' roll, are ever present.

My brother, Jerry Rosen, led me to Shelley Stewart, who greatly influenced the character of Red Dupree and helped me take this book to a new level. Shelley is an inspiration and played a pivotal role in what he calls the human rights movement. If I could, I would put a copy of *Mattie C.'s Boy: The Shelley Stewart Story* by Don Keith into the hands of everyone who thinks life has been unfair to them.

Thank you to my friend Julie Anderson, who came through for me with a coveted copy of *Record Row,* for turning me onto *Born in Chicago* and for introducing me to Syl Johnson, who graciously invited us to his home and shared his recollections of Chess, Vee-Jay and the Chicago blues of the fifties and sixties.

The original Maxwell Street sadly no longer exists, but thankfully blues musician Bonnie McKeown put me in touch with Steve Balkin, one of the leading experts on Maxwell Street. Over lox and bagels Steve explained the importance of what was known as Jewtown to Chicago and especially to the birth of the

Chicago blues.

Dr. Irving Cutler gave me a guided tour of the old Lawndale neighborhood and what used to be the Maxwell Street market. He also took me by the home that the Chess brothers grew up in on Karlov Avenue. His books have served as valuable reference material for me.

Along the way I was lucky enough to meet blues guitarist Chuck Crane and blues singer Gail Reid. Their insights and generosity and friendship are much appreciated. If you are in Chicago, go see them at Linda's Place — you can thank me later!

I'd like to thank Teddy Johnson, owner of Teddy's Juke Joint in Zachary, Louisiana. This is a must-see for those who love the blues. Teddy, you are the real deal. Thank you for your hospitality.

To Phil Ranstrom, who, thanks to a shipping error, hand delivered his brilliant documentary film *Cheat You Fair* and stuck around long enough for us to become friends.

My education in blues music began with a stack of CDs from Manny Utset, who is still patiently waiting for their return. My friend Chris Lee was good enough to read this manuscript, and his friendship and support are much appreciated. Thank you to Linda Yellin for her challah metaphor and to Trish Haywood for vetting this book for historical musical accuracy. Additional thanks go out to Jennifer Fisher for her early read and to Andrew Grant for helping me navigate through 1958 London.

I also want to express my appreciation to Joanne Steinback and Ed Finkelstein for their efforts and support for this project in its earliest stages.

A shout-out to those who came to my rescue when I needed a title — especially Stephanie Nelson, who spent much time brainstorming with me and the three people who all came up with the title *Windy City Blues:* Caryn Sandler Strean, Sara Jordan-Heintz and Berkley's own Executive Director of Publicity, Craig Burke — thank you, all! Great minds think alike.

I am extremely fortunate to have the support and wisdom of publishing's very best in my corner. My trusted agent, Kevan Lyon, continues to shepherd my career and soothe my panicky moments. Her assistant and fellow agent, Patricia Nelson, has been instrumental along the way with her razor-sharp eye. At Penguin Random House, the Berkley team is extraordinary, starting with Claire Zion, my editor, who has helped me grow with each book and was the first to say those magic words: "What about the blues?" Lily Choi, who gave us one final and thoughtful read. Craig Burke (again), Danielle Dill and Ryanne Probst, who all work tirelessly to publicize my titles, and Jeanne-Marie Hudson and Fareeda Bullert and all the wonderful folks behind the scenes in marketing who have done an outstanding job promoting my work. Thanks also to Yuki Hirose for her legal expertise. My local sales reps Stefan Moorehead and my dear friend and confidante Brian Wilson — thank you from the bottom of my heart.

Speaking of friends — Karen Abbott, Tasha Alexander, Stacey Ballis, Lisa Kotin, Kelly O'Connor McNees, Amy Sue Nathan, Marianne Nee, Javier Ramirez and the Sushi Lunch Bunch — you make the isolated writing life much less lonely. A special thought of thanks to the late Joe Esselin — you are deeply missed.

To my special girls, Sara Gruen, Brenda Klem and Mindy Mailman — I love you all.

Special love and gratitude for all the support of my family: Debbie Rosen, Pam Rosen, Jerry Rosen, Andrea Rosen, Joey Perilman and Devon Rosen.

To John Dul, who has been part of this book from the very beginning, who rode the Blues Highway with me and has taken me and this book further than I could have imagined — I love you.

Lastly, thanks to all the people who traveled near and far to make Chicago their home, bringing their music and traditions with them.

The blues had a baby and
they named it rock 'n' roll.
— McKinley Morganfield,
a.k.a. Muddy Waters

PROLOGUE:
"SWEET LITTLE ANGEL"

1933

She did her worshipping from the hood of a rusted-out Chevrolet in a junkyard on Twenty-ninth and State Street across from the church. Leeba Groski felt closer to God there than she ever did in a synagogue. It was a Sunday morning and she'd tagged along with the neighbor boys, Leonard and Phil Chess. They sat three in a row on the hood, their feet resting on the bumper while they listened to the gospel music pouring out of the church's open door and windows. Even in Chicago's August heat the piano music and voices gave Leeba goose bumps as she clapped and sang along to "Jesus Gave Me Water." Leeba didn't have a great voice, but when she sang you couldn't hear her accent. If she could, she would have said everything in a song.

She was seven years old when her family arrived from Poland. The only English word she knew back then was *okay*. So everything

15

was *okay.*

"How old are you?"

"Okay."

"Where do you live?"

"Okay."

"Stupid kike."

"Okay."

Now she was eleven, sitting in a junkyard singing without holding back, tapping her toes inside her hand-me-down shoes. Music so magical, it made her body move, her fingers snapping as effortlessly as her heart pumped, as her lungs took in air. As Leeba swayed to the music all else disappeared. Gone were the rows of decrepit autos, the chain-link fence, the scent of gasoline and the stench from the nearby stockyards. Even the empty liquor bottles and trodden trash on the ground vanished. All that existed in that moment was the music. She surrendered to it, letting it lift her up inside.

When the song ended, Leonard tapped her on the shoulder, offering her a Lucky Strike before cupping his hand around a match, blocking the wind while he lit his. He was sixteen and had been smoking for as long as Leeba could remember. Phil, four years younger and enamored of his big brother, patted down his flattop and reached for a cigarette of his own. Leeba contemplated trying one, until she became distracted by a young girl standing outside the church in a flowing white robe, the breeze catching her sleeves, billowing them up like angel wings. The young girl with skin the color of cocoa tilted her head toward the heavens and opened wide, singing "Move On Up a Little Higher." The words boomed from her with a force that seemed to shoot forth from the earth and move through her. Leeba watched, listened, astonished. Was *that* coming from her?

"Motherfucker," said Leonard, as that was his favorite word, suitable for any and all occasions and often employed as a term of endearment.

"Yeah, motherfucker," said Phil, nodding. He liked that word, too, mostly because Leonard liked it so much.

When the song was over, the singing angel kicked a cluster of pebbles that sent dust across the lot before she was summoned back inside the church.

"Boys, get back to work," Mr. Chess called out in a thick Yiddish accent. He owned the junkyard and Leonard and Phil worked there in the summertime and on weekends. "Boys," he called again. "We have lots to do."

One by one they slid off the car hood, the brothers darting their cigarettes to the ground. The music in the church had stopped. There was no piano, no singers, just barking dogs, horns honking in the distance and the preacher delivering his sermon. The

17

junkyard lost its sanctity and Leeba found herself back in a land of broken headlights and shattered windshields. Her friends had things to do, and Leeba was left with a long day to fill all by herself. Jacks, solitaire, her jump rope, a library book, the piano — she contemplated her substitute playmates.

Leeba left the brothers to stack tires and headed toward the bus, shuffling along in Cousin Eli's shoes. They were a size too small for him and a size too big for her, but her mother wouldn't spend the money for a new pair. *Why, when those are perfectly good?* Leeba polished and buffed them, but still they looked like boys' shoes that didn't fit. It was bad enough that she was taller than the other girls, taller than the boys, too. In the fifth grade she already stood five-four and she wasn't done yet. Other mothers urged their children to stand up straight, shoulders back. But fearing her height would scare off the boys, Leeba's mother never corrected her for slouching, her torso sunk in like a *C.* And even then she still towered over her class- mates. Her father said her long legs were a fluke. Even the men in her family — on both sides — struggled to reach five-seven.

Twenty minutes later the bus dropped Leeba off in a section of Chicago called Lawndale. The Groskis lived over there on a shady, tree-lined street where everyone knew everyone else. Their house in the center of

Karlov Avenue was a simple four-flat with a brick exterior. They had the first-floor apartment, three rooms for the four of them: Leeba's parents; her younger sister, Golda; and her. Compared to how they'd lived in the shtetl, their village in Poland, this was a castle. Uncle Moishe, Aunt Sylvie and Cousin Eli had the apartment across the hall.

Leonard and Phil Chess lived in the building next door on the second floor. Leeba's mother was the only person who still referred to them by their Polish surname, Czyz. She called the parents Cryla and Yasel instead of Cecile and Joseph. They never corrected her, but the boys, Lejzor and Fizsel, were quick to remind her that they only answered to Leonard and Phil. The Chess family had come over in 1928, a year before the Groskis, but to Leeba they were true Chicagoans who had American names and ate hot dogs and spoke English, their accents beginning to fade as beautifully as a setting sun.

Leeba entered the small foyer to the building where the wallpaper curled away from the corner seam. The hallway smelled of boiled cabbage. Her mother was cooking again. Leeba wiped her big shoes on the welcome mat with *Shalom* running across the burlap in black Hebrew letters.

"Leeba, iz az ir?" her mother called out when she opened the front door.

Leeba saw the tips of her mother's pink

19

slippers poking out of the kitchen alcove. *"Ya, Mama, ikh bin heym."*

Yiddish was the only language spoken in the Groski home because Leeba's mother had never learned English. She claimed she had no use for it, whereas Leeba found it a necessity, even if confounding. When was a *kernel* something that got caught in your teeth and when was it an army officer? Words like *choir, knife* and *gnat* — even more puzzling. She wrestled with words in her diary, in the poems she wrote, in the little songs she made up. She mentally rehearsed each time she spoke, wanting only to sound American.

With the church music fresh in her head, Leeba went into the living room and sat at the piano. It was a secondhand upright with keys as yellowed as an old woman's teeth and an F key that stuck in humid weather. Her father had splurged on the piano after her teacher at Theodore Herzl School realized Leeba could play by ear. If she heard a song enough times she could play it back note for note. How her fingers knew which keys to strike she didn't know, couldn't explain. From the age of ten Leeba had taken private lessons at the J.P.I., the Jewish People's Institute, on Douglas Boulevard. But even before that she had taught herself to play "Stormy Weather," "Sitting on Top of the

World" and other songs she'd heard on the radio.

She got her talent from her father, who had played in a klezmer band back in their shtetl. He still held concerts at their Lawndale home, where neighbors — all of them from the Old World — gathered in their living room to drink schnapps from mismatched shot glasses while Leeba played the piano. Her father accompanied her on violin and Uncle Moishe on the clarinet. Leeba was the center of attention those nights, relishing the admiring looks, the praise, savoring every moment before the song ended and everyone's focus went elsewhere. She knew that this — being able to play like she did — was the one thing that made her special. It was the tradeoff God had given her for being born too tall and with the curls that some called "Jew hair."

While Leeba sat at the piano, the gospel music from earlier played inside her head as her fingers instinctively found the notes, sounding out the melody for "Jesus Gave Me Water." She played that song over and over until her mother called her to dinner, where the rest of the family was already seated at the table, waiting on her. The usual chatter while they ate was lost on Leeba, who still heard the music playing inside her head.

Afterward, she stood next to her mother at the kitchen sink, drying the dishes while her mother washed. Golda was in the living room listening to *The Lone Ranger* on the radio while her father sat at the table building a model airplane out of balsa wood, the smell of airplane glue heavy in the air. While he assembled the pieces, Leeba's mother complained about the *schwartze*s who had moved to Lawndale.

"It's the Glucks' fault," her mother said. "How could they have sold to Negroes?"

"What I don't understand," her father said, pressing two glued sections together, "is why they would want to live in this neighborhood to begin with."

Golda, aptly named for her golden hair, so silky smooth it captured the light in ways that Leeba's never would, came and stood in the doorway. "Does that mean the *schwartze*s will go to my school in the fall?"

"But you don't need to mix with them," her mother said. "You stick to your own kind. You, too," she said to Leeba as she tugged the dish towel off her shoulder. "I am so angry with those Glucks for putting us in this position."

"What position?" asked Leeba.

"Never mind. Dry." Her mother handed her another plate. "I still can't believe it. *Schwartze*s in Lawndale."

The next day Leeba walked down Fifteenth Street to see what all the fuss was about. After listening to her parents, she, too, wondered

22

why a Negro family would want to live in the heart of a Jewish community, where synagogues and kosher butchers graced nearly every block. She turned down Kostner Avenue, a street lined with modest two-flats and factories.

When she arrived at the Glucks' old house, Leeba saw a cluster of young boys from the neighborhood up on their tiptoes, looking through the windows, hands cupped about their eyes, faces pressed to the glass. A peep show could not have been more captivating.

"Look at that radio."

"They have a phonograph player, too."

"Hey," Leeba called to them from the sidewalk. "What do you think you're doing?"

One boy grinned, big, toothy and proud. "We're watching the *schwartze*s."

"Get away from there." Leeba ran up on the grass to shoo them off, knowing that she, too, had gone there to "watch the *schwartze*s." It had seemed like an innocent adventure until those boys held up an ugly mirror. To cover her shame she posed as the protector, shouting louder this time, "Go on now. Get away from there. Leave these nice people alone." As the words left her mouth she bought into her own posturing, feeling superior, even a bit virtuous.

But the boys were defiant and didn't budge until they heard the jingle jangle of the Good Humor Man pedaling his bicycle truck down

23

the block, his handlebar bells trilling. The boys raced toward the curb, circling around the cart, digging into their pockets for coins.

Leeba was still on the lawn when the front door swung open and the newest resident of Lawndale stepped out on the porch. She recognized her right away: the singing angel from the gospel church. She was about Leeba's age and even prettier up close, with fine, delicate features, her hair every bit as curly as Leeba's.

A woman came out on the porch behind her, barefoot and dressed in a floral housecoat, her wiry hair pulled back in a plain gray kerchief. She started toward the steps, her toes teetering over the edge, her brown skin cracked white around her heels.

"Mama, go on back in the house."

The woman was already on the first step.

"Go on now, Mama. Back inside."

That time she listened and moments later Leeba saw her hovering near the window, watching.

"Don't mind her," said the angel. "She get like this sometimes." The girl pointed to the children gathered around the man in the white uniform. "Who's that?"

"The Good Humor Man."

She crinkled up her forehead, confused. It occurred to Leeba that this girl had never seen a Good Humor Man in whatever neighborhood she came from.

"He's selling ice cream."

"How much do it cost?"

"A nickel."

The angel turned and disappeared inside the house, closing the door behind her. Leeba felt ashamed, trespassing on this girl's lawn. She headed toward the curb where the boys were licking and slurping as their ice creams melted, dripping onto the pavement. Leeba had no money to spend on something like that. She had no extra money, period. Her weekly allowance had been cut back to a quarter since the Depression and she'd already spent her money the day before on 78s of Bing Crosby and Duke Ellington at the used record store.

She was about to head for home when the front door opened again and the girl came running down the lawn.

"Can I have one of them ice creams?" She handed the Good Humor Man a dime and turned to Leeba. "Ain't you having none?"

"I don't have any money."

The girl looked at the change resting in her palm and handed Leeba the nickel. "Well, here —"

Leeba hesitated. It seemed like such a grand gesture and she felt undeserving, especially given her motives for being there that day.

"Go on now, go get yourself an ice cream. You pay me back later."

The girls sat side by side on the curb and while they ate their treats Leeba said that she'd heard her outside her church the day before.

"How'd you learn to sing like that anyway?" asked Leeba.

The girl shrugged. "Just born to me, I guess." She looked down and Leeba worried about her cousin's shoes until the girl glanced up, indifferent, as if she hadn't noticed.

After they'd finished their ice cream Leeba brought her new friend, Aileen Booker, home so she could repay her for the ice cream.

As they came through the doorway Leeba's mother stepped out of the kitchen. *"Vas iz das?"* she asked, running her hands down the front of her apron, her eyes narrowing on Aileen.

Leeba explained about the ice cream and her mother shook her head, muttering as she went to the Maxwell House canister on the counter where she kept spare change.

"Is she mad?" Aileen whispered so softly she practically mouthed the words.

"Oh, don't worry. She can't understand you. She doesn't speak English."

"Oh." Aileen paused for a moment. "Well, then, what do she speak?"

"Yiddish."

Aileen made a face.

"Polish," said Leeba, which didn't appear to be much more of an explanation.

Leeba's mother fished a nickel from the canister and handed it to Leeba. "Give this to her and don't take money from her again. You understand?"

Leeba knew by her mother's tone that she was in trouble for something. She just didn't know what.

"Now send her on her way," her mother said. "She doesn't belong here."

But Leeba didn't want to send Aileen away. Other than the Chess brothers, Leeba didn't have any friends, let alone a girl friend her age. Leeba never fit in at school, teased because of her height, her accent, her hair, the *schmateh*s her mother made her wear. Aileen hadn't flinched at any of that — not even her shoes — and that alone won Leeba's unconditional devotion.

Later that night while Golda slept, hogging the covers on her side of the bed, Leeba listened to her parents through the thin walls.

"What can we do about it, Freyda?" her father was saying. "You want she should have friends and now she does."

"But a colored one?"

Leeba heard the bedsprings squeak and the thud of her father's heavy feet hitting the floorboards. "We can't tell her not to play with the girl."

"But you didn't see her. She's dark. We can't have Leeba running around with her."

Knowing that her mother didn't approve of

Aileen made this budding friendship all the more appealing to Leeba. Defiance was her weapon, the only way she could retaliate against her mother favoring Golda. For Golda there was money for shoes. For Golda there was everything. She was the family beauty, the child to hang one's hopes on, not the tall, gangly daughter with the wild curls. Leeba reached under the bed for her notebook and pencil and scribbled the start of a poem in the dark: *A nickel for a friend / A small price to pay* . . .

"We have to put a stop to this," her mother was saying, making Leeba pause her pencil. "What will people say?"

"It's not so *geferlech,* not the end of the world. Would you rather she run around with the Chess brothers the rest of her life?"

■ ■ ■ ■

ONE:
1947–1950

■ ■ ■ ■

One:
"So Many Roads, So Many Trains"

Red

All he brought with him was a suitcase held together with twine and his guitar — a secondhand Stella that he'd traded his pocketknife for when he was sixteen. That summed up his possessions as he rode the Greyhound from Merrydale to the train depot an hour outside of New Orleans. Everyone back in Merrydale knew him as Reggie Smalls, but an hour later, by the time he boarded the colored entrance of the Illinois Central train, he was Red Dupree. Change your name, change your life. "Red Dupree" had the sound of a real bluesman and that was what he was determined to become. A real bluesman.

It was only April but already hotter than a smoke pit, especially inside the train car. Red was six foot four, and when he sat down on one of the wooden seats his knees were nearly up to his chest. He was riding in the Jim Crow car along with the rest of the Negroes.

The other cars had nice upholstered chairs that reclined all the way back, but those were reserved for the white folks. Same was true for the only bathroom on board.

Red's legs were already cramping up and he was only an hour into his trip. There wasn't any room to stretch out, so he had no choice but to keep himself folded up, his hands tucked under his thighs for safekeeping, a habit he'd formed years before. As the train barreled through Yazoo City, Greenwood and Glendora, he looked out the window thinking those towns were all the same. The same lone gas pump at the filling station with another nameless colored man, old before his time, waiting in the hot sun for a customer to pull up. The same plantations that by fall would be nothing but cotton bolls, needing to be picked. More miles of track, more swamps and plantations. He saw men and women gathering corn and pecans, some cutting sugar cane. He could almost feel the sweat running down their backs and those cloth sacks getting heavier by the handful. Being a sharecropper was a dog's life and he wouldn't miss it at all.

He couldn't say the same for his mama, his sisters and the rest of his kin. It was hard leaving them behind. His mama had been so upset when they'd gone to the Greyhound station that she forgot the fried chicken and corn bread she'd packed for him. Oh, how she didn't want to see him go, especially since he was the only man in the family now. The year Red turned ten his father boarded a train heading north and never came back. Red had grown up on the spot after that. His father left them with no money and little food. Even with his mama and sisters taking over in the fields, Red had to do more than his share. Not wanting to quit his schooling, he'd get up at three in the morning, shovel grain in the buckets for the mules, clean the grub hoes and do his other farmwork before heading to class. He reeked of sweat and manure and no one wanted the desk next to his.

When Red's train arrived in Clarksdale, some passengers got off and others came on board. An older couple took the two seats across from him. She had tight gray curls sticking out beneath her hat, her white gloves clasping her pocketbook. Her husband had a cane, his dark brown fingers opening and closing around the curved handle. She smiled, asked Red how far he was heading.

"Chicago, ma'am."

"Chicago, huh? Ain't never been up to Chicago." She adjusted her hat and made a shivering sound. "Heard it get mighty cold up there in the wintertime."

"That's what they tell me, ma'am."

People warned him about the snow and the cold, but he didn't care. Chicago was the place to be. It was where everyone said he ought to go. Enough people say you got a gift and you start believing them. That was what happened when he began playing his guitar. One day Red was sitting on the porch fooling with a Robert Johnson song he'd heard on the radio, "They're Red Hot." He was just messing around when the neighbors started coming over, clapping and dancing. More and more folks joined in and even the stray cats that lived under the risers came out, lying on the grass watching. When Red realized he was the one drawing them all in, he was astonished. They had gathered around to hear him. That unleashed something inside him, something he didn't even know was there. He'd always thought of himself as a shy kid, but no more — that guitar in his hands was a power, a passport that he hoped would open the world to him.

Shortly after that he started playing at juke joints in Zachary, Louisiana, and Natchez, Mississippi, and even up in Clarksdale, where a lot of folks went to make a name for themselves before heading to places like Memphis, St. Louis and Chicago. Now it was his turn to try his luck, see what he could make of himself.

Red craned forward and saw all the picnic baskets in the Jim Crow car. They called this train the Chicken Bone Express because the colored passengers brought food on board since they weren't allowed in the dining car.

His stomach growled and he was sorry his mama had left that food back home. Wouldn't be the first time he'd gone hungry, though. He'd been raised on hunger pangs; he and his sisters would go out to the pump, cup the water in their hands and drink as much as they could hold just to fill the empty ache in their bellies. He leaned up against the window, gradually drifting off, and as the miles ticked by and the distance between him and Merrydale grew, he fell into a deep sleep.

Lost in that slumber he was a young boy again, sitting on the front porch of his granddaddy's cabin. He was begging the old man, who'd lost nearly all his teeth but could still sing, to teach him the guitar. Red had made himself a diddley bow the year before, but there was only so much sound he could get out of a piece of wire nailed to a board. He wanted his granddaddy to teach him the blues.

The first time he held the guitar and mimicked the E7, A7 and B7 chords his granddaddy just taught him, the old man smiled, letting nothing but his pink gums show.

"Put your hand up here, son."

Red did as he was told, pressing his seven-year-old palm against the old man's. Even then his fingers were long, nearly as long as his grandfather's.

"You got the hands of a bluesman. You protect them hands, boy. Don't be lettin' nothin' happen to 'em. With them hands you always be able to make money. You got that?"

"Yes, sir."

"And don't you go tellin' your mama I'm teachin' you the devil's music . . ."

The train whistle blew and Red woke with a start, his hands still tucked beneath his thighs, guarding them even as he slept. He opened his eyes and saw the flashing red lights of the crossing gates as the conductor came down the aisle, calling, "Now approaching Memphis Central Station. Memphis, this stop."

Red was stiff when he stood up. The smells of creosol and smoke blasted him in the face as he stepped down off the train. He had a half hour before they would be leaving again and he was starving. Across the street from the station a green and red neon sign for the Arcade Restaurant caught his eye. He dodged the streetcars and automobiles and went to the colored entrance around the back, where they had a couple of nicked-up tables and some folding chairs. There were mops and brooms leaning against the wall next to a bucket of gray sudsy water. He saw the front room, where the white folks ate, with its big blue and tan booths and stools at the counter that spun all the way around. He moved up to take a closer look at the jukebox — a big bubbler flashing colors as it spewed out Tex Williams's "Smoke! Smoke! Smoke! (That

Cigarette).” Red was fascinated. They didn’t have fancy places like this back home. He was tapping his foot to the music, breathing in the smell of grilled onions and barbecue.

“What you looking at, boy?” one of the waiters called to him.

Red froze up, that prickly feeling rushing up his spine.

“Stay back. We don’t need no trouble here. Go on now” — the waiter motioned with his hand — “get back where you belong.”

All that marvel from moments before vanished, like someone had just turned off the lights, shut down the music. Red saw the way that waiter was staring at him. He’d seen that look before. The first time was when he was six or seven. Little Reggie Smalls was walking with his mama when he stumbled upon a nickel in the road, its shiny edge glinting in the sunshine. There was no one else around who might have dropped it so he slipped it in his pocket. Moments later they passed a candy store and he wanted to get some chocolate, that nickel weighing heavy in his pocket. He started for the door, but his mama grabbed his arm.

“You can’t go in there,” she said.

“How’s come?”

She crouched down and looked him in the eye, her voice sounding annoyed, as if he should have known better. “ ’Cuz you’re colored and that store’s for whites.”

"You mean I can't have no chocolates just because I'm colored?"

"That's right."

But it wasn't right and before his mama could stop him, he had pulled away from her and marched inside the store. The woman behind the counter gave him a surly stare through a pair of glasses riding halfway down her nose. "We don't serve no niggers in here, boy."

As an adult he knew that couldn't have been his first brush with prejudice, but still he'd always remember that incident as the very moment he became conscious of his skin color and aware of how others — mostly whites — saw him as inferior. Now he was a grown man, standing in the Arcade Restaurant, and nothing had changed. And he knew being tall as he was did him no favors. They were scared of a six-foot-four Negro, but didn't they know he was scared of them, too? They had the law on their side. All he had was dark skin.

Another man, with a toothpick parked between his lips, came and stood next to the waiter. Soon a third man with a fat stogie joined the other two. Part of Red wanted to challenge them, but defiance had been beaten out of him long before. As a young boy he'd learned the hard way that giving a white man the wrong look — a poorly timed sigh, a smirk, a roll of his eyes, anything that might have been interpreted as questioning a white man's authority — was enough to get his hide whipped. It was easier, safer, to turn and walk away.

He hurried back to the train station, ignoring the rumbling in his gut. But three hours later, when the man sitting across from him on the train pulled out a barbecued sandwich, Red watched him like a dog begging for table scraps.

He eventually drifted off to sleep only to be awoken by the train whistle and the bells at another crossing gate. Red had no idea how long he'd been out. He was still pulling his surroundings into focus when he looked over and saw an older woman squatting down in the aisle relieving herself over a bucket. He turned away and couldn't look at her the rest of the ride.

By the time they reached Illinois he'd gone stiff again with the aches of a man twice his age, not a twenty-five-year-old. The sun was starting to set and he could see the lights of Chicago coming into view. And to think he thought Memphis was big. Here there were more train tracks than he'd ever seen in one place, a whole tangle of them crisscrossing each other. And the grain silos of the country-side had given way to smokestacks spewing dark clouds billowing into the sky. There were water tanks on the rooftops and the buildings were getting taller and closer together block by block.

By the time he stepped off the train at Chicago's Central Station that night, he didn't know which way to turn. The only thing familiar was that smell of creosol hanging heavy in the air. Even at his size he felt small up against the city, especially when he gazed at the giant clock tower outside the station. People bumped into him, rushing toward their friends and relatives, their arms opened wide. Red felt a twinge of homesickness. No one was there to meet him. He was on his own. And scared. This journey he had dreamed of for so long was now real and all he could think was, *What have I done?* If he had any sense he would catch the next train home.

Instead, he was swept along with the crowd, caught in the wash of the city. Just outside the station a couple of men in fancy suits with rings on almost every finger called out with promises of cheap rooms for let. Red took them to be shysters and kept walking. But he didn't know where to go, so he turned around and ended up back at the train station. That was where he'd sleep his first night. He didn't see signs that said "Coloreds Waiting Area" or "Whites Only," so he found a wooden bench toward the back, tucked his suitcase underneath and folded himself up like a stepladder. He woke cold and disoriented in the morning with his hands tucked deep inside his pockets, Stella at his side.

At least there was a bathroom in the station and again he didn't see any signs for "Coloreds" or "Whites Only," so he ventured inside and ran some water over his face and tried to clean himself up. His stomach growled and he was queasy from hunger, like when he was a child, living on cornmeal and salted potatoes. He needed food, maybe then he could think straight. He didn't have more than a hundred dollars — all the money in the world to him, but it wouldn't go far in a city like this. He had to get a job, find a place to stay.

He stepped outside, thrown off again by the city's welcome, a roaring thunder coming from the streets and sidewalks. Dirty and gritty. And where were the trees? The grass? The only green he saw was on the buses and taxicabs that clogged the roads along with the cars, one right after another. He gazed up at the skyscrapers, wondering if it was true that they swayed when it got too windy. All he knew was that nothing in Chicago stood still. Everything was in motion like an amusement park ride. He wanted to get on board but didn't know how. It was all going too fast.

A man selling city maps for a nickel apiece strolled up and down the sidewalk and called to Red, "Get your map of Chicago right here." He had a big gold tooth in front and wore a brown suit and a sharp fedora with a

41

blue feather rising from the band. "Everything you need to know — right in here — just five cent is all I'm asking."

"No, thanks."

The man came closer. "Where you from, son?"

"Merrydale, Louisiana."

"Louisiana, huh. What's your name?"

"Red. Red Dupree." It was the first time he'd said it out loud.

"You look like you could use some food, Mr. Red Dupree."

"Need a place to stay, too."

"Got any money on you?"

Red plunged his hand in his pocket, felt the lining, a handful of coins and a modest fold of bills worn to the texture of felt. "Not much."

"Then what you need to do is get yourself to Jewtown."

"Jewtown?"

The man pulled out a map and splayed it out flat against the brick wall. "You take this here road straight like this, see?" He traced his finger over a thick line on the map. "That'll take you right to Jewtown. You get anything you need there and you can get it cheap. You want food, clothes, a place to stay, you name it — it's in Jewtown. You need a woman — you need a drink — Jewtown's the place. And you're in luck. Today's Sunday and Sunday's the busiest day down in Jewtown. And, son" — he gave Red's guitar a thump with his knuckles — "you know how to play this thing?"

"Yes, sir."

"Then you get yourself to Jewtown and go make yourself some money."

"How do I do that?"

"You'll see. Just go on now. Go."

Red thanked him — for what, he wasn't sure — and as he was leaving, the man flashed that gold tooth and said, "Now, don't be forgettin' your map. You gonna need this here map. Just five cent is all I'm asking."

Red reached into his pocket and gave him a nickel before he started on his way, walking down Roosevelt Road. The green fields of Louisiana were long gone, replaced by dried-out grass peppered with trash. The dusty dirt paths of home had turned to paved streets. There were traffic lights and horns honking, brakes screeching. People sat on the stoops of storefronts and gathered outside the pool halls, liquor stores and laundromats.

As he walked along he heard music in the distance, growing louder as he passed a sign that said "Maxwell Street — Open-Air Market," but saw nothing for this Jewtown place. He thought he had to be getting closer when he came across a string of stores: Shapiro's Saloon, Hattie Rubinsky's Grocery Store and Siegel's Butter and Eggs. A lot of Jewish-sounding names, thought Red, but still not a single sign for Jewtown. At the next intersection he looked down Canal Street, where garment stores lined the street, dresses and trousers hanging from nails along the torn awnings. At Clinton Street he found still more canopied storefronts. He'd given up on finding Jewtown and turned down another street filled with three- and four-story buildings all butted up against one another, each with a storefront on the bottom. As Red came to a crowded intersection at Halsted and Maxwell Streets he saw makeshift tables crowding the sidewalks, piled high with everything from hacksaws to radios, all of it for sale.

Everywhere he looked there were whites and Negroes — all together, like it was no big thing. That would take some getting used to up here. It had been pounded into his head early on that he was to move silently through the white world, never causing trouble or calling attention to himself. That set up a tug-of-war in his mind, challenging his dream of being on stage and hearing his music on the radio. He had to remind himself that he wasn't trying to be Louis Armstrong or Charlie Christian or any other Negro musician playing for white audiences. He wanted to be a bluesman playing for other coloreds, and that was different. That was okay.

Red saw a man sitting on a wooden milk crate with a banjo, along with a man playing a washboard and another fellow blowing on a jug like it was a bass. It reminded him of a scene from back home. People were clapping and singing along and tossing money into a bucket near the banjo player's worn-down boots. And all the while, white men lined the sidewalks, calling out to folks, trying to sell them socks and umbrellas, nuts and bolts and fishing gear.

The smell of smoky sausages wafted past Red. He hadn't eaten since he'd left Merrydale and whatever was cooking and wherever it was coming from, he was going to find it. He ventured deeper into this Maxwell Street market, discovering different kinds of music on every block: jazz, swing, boogie-woogie.

There was one musician putting out a sound so wild, so unlike anything he'd heard before, that Red had to stop. It was coming from a young man playing a harmonica — a blues harp — but playing it in a way that Red had never heard before, letting out a string of *wah-wah-waaahs.* Cupping his hands around the harp, he was drawing and blowing, his cheeks puffing way out and then going concave as he inhaled, hitting notes that seemed like they were arising from inside him. That was a powerful sound coming from such a slight, scrawny-shouldered kid. Red figured he couldn't have been more than sixteen or seventeen years old. No one was paying attention to him, but Red stood transfixed. And though he couldn't really spare it, he reached in his pocket and tossed a few coins into the boy's empty cigar box. Anyone who could play like that deserved it.

The harp player nodded and Red hung around for one more song before he went off in search of food. People were waiting in line for something called a Maxwell Street Polish. A man in a grease-stained apron stood behind a grill that looked like a fifty-five-gallon drum sawed in half, with smoke rising up from the hot coals. He wielded a pair of tongs and Red watched him turn the thick sausage links before he grabbed a bun, smeared it with mustard and plunked a sausage down inside, topping it off with a heap of grilled onions. Red took his place in line and ordered one. Setting his suitcase down, he swung his guitar around by the strap so that it lay flat against his back and with one bite almost half the sausage was gone. The explosion of rich, hot food in his mouth made him hungry for more and he was already thinking of ordering a second one.

"Easy, now. You gonna get yourself a case of indigestion eatin' that fast."

Red looked up. It was the harp player. He noticed that he had a scar above his left eyebrow.

"You know, you the first person to hit me all day." He shook his cigar box, rattling

Red's tip.

Red took another bite of his sausage and nodded. "You're good, man. You're real good. Who taught you to play like that?"

The young man laughed and gestured toward Red's suitcase. "You new here, ain't ya?"

Red nodded again and licked the grease off his fingers. "Just got to town. Maybe you can help me. I'm looking for Jewtown."

The harp player burst out laughing. "Where the hell you think you are? This here *is* Jewtown. Maxwell Street — all these here streets — they all Jewtown 'cuz Jews own just 'bout every store around here." The young man dragged his shirtsleeve over his forehead to clear the sweat, and when he did, Red saw that he had a gun tucked down in the waistband of his trousers. "So you play guitar?"

"Huh? What?" Red was distracted, thinking about that gun.

"I asked about your guitar playing, man. C'mon now, show me what you got."

Red hesitated for a moment, finished the last bite of his sausage and licked his fingers, drying them on his pants. He reached in his pocket for a pick and placed it in his mouth while he brought his Stella around to the front. Holding the neck and feeling those strings beneath his fingertips was like meeting up with an old friend. Red played a few strings and reached over and adjusted the tuning pegs before pulling off a riff that made the harmonica player's eyes open wide.

"Damn," was all he said when Red played another riff and then another.

When Red began to sing an old Skip James tune, "Hard Luck Child," the harp player pulled the harmonica from his breast pocket and joined in.

When they finished, the harp player said, "Man, you in the pocket. I'll tell you what — first thing we gotta do is get you an electric guitar."

"Why do I need that?"

"This here's Chicago — ain't nobody gonna hear you without an amp. And then you and me, we gonna play down here together."

Red wasn't sure if he was offended by this kid's pushiness or grateful for it. His pride said he was the adult, he should be the one calling the shots, but he was too tired, bewildered and overwhelmed by the newness and bigness of Chicago to take the lead.

"You got a place to stay?" the kid asked.

"Not yet."

"You come stay with me till you find yourself a room or a woman. Tomorrow afternoon we get you an electric guitar and then you and me, we gonna make us a bunch of money."

The map man was right. Anything Red needed was right here in Jewtown.

"Say, what's your name?" asked Red.

"Walter. Walter Jacobs, but the boys 'round here call me Little Walter."

Two:
"Fishin' Pole"

LEONARD

Leonard parked his beat-to-shit Buick at the corner of Cottage Grove and Pershing on Chicago's South Side. He walked down the broken sidewalk cluttered with the previous night's empty pints and beer bottles.

"Morning, ladies." With a tip of his hat Leonard greeted the whores who worked that block.

"We been waiting for you, sugar," said one of the girls, running a finger down her cleavage.

"Not today, girls. Not today."

A few doors down, a man looking like he'd slept in his clothes smiled on the sly and mumbled, "Got a girl and a boy, Leonard. A girl and a boy."

One meant cocaine, the other was heroin, but Leonard never remembered which was which. "Not today, man. Not today."

Leonard crossed the street, pulled a key from his pocket and undid the padlock on the Macomba Lounge. He threw open the door and flipped on the lights. *What a shithole.* A long narrow room with a bar on one side, booths on the other, some crappy tables near the bandstand, a rib-pit kitchen in the way back. The place reeked of smoke and booze. The janitor hadn't come by yet so the joint was full of empty glasses, beer and whiskey bottles, overflowing ashtrays and cigarette butts floating in a sea of spilled liquor on the bar.

Leonard was picking through the slop when Phil showed up, the brim of his hat shading his eyes, first cigar of the day already clamped in the corner of his mouth. Phil was shorter and stockier, but no doubt they were brothers. Same light brown hair, same prominent nose and high forehead.

"I gotta put an order in this morning," Leonard said to him. "We're down to two cases of Old Crow and one of Old Grand-Dad."

"Better have 'em bring over some more gin and vodka, too."

Leonard and Phil had opened the nightclub a little over a year before, after Phil came home from the war. Leonard would have joined the army, too, if it weren't for his heart. They 4-F'd him — not fit to serve because of a weak valve. Bullshit — he could have done it. He'd been running a liquor store down on South State Street and that

51

took plenty of guts, too. Leonard had seen it all there: shoplifters, drunken brawls, hold-ups. Once he knew Phil was on his way home from the war, Leonard had sold Cut-Rate Liquor and got his ass out of there. Opening the nightclub seemed like a step up. They'd found a run-down restaurant in the heart of the Black Belt — Chicago's Negro neighborhood — but that didn't bother Leonard or Phil. Their father's junkyard had been in a colored neighborhood and, besides, property was cheaper in that part of town.

"Did you check under the stools yet?" Phil asked.

"Not yet."

Phil propped his cigar in his mouth and flipped the first bar stool upside down, looking for drugs. The dealers kept their cocaine, heroin, uppers and downers taped under the stools in case the cops showed up and frisked them. Problem was that usually by closing time some of the dealers were so strung out they'd forget to take their drugs with them. Checking the bar stools had become as much a part of opening up as turning on the lights.

"Bingo." Phil held up a package of powder. He went down the bar and checked the rest. They were clean, so he went to the john in the back and flushed it. Phil didn't want that shit lying around. Neither did Leonard, but it came with the territory.

The other clubs closed down around two

a.m., but that was when the Macomba was just getting going. They booked a lot of good acts and word got around. Other musicians came in after their gigs at other clubs. As far as Leonard was concerned, as long as people were coming through the door, they'd keep the Macomba open till dawn. Even if it meant shelling out a few twenties to make the cops look the other way.

The club was doing all right, but it wasn't bringing in the kind of dough Leonard wanted. And he wanted a whole lot of dough. Back when he was nineteen and so in love he couldn't see straight, he'd wanted to marry Shirley Adams, but her father said Leonard would never amount to anything and made her break it off. That changed everything for Leonard and sent him on a quest. He could thank Shirley's father for his drive, his ambition. Even now, more than ten years later, when he was married to Revetta with three kids, he still had this need to prove himself. He wasn't going to let anyone think of him as a loser ever again.

Leonard looked around the room and thought about how much he'd come to hate the goddamn nightclub business. The hours were long; the crowd was rough and raunchy. He wanted out, and since he'd gotten Phil into this mess, he had to get him out, too.

Leonard always kept his ears open, which was how he'd found out about Evelyn Aron and Aristocrat Records. She was a Jewish broad who'd started a record company with her husband's money. The label was struggling and Leonard saw an opportunity. He'd been holding off, waiting for the right moment to approach her, and looking around the decrepit club, he decided now was the time. He reached for the telephone behind the bar and pulled a matchbook from his breast pocket. After he lit a cigarette he looked at the telephone number scribbled inside the cover. Two more puffs and he picked up the phone and dialed.

"Got an act down here you gotta come see," he said.

"Who is this?" Evelyn Aron asked.

"Leonard Chess. I got a club — the Macomba Lounge. Maybe you heard of it?"

"No."

"If you're in the record business, lady, you gotta know about us."

"Who did you say you were?"

"Leonard. Leonard Chess. I gotta —"

"I'm sorry, Mr. Chess, but I really have to —"

"Wait. Don't hang up." Leonard drew down hard on his Lucky Strike. "You gotta come see this kid playin' here tonight. I guarantee you ain't seen nothin' like him."

"And what's so special about this kid, Mr. Chess?"

"He's gonna be a star."

54

Tom Archia was a sax player and singer who was starting to make a name for himself. People came into the club asking where they could buy his records. Leonard wanted to record him before someone else did. He saw recording Archia as his way out of the nightclub, and if Evelyn Aron came along with the deal, then so be it.

Later that night Evelyn Aron walked into the Macomba. Leonard took one look and knew it had to be her. She was the only white woman in the joint and she was wearing the largest goddamn diamond ring he'd ever seen, along with a fancy-schmancy dress that probably cost more than his customers made in a month. She was pretty, though, a redhead with alabaster skin, not a single freckle. She was about Leonard's age, maybe a few years younger — late twenties, he figured. The regulars were sizing her up and she had a glazed, uneasy look in her eyes that told him she was scared, and when he went over and introduced himself she seemed both relieved and shocked.

He laughed. "You thought I was a Negro, didn't you?" People always thought that after talking to him on the phone first. When Leonard arrived from Poland he was only eleven and didn't speak English. Growing up, he was always around colored people — hanging out with them at his father's junkyard and on the fringe of Lawndale where a few Negro families lived. White, colored, Leonard didn't care. He wanted to fit in and not sound like an immigrant. He studied the way people talked, mimicking their phrasing, picking up the slang, so that over time, even though he still spoke Yiddish, Leonard Chess sounded more like a Southern Negro than a Polish Jew.

"Admit it. You did think I was colored, didn't you?"

"No, no, no." Evelyn's cheeks were beginning to match her hair color.

"C'mon, relax." He laughed.

She didn't. He'd heard that she was one of those uppity German Jews, the kind that looked down on those who came over from Eastern Europe. He reminded himself that he didn't have to like her — this was business. So he got her a drink and showed her to a table near the stage. He noticed that at some point she had turned her wedding ring around so no one would be tempted by the stone.

It was showtime and the boys took to the bandstand, where Archia's shiny brass saxophone rested in the stand, waiting for him. He had a drummer, bass player and piano player with him. They opened with a number called "Jam for Sam." Bouncy as hell. Halfway through, Leonard saw the sweat beading up on Tom's forehead and spit bubbling up from his mouthpiece. The piano player was on his feet, his ass hovering a good six inches above the bench, fingers flying up and down the keyboard, while the drummer circled the skins with his brushes. The guy on the upright bass leaned in, his ear close to the fingerboard before he straightened up and spun it around real fast on the tail spike. The crowd loved it, dancing in their chairs, shoulders shimmying, fingers snapping. Leonard glanced at Evelyn to gauge her reaction. She was right in there with the rest of them, nodding, her fingertips tapping out the beat.

There was a burst of applause as Archia moved into the next number, singing about his "fishing pole." He was making eyes at the women who were swooning near the bandstand and each time he talked about his "long, long pole," Leonard saw Evelyn Aron blush.

Tom Archia was still singing when Leonard went over to her table, pulled out a chair and flipped it around to sit sailor style. "So what do ya say, Evelyn? You wanna partner up and make a record?"

"With you?" She looked amused and took a cigarette out of her gold case, waiting for Leonard to offer her a light. "Why on earth would I partner with you?"

"Because it's the smart thing to do."

"How so?" She shot a stream of smoke

toward the ceiling. If she was still nervous she was doing a hell of a job of hiding it just then.

"Take a look around this club," said Leonard. "You see all these people in here? They love race music, but nobody's putting out records for them. That's where you and me come in."

"No, thank you, Mr. Chess."

"What, you gonna keep recording the Sherman Hayes Orchestra and that polka player?"

She took a puff off her cigarette and shook her head as if he didn't know what he was talking about.

"Let me tell you somethin', lady. Your label, Aristocrat, is going down the tubes. It's a goddamn joke."

"Then why, Mr. Chess, would you waste your time with my *failing* label?"

"Because I can help you. You've already shelled out the dough for a license with the musicians' union and you're set up. The problem is you're recording the wrong music. I can turn your label around."

"And do you know anything about making records?"

"No. But you'll teach me."

"Just like that, huh?" She stubbed out her cigarette. "Thank you for the offer, Mr. Chess, but I think I'll pass."

With that she stood up and walked out of

58

the club.

Leonard thought he'd blown it, until one night a few weeks later when Evelyn Aron came back to the Macomba Lounge.

"Would you look at that?" Leonard nudged Phil, watching her flit in like she was a regular. Not a hint of hesitation as she marched up to the bar.

"Hello, Leonard. Nice to see you again."

"I don't believe it."

"I saw that Tom Archia was playing here again tonight. I thought I'd come give another listen. You don't have any objections, do you?"

"Be my guest. I'll even buy you a drink."

She ordered a dry martini and turned her back to Leonard while she leaned against the bar and watched Tom Archia and His All Stars perform. Leonard was trying to get a bead on Evelyn when two thugs up front started shoving each other back and forth.

Here we go again.

Before Big Gene, the doorman, could step in and break it up, Leonard saw one guy reach in his pocket and pull out a penknife, the overhead spotlights bouncing off its shiny edge. The band played through it while several women screamed, grabbed their pocketbooks and headed for the door. Plenty of men left, too. The first knife fight of the evening and half the place cleared out. But Archia and his boys were still performing.

Leonard would have expected Miss Prim and Proper to flee, but damn if Evelyn Aron didn't stick around, even ordered another drink.

The bouncer got rid of the fighters and when the band finished their last set Evelyn waltzed up to Archia with her business card and was out the door before Leonard could confront her. When Leonard asked Archia what Evelyn wanted, Archia snapped the latches shut on his sax case and said, "She's gonna record 'Fishin' Pole.' "

The next morning Leonard went down to the Aristocrat office — if you could call it an office. It was a small space adjacent to a paint store on South Phillips Avenue that Evelyn's husband owned. The room was cluttered with boxes of pressed records and stacks of *Billboard* and *Cash Box* magazines. And while the front of the building reeked of paint, all Leonard could smell as he headed toward the back was Evelyn's perfume.

"Well, this is certainly a surprise." Evelyn looked up from her desk as he stormed through the doorway.

"What the hell do you think you're doing?"

"Can I help you with something, Leonard?"

He was frosted and if she'd been a man he would have thrown her up against the wall. "What are you gonna do with Archia after you record him, huh? You think *you're* gonna sell a Tom Archia record? You think your rich country club friends are gonna listen to race music? Huh, do you?"

Evelyn didn't say anything. He saw a faint vertical line form between her eyebrows.

"No white record store is gonna sell a Tom Archia record," he said. "Nobody *you* know is gonna listen to 'Fishin' Pole' on their radio or put it in their jukeboxes. Now, I happen to know the people who can sell a Tom Archia record and I know the motherfuckers who wanna buy it, too."

Evelyn splayed her hands flat down on the desk as if admiring that colossal ring. He noticed a raspberry rash coming up on her neck. She raised her eyes. "Very well, Leonard. What is it that you want?"

What did he want? He wanted to buy his wife a ring as big as Evelyn's. He wanted to get his brother out of that godforsaken club. He didn't want anyone like Shirley's father to ever call him a loser again. "I want a cut of the action," he said. "I wanna be a record man."

Two weeks later, after the Tom Archia records were pressed, Leonard stood next to Evelyn in her office while she flipped through a clipboard of papers. "I've done some research," she said. "And I've drawn up a list of accounts for you."

Leonard read along over her shoulder, run-

61

ning his hand back through his hair. This was bullshit.

"Now, here are the distributors who sell to jukeboxes," she said, trailing a red fingernail down the page. "Here's a list of record stores and —"

"Let me handle this, would you?"

Evelyn dropped the clipboard to her side and jutted out her hip. "And how exactly are you going to handle it? Do you have a list?"

"I don't need a goddamn list. You want this record to sell? Then let me take it to the people who can sell the motherfucker."

"I absolutely hate it when you use that kind of language with me."

"I know you do."

She clamped her jaw shut. She was seething.

"Look," said Leonard, "there's a market for Archia. So let me go out there and make something happen."

"You are so cocksure of yourself, aren't you?"

He had to admit that yeah — hell yes, he was sure of himself. He didn't know where this confidence came from. He was no more qualified to sell a record than she was — in fact, she was a hell of a lot *more* qualified than him. But he had a gut feeling he could do this. "You can't afford to blow this chance, Evelyn. Now just let me sell the goddamn record."

"Okay, fine. We'll try it your way."

Leonard brushed past her, loaded up his trunk with Archia's "Fishin' Pole" and took off in his bucket of bolts. He had salvaged the Buick from his father's junkyard, put a few dollars into the engine and got the thing running. It looked like hell with its cracked leather seats, stuffing popping up through the corners. The ashtray was overflowing and the windows needed washing. But it was temporary. He promised himself that one day he'd own a new Cadillac and he'd keep it in mint condition.

Leonard was still steaming over Evelyn as he drove deep into the city's South Side. He didn't like her and she didn't like him, but they needed each other. He tuned the radio dial to WGES, one of the only stations that devoted a little airtime each day to race music. The Dozier Boys were playing and Leonard snapped his fingers to the beat. Now, *that* was Negro music. White people didn't get it. And for sure Evelyn didn't.

Leonard understood that when Negroes came up from the South it was no different from when he arrived from Poland. The Negroes came by train, and his family by ship, but it was the same thing. The Jews in their shtetls were just like the coloreds on their plantations. When Leonard heard guys from the South describe their sharecropper shacks, he thought they sounded like his

63

home back in Motele — three rooms, no heat, no hot water, no electricity. His father had brought them to America seeking a better life. It was the same for the Negroes coming north. Only life wasn't always easier in Chicago, whether you were a Negro or a Jew. White America didn't want either one of them here, which was why Leonard felt more comfortable with coloreds than with most white people. Evelyn Aron, Miss Hoity-Toity, would never understand. She'd been born in this country. She'd told him that her family had come over from Germany sixty years ago. She didn't know what it meant to arrive in a new city, let alone a new country, kiss your old life good-bye — no matter how shitty it was — and start over.

That was what he was thinking that day as he headed down Cottage Grove and into the ghetto, where people were sitting in the doorways of their tenement houses, the women fanning themselves, the children playing in the water shooting out of an opened fire hydrant. There was gospel and swing music blaring from radios set on the cement steps and on the window ledges. Leonard pulled up to the curb alongside a stretch of storefronts and opened the trunk. He grabbed a stack of records and went into Decker's Drugstore on the corner.

The uneven floorboards squeaked beneath his feet as Leonard swaggered in. The sweet smell of tobacco and something spicy hung in the air. Decker was a short, husky black man standing behind the cash register, reading the *Defender* — the Negro newspaper. Leonard saw the headline: "Call to End Segregation in Armed Forces."

Decker looked up and let the paper slump. He had a matchstick dangling from his mouth. "Whatchu doin' down here, Leonard?"

"Hey, you crazy motherfucker you," said Leonard with a handshake and a smile. He knew Decker from the Macomba. The guy loved the music they played at the club. After shooting the breeze Leonard said, "You sell records in here, don't you?"

"Depends on the record."

"Well, do me a favor and take a listen to this —" He held out the record to Decker.

" 'Fishin' Pole,' huh?"

"Just give it a listen."

Leonard followed Decker to the back of the store where there was a box of 78s with a sign that read: "79¢ Each, 3 for $2.25." There was a record player on the counter where customers could listen before they bought. Decker set the record on the turntable, swung the tonearm across and lowered the needle. "Fishin' Pole" with all its sexual innuendo filled the drugstore while Leonard made his pitch.

"That's Tom Archia you're listening to.

You've probably seen him at the Macomba."

Decker pulled the matchstick from his mouth and said, "Leonard, since when you in the record business? And the race record business at that?"

"You know me — the only color that matters is green. Now listen right here —" He cupped his hand to his ear as Archia sang about how he was gonna put his long pole in real, real deep.

Decker laughed. "Okay. All right. Give me a dozen and let me see what I can do."

"A dozen? You can do better than that."

Decker ended up with three dozen records and a money-back guarantee if they didn't sell. Evelyn wouldn't like that, but she knew that was how the majors did it, too. Labels like RCA Victor, Capitol and even the independents like Atlantic did everything on consignment. A record store could take five hundred copies, sell one and return the other four hundred and ninety-nine. God knew, he hadn't made the rules — but that was the way this game was played.

After Decker's, Leonard drove to the next stop and with more records from the trunk he went inside a barbershop. The whole place smelled of talcum powder and aftershave. The barber also knew Leonard from the Macomba, but he wasn't biting.

"Yes, I play music in my shop," he said to Leonard. "But no, I don't sell it and I don't *want* to sell it. And I don't want to play that particular song in here."

It went on like that, going in and out of stores. He also met with distributors who sold records for jukeboxes on the South Side. Some took a few dozen copies, others only one or two. By the end of the day Leonard had managed to clear out a couple hundred records.

But there was one more stop he had to make. He got back in his car and headed to Washington Boulevard where they broadcast WGES. They called this station the International House of Air. They had something for everyone: the Italians, the Irish, Poles, the Lithuanians and the Negroes. And when it came to race music the one they all tuned in to hear was Al Benson, the Old Swingmaster.

With a copy of "Fishin' Pole" in his hand Leonard found Al Benson in the booth, sitting before a microphone with two turntables, one on either side of him. He'd just finished playing "Old Man River" by the Ravens and broke in for a commercial message: "It's your Old Swingmaster here, Al Benson, from Chicago's great South Side . . ." He went on to advertise a dry cleaner's, then put on the next record. When the red light flashed off, he motioned for Leonard to come inside the booth.

"Hey there, motherfucker — how ya been?" Leonard gave Benson a hug. Benson, like the others, was a regular at the Macomba. "Got something for you," he said. "I want you to give it a listen. Give it some play."

Benson put another record on for his audience to buy himself more time while he listened to the Archia record. He leaned back in his chair with his arms folded, his toe tapping.

"It's good, Leonard," he said as he removed the 78, put it back in its sleeve and handed it to Leonard. "But I've got half a dozen tunes sounding just like it. And without that business about sticking his *pole* in places."

That was when Leonard reached into his pocket, put a twenty-dollar bill in the cardboard sleeve and passed it back to Benson. "Try listening now."

Benson gave him a nod and returned to his program. That was it. Nothing more was said, but not five minutes later, Leonard was back in his Buick, heading toward Cottage Grove, when he heard Benson come over the radio saying, "This is your Old Swingmaster, Al Benson, with a brand-new one from Chicago's own Tom Archia. Give a listen to 'Fishin' Pole.' "

That was all it took. A little face time and a twenty-dollar bill and "Fishin' Pole" was on its way.

Leonard knew that if the song was taking off in Chicago, it would go through the roof down South. So he hopped in his Buick and

68

went to radio stations and record stores in Tennessee, Georgia, Alabama, Mississippi and Louisiana. He got "Fishin' Pole" on the air and in stores and jukeboxes all across the South. Within a month, it became Aristocrat's first success, selling seventy-five hundred copies.

The day "Fishin' Pole" showed up on *Billboard*'s Jukebox Race Records list, hitting at number seventy-three, Leonard rushed into the Aristocrat office flapping the magazine in his hand. "Did you see this? Did you?" He plopped the magazine down on Evelyn's desk and pointed to the list. "Take a look at that."

"I see." She pressed her fingertips to her temples. "That — that's great."

"That's it? That's all you got to say?"

She looked up and he saw that she'd been crying and he didn't know what to do, what to say. He'd never seen her like that before.

She closed the magazine. "Charles and I are getting divorced," she said matter-of-factly as she plucked a tissue from her desk and dabbed her eyes.

Now Leonard really didn't know what to say. He felt bad for her, but the two of them had been at each other's throats from day one, so for him to suddenly turn into Mr. Compassionate felt phony as hell.

She cleared her throat, fisted up her tissue and pitched it in the wastebasket. "So, I suppose this makes you happy."

He was taken aback. "Why the hell would I be happy that your marriage is over?"

"Let's face it, we both know I can't do this alone. I need a partner. So here's your chance to buy out Charles and come on board."

THREE:
"NEED A LITTLE SUGAR IN MY BOWL"

LEEBA

Leeba had a job at a music store of sorts down on Maxwell Street. She worked six days a week, the Sabbath being her only day off. One Sunday afternoon she was on her lunch break, walking through the open-air market amidst the merchants and musicians, Negroes and Jews, the two most unwelcome people to call Chicago home. She thought about how Maxwell Street was the only neighborhood in Chicago that would have them both and how over time their cultures had braided together, like a challah.

It was a cloudless day and unusually hot for May. The market was packed. Leeba passed pushcarts piled high with everything from used tools to pots and pans and tables displaying hair combs and wristwatches. As she turned the corner, she saw Leonard jogging up to her, breathless and rumpled, pinpricks of sweat along his upper lip.

"There you are," he said, panting. "I've

been looking for you."

"What's wrong? Is everything okay?"

"Wait till you hear this. I'm going into the recording business and I —"

"What? Slow down."

"I'm a new partner at a record label."

She almost laughed. "What do you know about making records?"

"Not a goddamn thing, but I know a hell of a lot about making money. And I want you to come work for me."

"Me work for you?" This time she did laugh. "Not a chance." Leonard Chess was the biggest cheapskate she knew. In restaurants he pocketed extra rolls from the bread basket and always ordered sodas without ice so he'd get just that little bit extra. If she worked for him she'd end up a pauper.

She kept walking, surrounded by the sound of guitars and harmonicas accompanied by the cries of Yiddish peddlers. A merchant with long *payot*s hanging down the sides of his face tugged at her arm. He was selling used shoes and had a handful of laces hanging through his open fingers like spaghetti. She'd been raised in used shoes and side-stepped around him. She refused to make eye contact, the only way to maneuver through the market without getting caught in the schleppers' sales pitches.

"Oh, c'mon," Leonard said, jumping in

front of her and making her stop. "What do ya say?"

Leeba groaned and stopped to face him. They were standing next to a table of hood ornaments and car parts that may or may not have been stolen. The sunlight glinting off the hubcaps made her squint. "I already have a job. Besides, I know more about making records than you do."

"Exactly! Why do you think I want to hire you?"

Leeba worked at the Maxwell Street Radio and Record Store and the owner, Bernard Abrams, had a recording booth in the back with a Presto disc-cutting machine that turned out eight-inch lacquers. Abrams ran a little label out of there called Ora Nelle and each day Leeba watched the musicians come inside — after scraping together enough money playing out on the street — to make demos that they hoped would one day become records.

"C'mon, Leeba. It's not like you're getting rich working for a *chazzer* like Abrams. What's he paying you?"

"Fifteen."

"Fifteen dollars?" He blinked with exaggeration. "A week?" His eyes grew wider. "That's it?" His mouth dropped open, too.

"It could be worse." Actually, fifteen dollars had seemed like a fortune when she started. The first time Abrams paid her, she bought

73

two pairs of shoes.

"You'll make more money working for me."

"Oh, please. And how are you going to pay me?"

"I got money. I just borrowed a ton of dough from my old man to do this."

"How much is a ton?"

"Ten grand."

She hadn't meant to gasp, but it was a staggering amount.

"C'mon, you're always saying you hate that son of a bitch Abrams."

" 'Hate' is a very strong word." She waved a mocking finger at him.

"Admit it — you hate how he talks to you. How he's always flying off the handle, screaming at you. Come work with me instead. I already got the owner to record one of the guys from the Macomba and the motherfucker's starting to sell. I even got it played on the radio."

"Speaking of the Macomba, Len, what about the club?"

"Phil's gonna keep it running while I'm working for the record company. And I'll still help out in the evenings. And when the time's right I'll bring Phil over to the label, too. C'mon — you, me, Phil — what do you say? I need your help and, let's face it, you need mine."

She paused and raised a hand to her brow, shielding her eyes from the sun. "And how exactly is it that I need your help?"

"You want me to spell it out? C'mon, you're twenty-four years old. You're still living at home. I can't remember the last time you had a date or —"

"Good God, Leonard." Did he think she was single by choice? That she liked being half a foot taller than every available man in town? That she wasn't humiliated back in high school to learn that the only reason boys asked her to dance was so they could stare into her breasts? So yes, she'd been unlucky in love. And yes, she feared that she'd never marry, never have children, but why did Leonard need to remind her of this? Especially when her mother had tried to make a *shidduch* between them when Leeba turned fifteen and Leonard was twenty. It never would have worked. He was like a brother to her and, besides, Leonard was still broken-hearted over Shirley at the time. On their one and only date, Leonard took Leeba on a stakeout, the two of them sitting across the street from Shirley's house. They waited for a glimpse of her coming up the sidewalk, silhouetted in a window. *Anything!* Hours later when all the house lights went dark Leonard began to cry. A couple months later he met and married a beautiful girl from the neighborhood, Revetta Sloan. Leeba had been happy for him, but every time her mother saw Revetta and their three children

75

she would say to Leeba, "That should have been you."

"And excuse me," Leeba now said to Leonard, "but what does working for you have to do with my personal life?"

"I just thought this could be good for you. You'd meet some new people, make some money, you know . . . And c'mon, you love music. Remember when we were kids, all of us sitting around listening to the radio, you and Aileen making up songs? You used to play those dirty songs 'cuz your mother couldn't understand the words. Remember that?"

She laughed. She did remember it. She and Aileen would sit side by side at the piano, knowing that Leeba's mother, standing right in the next room, couldn't understand a word of those naughty little numbers, like Blind Boy Fuller's "Sweet Honey Hole" and Bessie Smith's "Need a Little Sugar in My Bowl." They themselves were too young to really understand what they were singing, but oh, how they had fun.

"I always thought you'd end up writing songs or playing professionally," said Leonard.

Leeba folded her arms across her chest and challenged him. "So, what — now you're offering me a job as a songwriter? As a piano player?"

"I didn't say that. I can't promise anything, but maybe someday we could do something with your music. Besides, you know how unorganized I am. I need someone I can trust, someone like you to run the office."

"Aha! So you want me to be your secretary."

He stopped before Jim's Polish Sausage stand and changed the subject. "You hungry? C'mon, it's on me."

The smell of sautéed onions enticed her. "Okay, but only because you're a record man now." She laughed. "Leonard Chess — the last of the big-time spenders."

"Nothing but the best for you."

She smiled and gazed at the links sizzling and spitting on the grill while the raw ones, strung together by the *pupik*s, hung down from the wooden racks, waiting their turn.

Once they had their sandwiches, he pinched a few grilled onions from his Polish, leaned back and dangled the translucent strands above his mouth. They went silent for a moment while they ate their sausages. He popped the last bite in his mouth and in between chews said, "So what do you say? Will you come work with me?"

She didn't answer because she was still stuck on the possibility of doing something with her music. All her life she'd been hearing melodies inside her head. She thought everyone was like that until her piano teacher pointed out that she had a gift. *A gift, huh?* She'd never thought about doing anything with it other than for her own amusement.

The idea of becoming a real songwriter was so lofty it gave her a stir, and she couldn't let it go.

"Will you at least *think* about it?" he said. "Please?"

The look in his eyes was so intense, the hope so palpable. That look alone could make him succeed. "Okay. All right, I'll *think* about it."

"That's my girl." He grabbed her by the shoulders, gave her a rag doll shake and kissed her on the cheek. "I gotta run — gotta meet Revetta."

"Go on." She laughed. "Get out of here."

Leonard went one way and Leeba headed back to the Maxwell Street Radio and Record Store. The musicians on the street were interspersed with the merchants. Armed with their instruments, they were vying for space and access to the storefronts that charged a dime or sometimes a quarter to plug in their amplifiers.

A young girl with tawny skin and braids sticking out like tree branches was playing an upright bass, singing along, slapping the sides of the instrument, stomping her foot to the beat. She reminded Leeba of Aileen and the time she came down here seeking fame and fortune. They were just twelve and Aileen had gotten it into her head that she could be discovered on Maxwell Street. Leeba had gone along because she always went along with Aileen's schemes. Aileen was the riptide whose current never ceased to pull Leeba in and under.

That day on Maxwell Street Aileen belted out Billie Holiday's "You Let Me Down" a cappella. Her voice was so big and bold she drowned out the banjo player across the way. He eventually gave up and joined the others who had gathered around, not believing that this sound was coming from a child. Even Leeba, who had heard Aileen sing hundreds of times before, was stunned. The crowd had obviously inspired Aileen, letting her unlock octaves and ranges and notes that she had never hit before. More people joined the crowd and by the end of the day Aileen had collected thirteen dollars and thirty-seven cents. Something had begun. The whole way home Aileen had talked about making records, being on the radio and going back to Jewtown to perform.

But that never happened because while the girls were down on Maxwell Street, Aileen's father had been killed in an accident at the steel plant where he worked. That changed everything for Aileen.

Leeba paused outside the radio and record store, noticing that the sign — "Radios — TVs — Records — Parts — Sales — Service" — was crooked. She stepped inside the cramped store, a hodgepodge of new and used instruments hanging from hooks on the pegboards along the walls. Near the front window, her eyes landed on the store's one true prize: a used baby grand. A Bösendorfer. She knew the handcrafted instrument had taken eleven months to make, two months longer than the making of a child. The previous owner had taken good care of it, having it tuned twice a year. The only flaw was a scratch on the fallboard, something etched in the black lacquer that reminded her of a lightning bolt. Abrams said he'd sell it to her for six hundred dollars and she'd been saving her money ever since, vowing that one day this magnificent instrument would be hers.

While Abrams was with a customer, Leeba circled around the baby grand using a soft cloth to clear traces of dust that had accumulated from the morning. She caught her reflection in the raised lid, her dark curly hair visible in the wood's luster. After dusting the piano keys, setting off a trickle of notes, she couldn't resist playing a few chords.

"Leeba!" Abrams scolded her. "Back to work." He was an impatient, barrel-chested man with a glass eye that stared lifelessly from the socket. Leeba never knew where to look when he spoke to her.

She went to the front counter, shoved the unneeded step stool out of her way and retrieved a radio from the top shelf where it was awaiting repair. She wrote up the ticket for that and another one for a record player.

When she finished, Abrams had her alphabet-
ize sheet music and sort screws and vacuum
tubes for the repairman.

Later that afternoon while she was replacing a violin string, a deep voice broke her
concentration.

"Excuse me, ma'am, mind if I plug in my
amp here?"

Leeba looked up — and *up, up, up.* He was
well over six feet tall. Then the rest of him
came into view — dark eyes, dark skin the
color of cinnamon. He held a power cord in
one hand and a guitar in the other.

"Would that be okay with you, ma'am?"

"Tell him it's twenty-five cents," Abrams
shouted over.

The guitar player set the cord down and
when he reached in his pocket and gave her a
quarter his hand brushed against hers — or
maybe she only imagined it had.

He went back outside after plugging in his
amp, and she stood by the front window
watching him. He had a long, square face,
and his lips had a pinkish cast to them. She
thought he was attractive, but once he started
with his guitar he became exceptional. She'd
never seen anyone play up so high on the
neck, finding his home along the tenth,
eleventh and twelfth frets, close to the sound
hole. He kept his eyes closed and each string
he picked and every chord he hit registered
on his face, eyebrows inching up on the high

notes and lips pursed firm on the lower ones. Then he began to sing with a low, gravelly growl of a voice that practically vibrated inside her chest.

After that it was hard to focus on work and Leeba found excuses to stand near the doorway and watch him. He had a harmonica player with him, a shorter, younger guy who performed stunts, squeals and rhythms on his tiny mouth harp that she didn't know were possible. That music made her want to move her body, made her forget about her miserable job, and that she only had a dollar and a quarter to last till payday. When she was listening to them play, she wasn't thinking about anything other than how good their music made her feel. She was still standing watching him when the guitar player looked back in her direction. She felt herself blush and had to turn away. She already knew that she would fall asleep that night picturing his face.

The following Sunday the guitar player was back. And he was back again the Sunday after that. Every Sunday for almost a month he came into the store, said hello, paid his quarter and handed her his cord. He seemed shy and polite until he started playing. She saw the way music transformed him. When he played he became charismatic, displaying the kind of confidence that couldn't be faked and couldn't be taught.

She lost track of time watching him, but she couldn't help herself. She knew white girls, especially white Jewish girls, weren't supposed to be attracted to Negroes. Maybe that was part of his appeal. Like the new tighter skirts she wore, knowing her mother disapproved of them.

On one Sunday Aileen happened to be in the store when the guitarist showed up. Leeba was standing off to the side with Aileen, who was pretending to be looking through the record bins, when they saw him walk through the front door.

"Lordy be," Aileen said, splaying her hand across her heart. "That is one long drink of water."

"Shh." Leeba gave her an elbow jab.

They heard Abrams coming up front and Leeba darted back behind the counter while Aileen flipped through the records. "I'm shopping," she said to Abrams. "See?" She held up a 78 as proof.

"Feh." Abrams swatted his hand through the air and muttered, "Troublemaker."

Leeba's pulse was racing as the guitar player made his way up the center aisle with his electric Gibson in one hand, his cord in the other.

"Mind if I plug in my amp?"

"Give it here." Abrams cut in front of Leeba and took over. "That'll be twenty-five cents."

Her heart sank as the guitar player politely paid Abrams and headed back outside. She waited, while her world stood still, hoping he'd turn back around. Just once. Just for a split second. But he didn't.

The week passed with her anticipation growing and on the next Sunday the guitarist came into the store asking again if he could plug in his amp. Abrams was nowhere in sight and so when he reached in his pocket for a quarter she stopped him.

"This one's on me." She smiled.

"Why, thank you, ma'am."

"Your music's swell," she said.

"Well, thank you again, ma'am."

He started to turn away and, not wanting him to leave yet, she blurted out, "How did you learn to play like that?"

He stopped, puzzled, as if he wasn't sure she was talking to him.

"Your guitar," she said, pointing to the Gibson in his hand. "Who taught you to play like that?"

"Oh. It was my granddaddy. He taught me to play." Again, he started to turn away.

"How old were you?"

"I'm sorry?" he said, despite there being nothing to apologize for.

He was obviously uneasy talking with her and she wasn't sure if it was because he wasn't interested or because she was white. "I was just wondering when you started playing — how old were you?"

"Oh, um, about six or seven."

"Six or seven. Wow." She leaned forward, planted her elbows on the counter and butted her chin against the heels of her hands. "You were really young when you started, huh? Did you ever study professionally?"

"Me?" He cracked a smile as if the suggestion was absurd. "Nah, after my granddaddy got me started I pretty much taught myself. I play by ear."

"Really?" She straightened up, delighted to have found some common ground. "Me, too."

He was about to say something — what, she'd never know, because the harp player banged on the storefront window.

"Well, I gotta get out there," he said.

"I really do think your music's swell."

"In that case I'll dedicate our first song to you. What's your name?"

"Leeba."

"Nice to know you, Leah. I'm Red. Red Dupree."

She didn't have the heart to correct him and followed him to the front of the store. Standing in the doorway, leaning against the jamb, she watched him dash off a guitar lick before he said, to no one in particular, "This one's for Leah."

"Leeba!" Mr. Abrams shouted. "Go help them." He pointed to a young couple circling the Bösendorfer. The woman had a lemon yellow pocketbook hanging off her wrist and a matching ribbon in her hair. "But don't talk price," Abrams said to Leeba. "That's my business."

Leeba felt imposed upon, and as she went over, she was offended by the way the woman glided her fingertips across the lacquered lid of *her* piano, leaving a trail in the fine dust that was ever present in the old shop.

"It's for our daughter," explained the husband. "She's starting to take lessons."

"We thought we'd surprise her," said the wife.

"That's quite a surprise," said Leeba. *They're going to give this magnificent instrument to a child — a beginner?* "But if she's just starting to play," said Leeba, "you don't need anything this elaborate. You could save a lot of money by going with an upright and —"

"Leeba!" Abrams flapped his arms. "*Gey avech.* Go away." He shooed her off and addressed the couple. "You'll have to forgive that salesgirl. She doesn't know from good pianos. And this right here" — he tapped the Bösendorfer's lid — "is one of a kind. How much you want to pay? No offer too small."

Leeba felt betrayed and sick at the thought of the piano selling. Abrams had promised it to her. She went back up front to watch Red Dupree, half listening to the music, half to Abrams's haggling. When the husband refused to go above five-fifty the couple left pianoless.

As soon as they were out the door Abrams stormed up to Leeba, sputtering mad. "What is wrong with you? You cost me that sale, you imbecile."

Imbecile? She was in no mood to be yelled at and turned away.

"I'm talking to you," he said, spinning her back around. "Do you hear me?"

"I hear you all right," she snapped. "You're screaming at me." She'd never talked back to him before and maybe she spoke up that day because she knew she had another job waiting for her with Leonard. Or maybe she'd just had enough. How dare he break his word and try to sell *her* piano out from under her?

"One more move like that," he said, "and you're finished. Kaput. You hear me?"

"Don't worry," she said. "There won't be a next time because you and I are kaput. I quit — *you* hear *me*?"

FOUR:
"CHI-BABA CHI-BABA"

LEEBA

The smell of Chanel No. 5 lingered in the air long after Evelyn Aron left the office, heading to the recording studio in her red convertible. Leeba had been working at Aristocrat for a month, ever since she quit her job at the Maxwell Street Radio and Record Store. She was making eighteen dollars a week now — three dollars more than she'd made with Abrams. On her first day Leeba told Evelyn that she played piano and did some songwriting, but Evelyn had been more interested in Leeba's typing skills.

Even so, Leeba found Evelyn fascinating. Smart, clever, so beautiful, so American. She got weekly manicures and wore red lipstick that rivaled her hair color. She dressed in tailored clothes and had diamond earrings and strands of pearls. She kept an extra pair of shoes tucked under her desk and Leeba would have tried them on had Evelyn's feet not been so tiny.

Leeba found it hard to believe that Evelyn was only four years older than herself. At twenty-eight Evelyn had already been through two husbands and owned a record business, although, except for the upright piano and the stacks of *Billboard* and *Cash Box* magazines lying around, nothing there suggested music. The office was just a storefront on Cottage Grove Avenue, but still it was a business and Evelyn owned fifty-one percent of it. Leonard had the rest.

After Leeba reconciled the checkbook, organized Leonard's expenses and scheduled Evelyn's beauty parlor appointment, the telephone rang for the first time that day.

"Aristocrat Record Company."

"I need you to do me a favor." It was Evelyn. "I'm over at the studio with Leonard and we forgot the contracts. Can you bring them to us at Universal?"

Universal Recording was in the Civic Opera Building downtown and there was a time when Leeba would have been too intimidated to venture there by herself. But here she was boarding the Lake-Ashland El at Garfield Boulevard like any other Chicagoan. She got off at the Clinton Street stop and walked the rest of the way along Wacker Drive, proud of how she'd learned to maneuver her way around the city, sorting out the tangle of elevated railroad tracks and bus routes, the many streets and boulevards that fed into

89

Chicago like veins to the heart.

She arrived at the Civic Opera Building. Inside, it was as ornate as a church, adorned in marble and gold. The Universal Recording studio was in a more modest section of the building, in the office tower on the forty-second floor. Leeba's ears popped on the elevator ride up.

She stepped into a lobby with a wall of framed gold records: "Peg o' My Heart" by the Harmonicats, Vic Damone's "You Do" and Al Morgan's "Jealous Heart." She was standing in the very place where those hits were recorded, thinking that behind each song, a voice had been plucked from obscurity. One day they were driving trucks or busing tables and the next day — bam — recording stars. And then there were the songwriters who created those lyrics and melodies that were so infectious and unforgettable. She was fascinated by the talent scouts who roamed the countryside and city clubs looking for that sound, that special something. Leeba was sure Aileen had it. So did that guitar player, Red Dupree. So did countless others she'd seen on Maxwell Street. The city was bursting with talent and she'd often wondered what determined who made it and who didn't.

Leeba waited in the lobby, watching people coming and going, moving in drum kits and amplifiers, microphones and reel-to-reels. A young man stood near her, guitar in hand, his case freckled with nubby putty-colored stickum where some decals once lived. Leeba saw the studio owner, Bill Putnam, coming down the hall, talking to a young man trailing behind him with a notepad in hand.

"Nah," Putnam was saying, "we can't record there. There's too much reverberation. We'll end up with an echo of the echo . . ."

Leeba recalled what Evelyn had said once about the lengths to which Bill Putnam would go to capture a particular sound. He'd been known to sneak musicians and recording equipment into the ladies' room so he could bounce the music off the marble floors and walls. He used to ask Evelyn for Wet Paint signs from her husband's store so he could tape them up along the hallways to keep people out while they recorded.

Leeba waited until the receptionist led her back to the studio. Evelyn, Leonard and an engineer were in the control booth seated in front of a plate-glass window that looked out onto the studio. This was the first time Leeba had been in a real recording studio and it was nothing like Bernard Abrams's booth at the back of his store. The engineer wore headphones as he dialed a series of knobs to the left and to the right. Stray coffee cups and smoldering ashtrays were stationed around. A big reel-to-reel machine on the far wall was going around and around, recording the Sherman Hayes Orchestra, all clustered together on the other side of the glass.

"Stick around," Evelyn said to Leeba. "You can get all the paperwork signed."

Leeba sat on a stool in the back, watching Evelyn, who had taken charge of the session. After another series of takes Evelyn spoke to the engineer about sound levels and phrasing. She guarded the speaker button, her lacquered nails resting on top of it. "Let's do another take," she said to the engineer.

He nodded and pushed a second speaker button. "This is 'Chi-Baba Chi-Baba,' take eleven."

Leonard didn't like take eleven, twelve or thirteen and it was a good thing that Sherman Hayes and his orchestra couldn't hear what he was saying inside the control booth. Leonard reached for the lyric sheet. "C'mon, Evelyn. 'Chi-Baba Chi-Baba'? These guys are a joke."

"I thought you said you weren't going to say anything." She glared at him. "What happened to 'Just let me come watch. I just want to learn more about producing.' What happened to that? Honest to Pete," she said under her breath, "times like this I question why I brought you on board."

"Because you need me, remember? If you'd get your motherfucking head out of your *tuchas* you'd know that."

"Enough." She pounded her hand on the console. "If you must speak, please refrain from sounding like a drunken sailor."

Leonard got up and sat off to the side, a cigarette dangling from his mouth. Evelyn was ready for another take. The orchestra started again, getting two measures in before she stopped them.

The engineer adjusted his headphones and said, "I think they need to tone down the saxophone and the trumpet. The clarinet, too."

"I think it's the tempo," said Leeba.

Evelyn spun around, eyes narrowing.

"I'm sorry" — Leeba said with a shrug — "but the tempo's too slow."

"She's right," said Leonard, back on his feet. "It sounds like a goddamn funeral march."

"It's supposed to be a fun song," added Leeba. "And they're treating it like a ballad."

Evelyn folded her arms across her chest. "Well, I see you both have it all figured out. Tell me, Leeba, is there anything else, with all your *vast* recording experience, that you'd like to add?" Evelyn turned to Leonard. "And what about you? I suppose you want to tell me how to do my job, too. We had an agreement. You do the sales and distribution and I handle the production."

"Whoa" — Leonard held up his hands — "I'm not saying another word. Scout's honor." With a cigarette scissored between his fingers he crossed his heart and looked at Leeba while he crossed his eyes, making her burst out laughing.

Evelyn shook her head, dismissing both of them as she pushed the talk button. "Let's go again."

The engineer hit a button and spoke into his microphone. "Rolling tape. 'Chi-Baba Chi-Baba,' take fourteen."

There were three more takes after that. Leonard paced, slapping his hands to his thighs. The clock was ticking and he didn't want to pay the overtime costs, which Leeba was calculating in her head. They had the studio booked at forty dollars an hour. The sidemen each got forty-one dollars and twenty-five cents for a standard three-hour session and Sherman as the bandleader got eighty-two dollars and fifty cents. Anything over three hours jumped the costs for everyone up to time and a half, according to the musicians' union.

Eventually even Evelyn realized that the last take was as good as it was going to get, so she pushed the talk button one last time. "Okay. We got it. That's it. Thank you, everyone."

The following week the pressed records arrived — thirty-five hundred copies of "Chi-Baba Chi-Baba." Leonard picked up a record and pursed his lips before chucking it back onto the pile. "Never should have pressed this many copies."

Leeba spent the next two days gluing labels, stuffing 78s into sleeves and backing them with cardboard before placing them into packing envelopes. While she assembled the records, Evelyn and Leonard drove around town — Evelyn in her red convertible, Leonard in his beat-up Buick, both their trunks loaded with boxes of "Chi-Baba Chi-Baba." They were trying to get the song into record stores, jukeboxes, drugstores and anywhere else they could think of. But more than anything they needed to get "Chi-Baba Chi-Baba" on the radio.

When Evelyn came back at the end of the day, Leeba knew she was exhausted. She sat with her jacket draped over her shoulders, her head cradled in her hands. A couple of jukebox distributors had said they would give it a try, and a drugstore had taken twenty-five copies, along with a beauty parlor that had agreed to take a dozen. Leonard, who had returned earlier, reported that he hadn't fared much better.

"Are you even *trying* to sell this?" Evelyn asked.

"The record stinks," said Leonard. "You give me something worth selling and I'll sell the hell out of the motherfucker."

"Really, Leonard, must you always talk like that?"

"What's wrong with the way I fuckin' talk?"

Leeba laughed. Leonard relished tormenting Evelyn, and in turn, Evelyn loved lording her fifty-one percent ownership over him. They argued for the sake of the fight, but in the end, Evelyn's extra two percentage points always won out.

A week later Leeba was at the office, typing a letter to Evelyn's furrier about storage for her mink, when she heard the familiar opening chords coming over the radio. Her fingers froze in place above the Smith-Corona. Even before the vocals started, she recognized the song immediately. It was "Chi-Baba Chi-Baba."

Evelyn heard it, too, and dropped down in her chair. She went pale. It was "Chi-Baba Chi-Baba," all right, but that wasn't the Sherman Hayes Orchestra. Leeba noticed red blotches sprouting along Evelyn's neck as the two of them listened, speechless. The disc jockey came on afterward and said, "And that was Louis Prima climbing the charts with his new hit, 'Chi-Baba Chi-Baba' . . ."

"Louis Prima." Evelyn closed her eyes, her shoulders rising and falling as she breathed. More blotches appeared, deeper, redder. Leeba didn't mention the upbeat tempo of the Prima version.

Evelyn rubbed her stomach. "I think I'm

developing an ulcer." She pulled a bottle of Bromo-Seltzer from her drawer. "I can't compete with Louis Prima." Leeba brought her a glass of water and Evelyn stirred in a spoonful of granules, the Bromo fizzing, misting up the insides of the glass just before she guzzled it down. "What are the odds — this can't be happening."

Two seconds later Leonard bolted through the front door looking rumpled, his shirt untucked, his trousers wrinkled, hair jutting out. "Did you just hear that?" He pointed to the radio. "It's the second time they've played that goddamn song in the past hour."

"Stop shouting." Evelyn propped her elbows on her desk and pressed her fingers to her temples. "I can't control who covers a song."

"Maybe one of these days you'll listen to me, huh?" Leonard picked up a copy of "Chi-Baba Chi-Baba" and sent it soaring across the room like a flying saucer.

FIVE:
"SHAKE FOR ME"

RED

Getting to know a new guitar — especially an electric guitar — was like getting to know a woman. After almost five months Red was still getting comfortable with his Gibson, learning her curves, how to hold her, touch her and please her so she'd give off the sound he wanted.

Buying that electric guitar had cleaned him out. Seventy-seven dollars and fifty cents, but at least that included the fifteen-foot cord. The amp was another thirty-four dollars. Red knew he had no choice if he was going to make it in Chicago, but going electric was a whole new sound. He was still getting used to having tone and volume controls to contend with and learning how to deal with the feedback. Sometimes he actually liked the distortion, though, and tried working it into the songs.

But despite the Gibson's fancy features, Red still preferred his secondhand acoustic.

In the quiet of his crappy little room, he'd sit on the mattress — flush with the floor — and lean against the wall and play his Stella. That took his mind off his lousy job at the brick-yard that still left him short after he'd paid his rent, always having to wonder how he'd eat from week to week.

Red and Little Walter had become regulars in Jewtown, playing out front of the Maxwell Street Radio and Record Store. When they weren't on Maxwell Street, they were at the musicians' union hall, a big recreation room with rehearsal booths along one side, card tables on the other and pool and Ping-Pong tables in the center. Two vending machines filled with cigarettes and candy greeted you at the doorway.

One day Red was sitting off to the side with Jimmy Rogers, another bluesman from Mississippi looking to break into the business. Jimmy was fiddling around, playing a few riffs on his new Harmony and talking about Aristocrat Records.

"They're putting out race rec— Shit. God damn it." Jimmy had dropped his pick inside his guitar. "God damn it," he hissed again, shaking it violently upside down.

Red could hear the pick rattling around inside, trapped.

Jimmy kept talking, while still trying to retrieve it. "They got a new owner at the label now." *Shake, shake, shake.* "It's that white man — Leonard Chess — from the Macomba Lounge."

Red knew the Macomba. It was over on Cottage Grove, and each time he went down there he was dazzled by the lights, the cars, all the action. Negro nightclubs lined both sides of the street, but the hottest spot on that strip was this little joint called the Macomba Lounge. He heard Archia got discovered there.

"God damn this thing." Jimmy was still shaking his guitar.

"Give it here," said Red. "I'll get your pick out."

"And how you fixin' to do that?"

Red grabbed a pencil off a nearby table. "Watch." He took Jimmy's guitar and gently shook it until he lined the pick up with the sound hole. Red stuck the eraser end of the pencil down through the strings and held the pick in place while he gave the guitar a quick flip. With it still turned upside down, Red pulled out the pencil and the pick dropped through the strings and landed in his hand. "Here you go."

"Damn." Jimmy looked impressed as he reached for the pick and his guitar. "Now, like I was sayin', if you boys was smart —"

"What do you mean, *if*? I *am* smart. I just got your damn pick out, didn't I?"

Jimmy laughed. "Then you and Walter need to go make yourself a demo and take it to

Aristocrat."

And that was what they did. The next day Red and Little Walter went to the Maxwell Street Radio and Record Store and talked to the owner, a Jewish guy with a glass eye. While Walter haggled over the price, Red glanced around the store at the brass horns, violins, maracas, concertinas and accordions mounted on the walls and at the beautiful baby grand up near the front. He kept looking around, eyes sweeping front to back, searching for that nice girl with the curly hair. It had been months since he'd seen her, but still each time he stepped inside that store his heart beat a little faster at the hope that she'd appear. She never did.

The owner led them back to the recording booth. A big sign over the doorway said "Welcome to Ora Nelle Record Company." It was nothing more than a closet with shelving along one wall, loaded down with sheet music. It was a tight fit with the two of them inside and it was hot and smelled of hair tonic. They recorded an old Charley Patton song, "A Spoonful Blues."

Red was sweating by the time they stepped out of the booth, but he was exhilarated. The owner handed him an eight-inch lacquer disc, his voice, his guitar playing committed forever in those grooves. This was the first real step he'd taken toward landing a recording deal.

■ ■ ■

The next day Red and Walter went down to Aristocrat Records. Red wore a suit he'd bought from a thrift store and freshly shined shoes. Walter slicked back his hair and put on too much aftershave. Red was anxious, nervous. So much was riding on Aristocrat wanting to produce their demo.

When they first got to the building, Red double-checked the address he'd jotted down. It didn't look anything like he'd imagined a record company would and he tried to shrug off his disappointment as they stepped inside.

". . . That's what I'm saying, mother-fucker . . ."

Red recognized Leonard Chess right away from the Macomba Lounge. He was on the phone, cussing someone out while a cigarette bobbed between his lips. An Admiral radio and phonograph took up most of his desk. There was a pretty redhead sitting behind a second desk, also on the telephone, plugging her ear with her free hand to block out Leonard. The third desk, a smaller one, was empty. They had a piano pushed against the wall, the bench piled high with magazines and newspapers.

As they stood there waiting, Little Walter couldn't keep still. He was twitchy, tapping his foot, jangling the coins in his pocket. Neither Leonard nor the redhead seemed to notice they were there. Or maybe they didn't care. The clock on the wall was frozen in time, stuck at a quarter past three. Red had no idea how long they'd been waiting.

"What are we supposed to do now?" asked Walter.

Red cleared his throat to get their attention. Nothing. He was thinking they should come back another time, when a young woman stepped out of the back room carrying a stack of folders. It took a moment before Red realized she was the girl from the radio and record store. That same surge of hope that he carried into the old Jewish man's store each week along with his amp cord suddenly flooded his body. There she was. Without thinking, Red started to smile. She looked up, startled, like he and Walter had scared her. She almost dropped her folders. Red quickly reined himself in, remembering that he was a colored man with no business even thinking of a white woman like that.

He drew a deep breath and set his mind right. "Excuse me, ma'am —"

She recovered with a smile. "Oh — oh, hi." She set the folders on her desk. "You're the guitar player from Maxwell Street. You're Red Dupree."

He was so surprised she remembered him that he was struck speechless.

While he wrestled to think of something to say, Walter spoke up. "We're here to see Mr. Chess. We got us a song for him to listen to, so you just tell him Little Walter's here." He raised the demo, shaking it like a tambourine.

She glanced over her shoulder in Leonard's direction.

". . . I'm done with polka music, mother-fucker . . ."

"He should be finished with his call soon," she said, looking back at Red. "Why don't you fellows stick around."

There were no chairs for them so Red and Walter stood there while the girl returned to her desk. Red felt her eyeing him when she thought he didn't notice and it would have been wonderful if she'd been looking at him with even a glimmer of desire, but he knew better. He was used to white folks keeping tabs on him in their place of business, afraid he'd steal something or start trouble.

"So," she said when he dared to let his gaze meet hers, "are you still playing in front of the radio and record store?"

"Sure are," said Walter before Red could speak. "Every week. Last weekend we was playing for the biggest crowd yet . . ." Walter kept talking until Leonard Chess finally got off the phone.

Setting the receiver down he looked at Red and Walter for the first time. "Who are you?"

"Leonard —" The girl stood up as she

made the introductions. "This is Red Dupree and Little Walter. They have a demo for you."

Red's chest went tight. His heart was pounding. This was it. This could be the moment that would change everything.

Leonard stubbed out his cigarette. "Okay," he said, his fingers impatiently summoning them over, "let's hear it."

"Yes, sir." Little Walter rushed forward and handed him the lacquered disc. "We have a big following down in Jewtown. Every Sunday folks down there be waiting for us and —"

Leonard raised his hand. "Spare me the sales pitch." Leonard looked at the label on the demo. "Another one from Ora Nelle Record Company, huh?" He put the disc on the Admiral turntable and dropped the needle.

It sounded different listening to it in front of Leonard Chess. All Red heard was the poor quality of the recording. The distortion amplified, the scratchy static. He felt himself shrinking under the girl's gaze, feeling her eyes on him. He started to sweat.

Eventually the redhead ended her telephone call.

"You hearing this, Evelyn?" Leonard said to her.

She came over and introduced herself just as the vocals began. She leaned on the desk, squinting as if that helped her hear better.

"Just guitar and harmonica?"

105

Red nodded. The best part — his guitar solo — was coming up and he didn't want them to miss it.

"No sax? No piano?"

"No, sir."

Leonard and the redhead exchanged looks just before Leonard raised the tonearm on the turntable and the music died. "Listen, fellas, a guitar and a harmonica do not a record make. Come back when you have a real band."

Six:
"Bilbo Is Dead"

Leonard

Leonard may not have had a hint of musical talent, but he knew how to spot someone who did. He booked all the acts for the Macomba and when it came to making records, he was learning to trust his gut. Just the other day a couple of musicians dropped off their demo — no sax, no piano, no nothing. He gave it a listen and turned them down. It was like that all the time, guys coming in off the street wanting to audition for him right at his desk. Some he liked and wanted to record, some he sent over to Phil at the Macomba and some, like that guitarist and the harp player, he sent packing.

But even more than his feel for talent, Leonard Chess had a head for business. Every other label, from the majors like RCA Victor and Capitol to the independents like Aristocrat, was putting out records by big bands and crooners. They all sounded alike. Especially the bulk of records Evelyn was producing. She insisted on putting out more Sherman Hayes records and had just signed a new act, the Dave Young Orchestra. Leonard bet they'd sell a couple hundred copies and soon be forgotten. "Fishin' Pole" was the only song right now bringing in any money for them.

Personally Leonard didn't have a strong feeling about race music one way or the other, but at least the songs coming out of the Macomba and other clubs on the South Side were different, fresh. It took some convincing, but after that "Chi-Baba" disaster Leonard got Evelyn to come down to the club to hear another young singer performing there. Andrew Tibbs was a good-looking kid with smooth dark skin, a thick wavy coif and a voice so clean, so sultry it made you sway along with him. The kid had charisma, too, and man, what he did to the women. He was shameless the way he'd look at them, suggestively sliding his fingers up and down that mike stand like he was hiking his way up under their dresses.

Evelyn agreed to sign him and two days later they had Tibbs in Studio A, the best room at Universal. They brought Tom Archia in to back him on the sax and another guy on piano. They had just finished laying down his first song, "Union Man Blues," and there was still some time on the clock so Evelyn pushed the speaker box in the control booth and asked Tibbs if he wanted to record something else.

Andrew pulled a crumpled paper bag with some handwriting on it from his pocket. "Wait till you hear this," he said.

Leonard propped himself on the edge of the control console. Evelyn lit a cigarette. The reel-to-reel was pausing off to the side.

"I'm calling this one here 'Bilbo Is Dead,' " said Tibbs.

Leonard pressed the speaker button. "Bilbo? You wrote a song about that mother-fucker in Mississippi that just died?"

"Yes, sir."

"You wrote the song on a paper bag?" asked Evelyn.

"The inspiration just come to me and I didn't have nothing else to write on," said Andrew as he smoothed out the paper bag on top of the piano and launched into the lyrics, a sarcastic farewell to his "old friend" Theodore G. Bilbo, senator from Mississippi, bigot and proud member of the Ku Klux Klan.

Leonard howled. "I love it." He leaned over and spoke into the mike, addressing Archia and the piano player. "How long will it take you fellas to learn this Bilbo number?"

Evelyn glared at him. "Are you crazy? They're making fun of a U.S. senator who just passed away."

"A senator who was a bigoted son of a

bitch. Not to mention anti-Semitic. I'm telling you — you have to put this record out. You just record the motherfucker and I'll sell it."

In the sweltering September heat, Leonard hefted up his suitcase and set it in the trunk of his Buick next to the boxes of records. Three thousand pressed copies of "Bilbo Is Dead." The first five hundred had already been dropped off at local deejays, record stores and jukebox distributors in Chicago — the same folks who had helped Leonard launch Archia's "Fishin' Pole" record.

Leonard closed the trunk and walked back across the lawn to where Revetta stood with Susie on her hip, five-year-old Marshall at her left and three-year-old Elaine at her right.

He patted Marshall's shoulder. "You're the man of the house while I'm gone. You take good care of your mother." He stroked the silky hair on Susie's head and reached for Elaine's chin, tilting her face up to look him in the eye. "You be a good girl. Listen to your mother." He leaned in and gave Revetta a loud kiss on the lips. "You need anything, you call Phil."

She nodded, but he saw she had her jaw clenched. And that killed him. She was used to him working long hours at the Macomba, but this would be his second road trip down South in a few months. He'd made the same trip when "Fishin' Pole" came out, and one thing that record taught him was that if Aristocrat was going to be successful they needed the South. There were thousands of Negroes down there who were hungry for race records. A huge market was just sitting there waiting for someone to develop it. Leonard didn't have any contacts in the South, no one he could ship the records to, so he had no choice but to do it himself.

"I'll be back before you know it." He got in the car, calling back through the open window, "Remember, if you need something, you go to Phil."

Leonard drove away, looking back through the rearview mirror until his family disappeared in the distance. He fiddled with the radio as he drove past Cottage Grove and out of the city.

The first night Leonard made it to Memphis, and after some barbecue at the Rendezvous he checked into the Hotel King Cotton on North Front Street and Jefferson. He sat on the side of the bed in his boxers and undershirt, reached for the telephone and called Revetta.

"I have a collect call from Leonard," said the operator. "Will you accept the charges?"

"No, operator, I'm sorry, I won't."

Good. Long-distance calls cost a fortune and Revetta knew the only reason to accept the call was if something was wrong. This was their signal, his way of letting her know he'd arrived. If there was something on his end, he'd call back a second time. On Sunday, when the rates were cheaper, he'd call and talk to her, maybe have her put Marshall and Elaine on the line, too.

The next morning, Leonard's first stop in Memphis was at WHBQ, where he met with the station's top deejay, a guy who called himself Piper Pete. Pete was a scrawny-looking guy with a long face and a blond crew cut. He spoke with a twang that he accentuated over the air. With sleeves rolled to his elbows, Piper Pete sat hunched over his microphone, the turntables at his side. While he had a long song playing over the air, Pete gave a listen to "Bilbo Is Dead."

"Well?" Leonard tried to read his face. "Isn't that something?"

"Oh, that's somethin', all right. I like the tune and all, and your singer's mighty fine. But I'm 'fraid I can't play that over the air."

"But you just said you liked it."

"Them lyrics." Piper Pete shook his head. "Well, you're just asking for trouble."

"But I know you play race music on WHBQ." Leonard reached into his pocket and slipped a twenty across the console. "And you *know* you got a lot of Negroes listening to you."

"Well, you do have a point 'bout that." Pete started for the money but stopped himself. "I sure am sorry, but I'm 'fraid I can't play that kind of music on this station."

Leonard moved on to the next station and the next, working his way from Memphis to New Orleans, hitting every station that played race music, even if for just a couple hours in the evenings. Those were the stations that had the reach — the stations they needed. But "Bilbo Is Dead" — even with a fistful of money — didn't interest them at WROX in Clarksdale or the radio stations in Jackson and New Orleans.

After a week, Leonard switched his strategy and decided to take "Bilbo" straight to the colored market. He turned heads as he walked through those Negro neighborhoods with a stack of records tucked under his arm, sweat trickling down his white skin.

"You with the police or somethin'?" asked a record store owner after he heard "Bilbo Is Dead." Leonard could tell he thought it was some sort of trick, a white man coming into his shop with a song like that. But Leonard assured him he meant no harm. The man took a hundred copies.

From there Leonard played "Bilbo Is Dead" in the barbershops and drugstores. He went into the diners and got the record put into their jukeboxes. Once they heard the song, there wasn't a Negro selling records who didn't want to stock it. But he still needed airplay so he traveled down to Broward

County in Florida and paid a visit to a small Negro station with a tiny audience, but, hell, it was radio. The deejay gave a listen and loved it so much he played it on the air while Leonard was still in the booth and then three more times in the first hour. Soon another station picked it up and then another.

Driving back up North Leonard must have heard "Bilbo Is Dead" a half dozen times on the radio. With each spin of that record, his pride swelled. *Look what this little* putz *from Poland just did. Only in America.* The song was working.

At least·it was for a little while. The day after he got back to Chicago, *Billboard* magazine called Aristocrat, wanting to speak to him. The voice on the other end sounded gruff and Leonard didn't catch the reporter's name.

"Is it true that you were recently in Tennessee to distribute a record about the late senator Bilbo?"

"Yeah, yeah. 'Bilbo Is Dead' by Andrew Tibbs. That's *T-i-*double-*b-s*. It's already climbing the charts."

The reporter laughed. "Then I guess you haven't heard."

"Heard what?"

"They're calling for a boycott of that song. People are up in arms over this record of yours. They want it banned in Louisiana, Alabama, Mississippi and Tennessee. We're running a story on it and I was wondering if you'd care to comment."

"You go ahead and print whatever you want," he said. "No such thing as bad publicity." Leonard hung up and didn't give it a second thought.

He spent the rest of the day making arrangements to have more "Bilbo" records pressed and shipped to stations and stores up North where Evelyn had established contacts. Everything was going great, even better than he'd expected.

But two weeks later Leonard arrived at Aristocrat one morning and Leeba handed him a stack of messages and said, "We got a call from a station owner in Rochester. He's getting complaints from listeners about the 'Bilbo' record. Their sponsors have threatened to pull their advertising if they play the song again."

"See?" said Evelyn.

"So what? That's one station." Leonard went over to his desk, shuffling through the message slips.

"One station up *North,*" Evelyn said, glowering at him from across the room. "This is Rochester, New York. We're not talking about the Deep South. People are offended. They don't want to hear it on the radio. They want the record off the air."

"It'll blow over. And like I said, no such thing as bad publicity."

115

Evelyn marched over to his desk and ripped the message slips from his hand. "I don't want *that* kind of publicity."

The following week, though, he got some calls from his colored customers at the record stores down South, saying they were too scared to sell the record anymore. They wanted their money back. That was followed by angry letters and telegrams from whites. The record was getting airplay in the northern sections of the country, but the more it played, the stronger the backlash. Leonard was beginning to question if *this* much publicity was such a good thing after all.

One afternoon Leeba put an urgent call through to him. Leonard assumed it was another reporter and picked up the extension. "Chess here."

"Leonard Chess?" said the caller.

"Yes."

"You're a dead man, you nigger-lovin' kike."

Leonard froze before he dropped the phone. Dropped it like a hand grenade. He was shaking.

He spent the rest of the day looking over his shoulder, certain that someone was going to jump him for putting out that record. There were more calls, more threats and more telegrams. Leonard tried not to let the panic show, but he was scared. More than that, he felt responsible. He'd been the one to push for the song and now he was fearing for himself and Evelyn, too.

He sweated it out for another week or so until thankfully the outrage began to subside. But by then the record sales had tanked. There wasn't a radio station south of the Mason-Dixon willing to play "Bilbo Is Dead" and the returns were already pouring in.

SEVEN:
"BROWN EYED
HANDSOME MAN"

LEEBA

Leeba and Aileen stood in the alley outside
the Lawndale Theater next to a door with a
sign that read "No Entry." It was a snowy
February afternoon and the wind was gust-
ing, blowing Leeba's curls into her eyes.
Aileen turned toward the door, trying to
block the blast of air long enough to get her
cigarette lit.

"Damn it," she said when the second match
blew out. She grabbed another blue-tip from
the box and struck it so hard the matchstick
broke in two.

"Give it here," said Leeba.

She got it lit, cupping her hand around the
flame, and while Aileen leaned in with her
cigarette the side door opened. A man
stepped out, letting Betty Grable's voice
escape. As he squinted into the daylight and
turned up his collar, Aileen and Leeba
slipped past him and ducked into the dark
theater, where just the flicker of light from

the projectionist's booth guided them to two empty seats. Leeba's feet began to thaw as she breathed in the buttery smell of popcorn.

Mother Wears Tights was the movie showing, and they had missed the very opening, but it didn't matter. Leeba and Aileen had already sneaked into this movie twice before. It was a musical and by now they knew most of the songs. When Betty Grable started performing "You Do," Aileen couldn't help but sing along.

"Shh." The woman in front of them turned around, finger to her lips.

Aileen let a line or two go by before she started up again with that voice of hers that boomed, echoing off the walls and ceiling. Leeba felt the whole audience shushing her this time, but Aileen kept singing until the usher came down the aisle with the beam of his flashlight leading the way.

He shined the light right in Aileen's eyes, making her squint, but not making her stop singing. Leeba could see the gold fillings in her back teeth. The usher was asking her to keep it down and Aileen stood up, took hold of his flashlight and held it like a microphone as she belted out the chorus.

Snatching his flashlight back, the usher said, "That's it. Let me see your tickets."

Their tickets. Leeba stood up now, too. "We were just leaving." She grabbed hold of Aileen, who continued to sing all the way up the aisle and through the lobby.

As they cleared the front doors, the two of them burst out laughing. "I guess this means we're gonna have to find us another theater, huh?" said Aileen as she scooped up a handful of snow, packing it between her gloved hands.

"Yeah, thanks to you," said Leeba, still laughing.

"But you gotta admit" — Aileen lobbed the snowball toward Leeba, who ducked out of the way — "I sounded good."

The two of them broke down laughing all over again.

Leeba could always count on Aileen for the unexpected. Aileen had a big, bold way of living. She made things exciting, always stirring up trouble or hatching some grand scheme, and Leeba fed off her friend's drama. It added color to her otherwise pale existence. They were still laughing as they boarded the 14/16 bus that went from Lawndale to the Maxwell Street area, where Aileen lived now, in a run-down apartment on Jefferson Street.

When they got off the bus they heard music in the distance and, despite the cold, they walked toward it, going the long way so Leeba could stop by the Maxwell Street Radio and Record Store and see her piano. She did that from time to time, paying a visit like you would to an old friend. She'd been working at Aristocrat for seven months now and had put money aside each week for it. When they went inside she was grateful for the warmth, but it came with that old musty smell that she remembered so well. She and Aileen walked over to the baby grand and Leeba was appalled to find boxes of vacuum tubes left on the lid and a pile of old newspapers on the bench.

When Abrams saw her he came over. "So she's back again, huh?" he said. "You ready to buy this time?"

"Almost. I've saved up two hundred and fifty dollars," she told him.

"The price is six — one, two, three, four, five, six," he said, holding up five fingers. "Six hundred dollars. You come back when you have the full amount."

"I don't like that old fuddy-duddy," said Aileen as they left the store. "Remember all those rotten things he used to say to you?"

Leeba didn't want to remember and changed the subject. "Before I forget, I'm bringing Evelyn to your gig at the Lantern Saturday night."

Aileen frowned. "Don't bother."

"Uh-oh. What happened?"

"It wasn't my fault." Aileen raised a pointed finger. "The club owner's a liar. He said I was drunk on stage. Said I was sloppy and 'not acting like a lady' and that is not true. I swear. I may have had a drink or two before I went on, but I wasn't drunk. But believe me, I got plenty drunk afterward. That's for sure."

"Why didn't you say something sooner?"

" 'Cause I knew you'd give me that look, like the one you're giving me right now."

Leeba couldn't help it. She knew Aileen had mastered the art of self-sabotage. Even as children Aileen would leave telltale signs of their mischief — her mama's lipstick and good shoes left out after they played dress-up; almost deliberately hitting the squeaky floorboard or letting the front door bang shut when she sneaked out of the house. It was like she wanted to get caught, as if she couldn't discern between attention and punishment.

As they walked, Aileen continued to insist that she wasn't to blame for losing her gig at the Lantern. "That owner had it in for me. I swear he never liked me. And I sounded good that night, too. I sure did . . ."

She was talking so fast and getting so wound up that Leeba couldn't catch half of what she was saying, but, knowing Aileen, she was pretty certain that she had been drunk on stage and she had been misbehaving. Leeba was disappointed. She'd been trying to get Evelyn to one of Aileen's shows, especially since Aileen was performing one of Leeba's songs, a number she called "Hop, Skip and a Jump," a bouncy tune fashioned after a Dinah Shore record. But still, Leeba wouldn't say anything. She wasn't sure if this was a weakness on her part or a sign of loyalty, but she found it hard to be critical of her friend. For anything. It was because of Aileen's past. First her father gets killed and six months after that her mother takes her own life and Aileen finds the body hanging in the bathroom, one end of a cord fastened to the towel hook, the other wrapped around her limp neck. At thirteen Aileen was sent across town to live with her aunt Effie, who had children of her own. She resented having to look after her dead sister's daughter, and she took it out on Aileen. How could you be hard on someone who'd been through all that? Leeba always made excuses, suspending her judgment when it came to Aileen.

"I'm sorry about your gig," she said to Aileen, who was now sulking, walking with her shoulders hunched forward, her head down, eyes to the ground.

Leeba knew her friend was moody, prone to sadness with an angry undercurrent. But ever since they were in their teens, it had been getting worse and now she noticed a pattern to Aileen's moods. Like hands on a clock Leeba watched Aileen move through the cycles. A bit of rage was always mounting below the surface and when that got loose there was no controlling her. Leeba had seen Aileen throw, kick and punch, saying horrible things she could not have possibly meant.

Those outbursts were followed by bouts of gut-wrenching sobs until all that was left was an ember, a flicker of hope. It would catch inside her and begin to burn brighter and brighter until the darkness was gone and life was grand again. That was when she'd go from sleeping all day to staying up three days straight. That was when she was going to make it as a singer and everything would be perfect. She could sing. *She could fly. She could do anything.* Until she couldn't. Something would knock her down and the sadness would return, followed by the anger and the tears until it gave way to those exhilarated bursts. But the next disappointment would be just around the corner and it would reduce her once again. Aileen seemed trapped on a carousel she couldn't get off, and it seemed to be turning faster and faster with every passing year. Leeba was scared for her.

They kept walking and the sound of an electric guitar and someone singing "See-See Rider Blues" pulled Leeba from her thoughts. Something in the playing, something in that voice, called to her and as they got closer she saw that, sure enough, it was coming from Red Dupree. He and Little Walter had drawn quite a crowd.

Leeba didn't say a word to Aileen. She didn't have to. Aileen saw the expression on Leeba's face and followed the direction of her gaze. "You got a thing for that guitar

124

player, don't you?"

There was no point in denying it. There was no point to any of it.

"Look at you," said Aileen. "You're blushing."

"No, I'm not. C'mon, let's go." But she couldn't bring herself to walk away. She couldn't take her eyes off him.

"Boy, oh boy," said Aileen. "Your mama won't like that at all."

"Since when have I ever done anything that my mama liked?"

Leeba entered the control booth at Universal the following Monday afternoon. Evelyn and Leonard were with the engineer, seated in front of the window looking out onto Studio A. The reel-to-reel was rolling and Leonard asked Leeba to stick around, keep an eye on the clock.

She liked being included on the sessions. It made her feel like she played a role in the music they were creating. Granted, it was a small role and she wanted to do more. She'd been writing songs in the evenings and on the weekends, so excited to play them for Leonard and Evelyn. One day, she thought she had hit on something, only to have Evelyn fold her arms and say, "It sounds like Doris Day."

"I know," said Leeba. She'd done that intentionally. "It'd be perfect for Aileen."

"See, that's your whole problem," Leonard had said. "You gotta quit trying to sound like everyone else. You need to develop your own sound. And I know you love Aileen, but —"

"Girl singers don't sell records," Evelyn had said.

That was the end of that song. Their rejections stung, each one more than the previous, as if the cumulative effect was mounting evidence that she had no talent as a songwriter. She probably would have given up altogether had it not been for her time in the studio. Those sessions inspired her to keep going. She grabbed a coffee from the pot in back and sat off to the side on a stool, watching the magic take place.

Since the "Bilbo" fiasco six months before, Leonard had been pushing to record more race records. Evelyn may have had her doubts about Negro music, but Leeba liked this new sound Aristocrat was going after. The rhythm was infectious. It got into your system and it wouldn't let go. The only other time she heard this kind of music was down on Maxwell Street.

That day they were recording a piano player named Sunnyland Slim. He wore a bowler hat and had the longest, most slender fingers Leeba had ever seen. He'd come up from the Mississippi delta and all you had to do was look into his sad, soulful eyes with their ashy circles underneath to imagine what he'd been through. Sunnyland Slim had arrived in Chicago about five years back and everyone said he was the best piano player in town. From time to time he sat in at the Macomba. That day Slim brought Ernest "Big" Crawford with him, a large, beefy man who held his upright bass close around the middle like he would a woman.

Sunnyland Slim and Big Crawford were on the other side of the glass, laying down a song, "Johnson Machine Gun." After a few takes, Leonard turned to Evelyn. "Something is missing. It needs a little *duh-duh-duh-duh.*"

" '*Duh-duh-duh-duh*'?" Evelyn cocked an eyebrow. "Could you be more specific?"

"I don't know what the hell it is. You know: *duh-duh-duh-duh.*"

"Would that be guitar?"

"How should I know? I just know that's the sound this needs."

Evelyn rolled her eyes and hit the talk button so the musicians could hear her inside the studio. "Hey, guys, what do you think about adding a guitar?"

Sunnyland Slim played a few chords and smiled. "I got just the cat."

He came into the control booth and made a telephone call. Fifteen minutes later a man wearing dusty overalls and an even dustier overcoat walked in with a guitar strapped to his back. He had a flat wide forehead, a full head of wild hair and a mustache so thin it looked drawn onto his dark skin. Sunnyland placed his hand on the man's shoulder and made the introductions. "This here's Muddy. Muddy Waters."

No time for pleasantries. Leonard ushered them into the studio and they went back to recording "Johnson Machine Gun." Only this time, with the addition of the guitar, Leeba saw Sunnyland Slim and Big Crawford come to life. She watched Sunnyland's foot stomp to the beat, his left hand vamping while his right hand hit the keys so hard they gave off a tremor. His fingers were flying so fast his movements blurred before her eyes. But as much as she admired his playing, Leeba had to admit it was the addition of that guitar player that made all the difference, and they nailed it on the first take.

Since there was still time on the clock, Sunnyland said, "Let me try a little something. We been foolin' with this here number —" He played a combination of chords. "Tell us what y'all think."

They weren't rolling tape when Sunnyland kicked off the introduction and the guitar player jumped in with a lick that twisted and whined while his fingers raced over the strings, up and down the neck. It gave off a shock of reverb that sounded like a mechanical voice speaking. The guitarist, this Muddy guy, was sitting in a folding chair playing so hard he made the legs rock back and forth.

He was playing up high on the frets, close to the sound hole. The only other person she'd seen play like that was Red Dupree. Muddy's brow began to glisten with sweat and when he started to sing about a gypsy woman his voice grew so guttural and so intense he sounded unlike anyone else they'd ever recorded.

When they finished the song, Leeba was sure that they were going to record Muddy, but instead Evelyn signaled the engineer, who hit the talk button and said, "That's a wrap, fellas."

Leonard and Evelyn were both running late and asked Leeba to stick around and handle the paperwork, so she stayed back in the control booth with the contracts. Big Crawford and Sunnyland Slim signed theirs and were out the door, but Leeba noticed Muddy shuffling through the pages, picking up the pen and setting it down and picking it back up again.

"Do you have any questions about the contract?" asked Leeba.

"Can't I just have my moneys?"

"That's what the paperwork is for, so you'll get paid. Just go ahead and sign right there." She pointed to the line.

"I don't wanna sign no papers." He hoisted up his guitar and she thought he was going to leave.

"But you won't get paid and we can't

release the record unless you sign them. It's a standard contract," she said, trying to reassure him. "The musicians' union drew it up. Not us. And it's for your own protection. I swear it is." She held out the forms to him.

"What is all this?" He shuffled through the pages, scanning them again, turning the forms over. That was when Leeba realized what the problem was. Muddy Waters couldn't read.

She didn't want to embarrass him so she took the pages from him and led him over to a chair in the control booth. "Honestly," she said, "no one ever understands these forms. See this right here" — Leeba pointed out key sections — "this says 'Session Agreement' and it explains that you recorded one song on today's date. It's got the studio — Universal Recording Company — see?" She moved her finger down the page. "And there's Evelyn's and Leonard's names right there. And over here — that's the title of the song. This part over here is just a bunch of gobbledygook. No one ever reads that." She smiled. It was true. "But this down here is important." She pointed to a checked box. "It says 'Type of Session: Standard. Three hours.' And this part over here says 'Session Fees: forty-one dollars and twenty-five cents.' If all that is correct then you go ahead and sign it."

He took the pen and marked an X on the signature line. Without looking at her he said,

"I ain't stupid, you know."

"Oh, I know you're not. Anyone who can play a guitar and sing like you did today is anything but stupid."

"I just never had no schooling. Ain't never learnt my letters."

"When I first came to this country I didn't know how to read or write in English, either," she said. "I couldn't even speak it."

"You soundin' all right now."

"That's because I've been here a long time. But in the beginning I had to learn it all. If you want, I can show you how to write your name. It's not hard." Leeba took a clean sheet of paper and drew an *M*. "Now you try. Up down, up down."

Muddy paused for a moment before he mimicked what she did, letter by letter, until they had his name spelled out.

"See, that's you. That's your signature. Muddy Waters."

He smiled, proud, more impressed by this than by what he'd done in the studio that day.

"And now I have to ask — how'd you get the name Muddy Waters?" He laughed for the first time and gave her a big, wide smile. "My grandmama gave me that name on account of me always playin' in the mud. I don't know where the Waters part come from. That got picked up 'long the way."

"What's your real name?"

"McKinley. McKinley Morganfield."

Leeba gripped his hand. "Well, you keep practicing your signature because, Muddy Waters, I have a feeling you're going to be signing a lot of contracts."

EIGHT:
"YOU'VE GOT TO LOVE HER WITH A FEELING"

LEEBA

Leeba passed a newspaper boy on the corner selling the evening edition of the *Daily News*. It was a Friday, the middle of March. The air was still cold but the days were gradually getting longer, giving Leeba a little extra time to make it home before sundown for Shabbos.

Rush hour had begun, the traffic backing up on Cottage Grove as people scuttled about, the men with their attaché cases and overcoats buttoned high, the women adjusting their hats and gloves. Leeba spotted a tall colored man at the corner and her pulse lurched. His back was to her and all she could see was the broad shoulders, the guitar case in his hand. She quickened her step and as he crossed the street she saw the man's face and stopped. Her heart sank a little and she was dumbfounded by her disappointment. It wasn't him. It wasn't Red Dupree.

She climbed the stairs of the El platform, paid her seven-cent fare and stepped on board the crowded train, standing the whole way, holding on to the ceiling strap. As she swayed back and forth while the car skated across the tracks, she wondered what had become of that guitar player. She knew Leonard had no interest in recording him, but his music haunted Leeba. Sometimes, when no one was in the office, she would listen to his demo, close her eyes and feel the power of his guitar playing surrounding her, his deep raw vocals pressing against her ear.

She got off at the Pulaski stop and as she walked up Roosevelt Road she passed Rosenblum's Bookstore, Silverstein's Delicatessen, the kosher butchers and the synagogues. This neighborhood, here among her people, was where she was supposed to feel most at home and yet so often she felt that there was no place she belonged. She came from an Orthodox family and yet she found herself on the fringe of Judaism. Leeba considered herself to be an American first — a Jewish American rather than an American Jew.

When she made it home that afternoon Leeba's mother was in the kitchen. The scent of sautéed onions and garlic hung heavy in the air, with a slight hint of airplane glue from her father's latest model. She watched her mother dunk a used tea bag — probably weak from the three or four previous cups — in the steaming water, her slippered feet impatiently tapping the checkered linoleum floor.

Her mother lifted the tea bag from the cup and placed it on a spoon, wrapping the string around it to squeeze out the last drops. Mustn't waste a tea bag with a little life left in it. When she looked up, Leeba saw the circles under her mother's eyes. Those crescents were always there, though, no matter how much sleep she got. It was a family trait and now that Leeba was older she could see the hereditary darkness forming beneath her own eyes as well. They did her no favors. No one ever called Leeba Groski pretty or beautiful, especially when compared to Golda, petite, three years younger, and already married. It was still daylight, but her mother was anticipating the sunset.

"Vos iz di shbs goy do azoy fi?" She pointed toward the bedroom.

"Oy, Mama." Leeba rolled her eyes. "The Shabbos Goy is here early because she's also my friend."

Even after all these years, her mother still referred to Aileen as their "Shabbos Goy." Every Jewish family in Lawndale had one. A Shabbos Goy was a gentile who came over on Shabbat and performed those chores that Orthodox Jews like the Groskis were forbidden to do: turn on and off the stove, the lights — even the icebox was off-limits because the light came on when they opened the door. Leeba's mother paid Aileen a dollar a week to do these things and when Aileen finished with their house, she went across the hall and did the same for Aunt Sylvie and Uncle Moishe and then over to the Chesses' house and from there to the Berkowitzes' and so on and so on, down the block. She'd been doing it for years even though she wasn't in the neighborhood anymore. She just jumped on the 14/16 bus, a straight shot from Maxwell Street to Lawndale.

"I'll be right in to help with dinner, Mama. I'm just going to get changed first and talk to Aileen."

"Put on something nice," her mother said. "And do something with your hair. We're having company."

"Who's coming?"

"Just Avrom Yurzel."

Just? Leeba had known Avrom from her days at Marshall High School. He'd been popular, handsome, athletic, the kind that dated those girls who hogged the bathroom mirrors between classes to reapply their lipstick and rouge. Leeba had been infatuated with Avrom, sometimes following him home from class, feigning interest in a neighbor's flower bed if ever he turned around. He was a tailor now with a shop on Maxwell Street. He was also a recent widower, his wife having died of a rare heart condition three months before.

"Mama, don't you think it's a little soon to be inviting him over?"

136

"The man has to eat. And besides, it's Shabbos."

It was no use. Her mother was determined to rustle up every available male in Lawn-dale: old, young, sick, healthy, rich, poor, divorced, widowed. Her daughter was twenty-five and still single — it was a *shand,* what would people think. This was an old hurt between the two of them, scabbed over and picked at for so long it would never heal right.

Leeba went down the hall to her bedroom and there was Aileen, sitting on the side of the bed, legs crossed with the top one swing-ing back and forth while she leafed through a magazine.

When she saw Leeba she dropped the magazine and sprang to her feet, grinning. "Guess what? I got me a new singing gig. Down at the Trigger Club. They're gonna start me off two nights a week."

"That's good."

Aileen's shoulders sank. "That's it? That's all you got to say?"

"I'm sorry." Leeba closed her bedroom door and leaned against it as if needing to support herself. "Mama just told me she invited Avrom Yurzel — remember him? She invited him for dinner. Tonight."

"Didn't his wife just pass?"

"You think that would stop my mama?"

"She sure is wanting to marry you off."
Aileen plopped back down and stretched out

on the bed.

An inexplicable dread filled Leeba as she lay down next to Aileen, resting her head on her shoulder. "This is going to be humiliating."

"It'll be okay," said Aileen as she brushed her fingers back through Leeba's hair. "Tell me something, you still thinking 'bout the guitar player?"

Leeba closed her eyes and there he was for reasons even she couldn't grasp. "Every day." She wouldn't have confessed that to anyone but Aileen, because her longing for this practical stranger embarrassed her. Did her heart know something she didn't or was it just her desiring something she couldn't have? Leeba looked at Aileen. "Have you ever been attracted to a white man?"

"When we were growing up I used to think Leonard was pretty cute." She laughed and wrapped one of Leeba's curls about her finger.

"Seriously, have you?"

"Sure," said Aileen. "I see handsome, sexy white boys passing by on the street all the time. I see 'em coming and I watch 'em go."

"But what if you met someone — you know, someone special?"

Aileen gave her a skeptical look.

"I know it sounds crazy," said Leeba, "but I feel something for him."

"Girl, every woman who looks at that man

is gonna feel something. It's called love. L-u-s-t, love."

Leeba laughed, insisting that it was more than that. "It's his music. It's the way he carries himself. I can't explain it."

"Want my advice? Forget about him. Things between men and women is complicated enough — you don't need to go borrowing trouble."

Leeba got up and went to the closet, screeching hangers across the rod as she sorted through her clothes, pulling out a navy blue utility dress with squared shoulders. She slipped it on and turned her back to Aileen for help.

Aileen scooted off the bed and zipped her up. She glanced out the window and said, "Only half an hour till sunset. I gotta get ready to make my rounds. I got a whole lot of stoves to turn off and lights to turn on." She laughed and pressed her forehead to Leeba's. "Good Shabbos," she said.

Leeba responded with a smile and her customary "And God be with you, till we meet again."

After Aileen left, Leeba went down the hall to use the bathroom and afterward lifted the lid on the tank and pulled on the chain to make the toilet flush. They had one toilet in their apartment and it had been broken for so long that the extra step no longer fazed her. Leeba's father had been saying he'd get to it, like the doorbell that no longer sounded and the radiator that clacked all winter long.

She looked in the mirror and brushed her hair, only making the curls and ringlets frizz up more. She was reminded of the time Aileen put pomade in her hair. The two of them had locked themselves in the bathroom while Aileen braided Leeba's hair just like she wore her own, in neat, tight rows.

When Leeba had tried sneaking out of the apartment, her mother blocked the door. "You're not going anywhere with that hair," she'd said. "You look like a *schwartze*." Her mother had pulled her over to the kitchen sink, ran her head under scalding water and tried to undo the braids. The next day she took her to the beauty parlor and had Leeba's hair cut short, cropped against her head. Now she wasn't just taller than the boys, but her hair was shorter than theirs, too. And her mother wondered why she had no dates.

Leeba set her brush down. It was no use. She pulled her hair back, holding the curls in place with a set of combs, and went into the kitchen to help her mother.

She'd just finished setting the table when Golda and her husband arrived. Even seven months pregnant with a belly out to here, her sister was beautiful. Her golden brown hair was pulled back in a loose bun, a few silky strands hanging down. And it only made sense that Golda would have married a man as handsome as Ber Lefkowitz. Dark haired, dark eyed, with broad shoulders, like Avrom he'd been one of the most popular boys in the neighborhood. Ber and his father owned a furniture store and Golda's big home on Independence Boulevard was *ongepotchet,* overdone with decorative pillows and lampshades, gaudy artwork and statuettes.

"So I heard Mama invited Avrom." Golda walked around the table, straightening a napkin here, a knife there. "Whatever you do, don't mention the dead wife." Golda plucked a glass from the table and held it out to Leeba. "There's a spot on this one."

"Kitchen's right there where it's always been." Leeba pointed over her shoulder.

Golda gave her a harsh look. This was about so much more than a spot on a glass.

"Fine." Golda narrowed her eyes. "I'll do it myself."

"Fine."

Moments later Avrom arrived, followed by Aunt Sylvie and Uncle Moishe. Cousin Eli had long since moved out of the neighborhood and rarely joined them anymore for Shabbat. Leeba's mother brought out a tray of mismatched shot glasses while her father opened a bottle of schnapps. Her mother drank to Avrom while the others toasted the Shabbos. The schnapps was strong and Leeba felt its heat rising up to her sinuses and spreading down the back of her throat. Uncle

141

Moishe raised his empty glass, coughing while comically pounding his chest.

Just before sunset everyone took their seats at the table, lighting the candles and saying the prayers over the bread, the wine. Uncle Moishe sat at one head of the table and Leeba's father at the other. Both brothers were balding and had the same dark round eyes that always made them look taken by surprise, along with the sloping nose that Leeba had inherited. Aunt Sylvie had been a head turner in her day, but now she was plump and doughy, standing barely five feet tall.

Avrom tasted the chicken soup. "Delicious," he said as he dabbed his lips with his napkin. "Did you hear that they're holding a big Zionist meeting this Sunday?"

"It's going to be at Temple Beth Shalom," said Ber.

"Leeba made that soup," her mother said, tapping Avrom's arm.

"Three hundred people they're expecting for this," her father added.

"She's a wonderful cook, you know," her mother said.

Avrom smiled at Leeba. "It's delicious."

"Well, thank you." She smiled back. But she did not make the soup, and as soon as her mother went into the kitchen, Leeba followed her. "Don't be so obvious," she said. "Quit trying to sell me."

"A little sell is such a terrible thing?" her

mother said. "Would it kill you to encourage him a little?"

Leeba wadded up a dish towel and threw it on the counter before returning to the table with the brisket.

After dinner they all bundled up and went to shul for Friday night services, and on the way home Leeba found herself walking next to Avrom, the two of them trailing behind the others. Every half block or so her mother glanced back at them.

"You do know she's planning a *shidduch* here, don't you?" Leeba said, finger waving to her mother, who abruptly faced forward.

"Of course." Avrom laughed. "That's what mothers do. Anyone with a daughter over the age of twelve has invited me for dinner. You can't imagine how many Shabbat dinners I've attended. I had six Passover Seders and I'm already booked up for the High Holidays."

They laughed and lapsed into an awkward silence as they walked beneath the street-lamps. The tree branches swayed in the breeze. A dog barked somewhere in the distance. She could think of nothing to say.

"The truth is," he said eventually, "I'm not ready for any *shidduch*s. I'm sorry. I hope you understand."

"No apologies needed. I'm sure you must miss your wife terribly." She offered him a sympathetic smile. As they walked along in silence the ache in her chest grew stronger.

The truth was that she was lonely. Yes, she'd been caught up lately in thoughts of Red Dupree, but that was a fantasy. Nothing would ever come of it and she knew it. And after years of denying, of doing her best to suppress any need, any want, she knew deep down that she longed to fall in love. She wanted a family of her own and, looking at Avrom, she felt a twinge of disappointment. She didn't necessarily want him, but it would have been nice to at least be wanted. By someone.

NINE:
"SWEET HOME CHICAGO"

RED

Red stumbled over to the sink and stared into the rust spot where the faucet dripped. The ice-cold water he splashed on his face hit his skin like needles. The light coming through his only window had changed since he'd lain down and now the sun was casting long shadows across the spider-cracked walls. No one could tell him that his family's shack back home was any worse than this dump he was living in on Canal Street. They called it a kitchenette. Just one room, with a bathroom down the hall that everyone on the floor used and no one bothered to clean. Didn't have a drop of hot water in the place. Cockroaches were a given, in the drawers, the closet, camped out in every dark corner. The occasional mouse or rat scurrying across the floor was no big deal. He slept on an old mattress he'd found out in an alley, thin and lumpy, but it was better than sleeping on the hardwood floor.

He hadn't meant to doze off. He and Walter had been playing late the night before at the Tuxedo Lounge and Red had been dragging all day on his job at the brickyard. When he got home from his shift, he lay down on the mattress and opened the *Defender* to read about Blatz Brewery hiring an all-Negro distribution company. He drifted off while he was reading.

He splashed more water on his face. Man, he was beat. And to think he thought sharecropping was hard. Trying to make it as a musician was nothing like he'd expected. Working all day and gigging all night, grabbing an hour or two of sleep here and there. Dropping off demos to people who didn't listen or didn't like what they heard. He was getting himself worn through and at the end of each week he barely had enough rent money. Chicago was supposed to be the place where magic happened. So where was it? Back home everyone told him he was something else, but up here he was just *someone* else. Everybody had a guitar or a sax or a harp and everybody was damn good. But it took more than just being good.

He stared into the basin, wondering what his mama and sisters were doing at that very moment. He pictured them sitting on the porch, their radio tuned to the gospel station, while his friends across the way drank beers and listened to the baseball game, cheering whenever Jackie Robinson got up to bat. What would they say if they saw him now? Red couldn't help but remember those big dreams he had about coming to the city. He'd pictured himself making lots of money, living in a big house and driving a fancy car. He'd been in Chicago for a year and thought for sure by now he'd be making records and hearing his songs on the radio. It was easy to get discouraged.

And yet there were things about Chicago he'd never give up. Knowing he could walk through the front door of a restaurant and sit wherever he liked was a feeling he never wanted to lose. It gave him the dignity he'd been denied in the Deep South. No "White Only" and "Colored" signs to remind him that he was second class in the eyes of white folks. Here he had an actual library card and was free to take out any book he wanted. Back home they didn't have many books so he'd read newspapers instead. He read every paper he could get his hands on — didn't matter if they were a day or two or even a week old. He just liked seeing those words, saying them inside his head. He read a lot of articles about Chicago and now that he was here he was taking advantage of the city. Especially the nightlife, the clubs, the music — if he had the time and the money he could have seen a different player each night. That energy was what kept him going. Red reached for a towel to dry his face and when he opened his eyes he jumped back startled, hands raised, heart hammering. Little Walter was pointing a gun at him.

"Man, put that thing away. You scared me half to death." Red's hands were still up in surrender.

Walter found this funny. He was laughing. "Big-city livin', brother. You gotta remember to lock your door behind you. Never know who might come and getcha." He howled and twirled the trigger guard around his finger like a cowboy.

At times Red questioned what he was doing with Walter. The kid couldn't pass up a prank or turn away from a challenge even when he had no chance of winning. The scar above his eyebrow and the signs of a nose broken in too many places were proof of that. Yet he'd come to Red's aid when he first arrived in town. He'd always be grateful for that and in turn Red took it upon himself to keep an eye on Walter. After all, Walter was still a kid, nine years younger than Red, and he needed someone to set him straight when he got out of hand. But more than anything else Little Walter was the best harp player Red had ever heard and the two of them were developing a small following around town.

Walter gave the gun another twirl on his finger.

"Stop doing that. What's wrong with you,

man?" Red threaded the towel through the rack. "Why are you carrying that thing anyway?"

"Maybe 'cuz I ain't big and tall like you," said Walter as he stuffed the pistol into his waistband. He looked in the mirror hanging off a bent nail and brushed his palms through his hair. "C'mon now, hurry up. We already gettin' a late start."

That night Red and Walter went down to the Macomba Lounge to hear Tom Archia play. The outside of the club wasn't much to look at, just a sign and a doorman, Big Gene, who was even taller than Red. Red and Little Walter went inside and the place was swarming with prostitutes and drug dealers. If you could get past that, you could sit down with a slab of ribs and listen to the best music in the city. Leonard Chess and his brother packed them in seven nights a week.

When they first arrived Red saw Leonard at the bar. "Working on a new demo for you, Mr. Chess," he said.

"Yeah, you do that. What'll it be?"

Red might as well have told Leonard he liked his tie. The man just didn't care about Red's music. So he ordered a whiskey and joined Walter at a table up front. They were listening to Archia singing "Fishin' Pole." Red had seen Archia perform it at the Macomba before and had heard it on the radio at work when the boss man wasn't around and they switched the dial to the Old Swing-master on WGES.

Red was enjoying the show, when a couple of whores sidled up to their table. Walter started working on them, trying to get a freebie. "C'mon, baby," he said to the one girl who had lipstick on her teeth. "Just as good for you as it is for me."

"Now, if I give it away to you, I gotta give it to your friend here, too." She gave Red a seductive glance.

"You ain't gotta give me nothing," said Red, tucking his hands beneath his thighs. "I'm not interested."

"What's the matter?" she said, purring into his ear. "Don't you like girls?"

"I don't like girls I have to pay for."

Eventually the hookers gave up and moved to the next table. The hour turned late, but the Macomba was just getting started. The place was elbow to elbow with musicians. They'd come inside, set down their guitars and horns just long enough to put a drink between them and their last gig before they'd go on stage to jam with Archia. It was that kind of place and Red liked it because you never knew who might show up. He'd seen Big Joe Turner there and Tampa Red, too.

It was going on three in the morning and Little Walter was on the verge of passing out when he saw something that sobered him up fast.

"Lord have mercy." Walter whistled through his teeth. "Would you take a look at that."

A woman came into the club and everyone turned her way. She had a presence that commanded the room. Even the women's eyes were glued to her. She was a beauty, tall and curvy with skin so light she could have passed for white.

Walter didn't waste any time. He swaggered over and sweet-talked her into coming back to their table.

"Red Dupree," said Walter, "say hello to Miss Mimi Cooke." Walter held out the chair for her while Mimi held out her hand to Red. "Let's get this little lady a drink. Whatchu drinkin'?"

"Martini. Gin. Splash of vermouth."

She was still looking at Red even though she was talking to Walter.

"You heard her," said Walter, giving Red a jab. "Go on now, get our friend here a drink. And I'll take another while you're at it."

Red knew Walter was a mean drunk and if you challenged him you were only asking for trouble. Even though Red shouldn't have wasted what little money he had on a round, it was easier to get the drinks. As Red stood up he felt Mimi's eyes scanning all six foot four of him. The way she smiled undid him.

He thought maybe Walter hadn't noticed until he said, "Go on now, Red. Go get us them drinks."

As pretty as Mimi was, Red wasn't going near that and not because of Little Walter. Women like Mimi were trouble. Too beautiful for their own good. Red knew a woman like that would spend your money, sleep with your best friend and still make you want her even as she was breaking your heart.

Besides, plenty of other women wanted to keep Red company. Seemed like all he had to do was pull out his guitar and they came around like bees to honey. He wouldn't have believed it possible back when he was a boy reeking so from the fields that none of the girls would sit next to him in school. And even on Sundays after he'd bathed and put on his clean church clothes he'd carried the shame of his own stink, afraid to even smile at a girl.

He was seventeen before he'd ever been kissed and it was by an older woman from the neighborhood that he'd only known as Miss Washington. But when she'd reached for his hand and led him to her bedroom, where a red scarf was thrown over a lamp, casting a moody glow, she told him to call her Jasmine. He'd stayed in her bed that night, incense burning and scented oils on the nightstand. Just before dawn he sneaked back home, falling into a deep, satisfied slumber, only to wake the next morning convinced that he was in love. And his feelings multiplied each time he thought of her, every time he saw her. Before he knew it she had taken custody of his heart. He'd been sneaking in and out of her place for a month when she put a stop to it. She'd met someone, someone older who played guitar in the juke joints around Merrydale and Monticello.

Red had been crushed. He'd gone home and cried like a baby, his innocent heart open and raw. When he couldn't get up to do his chores or go to school the next day, his mama checked his forehead for fever. He'd moped around for weeks and the only thing that made him feel better was picking up his Stella. He'd been sure there'd never be another Jasmine until he started performing. Then the girls came to him. He didn't have to say a word. They were smooth and silky with curvy bodies; some smelled like vanilla or wildflowers; others were musky, citrusy — always different, each one a new present to unwrap.

So why was he so disappointed in the mornings, eager to find his clothes and leave? Sometimes he caught himself thinking about that woman from Aristocrat. He'd seen her one day that winter when he was playing in Jewtown, but she didn't seem to notice him. Just as well. White women equaled danger. His friend Boggs back home took up with a white girl and when her kin found out they bashed his head into the side of a tree. Boggs was never the same afterward. He talked slow and forgot his thoughts, couldn't even tie his own shoes, and all because of a white woman. Red wasn't about to risk that. Even if they were up North now. He glanced back at the table. Mimi smiled at him. Red didn't know what he was looking for, but he knew it wasn't Mimi Cooke.

He went back to the table with the drinks and set them down, sliding the martini to Mimi and the whiskey over to Walter.

"So where'd you come from, Mr. Red Dupree?" Mimi asked, her lashes fluttering over the rim of her glass.

"He's from Louisiana," answered Walter. "Been here, what now, 'bout a year?"

Red kept quiet. He knew Walter was trying to get Mimi's attention.

"And what about you?" asked Walter. "You ain't from around these parts. I would have remembered you. That's for sure." He clanked his glass to hers.

"I'm from Alabama. Montgomery."

"Alabama? So what you doin' up here in Chicago?"

"Singing."

"You a singer, huh?" Little Walter reached for her hand. "I bet you do sound good."

She laughed, pulled her hand away and took out a cigarette. Walter lit a match for her, but she ignored his gesture, leaning over the candle instead and giving Red a clear view of her cleavage. "I do sound good," she said, looking in Red's direction. "So what do you boys do?"

"I'm a musician," said Walter.

"Walter here's the best harp player I've ever heard," Red said to bolster up his friend.

"And I sing, too," said Walter, nodding. "Don't forget, I ain't just a harp player."

"What about you, Red Dupree?" She raised her martini to her lips, fanning her lashes some more. "I suppose you're a musician, too?"

"I play guitar."

"And I bet *you* sound good, Mr. Dupree."

Walter's eyes shifted between Red and Mimi. Red felt the table shaking as his friend bobbed his leg up and down. Yep, Walter was twitching, getting ready to spring, and Red didn't want to be anywhere near him when that happened.

"Well," said Red, standing up, "I'd best be going."

"Oh, don't." Mimi reached out and touched his arm. "We were just getting to know each other."

Walter's leg was bouncing up and down so fast now Red could see the whiskey in his glass rippling. Red watched the veins in Walter's neck jumping and his face had broken out in beads of sweat.

"Another time," said Red.

"Yeah, that's right." Little Walter sprang to his feet, staggering while he knocked the table over, drinks and candle flying as he whipped out his gun. "You better damn well make it another time."

Mimi screamed, jumped out of her chair and ran to the other end of the bar. Walter threw his head back, raised his gun and fired three quick shots into the ceiling. *Pop. Pop. Pop.*

The band stopped playing and people ran for cover as plaster rained down on Little Walter. Big Gene and the Chess brothers rushed over as Walter dropped the gun to his side, laughing, clutching his sides like it was the funniest damn thing.

"Aw, c'mon, Red" — Walter was still laughing — "I ain't gonna shoot you." He dropped down in his chair next to the overturned table and snapped his fingers, calling out, "Let's get us a drink over here."

Red looked around the club. Mimi was gone. Everyone else had gone back to their conversations. The band went back to playing the rest of their set. It was just another night at the Macomba.

TEN:
"I CAN'T BE SATISFIED"

LEONARD

Nine o'clock in the morning and Leonard was on a stepladder with a spackling knife in his hand, a bucket of plaster resting on the top rung. He was spreading it like cream cheese across a bagel. Another hole needed to be patched at the Macomba. Some stupid fuck — that harp player — pulled a gun and fired off a few shots the night before. A week or two ago, another jackass had put his fist through the wall. It was always something.

A year back, when Leonard first started working with Aristocrat, he was certain his days as a nightclub owner would have been over by now. Instead he was working two jobs, hoping the club money would keep the record label going and eventually turn a profit.

Phil came up from the back of the club and propped his foot on the first rung of the ladder. "We should close the club at two a.m. like everyone else," he said.

"But it's that two a.m. to six a.m. crowd that pays the bills." Leonard spread the last smear of plaster and made his way down the ladder.

"And that's the same crowd that gives us trouble. Revetta and Sheva want us out of this racket — you know that, don't you?"

"I'm working on it." Leonard dusted the dried plaster off his hands.

"Let me ask you something," said Phil. "When was the last time you sat down and had dinner with your family?"

"I don't even remember the last time I saw my kids before they went to bed. If I'm lucky, I see them in the morning when I'm coming home from work and they're just getting up."

"What kinda life is this, huh?"

"I'm working on it," Leonard said again. "I'm gonna get us out of here."

Phil didn't say another word and went about his routine of looking under the bar stools. He found a few packages of drugs and went to the john and flushed them.

As far as Leonard was concerned, Evelyn Aron should have been kissing his *tuchas*. That was his thought later that morning as he unlocked the front door at Aristocrat and flipped on the light switch at 5249 South Cottage Grove.

Leonard lit a cigarette and swung his legs up on the desk while eyeing the ledger with a frown. The numbers didn't lie. They were always coming up short. It was the nature of their business. The studios and record pressers wanted their money up front, and each time they put out a new record it would be at least six months before they'd see any revenue from it. And then there were returns, like after the "Bilbo" disaster. They'd already tried for a loan and had been rejected by every bank in town. They were on their own to keep the label afloat.

The front door opened and the sounds of the street filtered in along with Leeba, who was carrying a bag with a newspaper sticking out the top. She shimmied off her sweater, reached inside her tote and plunked a hard-boiled egg down on his desk.

"You need to eat some protein," she said.

"And good morning to you, too." He picked up the egg and set it aside. "I already have a mother, you know."

"And you don't listen to her, either."

"Like you listen to yours?"

"Don't remind me."

"Aw, what's the matter, *bubelah*?" he said mockingly, getting up from his desk and going to Leeba, cupping her face in his hands. "Such a *shaineh ponem,* such a pretty face. Don't you worry, I will make a *shidduch* yet! I'll have men lining up outside the door, waiting to come for Shabbos dinner."

Leeba wiggled away from him, laughing.

"Very funny."

He was about to say something else, when Evelyn showed up in some ridiculous-looking hat and a getup that must have cost a fortune. He'd never seen that dame in the same outfit twice and yet she was always crying poor.

He waited till she got her coffee and settled in before tackling the payables. They sat with Leeba, who announced the new total after each check was cut. When they hit a balance of thirty-three dollars and seventeen cents left in the account, Leonard said, "We gotta do something to break out of this rut. We need to take a risk."

"Oh, another risk like 'Bilbo Is Dead'?"

"What? You think 'Chi-Baba' was any better?"

"Truce!" Leeba stood up between them, arms outreached.

"Okay, all right." Evelyn backed off. "Lee Monti has some new polka music he wants us to hear."

Leonard was done with polka music. His gut told him that the way to make their mark was with race music. "Don't we have a session coming up with that one guitar player we recorded?" he asked. "You know that guy, Dirty Rivers, or something —"

"You mean Muddy Waters?" said Leeba. "That's tomorrow."

"Do we even have the money to cover the session?" asked Evelyn.

"Hell, I'll pay for it out of my own pocket if I have to. I just hope that motherfucker's worth it."

The next day Leonard and Evelyn were at the studio with Muddy, backed by Sunnyland Slim on piano and Big Crawford on bass. Leonard brought Leeba along to handle the paperwork and to keep an eye on the clock so they didn't go into overtime.

The first song they laid down, a number called "Good Lookin' Woman," sounded too much like other songs he'd heard. Leonard leaned over the control console, watching through the window, trying to keep the stomach acids at bay. After another two takes he told everyone to take a break.

Sunnyland Slim and the engineer stepped outside for some air, but Muddy and Big Crawford stayed back in the studio and started fiddling around. Leonard was adding up the costs in his head: more money down the drain.

He looked through the picture window and watched Big Crawford laying down a syncopated bass line. Muddy adjusted the tuning on his electric guitar and slipped a three-inch metal pipe on his little finger and started sliding it up and down the neck of the guitar, giving off a whining, piercing feedback that hurt Leonard's ears. He'd never heard a guitar make that kind of noise. It sounded like a mistake, and once Muddy started singing, it got even worse.

"What the hell is that?" he said to Evelyn.

"You said you wanted different. And that's *definitely* different." Evelyn smiled and lit a cigarette. "I like it."

The engineer came back in from his break and Evelyn told him to roll tape.

"Wait — whoa, whoa. I ain't paying for this."

"Fine. Then I'll pay for it." She turned to the engineer. "Go on, roll tape."

Muddy started at the top and Leonard slapped his hands to his head. This was bullshit. It reminded him of that other guitarist, that Red Dupree. Leonard pressed the talk button and stopped Muddy in the middle of his song. "What the hell are you singing? Sounds like you've got goddamn marbles in your mouth."

Evelyn pulled Leonard's hand from the talk button and said, "Don't listen to him, Muddy. I want to see where this song goes."

"You're kidding me, right?" said Leonard. "It's just a guitar and bass."

"But aren't you listening to the words?"

"Words? What fuckin' words? I can't understand a goddamn thing he's singing."

"I think they're onto something," said Evelyn.

"C'mon now, Lenny." Leeba got up and stood in between them. "Just give it another listen. It's definitely a different sound. It's what you say you've been wanting."

Leonard dragged his hand back through his hair, took a deep breath and plopped down hard in a chair. He sighed, deflating like a tire losing air. "You realize that if we do this and the record flops we'll be out of business."

"Yes," said Evelyn. "But at least we'll go down fighting."

Before the session was over, Leonard and Evelyn agreed to record two of Muddy's songs: "I Can't Be Satisfied" for the A-side and "I Feel Like Going Home" for the B-side. After about two and a half hours, they had it in the can, but Leonard wasn't ready to pull the trigger and release it.

"What are you waiting for?" Evelyn asked the next day. She leaned over his desk, her diamond necklace swaying back and forth like a metronome. "You know I could override you and do this."

There she went again, lording her fifty-one percent over him. "Yeah, but we both know you won't." He didn't know that at all, but he was taking a chance. "You won't because without me you won't be able to distribute it."

Evelyn clenched her fist and narrowed her eyes. He knew she wanted to slug him and tell him to go fuck himself, but Evelyn Aron didn't do that sort of thing, so instead she said, "I'm telling you, you're wrong about this record."

"Yeah, well, I sure as hell know that Muddy Waters ain't the answer to Aristocrat's problems."

ELEVEN:
"OLD BUTTERMILK SKY"

LEEBA

Leeba walked into Aileen's kitchenette on Jefferson Street and found her sitting on the floor, her hair held back with a scarf tied at the nape of her neck. She was staring into a droopy houseplant in a cracked clay pot. There were fruit flies everywhere, hovering above the leaves, clinging to the mirror, lingering above the drain in the kitchen sink. Aileen seemed agitated by them, as if they were some sort of enemy. One crawled along the floor and she squished it with her finger.

"What's wrong?" asked Leeba. "Did something happen?"

Aileen nodded, her eyes fixed on the flies, crushing another one that landed near her foot. "J.J.'s back."

"J.J.? I thought you told him to get lost."

"I did. Twice." No matter how hard she tried, Aileen couldn't get rid of J.J. After two years she'd broken it off, but he refused to accept that it was over. "He's telling me we're

165

meant to be together and all kinds of hogwash like that . . ." Aileen killed another fly. "I'm sick and tired of everything. Sick to death of nothing going my way. You know what I made in tips last night at the Trigger Lounge? Three lousy bucks. Damn cocktail waitresses made more than me. Don't you ever get sick of everything being so damn hard? Sick of writing songs that no one wants to hear?"

Leeba thought about the music she'd been writing. Basically mimicking songs on the radio by singers like Dinah Shore and Peggy Lee. She'd always heard music inside her head, but lately that music was starting to change. Now it was the music of the delta. But that was Negro music and it felt off bounds to her. She pushed it down, denied it, but still the tunes kept surfacing.

"Well?" asked Aileen, hugging her legs to her chest.

Leeba recalled the session she'd been in with Muddy Waters, Sunnyland Slim and Big Crawford. "What I'd really like to do is write something new. Like the stuff Leonard's recording. That kind of music makes you have to move, have to dance. It's wild and exciting and you can't get enough of it. It makes you come alive." She sighed. "I'd love to try and write some blues."

"So what's stopping you?"

Leeba laughed. "I'm a white, Jewish girl, remember? I can't do blues music."

"Ah, excuse me. Have you taken a good look at Leonard and Evelyn? Last I remember, they was white."

When Leeba got home that day she went straight to the piano. Instead of suppressing it, she let her fingers feel the energy and the music welling up inside her. She reached for a pad of paper and scratched down notes and phrases, propping the pencil between her lips while she played a verse and then the next one and the one after that.

The following Saturday evening, the song she'd started writing was still in Leeba's head, competing with the sounds of the band playing and the crickets chirping. A breeze set the paper lanterns swaying on the rooftop overlooking Douglas Boulevard.

Leeba was attending a dance at the J.P.I., the Jewish People's Institute, but she wasn't planning on staying long because Aileen was waiting for her at a club on the other side of town. The only reason Leeba agreed to go to the dance at all was to pacify her mother. She'd been to the J.P.I. dances before and it was the same every week. Every Saturday night, after the Sabbath, all the single Jewish men and women in Lawndale could be found there, hoping to meet their *besherit,* their one and only.

A few months shy of turning twenty-six, Leeba was among the oldest women going to those dances and with each passing week it grew more humiliating. Other girls had been picked off like ducks in a shooting gallery, but here she was, still standing, still waiting.

At that moment she spotted Avrom Yurzel standing across the way, brushing crumbs off his lapels. She was surprised to see him there because Avrom wasn't a regular at the J.P.I. dances. In fact, that was the first time she'd seen him since her mother invited him for dinner some three or four months back.

He came up to her just as the band began playing "Night and Day."

"It really is you," she teased. "I thought I was seeing things."

He smiled and plunged his hands in his pockets. "I had nothing going tonight. Thought I'd wander over here. See what all the fuss is about. I've never been to one of these before."

"Believe me, you haven't been missing a thing."

They made small talk for a few minutes and when the band started playing "Ole Buttermilk Sky," much to her surprise Avrom asked if she'd like to dance. He was about an inch shorter than Leeba, but that didn't seem to faze him.

"So what are the chances of your mother inviting me back over for dinner?" he asked.

"I thought you were booked up through Yom Kippur."

168

He stopped shuffling his feet and stood back, a smile on his face. "I'll break my plans."

She was confused. Was he flirting with her?

"Or if you prefer," he said, pulling her in close, running his hand along her back, "we could have dinner, just the two of us."

Oh my, he was *flirting.*

Leeba and Avrom shared another dance — ironically it was to a rendition of "Chi-Baba Chi-Baba," which everyone from Louis Prima to Perry Como to Peggy Lee had recorded back in '47 when the Sherman Hayes Orchestra did it.

"Well, thank you," she said when the dance was over. "This was fun but I have to go."

"Not yet. It's a nice night. Come, take a walk with me." He held his hand out to her.

The next thing she knew, she was standing in the middle of Douglas Park kissing Avrom Yurzel. Mostly because he *was* Avrom Yurzel and as a young girl she had dreamed of this moment while kissing her pillow. The opportunity had presented itself and she had to see her fantasy through. But did she like Avrom? Did she feel something for him? *Anything?* And why was she wishing he was Red Dupree instead? She let Avrom kiss her again before she pried herself away.

"I'm sorry." Her hands pressed against his shoulders. "But I really do have to go now. I'm meeting a friend."

"Don't leave." He ran his fingers through her curly hair.

"What has gotten into you? I thought you weren't ready to —"

"Shh." He leaned in to kiss her again, but she backed away.

Here was a nice Jewish boy wanting to kiss her, maybe court her, maybe marry her and give her children, and she wasn't interested. Or maybe she was just being smart. "C'mon, Avrom," she said. "I know you're lonely, but you don't really want *this.*" She indicated the two of them.

He dropped his hands to his sides and furrowed his brow. "I'm sorry. Weekends . . ." His voice faded for a moment. "They're hard for me."

"It's okay. I understand."

He plunged his hands into his pockets and cocked his head to the side. "I don't want to go back up to that rooftop. Would it be okay if I came with you tonight? I won't try anything, I promise."

She smiled. "Okay."

As they slid into the backseat of the taxicab, she leaned forward and gave the driver the address. "Three fifteen East Thirty-seventh Street."

"East Thirty-seventh?" Avrom hiked up his eyebrows. "That's on the South Side. Near Bronzeville."

"Actually, it's *in* Bronzeville," she informed him.

"Not a great neighborhood, Leeba. Why are we going all the way to the South Side?"

"I'm meeting my friend Aileen at the Sunset Café. You remember Aileen, don't you? She went to Marshall High."

"You mean the colored girl you ran with?"

"I'm meeting her at a black-and-tan club." A black and tan was one of the few places where Negroes and whites were free to socialize together without anyone raising an eyebrow, let alone a fist. A black and tan was different from a place like the Macomba. That was a Negro club and it always took a good five minutes or so before everyone got comfortable having a white girl at the bar. But the black and tans were easy to slip in and out of. Leeba and Aileen had been going to them for years, sneaking in before they were old enough. Those were the clubs Aileen first performed in, the clubs where Leeba learned to swing dance and where she'd had her first martini.

"A black-and-tan club, huh?" Avrom ran his tongue across his teeth, making a sucking sound.

"It has some of the best jazz in town. But if you don't want to go, that's fine," she said. "I can drop you somewhere else or —"

"No, no." He straightened his necktie. "I'm going. I'm just surprised is all."

"Don't say anything to my mother. She'd have a fit."

"Not a word. Promise."

Leeba knew her mother would be furious at her for discouraging Avrom's advances, but then again, her mother was always furious at her for something. She'd never understood why until a few years ago when Aunt Sylvie explained *everything*. According to her aunt, her mother, Freyda Bartosz, married Jakub Groski when she was twenty-three — ancient compared to the other girls in the shtetl. But at last her *besherit* came along. Jakub the musician, the mason, her savior. She couldn't have been happier. Until Leeba came along. Jakub, so dazzled by this little girl, couldn't walk past her without scooping her up in his arms, never missing a chance to bounce her on his knee. Baby Leeba had captured her father's heart completely and her mother found herself competing with her newborn for her husband's affection. Over time she became jealous of her own baby. The resentment grew until Golda came along and Freyda decided she would show Jakub what it felt like to be second best.

Leeba and Avrom heard jazz coming from the club as their taxicab pulled up. The music swelled, growing louder as they entered the crowded café. Avrom was uneasy, Leeba could tell. He wore the same expression on his face that she'd seen plastered on the rare white face that dared to enter the Macomba. It was a bright cheery mask that said, *See, I'm here. I'm not a bigot.* But she saw beneath the mask. He was self-conscious and trying too hard to appear as if he didn't notice that half the people there were Negroes. Didn't he understand that the mix was the whole point of a black-and-tan club? Leeba and Avrom weaved their way through the packed room until they found Aileen sitting at a round table near the stage, nursing a drink. She looked up, stunned when she saw Avrom.

Leeba sat down and said under her breath, "Close your mouth. I'll explain later."

After Avrom ordered drinks he announced a little too enthusiastically, "Your people have a way with music. It's lively. Very lively."

Aileen burst out laughing. "You ought to take him to the Macomba or the 708."

"One step at a time," said Leeba.

Avrom took a long glug from his drink and gradually began to relax. They were listening to the music when Leeba spotted J.J. stumbling over to the table, drink in hand and already looking sloppy.

"Oh no," Leeba groaned. "Did you tell him you were going to be here?"

"No." Aileen shook her head. "I swear I didn't."

"Allow me to introduce myself," said J.J., looking at Avrom. "I'm Johnson Junior, but

173

you can call me J.J. And I see you've already met my woman."

"Knock it off, J.J.," said Aileen. "I'm not your woman. And Avrom is Leeba's date."

"Date?" Leeba looked at Avrom and laughed. "This isn't a date."

"That's right. We already established that. This is not a date." Avrom's eyes stayed on J.J., who was wrestling with a chair at the next table.

J.J. finally got the chair turned around and clumsily dropped into it. "Now see here," said J.J., draping his arm around Aileen's shoulder, "this here's the way it's s'posed to be. Me and my woman."

Aileen shifted in her chair. "I hate it when you say shit like that to me."

"Now, baby, don't be like that," said J.J. "I got you somethin'. Somethin' real special." He reached into his pocket and pulled out a bracelet, shimmering, dangling off his fingers. "What do you think of that?"

"I think you stole it," said Leeba.

J.J. turned to Aileen. "What you doin' hanging round with her all the time?"

Aileen ignored him, stood up and reached for Avrom's hand. "C'mon. Let's dance."

"Dance?" Avrom looked as if she'd asked him to commit a crime.

"Go on," said Leeba. "She's a good dancer."

Leeba sat back and watched Avrom. He was

as stiff as cardboard at first, but later, after two and a half glasses of whiskey, he began to lose his inhibitions on the dance floor. Soon he was clapping, shimmying his shoulders and thrusting his hips. At one point he looked up at the ceiling, raised his hands high above his head and yelped so loud Leeba heard it above the music.

When they came back to the table Avrom had sweat on his brow and upper lip. As he unknotted his necktie and slouched down in his chair, he said with full sincerity, "This place is great."

Twelve:
"Pistol Slapper Blues"

LEONARD
A month after they had Muddy Waters in the studio, Evelyn was still harping on Leonard to release the record. But Leonard had doubts. He added up the costs of pressing the record, plus the time and money needed to distribute it. Aristocrat barely had enough dough to carry them through the end of the month. He was pretty much resigned to the fact that the label had failed and that they were going out of business. He was hoping for a miracle and, as far as he was concerned, Muddy Waters and his down-home delta blues wasn't it.

That was on Leonard's mind one June afternoon when he stopped by the house before heading down to the club. He had just dropped off some money so Revetta could pay the electricity bill and as he was about to head back out to his car, he passed Marshall sitting at the foot of the stairs in the front hall, sulking, pounding his fist into his baseball mitt.

"How you doin' there, sport?" Leonard asked.

The boy shrugged, eyes kept low.

"Hey, what's the matter?" But as soon as he asked he remembered. Leonard felt like a shit. He'd forgotten that he had promised Marshall they'd go to a White Sox game that day. The kid had probably been waiting for him all afternoon. Raised in a houseful of girls, Leonard knew how much his son needed to spend time with him. He knew it and yet it never seemed to happen. Phil managed to set aside part of his day for his kids and wife. He took Sheva out to dinner at least once a week before heading into the club. He gave Terry piggyback rides around the dining room table and read Pam bedtime stories.

Leonard looked at his boy and did the only thing he could think of. "Hey, Marshall," he said, "wanna come to work with your old man tonight?"

The boy was already on his feet, a smile stretched across his face. Leonard called out to Revetta, "I'm taking Marshall with me to the club."

His hand was on the front door when Revetta darted out of the kitchen, her fingers tangled in a dish towel. "Len, he's five years old."

"Don't worry. He'll be fine. It doesn't get rough down there until late. I'll have him home long before that."

"And what about school?"

"He's in fuckin' kindergarten. What's he gonna miss? So he goes in late one day."

"I want him home by ten."

"Ten. Okay."

"I mean it, Len."

"Ten o'clock. I promise."

Revetta slung the towel over her shoulder and leaned against the doorjamb, looking at her son. "You want to do this, Marshall? You want to go down to the club with your father tonight?"

All Marshall could do was nod, his cheeks about to burst from smiling so hard.

When they got to the Macomba, Leonard propped Marshall up at the bar and gave him a Shirley Temple with an extra cherry. Between him and Phil they kept a close eye on him. He was a good boy, happy to sit there with his elbows on the bar, sipping his drink and watching the grown-ups, listening to the music. Everyone who came up to the bar stopped to muss Marshall's hair or pat him on the back. The kid was in heaven.

Leonard went about his business but watched the clock. It was a quarter past ten and they should have been going, but the kid was having such a good time and the crowd was well behaved. At the end of Tom Archia's set he'd take Marshall home. Besides, Revetta knew ten o'clock for Leonard really meant eleven, eleven thirty. No big deal.

Not long after that, some drunk near the bandstand shoved the guy next to him. *Ah shit,* thought Leonard. *Here we go.*

The drunk threw the first punch and Leonard whistled, motioning to Big Gene that there was trouble on the floor. Phil was already in the thick of it, trying to pull the one guy off the drunk. Marshall twisted around on his stool, not wanting to miss a second of this. Between Big Gene and Phil they got the guys separated. It was over, and things had started to calm down, when out of nowhere two other guys pulled guns and started shooting up the place. Bullets were flying, ricocheting off the ceiling fans, the light fixtures. Bottles behind the bar were exploding. Everyone was screaming, taking cover.

Leonard's only thought was *My boy! My boy's in here.* He lunged for Marshall and pulled him behind the bar. That probably scared the poor kid more than the gunfire. Leonard was shaking as he pushed Marshall to the floor, shielding him with his own body. He heard more bullets and more glass breaking. The floor was a swamp of liquor draining from the broken bottles on the shelf above. Round after round the shots kept going. Through the years they'd had a knife fight here and there, a few guns pulled, even a few shots fired inside the club — but Leonard had never seen anything like this before. Leonard knew he was crushing Marshall, but the kid didn't let out a peep, didn't cry, but Leonard sure did. When the gunfire subsided and he heard the squeal of the police sirens outside, Leonard rolled off of Marshall, leaned against the wall behind the bar and sobbed into his hands.

Revetta was going to kill him when she found out. That was all he could think as he told Phil to handle things at the club while he rushed to get Marshall home.

Leonard hardly slept that night. What the hell was he doing in that line of work? And what was he thinking taking Marshall down there? He knew that place was dangerous any time of day. He had to get the hell out of that nightclub. He had to get Phil out of there, too. He had one more chance to make something happen with Aristocrat and now was the time to do it.

The next day Leonard went into the office and said to Evelyn, "Okay. I'm ready. Let's release the goddamn Muddy Waters record."

Three thousand pressed records arrived at the office by the end of the week, and each one of those 78s needed to be labeled, stuffed into a cardboard sleeve, stacked and counted. Some of them had to be boxed up so they could be shipped to distributors in the South and along the East Coast.

Leonard loaded three cases of records into the back of his Buick and began making the rounds. His first stop was to see the Old Swingmaster at WGES. Leonard had talked the record up ahead of time, borrowing from Evelyn's enthusiasm because he still hadn't found any of his own. "A completely different sound" was what he'd said to Benson over the phone. "This is really something special. You gotta hear this."

An hour later Leonard stood in the studio while Al Benson leaned back in his chair and closed his eyes, ready to listen. Leonard dropped the needle and halfway into the first verse, the Old Swingmaster opened his eyes. When they got to the chorus he sat up and smiled.

Leonard was bewildered. What did everyone else hear in this music that he was missing? Could his instincts be *that* off? But he was a salesman, natural born, and so he played it to the hilt. "What'd I tell you?"

"You got something here," said Benson.

Before Leonard made it back to his car, Benson had "I Can't Be Satisfied" on the air. But what really surprised him was that by the time he pulled up to the curb outside Aristocrat, the Swingmaster was playing it again.

When he walked through the front door, Leeba pointed to the radio on her desk and said, "Are you hearing this?"

WGES had so many requests that day, and Benson had played that song so often, that by the next morning stores had sold out and people were calling the office, asking how soon they could get more records. Leonard got on the horn with Art Sheridan, the record presser, and ordered ten thousand copies.

Leonard still couldn't understand a god-damn thing Muddy was singing on that record, but he understood that they were onto something that was going to save Aristo-crat and make them a lot of money.

Walter dragged his sleeve across his mouth.

"I saw it all right."

Walter pounded on the bar. "Let's have us some service over here, huh?" He had already drained his flask on the walk over.

The next day as Red was coming home from work, he saw Walter tearing down the sidewalk. Sober for once.

"You know that cat who was hanging 'round us at Jewtown yesterday?" said Walter. "You know who that was? That was Muddy Waters."

"How do you know it was him?" Red thought that guy looked familiar. He had heard Muddy's records over the radio and had even gone to see him play in clubs around town, but he hadn't put two and two together.

"Last night, after you left the bar, he come lookin' for us. He's puttin' a new band together — all electric guitars — he wants you on guitar and he wants me on harp. Said to bring you 'round so we can start rehearsing."

Red paused, letting this sink in. Playing alongside someone like Muddy Waters meant exposure — the kind of exposure he'd dreamed of back in Louisiana. This was his chance to make something happen. He never would have guessed that his big break would come in the form of Muddy Waters. He gave himself a moment, wanting to mark in his mind the last moments of his old self, saying good-bye to that part of him that had been conditioned to play himself down. He no longer had to be a Negro afraid of calling attention to himself in a white world. Now all that was behind him; he could let himself all the way out.

"Go get your guitar," said Walter. "They's waiting on us at the rehearsal studio."

Red ran up to his kitchenette, grabbed his guitar and amp and went with Walter to a small building down on West Thirteenth Street. It was nothing fancy. A warped floor, sheets tacked up on the windows, exposed beams and naked bulbs along the ceiling. Aside from the drum kit and piano, it was just a couple of folding chairs and wooden crates. Pints of whiskey were being passed back and forth between the musicians.

Red and Walter shook hands with Muddy and were introduced to the rest of the band. Elgin Evans was a drummer with light skin the color of caramel and a deep, gravelly voice. Otis Spann, the piano player, had a mustache and wore his hair slicked straight back. When he smiled he was all teeth.

They rehearsed for almost three hours without taking a break. Elgin beat those drums, his sticks propelled by some force deep down inside him, and Otis Spann kept a cigarette — one after the other — pinched between his lips the entire time he played piano. Walter was blowing a double cross harp, his head rocking from side to side, his foot stomping to the beat. Red paid close attention to Muddy — how he used his fingers, never a pick, and how the slide on his pinky could deliver a shrieking open A. Red watched how he twisted the strings, making a single note cry out for more, working with the feedback and reverb, never trying to quiet it. Red had a few of his own tricks, but each time he got a little too fancy, Muddy would come in with a strident guitar lick. The message was clear: Muddy was the bandleader and ain't no one about to upstage him. Especially not Red Dupree.

Fourteen:
"Ain't Gonna Give Nobody None of My Jelly Roll"

LEEBA

When Leeba and Aileen entered Lyon's Deli on Maxwell Street they were greeted with the smell of grease and fried onions. Hard salamis hung from hooks in the ceiling behind the cash register. Leeba heard a tall, young colored boy behind the counter speaking Yiddish to a Jewish merchant ordering pickled herring. There were at least as many Negroes in there eating kosher beef and noodle kugel as there were Jews.

Leeba and Aileen placed their orders at the counter and took a table for two. Aileen had just come from work and Leeba saw, lurking beneath Aileen's jacket, her gray button-down uniform with "Knickerbocker Hotel" monogrammed across the breast pocket. While they were waiting for their food, Aileen brushed crumbs off the table and resituated the napkin holder, straw holder, the salt and pepper shakers, too. She didn't seem to be able to hold still while Leeba told her about the new song she was working on.

"This is the blues stuff you're trying to do, right?" asked Aileen.

"Yeah, but I'm stuck. I don't know how to end the song."

"What's it about?"

Leeba rolled her eyes. "Infatuation. Heartbreak. Love gone bad."

"Sure sounds like the blues to me." Aileen laughed and blew the paper wrapper off her straw. "So when you gonna let me hear this song?"

"Whenever I finish it. If I ever finish it."

"And you're positive you don't wanna get up on stage and perform yourself?" Aileen gave her a look of disbelief. "The only time I feel alive is when I'm on stage."

"I'm a behind-the-scenes kinda gal." Leeba thought about those neighborhood concerts her father had put together in their living room, when she'd been the center of attention. It had meant so much to her then, but now she couldn't imagine wanting that. "I'd be a nervous wreck playing in front of a crowd."

After lunch Leeba and Aileen made their regular pilgrimage to the Maxwell Street Radio and Record Store so Leeba could see her piano. It was a crisp fall day and the sun was shining but the air was brisk. As the girls walked through Maxwell Street, the music swirled around them. The different beats and bass lines moved through Leeba's body, causing her to pace her footsteps to the changing tempos. They kept walking down the crowded sidewalk, and when they came to the Maxwell Street Radio and Record Store, Leeba noticed something in the front window that made her mouth go dry. She felt like she had swallowed a fist.

"What is it?" Aileen asked. "What's wrong?"

Leeba rushed inside the store, hoping that it wasn't true. But there it was on the raised lid of her Bösendorfer: a red ticket with thick black lettering. *Sold.*

Aileen caught up to her. "I thought that old geezer was gonna sell it to you."

"So did I." According to Abrams, "a sale is a sale," so even after she'd quit working there, he had agreed to save it for her. She'd even made arrangements to keep it at Aunt Sylvie and Uncle Moishe's since they had more room. Leeba stood before the baby grand, something heavy stacking up in her chest. She'd saved five hundred and thirty-five of the six hundred dollars needed to buy it and now it was for nothing. Leeba swept her sleeve over the lid and bench to clear the thin layer of dust clinging to its lacquered surface.

"C'mon," said Aileen. "Let's go."

"Not yet." This was her last chance with her Bösendorfer. A proper parting was needed. She sat down and tinkered with the keys. "It needs tuning. Hear that?" She played a chord and smiled sadly. "Just a little off, just a little sour." Still, each note hollowed her out, echoing inside her. She played a few more chords before settling into an old Spencer Williams song. "Remember this one?"

Aileen laughed as Leeba played the intro and began to sing "I Ain't Gonna Give Nobody None of My Jelly Roll." They used to sing that song full of sexual innuendoes when they were too young to know what it meant. But now Aileen was singing it fully aware and shameless. And Leeba, knowing she'd never play this instrument again, let her fingers take over, her foot pumping the damper pedal. They drew attention from a handful of customers inside the store, who gathered around, shuffling back and forth, smiling, some even blushing. When Aileen got to the line about not letting anybody taste her jelly roll, Bernard Abrams burst through the circle, flapping his arms.

"Hey-hey! What do you think you're doing? You can't waltz in here and start playing."

He grabbed hold of Leeba's arm and yanked her to her feet. Aileen started to cuss him out and Leeba found herself trying to calm them both down. When the yelling subsided, Abrams, still holding tight to Leeba's arm, escorted both of them to the doorway.

Leeba glanced back over her shoulder at the piano. "Just tell me one thing," she said to Abrams. "Who bought it?"

"A radio station."

This disappointed and saddened her even more. How cold, how empty. It was like turning a child over to an orphanage. Her baby grand needed a rightful owner — someone who would love and care for it. "But you knew I was saving up for it," she said to Abrams. "How could you have sold it? And to a radio station."

"Six hundred and fifty dollars. That's how I sold it."

Leeba was so distraught when they left that at first she didn't notice who had started playing out front. But she heard the music and suddenly she stopped, her breath caught in her chest. She reached for Aileen's arm and gestured toward Red Dupree. He was there on the sidewalk with Little Walter, his guitar case already filling with dollar bills and coins.

"Damn, he's good," said Aileen. "So is his harp player."

Leeba nodded. She didn't want to speak. She just wanted this moment to listen to him play and watch him in all his glory. When that wasn't enough and she needed an excuse to get closer, she pinched open her pocketbook and took a bill from her wallet. Working her way through the crowd, she went up, her heart beating out of sync with the music as she placed her dollar in his guitar case. She

194

paused, hoping he'd notice her, thinking maybe he'd recognize her from the store or Aristocrat, but he was too lost in his music. He never even looked at her.

Leeba retraced her steps and stood once again next to Aileen. The swarm of people around Red Dupree and Little Walter had grown even bigger. She waited and listened to two more songs before she let Aileen lead her away, feeling as foolish as a schoolgirl.

But it wasn't all for nothing because when she got home that day she went straight to the piano. She had finally found the ending to her story, the hook for her song: "No, not a romance. No, not a chance."

Two days later, she played the song for Aileen. Though Leeba's voice wasn't right for the style, she closed her eyes and sang with conviction, feeling every note, every phrase. While her eyes were still closed, she heard Aileen begin to clap along with the beat. She moved into the chorus, the hook. *"No, it's not a romance. It don't stand a chance."*

When Leeba played the last note Aileen let out a laugh. "Girl, I do believe your lily-white ass is playin' the blues."

The following week Leeba and Aileen performed the song for Leonard and Evelyn in the Cottage Grove office during Aileen's lunch break. She didn't look like a blues singer, dressed in her hotel maid's uniform, her hair tucked beneath a scarf, but she sure did sound like one. While Leeba played, Aileen began to sing, turning Leeba's skin to gooseflesh. This was Leeba's song — she'd created it — and Aileen's voice was perfect for it.

Leeba saw Evelyn whispering to Leonard. He nodded while Evelyn toyed with her earring and whispered something else. When Aileen finished singing, neither Evelyn nor Leonard said a word. The room went silent. Leonard had an opinion about everything and the longer he went without speaking up, the worse his verdict.

It wasn't until Leeba prompted them that Leonard pinched the end of his cigarette and drew a deep inhale. "Aileen, you know I've always said you got a great voice. And, Leeba, I like this new direction. This blues style ain't exactly what I was expecting, but . . ." He paused and scratched his head. "But . . ."

"But?" Aileen's voice sounded small and frightened, nothing like the big booming one she'd just sung with.

"But like I've said before" — he raised his hands, palms up — "girl singers don't sell records."

Leeba watched Aileen's shoulders slump forward. "What about Ella Fitzgerald?" Leeba said. "And Billie Holiday? Dinah Washington?"

"What Leonard really means," said Evelyn,

"is that there's nothing wrong with your singing. Or your song, really. There's just nothing *special* about either one. And Leonard's right, girl singers don't sell."

Leeba was disappointed, but not like Aileen. She could tell that rejection hit her hard. She was on the verge of tears.

Leonard knew it, too, because he went over and put his arm around her. "You got the pipes. You got the look." He turned back toward Leeba. "You girls just need to come up with the right material."

Aileen nodded and sucked in her lower lip.

Leeba walked her outside just before Aileen broke down and sobbed.

"I'm so damn stupid," she said, wiping her hand across her eyes. "I thought maybe — maybe this gonna be my big break. I'm such a damn fool. I hate my life. Nothing ever works out for me. Ever."

Leeba wasn't happy, either, but she pushed her disappointment aside to keep Aileen from sinking. "You heard Leonard. We just need the right material. We can't give up."

"Maybe you can't, but I'm done." She looked at Leeba as the tears rolled over the rims of her eyes. "I'm so tired. I didn't think it was possible to feel this tired. This beat up. All I ever hear is no. I can't take it anymore."

"Don't think like that. We'll keep working on more songs. We'll get there. I promise."

Aileen glanced over Leeba's shoulder. "Oh

no, somebody's coming."

Leeba turned around. It was Muddy Waters walking up the sidewalk in a handsome suit and tie. His pompadour proud and high, a far cry from the man in the dirty overalls she'd met at Universal Recording a year and a half before. Ever since that day she helped him sign his name the two of them had formed a special bond. He was always bringing flowers for her desk or giving her chocolates. And it wasn't that he was sweet on her; he was just showing his appreciation. She waved while Aileen covered her face in her hands and turned toward the side of the building, her shoulders shaking.

"Hey there, now," Muddy said. "What's the problem here?" He tilted his head, trying to get a closer look at Aileen.

"It's okay," said Leeba. "Just having a bad day is all."

"See now, the good thing about them bad days is they don't last but for twenty-four hours."

When Aileen lifted her head and glanced back at Muddy her shoulders began to shake even harder. Leeba thought he had broken her, until she realized Aileen wasn't crying. No, she was laughing.

Slowly she turned around and fluttered her lashes, a thin smile rising up on her tearstained lips. Muddy didn't take his eyes off her and Leeba could feel the air pulsing between them. It was like she was intruding on an intimate moment. Something powerful had just started and Leeba wasn't sure if this was a good thing or not. For either of them.

FIFTEEN:
"PAYING THE COST TO BE THE BOSS"

LEONARD

It was one of those Indian summer days in October with temperatures in the high seventies. Leonard walked around the car one more time, a Cadillac Coupe de Ville, midnight blue with chrome trim, tail fins, power windows and a V-8 engine. This automobile was nicer than some people's homes. It set him back three thousand, four hundred and ninety-six dollars, but he needed a new car and had wanted a Cadillac his whole life. Muddy's record was selling and soon they'd start making some money. He worked hard. Didn't he deserve this one bit of luxury? He ran his hand along the hood. What a beauty. He shook the dealer's hand, opened the door and climbed inside. The leather was soft as suede and the smell intoxicating. He gripped the steering wheel, revved the engine and took off, leaving his junkyard Buick behind forever.

Leonard rolled down the windows and

200

blasted the radio as he drove along Douglas Boulevard, going slow just to watch heads turn. There was nothing subtle about the car and when he came to a red light, he pulled up alongside a mint green Starlight Coupe Studebaker. The freckly-faced young man behind the wheel looked over at Leonard's Cadillac longingly. At the next light Leonard looked through the rearview mirror and was disappointed to see that the couple in the car behind him were more engrossed in their conversation than his car.

As he turned onto Millard Avenue he crept past the greystones, keeping his eyes wide open. He knew where the apartment was and would be lying if he said he hadn't gone out of his way countless times before to drive by it. It was a small building, nothing special. He had Revetta in a bigger place and on a better block. Leonard pulled up a few doors down and threw the car in park. Idling in his showpiece, he lit a cigarette and gazed through the rearview mirror. There was a Chrysler parked out front. A '45 with rust spots on the side panels. *C'mon, Shirley. Just come outside. Just this once . . .*

Two cigarettes later he saw a man, about his age, walking up the sidewalk with a briefcase, his eyes shielded by his fedora. Leonard had heard that the husband was a door-to-door salesman. He watched him walk up the front steps and fit his key in the door.

201

When the man had gone inside, Leonard squeezed his steering wheel. The sun was going down; the streetlights had come on. It was time to go home.

When he got there he stayed in the car, honking the horn until Revetta came to the door. He called to her through the open window, "Don't just stand there. Come take a look."

She disappeared from the doorway and reappeared a moment later pulling on her sweater, the front door clapping shut behind her. Leonard turned off the engine and got out of the car, watching her walk around it twice before she said a word. Her mouth was agape. He didn't have a clue what was going through her mind. He was prepared for her to demand he take it back.

"Is this yours?" she asked at last.

"It's *ours*. What do you think?"

"It's beautiful, but, Lenny, can we afford this?"

"Of course we can afford this." He said it with such conviction he almost believed it.

She wrapped her arms around him and kissed him hard.

"Go get the kids. Let's go for a drive."

She rushed into the house and woke up the children, and all of them, still in their pajamas, piled into the backseat and went for a drive. Susie slept through the whole thing.

■ ■ ■ ■

A few weeks later Leonard sat across from his father at the card table in the front room of the apartment on Karlov Avenue. Joe Chess shuffled the deck. Normally they played pinochle with Phil and their neighbor Moishe, but that day it would be gin rummy, just the two of them.

"You trust that Evelyn broad?" his father asked, snapping the deck before he dealt the cards.

"She's a pain in the ass, but yeah, I trust her."

"So where the hell's all the money? You're telling me the business is doing better. You tell me you have hit records. I see you driving around in a new car — a Cadillac no less — and —"

"Dad, it's not —"

"*Shah.* Let me finish." He fanned out his cards. "Your brother's too proud to ask so I'm asking for him. Can't you find something — *anything* — for Phil over at Aristocrat?"

Leonard had known this was coming.

"Gotta be something over at that company he can do," his father said.

"The problem is, we can't pay Phil. Not like the kind of money he's making now at the club."

"I see you made enough money to get that

new car."

A dagger of guilt stabbed Leonard. Ever since he'd bought that car, people had assumed he was on easy street. And yes, that was the whole idea behind getting a Cadillac; but at the same time that image meant having to explain and apologize. Phil never said a word about the car other than "Mazel tov, motherfucker. You always said you were gonna get one of these."

His father grunted. "I think you should share some of the wealth with your brother."

Leonard laid his cards facedown. Yes, Muddy's records were selling, but it wasn't that simple. The record business was an up-front business — studios, musicians and record pressers all got paid at the time of service. And even after Leonard got a record out to the stores and deejays and jukeboxes, he knew they could come back as returns. He had tried before to explain all that to his father, but the old man saw only that Leonard was driving around in a Cadillac.

"It's complicated, Pop. But Evelyn and I are talking about getting a loan."

"I thought you already tried to get a loan."

"We did, but the business is healthier now. Don't worry, Pop, I haven't forgotten about Phil."

Leonard stood outside the Macomba Lounge and handed Muddy a check for two hundred

204

dollars along with a set of keys to a brand-new Cadillac of his own. He'd bought the second Cadillac for Muddy out of guilt, knowing he could have never owned a car like that himself if it hadn't been for Mud.

"It's all yours, motherfucker," Leonard said.

Muddy took the check and the keys. "Now, what was that you was sayin' 'bout my havin' goddamn marbles in my mouth?"

They both laughed. Muddy tossed the car keys in the air and snatched them in his fist.

Leonard waved to Aileen, who was leaning against the passenger-side door waiting. "Go sit inside the car," he called to her. Aileen and Muddy had been inseparable for the past few weeks and Leonard had his concerns. "Be careful with that one," he said to Muddy. "She acts tough, but she's fragile. Spun glass."

"Don't you be worrying 'bout that."

"I hope you told her you're married."

"Like I say, don't you be worrying 'bout that."

Leonard stood back and watched Muddy and Aileen drive off in that shiny red automobile. It was the middle of the day and the drug dealers and streetwalkers were already out in force, the ladies propositioning the men walking by, driving by. The sidewalks were littered with empty whiskey pints and beer bottles, used syringes, someone's brassiere. A story behind every item. The clouds hung low in the overcast sky, making that grungy neighborhood look even more dismal to Leonard.

It started to drizzle as he chucked his cigarette to the curb and went back inside the Macomba. Remnants of the previous night's brawl were evident. A couple of drunks had gotten into it at about four in the morning and started smashing up the place, throwing chairs and heaving tables at each other. They'd had their share of fights in the club, but aside from that night of the shooting when Marshall was with him, they'd never seen anything like this. The club drew a bad element that was getting worse all the time. They never knew when some drunk or junkie was gonna start a fight, pull a knife or a gun. He walked through the carnage wondering if they'd be able to salvage any of the furniture.

Phil was on the phone with the insurance company trying to determine if the damage would be covered. "I've been on hold with them for the past half hour," he said to Leonard, removing his hat long enough to wipe his brow and repositioning it on his head.

Leonard looked out at the club. The lights were flickering because of a short in the system. They'd had an electrician come look at it, but he had told them they needed to rewire the place to the tune of five hundred bucks. Maybe more.

Phil slammed down the telephone. "God-damn insurance agent. They're gonna jack up our premiums. We're better off replacing all this crap ourselves."

"Listen," said Leonard, "Evelyn and I got a meeting with the bank later this afternoon to see about a loan. Once that comes through, you and me are out of here. I promise."

Phil didn't acknowledge Leonard. It was as if he'd heard it too many times before.

Leonard was trying to think of a way to re-assure Phil, when someone pounded on the front door.

"Hold on. Hold on." Leonard unlocked the door and there was Leeba, panting hard, try-ing to catch her breath.

"I've been calling you for the past hour. Your line's been busy."

"What's wrong — what's going on?"

"It's Evelyn." She stepped inside, shaking rain off her umbrella. "She never came into work today. I can't find her anywhere. No one's seen her since yesterday afternoon. No one knows where she is. She's missing."

Sixteen:
"Worried Life Blues"

Leeba

Before Leeba had gone to get Leonard at the Macomba that Friday, she'd already telephoned everyone she could think of. Evelyn's mother, her friends, even both her ex-husbands. No one had seen or spoken to her since the day before. On their way back to the office, Leeba and Leonard agreed it was time to go to the police.

As they were keying into the office they heard the telephone. Leonard tripped the lock and Leeba rushed to her desk, grabbing the phone on the fifth or sixth ring.

"Hello? Hello!"

It was a long-distance operator with a collect call from Evelyn. "Will you accept the charges?"

"Yes." Leeba clutched the phone with both hands and called across the room to Leonard. "It's her. It's Evelyn."

Leonard perched himself on the edge of her desk. "Where the hell is she?"

"Shh, I'm on hold." It seemed like an eternity before the operator put the call through. "Evelyn? Are you all right?"

"Oh, yes, yes. I'm fine."

She sounded calm, serene, and the way she'd tossed in that "oh" so casually threw Leeba.

"Where are you?"

"I'm in Vegas."

"Las Vegas?"

Leonard's eyebrows spiked high on his forehead. "She's in Las Vegas?" He twisted out of his coat and thrust out his hand. "Give me the phone."

Leeba pulled it out of his reach and kept talking, plugging her free ear to block Leonard's yelling. "What are you doing in Las Vegas? We've been looking all over the place for you."

"So sorry. This is the first chance I've had to call." Evelyn paused for a long exhale. She sounded so blasé and Leeba could picture her lying there on some chaise, taking a long luxurious puff off her cigarette, shooting her smoke to the ceiling. "I didn't mean to worry anyone."

"What are you doing in Vegas?" Leeba asked again. "You have a meeting with the bank in an hour."

"Oh, I know, I know," said Evelyn with a *silly me* laugh. "I completely fouled that up, didn't I?" She was annoyingly giddy. "We'll have to reschedule. It's no big deal."

Leeba looked at Leonard pacing back and forth. "I can't believe she's doing this."

The room grew stiflingly hot. Raindrops had collected on the floor from Leeba's umbrella. She unbuttoned her coat and yanked her scarf free from about her neck. "Evelyn, what is going on? This isn't like you. You sound funny."

"Everything's fine. Never better, in fact. I'm just calling to let you know that I'll be back on Wednesday."

"Not till Wednesday?"

Leonard lunged for the phone. "Let me talk to her."

Again Leeba pulled the phone out of his reach. "Evelyn, you still there?"

"I'm here. I'm just calling to let you know I'll be back on Wednesday. We flew out here last night. We got married, Leeba. I'm on my honeymoon."

"Married? To who?"

Leonard stopped, his eyes about to bulge from their sockets as he kicked a wastebasket, sending papers skittering across the floor.

Evelyn laughed again. "What do you mean, to who? To Art Sheridan, of course."

"Oh." Leeba's mouth dropped open. She was dumbfounded. Art Sheridan was a record presser. Leeba had had no idea there was anything going on between Evelyn and him.

She congratulated Evelyn, hung up the

phone and turned to Leonard, who blurted out, "I'm gonna kill her. When she gets back here I swear I'm gonna kill her."

Evelyn returned from Las Vegas with sunburned cheeks and a few freckles across her nose. She waltzed into the office the following Wednesday with her pocketbook swinging from her arm, her new diamond ring catching the light.

"Well, hello there," she said. "I'm back."

Leeba and Leonard had already been in the office for hours, buried beneath a stack of invoices, trying to figure out which ones had to be paid and where they were going to find the money for them. Leonard slapped his pen to his desk and pushed himself out of his chair.

"You got some nerve, lady."

"Oh, Leonard, calm down. Your face is all flushed. It's not good for your blood pressure to get so worked up."

"You're what's not good for my blood pressure. We rescheduled the meeting with the bank for tomorrow afternoon and you better be on time. We need this loan."

"I'm very much aware of our financial needs. I'll be on time."

The next day Leeba watched Leonard pacing about the office. It was raining again that day and his shoes were squeaking, wet from having stepped in a puddle earlier. His suit jacket was rumpled and his tie was a mess.

"Did Revetta let you walk out of the house looking like that?" Leeba smiled. "Come here." She flipped up his collar and loosened the knot in his tie and started over again. "Did you eat breakfast today?"

"Does she think she's still on her goddamn honeymoon or something?"

"Calm down. She'll be here." Leeba finished knotting his tie and patted his shoulders. "There. Perfect."

Twenty minutes later, when Leonard was about to explode from anxiety, Evelyn sauntered in, dressed in a smart suit and one of her high-fashion hats. Standing next to Leonard in his wrinkled shirt and outdated two-piece suit, his tie too narrow, Leeba thought they appeared every bit the mismatched partners that they were.

"Well," said Evelyn, inspecting her makeup in her compact before closing it with a snap. "Shall we go?"

After they left, Aileen called from a pay phone at work. Leeba could hear the elevator cars dinging in the background and pictured Aileen standing in the booth, keeping a lookout for her boss. Leeba cradled the receiver between her ear and shoulder and scanned the ledger while Aileen prattled on and on about her favorite subject: Muddy. She never tired of him, fascinated by everything from his silky conk to his cuff links.

That day it was all about his new Cadillac. Aileen was talking nonstop about the interior, about how smooth the ride was and how people stared when they drove by . . .

"And did I tell you he said I could borrow it whenever I want? Me, driving a Cadillac. Can you believe it?"

Silence. The phone was pressing into Leeba's shoulder. She switched ears.

"Are you there? Leeba?"

"Yep, I'm here." She drummed her pencil against the ledger.

"What's wrong?"

"Nothing." She drummed faster.

"Something's bugging you."

Aileen was going to force it out of her. "Okay, listen, I like Muddy, I do —"

"But?"

Leeba hesitated.

"If this is 'bout him being married, I keep tellin' you, she's just a common-law wife and besides — Oh shit, my boss is coming. I gotta go, but I'll call you back. I got something to tell you. Something big."

Aileen hung up on her and Leeba had to admit she was relieved to be off the phone. She couldn't listen to any more talk about Muddy. She wasn't in favor of their relationship. He was married. It was wrong. And yet Aileen was happier than Leeba had ever seen her. But it was borrowed happiness and that worried Leeba. She would have felt better knowing that Aileen had gotten there on her own and not just because Muddy had come into her life. That smile on her face was Muddy's; the sparkle in her eyes belonged to Muddy. Everything was on account of Muddy.

Leeba got busy with some paperwork, and two hours later Evelyn was back. She swept in through the front door, shaking out her umbrella before peeling off her hat and plunking it down on her desk.

"Well?" said Leeba. "What did the bank say?"

Evelyn shrugged. "We're a bad risk." Her mouth turned downward.

"Where's Leonard?"

"Oh, I don't know." Evelyn looked around on the floor as if searching for something she'd dropped. "He was just behind me." She sat down and fiddled with her stockings, her leg extended, toes pointed. She shuffled through some message slips and then pulled out a bottle of nail enamel and began polishing her nails at her desk.

Leeba never thought she'd see the day when Leonard Chess behaved more professionally than Evelyn Aron. And where was Leonard anyway? She grabbed her coat and umbrella and went outside to look for him.

It had been raining off and on all day and everything was soaked, the streets and sidewalks covered in wet leaves turned orange, red and yellow. It didn't take long for Leeba to find Leonard. He was in the parking lot across the street, sitting in his Cadillac. She looked through the window and saw that he had his head in his hands. She knocked on the glass and his head snapped back with a start.

"What are you doing out here?" she asked, after he'd unlocked the door and she'd slid into the passenger seat, rain from her umbrella pooling at her feet.

He squeezed the steering wheel and looked straight ahead. "I can't believe the bank turned us down. I'm screwed."

"What are you talking about? Muddy's new record is selling like hotcakes."

"Do you realize how long it's going to be before I see a dime of that money?"

"There's other banks," she said. "You'll get a loan to carry you until the money comes in. It'll be okay."

He shook his head. "I never should have bought the Cadillacs. I was a fool counting on that loan. I'm in over my head. I owe everybody money." He was breathing hard, fogging up the windows. "We barely have enough money to take Muddy back into the studio. And you should have seen Evelyn with those bankers — she doesn't give a shit."

Rain collected on the windshield, blurring their view of everything. Leonard had always complained about Evelyn, about their cash flow, but this time Leeba sensed that he really couldn't see his way out of this mess any more than he could see outside his front window.

"You'll turn things around," she said. "You've never walked away from a challenge. Not in all the years I've known you."

"You really think I can make this work, huh?"

She reached over and put her hand on top of his. "Not *think*. I *know*. I know you can."

He was still staring out the windshield. He didn't speak. He looked doubtful.

"C'mon now, motherfucker," she said. "I believe in you."

He turned and shot her a stunned look. "I don't believe it. Leeba Groski said 'motherfucker.' " He burst out laughing and reached over and hugged her.

The two of them sat there laughing until the rain eased up and it was time to go back into the office.

"Your little friend's been calling here," Evelyn said to Leeba. "I told her you weren't here so what does she do? She calls back two seconds later. She's *meshuge,* that one."

Leeba knew how Aileen could get, thinking she could *will* the universe to comply at her urgent insistence. Leeba was hanging up her raincoat when the phone rang again. She answered, not surprised that it was Aileen calling yet again.

"I only got a few minutes before my break's up," Aileen said. "You are not gonna believe this."

Aileen was talking way too fast and too loud, going on and on about Muddy and his band and all his gigs. Leeba was only half listening until Aileen mentioned the guitar player.

". . . You know the one. The real tall one you like, that guy down on Maxwell Street."

"You mean Red? Red Dupree?"

"That's him. He's playing second guitar now in Muddy's band. And he's got that harp player with him, too. Now, Muddy says that boy's trouble, always acting a fool . . ."

Aileen was still rambling on, but all Leeba could think about was seeing Red perform. She could just look at him. Listen to his music. Maybe go up during his break and say hello. Maybe talk to him, get to know him. Maybe they'd become friends. Maybe more . . . *Maybe. Maybe. Maybe.*

With that tidbit of information an otherwise rainy fall day had just turned bright.

SEVENTEEN:
"GOT MY MOJO WORKING"

RED

Red got up on stage at the 708 and looked out past the spotlights, blinding hot circles of blues, yellows and whites. Through the clouds of smoke the audience slowly came into focus. He'd been in Mud's band for almost six weeks now and they'd played all over town, places like the Flame Club, Theresa's Lounge and Silvio's. Muddy pulled in larger crowds than Red and Walter were used to, but it didn't shake him. No, Red watched the way everybody locked onto Muddy and it only made him that much hungrier to have those eyes on him.

Red figured he was paying his dues, playing in Muddy's shadow, and he wasn't complaining. He wasn't even complaining about not playing on Muddy's records. Muddy said the people at Aristocrat, Leonard and his partner, didn't want to record him with a full band because it would be too expensive.

So Red made do with gigging. But it was

hard work. The night before, after their final set, Red had stumbled back to his room, kicked off his shoes and flopped down on the mattress just as the sun was coming up through the torn blinds. He'd barely shut his eyes before he had to get back up and head to the brickyard. It was grueling, but he was making money now. Playing with Muddy put an extra sixty-five or seventy dollars in his pocket every week.

The 708 was packed that night and Red eyed the audience. The only place he knew that was rowdier and raunchier than the 708 was the Macomba Lounge. Red was playing rhythm guitar on "Mean Red Spider" and held his pick between his lips until Muddy turned the guitar lead over to him. Then Red launched into his solo, measured at first before building to a frenzy, his fingers playing higher and higher on the neck. Otis Spann came in on piano, pounding the keys hard and rocking back and forth so much that Red thought the bench legs were gonna bust on him. Big Crawford's fingers were swollen plump as prunes from slapping his upright; and Little Walter, menace on the stage, swept from one end to the other, drawing on his cross harp.

On the next tune, "Screaming and Crying," it was Muddy who really let loose. Red saw the sweat glistening on the man's face, the spit bouncing off his microphone as he sang.

There was a group of women in the front row and he was playing to them, coming on to them, bumping and grinding his hips. He was teasing the hell out of them, making them swoon with each thrust in their direction. When Otis took the piano solo Muddy turned his back to the ladies. He winked at Red as he reached for a bottle of beer resting on the stool, corked it with his thumb and gave it a good shake. Then Muddy opened his fly, tucked that loaded bottle inside his trousers. When he turned back around he let those ladies have it, shooting a spray of beer foam all over them. They were cheering him on, licking the suds off their fingers. That was how they finished the first set of the evening. Red couldn't figure how Muddy was going to top that.

While they were on break Muddy cozied up to those ladies, their skin still shiny wet with beer. When it came time for their next set, Otis had to call him back on stage. Twice. They were in the middle of one of Muddy's hits, "I Feel Like Going Home," when Red noticed Muddy's woman coming into the club. That would straighten Mud up right quick, because Aileen wouldn't stand for his flirting.

She had a white girl with her — that girl from Aristocrat Records. Half the crowd turned to look. They weren't used to seeing whites in a place like the 708 and especially not white women. He hadn't realized before how tall she was and yet she walked with her shoulders stooped forward. She seemed more self-conscious about her height than her skin color.

When they finished the set, Red and the rest of the band sat at a table near the stage. Aileen came up and flung her arms around Muddy and kissed him hard, practically lapping up the sweat coming off his face. She had it bad for him and Red wondered if she knew about Muddy's other women — Sallie Ann down South, Geneva up here, and he'd lost count of the ones in between.

Red, at the far end of the table, was startled when Aileen's friend leaned over and said, "Red Dupree, right? We've met before. At the radio and record store and then at Aristocrat."

He was surprised that she spoke to him, let alone remembered who he was. "Yes, ma'am. I remember."

" 'Ma'am'?" She laughed. "Please, my name's Leeba."

"Sorry, ma'am. I mean Leah."

"Not Leah, Lee-*ba*. With a *b.*"

"Lee-*ba*? What kind of name is that?"

"Polish."

The only Polish people he knew were a handful of store owners in Jewtown and the guys from the brickyard. They all spoke with such thick accents it was hard to understand them. But she wasn't like that. "You're Polish?"

"I am." She jiggled the ice in her glass and took a sip. "And what about you?"

"Me?"

"Yeah, you. Where are you from?"

Why did she care where he was from? And why did she get up from her seat and come sit closer to him? He could tell she was tipsy, one drink away from something she'd regret the next day.

"Well?" She tilted her head and one of her curls fell across her cheek.

If she was a colored woman he'd say she was making a play for him. If she was colored he'd know what to do. But she was making him nervous, self-conscious. He watched her swirling the ice in her glass and the more he looked at her the more he appreciated her features, the dark eyes, strong nose, perfect skin, and the way her curls framed her face. She was a different kind of pretty, the kind that snuck up on you.

"Aren't you going to tell me?" she asked. "Where'd you come from?"

"Merrydale."

"Merrydale? Where's that?"

"Louisiana. Not too far away from New Orleans."

"Oh."

There wasn't anything more to say after that. She got quiet and so did he. She was still looking at him, though, and he cracked, turned away. But from the corner of his eye he sensed she was still watching him.

"Aileen told me you were playing in Muddy's band now," she said before she leaned in closer and whispered, "I think you should be the bandleader."

"You're gonna get me in trouble with the boss if you keep talking like that." He laughed, forgetting himself for a moment.

"Well, it's the truth." She took a long pull from her drink, tilting the glass back, the tip of her pink tongue tickling the ice cubes. "I think you should audition for Leonard and Evelyn."

"I already gave them my demo. Long time ago."

"Yeah, but your demo doesn't do you justice. And they're going for a different sound now. Leonard wouldn't have even recorded Muddy back then. I think you should come in and play for them. Live. No demo. No Walter. Just you and your guitar."

Muddy came up and slapped him on the shoulder. "C'mon, man. We're on."

They were playing "I Can't Be Satisfied" and Red launched into another solo, giving Muddy's slide guitar a break. Red closed his eyes as his fingers were plucking and strumming. He felt the sweat collecting on his forearms and trickling down the back of his neck. He was drained and exhilarated, giving up every part of himself for that song. People were clapping and that was when he opened his eyes, searching through the audience, past the paisley swirls of smoke up near the lights, until his sight landed on the girl. She smiled at him or he thought she did. He wasn't sure.

She stayed until after the last set and even lingered for a few minutes after Aileen had left out the side door with Muddy. Little Walter said something to her, but her eyes held on Red. She was still watching him even as she reached for her pocketbook and began drifting toward the door. But then, just when he thought she had gone, he saw her walking back, heading straight toward him.

"Come by and see me some time at Aristocrat," she said. That was it.

He was too stunned to remember his response, but he'd never forget the way she turned back around at the door and this time when she smiled, he knew it.

Eighteen:
"Something's Got a Hold on Me"

Leeba

Leeba rolled over, squinting at the daylight streaming through the bedroom window. She heard some commotion outside her room but couldn't be bothered with it. Her head felt heavy, her eyes burned, her mouth was as dry as dirt. Snippets from the night before floated back to her. Why did she have that last drink? Ah yes, she was nervous. She tried to recall her conversation with Red Dupree but drew a blank. The only part she remembered was telling him to come see her at Aristocrat.

She was thinking about all this when she heard her mother shout, *"Du zaist nit ir brengen az in do."*

"Don't you bring what in here?" Leeba asked as she pulled on her bathrobe and went out to the living room. Her mother was glaring at a deliveryman attempting to wheel an enormous box into the apartment.

Turned out to be a television set. A ten-inch Emerson in a handsome wooden cabi-

225

net. Leeba had won it, the grand prize for a contest she didn't remember entering. Her mother had almost refused to accept it, but before she'd let Leeba leave for work that day, the two of them — her mother like an ant lifting twice her body weight — re-arranged the living room furniture to make space for it.

That night when Leeba came home from work, the TV was blaring and there they were, four in a row on the davenport, her parents, Aunt Sylvie and Uncle Moishe, eyes glued to *The Texaco Star Theatre*. Light from the TV screen flickered across their faces.

"Come see this," her father said, scooting closer to her mother and patting the cushion.

She squeezed in beside him. The others, even her mother, who couldn't have fully understood everything since it was in English, stared ahead, engrossed. But Leeba, still nursing her hangover, couldn't focus on the program because she couldn't stop replaying images from the night before. What had she said to Red Dupree? Did she make a full confession? Tell him she dreamed about him? She cringed and vowed to never drink bourbon again.

A commercial came on for Band-Aids that showed a housewife applying the adhesive strip to an egg, demonstrating how effectively they would stick to the skin. Her mother and Uncle Moishe found this fascinating. Both of them inched forward as if to get a closer look. Leeba glanced around, noticing her father's half-built model airplane waiting for him on a sheet of newspaper covering the dining room table. After the television program was over Leeba excused herself, went into her bedroom and immediately fell asleep.

The following night when she came home from work everyone had already taken their places on the davenport and once again her father made room for her and patted the seat cushion beside him. While the others watched *Kraft Television Theatre,* Leeba watched the future unfold. Here she would sit night after night, growing old, with her parents and relatives growing even older, watching television shows with the volume up too high.

She thought about how normally, on a night like tonight, she would have been with Aileen, but her friend was spending all her free time now with Muddy. Leeba caught herself thinking about Avrom Yurzel and wondering if she'd done the right thing by not pursuing the relationship.

The next morning before she left for work Leeba saw that her mother had moved her ironing board into the hallway so she could watch the TV, which depressed Leeba more than she could say. There was no programming on at seven in the morning, just a screen with a test pattern that her mother watched while she ironed. Leeba felt a rare tenderness toward her and went over and kissed her cheek.

Her mother was startled by the gesture. "What was that for?"

"Just because. I'll see you later tonight."

Her mother didn't say anything more. She just went back to her ironing, back to the TV test pattern. As Leeba made her way into the office she had a feeling the TV she'd won was going to take over their lives and that her father would never again build another model airplane.

When she got into the office she was thankful that it was quiet there that day. Leonard and Evelyn were at Universal Recording for a Five Blazes session that once again Leonard was paying for out of his own pocket. Leeba glanced at the ledger, wondering if they had enough money for that week's payroll and upcoming royalty payments. She closed the book and organized a stack of bills, making lists of what needed to be paid and what was past due.

She was still sorting through everything when she looked up and felt her heart skip. Red Dupree was coming through the front door. Yes, she'd told him to come see her, but she'd been drunk and bold that night. She never expected him to follow up on it and yet just a few days later here he was. Now she didn't know what to do. She stared at the guitar in his hand, her heart hammering, the blood rushing through her ears.

"You said I should come on by. So I came to play for them." Red gestured with his guitar.

"Leonard and Evelyn aren't here right now."

"Hm." He glanced at his guitar. "Okay, then. Well, another time." He started back toward the door.

"No, no — don't leave." She got up from her desk. "You can wait for them. They should be back soon. Come — sit. Want some coffee? A Coca-Cola?"

He set his guitar down and shook his head, but she got him a bottle of soda pop anyway. He took off his jacket and as she handed the bottle to him she couldn't keep from staring. She thought him magnificent. He stirred her, and those fantasies of him kissing her, touching her, made her flush. She wondered if it showed, if she was giving herself away. She gestured and he took the chair opposite her desk, tucking his hands beneath his thighs.

"What is it that you do around here?" he asked.

"A little bit of everything. I call deejays and make sure they're giving us the airtime they promised Leonard. I talk to the distributors — make sure they're getting the records in the jukeboxes and the record stores. I do a little songwriting here and there," she said, hoping to show him they had something in common. "Nothing that they've recorded," she explained. "At least not yet . . ." Now she worried that she was rambling. "But mostly I keep Evelyn and Leonard from killing each other." She laughed self-consciously, sensing him drifting from her, his eyes looking everywhere, at everything but her. "Are you okay?" she asked, feeling desperate to reel him back.

"What?" He glanced at her, almost startled, as if he'd forgotten she was there.

"Is everything all right?"

He didn't respond and she watched him take a sip of Coke, his Adam's apple moving up and down with each swallow. There was a long silence and each time he let his eyes meet hers, he grew shy and turned away. She seemed to be making him nervous. But he was making her nervous, too. Why — out of all the men in this city — did she have to want him, the one person she could never have? But the thought of touching him — just once. To know what it felt like to be in his arms — just once. To kiss him . . .

"So," he said setting the bottle down, "you say you do some songwriting." He gestured to the Wurlitzer upright in the corner. "Do you play?"

She nodded.

"Well, then, c'mon now." He got up and walked over to the piano. "Play me one of your songs."

After some mild protesting she went over to the piano and he stood with his elbow on the lid. When she played the intro of a song, the look on his face made her stop. "What?" Her fingers froze in place. "Is it *that* bad?"

"No, no." He laughed. "I just didn't take you for a blues player, that's all. C'mon now, keep going."

She played another stanza and stopped. "How am I doing? Any pointers?"

He thought for a moment. "Well, yeah," he said, laughing again, "I got a pointer for you. Now, don't take this the wrong way, but there ain't no blues players by the name of Leeba. We have to fix that. What's your last name?"

"Oh, if you don't think Leeba sounds like a blues name, wait till you hear this — it's Groski."

He made a smacking noise with his lips. "You gotta change all that. See now, my real name's Reggie Smalls, but that sounds flat to me, so I changed it to Red Dupree. Change your name, change your life."

"So what should my blues name be?"

"Hmm." He studied her face as if setting eyes on her for the first time. She felt vulnerable, exposed. It made her self-conscious. He was taking her in and it unnerved her.

"Well," he said, "if it was up to me, Leeba Groski, I think I'd call you Leah. Leah Grand."

"Leah Grand." She tried it on. "Leah

231

Grand. Leah Grand." She chanted it aloud, spinning the name inside her head. It sounded sophisticated, confident, American. She liked it. She liked it very much. *Change your name, change your life.*

"Well," he said, rubbing his hands together, "that takes care of your name. Now let's talk about your piano playing." He came over and sat beside her on the bench. He smelled oaky, spicy. "Your playing's fine, but what you wanna do is get a little more of *you* in there."

"How do I do that?"

"You feel it. That's what the blues is. It's all feeling."

He placed his long tapered fingers on the piano. "You get your bass line working with this hand, like this, see" — he had his left hand laying down the rhythm — "and then you come in with some chord changes with your right hand."

She was mesmerized. Something came over her — it had been building up inside her for days, for weeks, forever. She went with it, placing her fingers lightly over his. There she was at last, touching him. His hand went stiff beneath hers and the room fell silent. They were facing each other now, their eyes locked. With her free hand she brought her fingers to his face, surprised by the smoothness of his skin. There was no turning back now. She couldn't help herself. She leaned in and kissed him, letting her arms circle around his shoulders. She was the aggressor, but he was allowing it, or maybe he was just too stunned to stop her. She was still kissing him when she heard Evelyn and Leonard coming through the front door.

". . . that's bullshit, Evelyn, and you know it."

Leeba had already pulled away from Red and both of them bolted up, looking like a couple of kids caught playing with matches. Evelyn and Leonard didn't even notice that they were there.

"I'm sick and tired of you saying that," said Evelyn. "We've been through this a million times." She flung her coat and hat onto the desk.

"Evelyn? Leonard?" Leeba interrupted their argument. Her face was flushed, her lips still hot. "You remember Red Dupree? He's a guitar player. He's in Muddy's band."

Red crossed the room and shook both their hands. "Good to see you both again."

"He's here to audition for you."

"Not a good time," said Evelyn, shaking her head. "Nice seeing you, Red, but really not a good time."

Red shrugged on his jacket and reached for his guitar case slumped against the wall. "I'll come back another day."

Leeba expected them to say something in return. Just to be polite. They didn't and she watched Red walk out the door while Leonard and Evelyn went back to bickering. Leeba froze for a moment, gathering her thoughts. *Let him go,* she told herself. It would never work. She didn't even know how to frame *whatever* this was in her mind. He couldn't be a boyfriend. There was no way she could bring him home for Shabbos dinner, or walk down the street with his hand in hers. She could never marry him, have his children. But she wanted him. She wanted him with a desire so deep she could swim in it forever. So despite all that she knew about why it was impossible, she couldn't fight it. With a jolt she grabbed her coat and pushed through the front door, letting a blast of crisp fall air and sunlight hit her face. She looked to the left and to the right — and there he was.

"Red, wait —" She took off after him, catching him as he was about to turn the corner.

"Sorry about what happened in there," he said sheepishly, setting his guitar case down, stuffing his hands inside his pockets. "I shouldn't have done that."

"You didn't do anything. It was me. I'm the one who kissed you, remember? And I'm not sorry I did."

He glanced down at the sidewalk before looking into her eyes. "This is trouble, you know."

She smiled. "I know."

NINETEEN:
"MY SWEET LOVIN' WOMAN"

RED

Red looked at the clock on his nightstand. It was a quarter till nine. If he was going to meet Leah he'd have to leave now. The day before, after she'd kissed him, as they were standing on the sidewalk, they had made plans to meet the following night at a black-and-tan club. Now he was losing his nerve.

He'd been just as apprehensive when he went down to Aristocrat — and that was before anything had happened. He told himself he was going to audition, but in truth he wanted to see her. He knew now that the attraction was mutual, but he didn't know what to do with that. What was the point of seeing her again? He waited until the last minute, watching the second hand on the clock ticking away and knowing that even though the odds were stacked against them, he was going anyway.

Thirty minutes later he got to the club and through the crowd and haze of cigarette smoke he saw her. Actually he saw her curls first, the spotlight catching the edges, framing them in cobalt blue shimmer. She was sitting at a table by herself, a drink in her hand, her eyes on the stage, watching the jazz trio. Again something nagged inside him, telling him to turn around. But instead he walked over to her. She seemed surprised to see him, as if she'd forgotten that they'd planned to meet. His head filled with new doubts; maybe he'd misinterpreted it all and was stepping over a line. He was about to apologize when she smiled, her face and eyes opening wide to him. She gestured to the chair. He sat self-consciously, ordered a drink and smoked a cigarette, struggling to hear what she was saying over the music.

When the band played a softer, slower song Leah stood up and asked him to dance with her. They were both awkward, stiff and standing about as far apart as they could and still technically be dancing together. Red couldn't help it; taking a white woman in his arms went against everything he'd been taught, everything he'd been warned against. But once Leah relaxed she closed the gap between them. He felt the heat of her body and smelled the soft florals of her perfume. He wanted to run his fingertips through her curls but didn't dare. When she rested her head on his shoulder he was sure she could feel his heart pounding.

The band went on break and without the music Red was lost again, coming back to himself and not knowing what to do. He told her he needed a minute and went down a long dark hall toward the men's room. He stepped inside, splashed water on his face and looked in the mirror. *What are you going to do with this now?* The smartest thing would be to thank her for the dance and leave.

That was what he planned to do; only when he opened the door she was standing there. Standing alone in a long, dark empty hallway, waiting for him.

"I need to kiss you again," she said.

He saw her again the following week. The two of them met at another black-and-tan club and this time Red was more relaxed, especially after his second cocktail. They were talking about all kinds of things and began trading stories of what it was like being a minority in Chicago, both of them surprised by how similar their experiences were.

"See, everyone thinks that Negroes and Jewish people don't have anything in common and that's where they're wrong," said Red, sitting on his hands like he normally did. But this time he also did it to keep from reaching over to touch her. "The truth is," he continued, "I think Negroes and Jews in Chicago recognize that we need each other. Almost everyone I know who came up from the delta has worked for Jewish businessmen at one time or another. They gave us jobs and we gave them labor. The Jews have been good to us Negroes. Look at what Leonard and Evelyn have done for Muddy. I've always gotten along with Jewish folks and they never had a problem with me, neither."

He saw her turn out her bottom lip. "Well, you haven't met my mother."

"Your mama?" He laughed. "She wouldn't approve of this here, huh?" He indicated the two of them.

"Whatever 'this here' is," she said, smiling, "no, she wouldn't approve. My mother thinks we should all stick to our own kind. Jews with Jews and Negroes with Negroes. She's never understood my friendship with Aileen. And oh, you should see how she acts toward her. She's rude, dismissive — it's like Aileen's not a *real* person and it makes me furious."

"I guess some folks are just scared of anyone who's different."

"Is it fear or just plain hypocrisy? My mother treats Aileen and regards other Negroes with the same kind of disdain and disrespect that she complains the Jews always get. But she refuses to see it that way."

Red sat back and listened to her talk, realizing he'd never had a conversation like this before with a white person, let alone a white woman.

"The part that really gets me," she was saying now, "is when someone takes one look at me — sees that I'm Jewish — and without knowing a thing about me they decide I'm a second-class citizen. You hear all the horror stories coming out of Europe about what happened to the Jews there and you'd think people here would be different now, but they're really not. I can't tell you how many times I've been accused of having horns, or been called a 'little Jew girl,' a 'dirty kike.' It's a slap in the face."

"Same thing when someone calls me a nigger. It makes my blood boil and takes all my self-control not to put them through a wall."

Later that night he felt closer to her than he could have thought possible. Yes, they came from different worlds, but they understood each other. They held each other tight on the dance floor and before the evening was over she said she wanted to see him again.

After two more weeks of meeting at black-and-tan clubs, he brought her back to his kitchenette, painfully aware of the stench of beer and urine in the hallway. As he let her inside he glanced at the broken window blinds, naked bulb overhead, the mattress lying flat on the floor.

"Sorry I don't have a nicer place."

She didn't say anything. It was like she hadn't noticed, or maybe she didn't care. She just smiled and stepped forward. This was it.

They were alone now, just the two of them, and it didn't matter that he was black and she was white. He was a man, she was a woman and he wanted her. Meeting her halfway in the middle of the room, he kissed her, kissed her full-on, the way he'd been wanting to. He went on kissing her while he walked her backward until her spine was pressed against the wall. He unbuttoned her blouse and ran his fingertips over her pale skin and along her collarbone. She reached behind and unhooked her brassiere, sliding the silky straps down her shoulders to offer her breasts to him. At first all he could do was look, admiring the faint blue veins fanning out from her pink nipples. He'd never seen anything like that before; it took his breath away. He went on kissing and exploring every inch of her, loving the way she felt in his arms, the way she smelled, the way she tasted, the way she moaned, responding to his touch. He made love to her that night and afterward the look on her face was one of surprise.

"I thought you'd be shy," she said, rolling onto her side, propping herself up on one elbow.

"Now, what would make you think that?"

"You're always so polite and —"

"Oh." He nodded. He got it. Wrapping one of her curls about his finger, he said, "I've never been with a white woman before. Back home a Negro man can't even look at a white girl. They'd string you up for that. It took me a long time when I got here to even be able to look a white person in the eyes."

"So if I hadn't made the first move, what would you have done?"

"Thought about being with you. Would have thought about that a lot. You gotta understand, this sort of thing doesn't happen down South."

She smiled. "Good thing we're not down South, huh?"

He made love to her once more before she dressed and went back home where she belonged.

He saw her again and again, but as a mixed couple, they couldn't go anywhere other than a black-and-tan club. Not that they *couldn't*. They could have gone into a restaurant together, but they certainly would have turned heads, and it could have provoked nasty comments and disapproving looks from the owners and other patrons. That right there would have spoiled their time together. It was just easier to sneak her back into his kitchenette and each time he did it grew more intense.

One night two months after they'd started seeing each other they lay together on his mattress, their naked bodies cooling as they took in the quiet of the room.

"You hear that?" he said eventually.

"What?" She sat up and looped her arms about her legs.

"That." He pointed toward the ceiling. There was a *thump, thump, thump* coming from overhead. "That's old man Pacer in 407 with his cane. He must have just come home. And wait, there's gonna be a squeak in a second." He paused and there it was.

Leeba laughed. "How did you know that?"

"That's his closet door." Red smiled. "Sometimes when I can't sleep I listen to all the sounds around me, try to figure out what they are. Try it. Close your eyes. Tell me what you hear."

She leaned back, eyes shut, her curls fanning out across the pillow. "Let's see, I hear a dog barking, some footsteps . . ."

"C'mon —" He gave her a playful jab. "You can do better than that. The walls around this place are paper-thin. Listen harder. Tell me what you hear."

She closed her eyes again and he watched her concentrating, a thin line forming between her brows. "Ah." She smiled. "I hear a screeching sound, like hangers going back and forth in a closet."

"That's it. There you go. What else?"

"Hmm . . ." She grew quiet for a moment. "I hear something like a coffee percolator coming from next door. It's belching, making that burping sound."

He smiled, leaned forward and kissed her.

"See, I knew you had musician's ears."

She opened her eyes and kissed him back. "I'm fascinated by you, by the way your mind works."

"And how do you think my mind works?"

She stroked his cheek. "It's like you see music and sound in everything. I can tell that's how you relate to the world around you. It's everything to you."

He glanced down at her breasts then into her eyes. "It's not *everything.*"

She laughed and he laughed because she was laughing and soon they couldn't stop, both of them oozing tears from their eyes.

When silence filled the air, she turned to him and said, "I love you."

They looked at each other equally shocked by her confession. He saw the blush rise up on her cheeks and as she started to turn away, he stopped her, cupping her face in his hands. His heart was pounding. He'd never said those words to anyone before. He wanted to say them to her, but instead he kissed her.

They made love again and somehow it was different this time, knowing how she felt about him. The sex was sweeter, exciting, but more tender, too. Afterward, he got up to get them some water and turned on the radio. They lay side by side listening to Amos Milburn's "Roomin' House Boogie."

She rolled onto her back and said, "You know what I love about music? It's not like reading a book or watching a movie or a play. You don't have to think or try to figure it out, or work for it. With music you don't have to do a thing. You just listen and it does it *to* you. A good song can change your mood. Change the mood of a whole room. It gives so much and it asks nothing in return. You know what I mean?"

He knew exactly what she meant. He kissed her and before he could stop himself, he blurted it out: "I love you, too," he said. "I really do."

She stroked his face and pressed her nose to his. They stared into each other's eyes for a long time until she finally spoke. "Will you do something for me?"

"Anything."

"Will you show me how to play a blues riff on the guitar?"

He laughed. "You mean you want to learn to play the devil's music?"

"Why do people call the blues that?"

"The devil's music? 'Cuz it's evil." He laughed. "At least that's what my mama always said. And she never even heard Robert Johnson's playing."

"Robert Johnson wrote 'Sweet Home Chicago,' didn't he?"

"He did a lot more than that. Robert Johnson was the greatest bluesman in the delta. Nobody played a guitar like him. When he first started playing, though, he wasn't any good. But he wanted to play that guitar so badly that he went down to what they call the crossroads in the delta. He went there at midnight because that's when the devil shows up. And he made a deal with Lucifer. 'Let me play this guitar the way I want and you can have my soul.' After that, Johnson became a legend. He changed the sound. He was one of the first ever to take a bottle and slide it across the neck of his guitar. He's the one who made slide guitar what it is today."

"So the devil granted him his wish."

Red nodded. "Johnson started making records — and everybody wanted to play like him. That's how Muddy learned to do what he does. Lots of other folks, too. But old Lucifer kept up his end of the bargain. Not long after that, poor Johnson turned up dead. Gone by the age of twenty-seven."

"What happened?"

"Nobody knows for sure. One of the great mysteries of the delta." He got up and brought his Stella over to the mattress and handed it to her. "Now, the first thing you have to do is get comfortable holding a guitar. Find the right spot."

She sat up, naked and cross-legged, and settled in with the guitar.

"Now, it's different from piano because all you have here is six strings. The low E — that your top string."

"This right here?" She plucked it.

"And next is the A string, the D string, G, B and back to E."

"Okay."

He showed her a series of notes, a classic blues riff. "Just keep practicing that."

She tried it once and laughed. "That sounds terrible. That's nothing like a blues riff."

"Sure it is." He took the guitar from her and played the same sequence and there it was, the blues.

She lay back down on the mattress and closed her eyes. With a smile rising up on her face, she told him to keep playing. "Never stop."

TWENTY:
"ROLLIN' AND TUMBLIN'"

LEONARD

"Aren't you going to say anything?" Evelyn asked.

Leonard had his back to her. He was looking out the front window, watching the guys load their amps and guitars in the back of Muddy's Cadillac. They'd just finished rehearsing a new song, "Rollin' and Tumblin'." Leonard had wanted to lay it down at Universal and release it after Christmas. Now he wasn't sure.

"Well?" Evelyn called to him. She was seated at her desk, hands folded.

Leonard didn't know how to answer her. Her news was still sinking in. She'd just told him that she wanted out of the business.

"Let's face it, Leonard. You and I are horrible business partners. If we stay in this together we're going to end up killing each other." She undid her hands, opened her desk drawer and began removing items and setting them into a box: an engraved fountain pen, a tube of lipstick, a letter opener. "I'm married now," she said. "Art and I want to focus more on distribution than producing. Besides — and believe me, I never thought I'd say this, but I think you're more cut out for this business than I am."

Leonard tried not to smirk. Even with Evelyn and her fifty-one percent, everyone still looked to him for answers. *What do I record next? Why isn't my record selling better? When are you putting another ad in the trades?*

"So what happens now?" he asked.

"I'll sell you my half of the company."

Leonard didn't respond right away. He had to play his next move just right. He let a moment of silence pass. "What makes you think this company's worth anything? We didn't get the bank loan; we can't finance the operation. This label'll be shut down within a month after the next round of bills hit." He was setting her up, acting as if he had no interest in buying her out.

She reached for a cigarette and took her sweet old time lighting it. He could tell she was jockeying for position, too, keeping him waiting. What a game.

"Look," she said, "we both know that Muddy hasn't written his last hit. Neither have the others. Those artists are under contract with Aristocrat. This company is still worth something."

He knew she was right. They were growing

a winning roster of talent. Sooner or later one of them would have another big song and the money would come rolling in. "Okay, fine. I'll tell you what — I paid ten grand for my half of this company when I came on board. I'll pay you another ten grand for your half."

"Oh, c'mon, Leonard!" She laughed. "You need to sharpen your pencil."

She threw out a number. He countered. They went back and forth a few more rounds and Leonard told her he'd have to think about it.

When he left Evelyn that day Leonard went straight to the Macomba Lounge. It was three in the afternoon. A few of the regulars were already hunched over the bar, but otherwise the place was quiet. The lights were turned up and Leonard could see all the blemishes, the stains on the carpet, the cigarette burns on the floor, the banged-up walls where the paint was chipped and cracked.

Leonard sat with Phil at the far end of the bar, two glasses and a bottle of scotch between them. It was one of the few times that Leonard drank, but he needed to that day. If he couldn't come up with the money to buy out Evelyn that meant he'd pretty much pissed away the last three years of his life.

Leonard flipped open the lid on his Zippo and lit a cigarette before snapping it shut with a loud clack. "Evelyn might as well be asking for a million dollars."

Phil adjusted his hat, shook his head. "I don't know what the answer is. We already tried to sell this place once. We couldn't give it away, remember?"

Leonard nodded. It was true. The brothers had tried to unload the club before, but got no takers. The building was falling apart. The roof leaked. The plumbing was shoddy. They needed to have the place rewired. None of it was worth their while. Even if they could have sold the club afterward, they never would have recouped their investment.

One of the bums at the other end of the bar called to them, holding up his empty glass, swaying back and forth. "Hey, how 'bout another one?"

"Hey, how 'bout you payin' for it this time?" said Phil.

Leonard left Phil a couple hours later and headed for home. He'd recently moved his family out of the old Lawndale neighborhood and into a better apartment on Drexel Boulevard. Coming up the sidewalk, he looked at the turrets along the roof of their building. It was a larger apartment than what they'd had before. Marshall had his own room now instead of having to share with his sisters. And Revetta, his Revetta who never asked for a thing, now had a larger kitchen than her mother, with a separate dining room.

Revetta had decorated every inch of the place — her grandmother's plates displayed along the wedge in the kitchen, knickknacks on the built-in bookcases, pillows on the davenport that matched the green chairs in the corners. He knew what it did for her to have her mah-jongg games and her Sisterhood and Hadassah meetings there. He couldn't take that away from her, tell her that he'd failed, say they had to pack up and go back to Lawndale. No, he couldn't do that.

As soon as he made it through the front door, the kids abandoned their marble game on the living room rug and charged toward him.

"I didn't expect you home for supper." Revetta leaned in to kiss him and pulled back, her brows knitted together. "Were you drinking?"

"Just one," he lied.

"Why? What's wrong? Did something happen?" She looked at the children. "Go — go to your rooms until I call you for dinner. And pick up those marbles."

He walked her over to the davenport and told her about Evelyn leaving the company. She listened carefully as she always did and when he was through talking and had ground out his fifth or sixth cigarette she folded and unfolded her arms.

"What are we going to do?" she asked. "We're a month behind on rent as it is."

"I don't know. Maybe my father —"

"You can't borrow any more money from him. Lenny, you haven't even finished paying him back everything you borrowed the last time."

He leaned forward and dropped his head to his hands. He felt Revetta's breath on his neck and her fingers sifting through his thinning hair. He closed his eyes, taking in her touch. Dear, sweet, beautiful Revetta. What did he do to deserve her? And how was he going to take care of her and the kids? What about Phil? And Leeba? What about the guys like Muddy and Sunnyland Slim? They were family to him now, too. He was everyone's protector, always had been; and now he didn't know what to do. He couldn't see his way out of this one.

The Macomba wasn't the answer. There was no way to make a decent living there without killing themselves or, worse, getting themselves killed in the process. He didn't want to go back to the liquor trade — those people were even worse than the thugs at the club. What else was there? Leonard had gotten a taste of the music business. He liked it, thought he could do well in it — especially without Evelyn standing in his way. He sat with his head in his hands.

"I know you're probably not going to want to discuss this," she said, "but I spoke to the lawyer again today. He says you still didn't sign the papers."

"Now?" He raised his head, glowering at her. "You're bringing this up now? Your timing stinks."

She pulled away from him, stood up and crossed the room. "I just don't understand why you won't sign it."

" 'Cause I don't want to sign my death certificate."

"Signing a will is not a death sentence. It's called being responsible. Being smart."

Being smart was not giving himself a *kenahora* and tempting the evil eye. His mother taught him that. She was even more superstitious than he was. Spit three times to ward off bad luck. No shoes on the counter, no hats on the bed, no opened umbrellas indoors, no buying a crib or even a diaper or uttering a "mazel tov" before a baby was born.

"Leonard, you have a family now. You need to have a will."

"You're right," he said. "I don't want to discuss it."

Twenty-One:
"I Be's Troubled"

LEEBA

On a bitter January afternoon just after New Year's, Leeba and Red stopped into a drugstore on Wabash and Adams so he could get a pack of cigarettes. It was nice and warm inside so they took time to browse, giving themselves a chance to thaw before facing the blustery cold again.

When they turned down the first aisle Leeba noticed the owner, a white man with a bad toupee, was following them around, casting a suspicious eye on Red. Leeba tried to ignore him until another white man came up to her, cutting right in front of Red. "Ma'am, is this Negro bothering you?"

Leeba was dumbfounded. All she could do was shake her head. "No. No, he's not bothering me." Choking back her rage she stormed out of the drugstore.

"It's okay," Red said, following her outside.

"No, it's not. That owner was watching you, acting like you were going to steal something.

254

And that — that other guy . . ." She couldn't finish the thought. She was sick of whites trying to save her from her boyfriend. Why couldn't anyone just accept at face value that they were a couple?

She had gone into this relationship knowing it would be challenging. But three months later she was just beginning to understand how difficult it would really be.

It was starting to snow now. Big wet flakes that hit the pavement and spread. She glanced over at Red, his hands stuffed in his pockets, collar turned up, teeth gritting against the snow and cold. "C'mon." She gestured toward the El platform overhead. "Let's go back to your place."

Red's kitchenette was dark and cold. The furnace was on the fritz so the radiator sat idle. With their coats still on and the lights still out, Red brought his hands to her face. There was the shock of cold fingers followed by the heat from his kisses. She wrapped herself around him. They didn't make it to the mattress. The counter along the kitchenette would do fine.

Their love was still new and the sex was urgent, hungry. The thing she looked forward to more than anything else. This, too, was unfamiliar. This kind of craving. Now she understood Aileen and Muddy for she, too, was one of the lovestruck.

Afterward she pulled on her clothes to ward

off the draft and made them each a cup of tea. She stood near the stove, stirring a spoonful of honey into the mugs, and he came up behind her.

"I love these little blue veins," he said running his hands over her pale skin.

She set the spoon down and glanced at the backs of her hands, having never noticed them before. Now they were something to marvel. She leaned back into his chest, her spine straight, shoulders back. She'd been that way, standing taller, owning her height, since he'd come into her life.

They drank their tea, standing side by side near the stove. It was warmer there, farther away from the window. Leeba couldn't have been happier. She was in love. And grateful. Crazy, gushy grateful because she never thought this would happen to her.

Leeba rinsed the teacups in Red's sink and set them on the drain board to dry. She went over to him and looped her arms about his waist. One last kiss before she let herself out, ignoring the stares from his neighbors.

About a week later Leeba and Aileen went to the Macomba Lounge. Muddy's band was playing that night, getting ready to go on when they walked through the door. The usual drug dealers were parked on their bar stools doing business and the prostitutes were working the room, too. The guy who worked the rib pit in back was bringing out slabs of barbecue. Leeba and Aileen hadn't made it past the bar when Little Walter rushed over.

"What're you doing here, Aileen? You can't be here."

"What are you talking about? I came to see Muddy." She started toward the stage.

Little Walter grabbed hold of her arm. "I'm telling you, you can't be here. Not tonight." Little Walter craned his neck toward the bandstand. "Muddy's woman's here."

"*I'm* Muddy's woman."

"You know what I mean, girl. His wife's here."

Leeba knew anything could happen now. Aileen got that look in her eyes. The storm was rolling in. She went to Aileen's side. "C'mon. Let's just go. We'll —"

Aileen pulled away. "I ain't going nowhere." She stared Little Walter down. "I'm not gonna be the only one in misery tonight. Let him look out from that stage and see me sitting here, like some big bad secret about to come out."

Walter was bewildered. "You crazy, woman, you know that."

Leeba watched him walk back to the bandstand shaking his head. A stool opened up at the bar and Aileen sank down and ordered a gin straight up.

The band started playing and Leeba hung back with Aileen, watching Red on stage in a dark suit and tie. He was seated on a cane-back chair off to the side. Muddy was sitting front and center, a pint of Old Grand-Dad parked near his stomping foot. Amazing he hadn't knocked it over. They were playing "Rollin' Stone." Red, strumming steadily, set the rhythm that the drums, harp, bass and Muddy's slide played into. The crowd was clapping, swaying back and forth.

Aileen slithered off her bar stool and slinked over to the telephone booth to make a call. Leeba watched her leaning against the door, fingers splayed against the glass, nodding to whoever she was talking to on the line.

She was so focused on Aileen that at first Leeba didn't pay any attention to the two women nearby, one on either side of her. They didn't say anything as they moved in closer and sized her up. The men in the club didn't make Leeba nearly as uneasy as the women. Being the only white female in the room usually didn't faze her. But now she was self-conscious and caught herself trying to compensate for her privileged skin color. She turned to the women and smiled. Neither one smiled back and Leah Grand was Leeba Groski once again, the sting of their rejection reminding her of the kids on the playground snubbing her because of her accent, because of Eli's shoes, because she ate stuffed cabbage leaves for lunch instead of peanut butter and jelly. Even after all this time, it still affected her and made her burrow into her old self.

"What do you think you're doing here?" said the woman on her left.

"Just came to hear some music, that's all." She looked at Aileen, who had returned to the bar.

"We saw you talking to that harp player." The other woman folded her arms across her chest. "Is he your man?"

"Walter?" Leeba could have laughed. "No. No, I'm not with Walter. He's just someone I know."

She sensed where this was going. They wanted to make sure she wasn't there for any of their men. It was one thing to lose a good man to another colored woman, but to a white girl — that was unacceptable. Leeba wanted to shout it from the stage that she was there for Red Dupree, but she couldn't say a word.

The two girls were still at her sides and Leeba knew they wanted to make her so nervous that she'd leave. They were doing a good job of that, but she wouldn't abandon Aileen. Her friend was going to fall hard and Leeba would have to pick her back up.

Muddy and the boys were in the middle of "I Be's Troubled" when Red looked out at Leeba and her heart ripened. There was a secret language between them and she knew

259

he was every bit as lost in the wonder of them as was she. So unlikely they were. So forbidden. And yet so right. Oh, how she loved the striking contrast of their skin and the way his body fit around hers when they lay together on their sides. How they shared their love of the blues. How he saw the world as music: the spines of books lined up on a shelf were piano keys to him, the finials on a fence were guitar frets. And oh, how he made her laugh, made her melt. All this and more flashed between them with just a glance. And in the midst of this private moment Leeba heard a familiar voice.

She looked over her shoulder and there was J.J. That must have been who Aileen called. Leeba watched her perk up, making a big show of smiling and wrapping her arms around him, kissing him long and hard on the mouth. J.J. was eating it up and Leeba could see Muddy getting irked by the display. She could hear it in his voice, in his playing. His vocals grew tighter, scratchier, his guitar licks fiercer, sharper.

When the band finished their set, Red swaggered up toward the bar, people clasping him on the shoulder, shaking his hand as he made his way through the crowd. Leeba felt the girls next to her watching him coming closer.

Red leaned in to her, all that stage heat coming off him. He whispered, "Been thinking about you."

"I've been thinking about you, too."

She was so focused on Red that she hadn't realized Muddy was there, too, talking to Aileen. "Entertainment supposed to be up on stage," Muddy said. "But I see you putting on a real show down here."

"None of your business what I do," she said.

"What's your point, woman?" Muddy said to Aileen. "What you tryin' to start?"

"She's with me now, see." J.J. stood up, eye to eye with Muddy. "You got somethin' to say, you say it to me."

"Ain't nobody talkin' to you." Muddy turned toward Aileen. "What you tryin' to do? You tryin' to make me jealous — with that clown?"

"Who you calling a clown?" J.J. muscled in on Muddy and that was when Muddy snapped, shoving J.J. so hard against the bar that a half dozen bottles and glasses went flying. Muddy had his fist drawn back when Red grabbed him from behind.

"C'mon now," Red said, holding Muddy back.

J.J. was still pushed up against the bar, afraid to move.

"Calm yourself," Red said to Muddy. "Don't be forgetting, you got kin here."

Leeba looked over and there was Muddy's wife. She was yelling at him, screeching, "Who is she? And don't lie to me."

Muddy let go of J.J. and went over to his

wife. "C'mon, baby," he said, running his hands up and down her arms. "She's nobody. Just a fan."

"Just a fan, my ass," said Aileen.

J.J. stepped up and put his arm around Aileen's shoulder. "Let's go. C'mon."

Aileen shrugged his arm off her. "To hell with you both." She grabbed her pocketbook off the bar and brushed past Muddy and J.J.

Leeba turned to Red, flustered. "I have to go with her. I have to make sure she's okay."

Leeba started after Aileen, when the two women who'd confronted her earlier blocked her way by the cigarette machine up front.

"Just came to hear some music, huh?" said one.

Leeba didn't know what to say. A sharp, pungent smell came to her, something acrid, like singed hair. She was still working up her defense when the girls backed off, their faces filled with alarm. Something was wrong. Terribly wrong.

Like a chain reaction, one by one Leeba and everyone else inside the Macomba Lounge became aware of the club filling up with smoke. Gray and hazy smoke one moment, and thick, black, rolling plumes the next. Leeba couldn't speak other than to gasp as a burst of flames erupted, dancing across the bandstand.

TWENTY-TWO:
"SMOKE STACK LIGHTNING"

LEONARD

It happened so fast, Leonard was in shock. Flames were still shooting into the sky and smoke was clouding, fogging everything. He couldn't get over how quickly it had exploded, devouring everything.

He remembered Muddy's band had just finished their first set and gone on break. Something had been happening between Muddy and another guy at the bar and one of Muddy's sidemen, the guitar player, Red, had stepped in and broken it up. It was right around then that he first smelled something burning. He thought it was something in the rib pit. But the next thing he knew the back end of the club was engulfed in flames. It had gone up like a matchstick. Everybody tore out of there, pushing and shoving. Leonard rushed back and opened the side door, hoping and praying that everyone got out. The smoke grew thicker, darker, and soon he couldn't see anything. His eyes stung and his throat closed up. He was groping through the haze, hacking so hard his lungs felt squeezed. He heard someone calling from behind. "C'mon, let's go. Let's go." He realized it was Phil, who had him by the waist, pulling him so that his feet barely skimmed the floor.

The sirens were now squealing in his ears and the whole area was crawling with firemen armed with axes and hauling hoses. Leonard must have counted a half dozen fire trucks blocking the intersection of Thirty-ninth and Cottage Grove. Flashing lights everywhere. People from the neighborhood and nearby clubs lined the sidewalks, watching. The air was thick with smoke and the sky lit up with flames.

Was Phil sure that everyone got out? Was anyone hurt? A whole new wave of panic shot through him. Without thinking, he started back toward the club. What he was going to do once he got there, he didn't know. It wasn't rational. He wasn't rational. He got as close as the sidewalk before the police pushed him back.

"But — that's my club. I gotta make sure everyone's out."

He couldn't remember what they said, but it was clear they weren't letting him any closer. Through the smoke he saw the familiar faces of the drug dealers, the pimps and the whores. They were shivering in the cold January air but they were okay. What about the others? Leonard raced through the crowd until he saw Muddy and his band off to the side, smoking cigarettes and passing around a couple flasks. Leeba and Aileen were there, too, along with Muddy's wife. Phil was with them.

"Everybody okay?" asked Phil. "Anybody hurt?"

Leonard watched his brother checking in with them one by one. Leonard was at a loss. For once he had nothing to say. He seemed to separate himself from what was happening. Everything went still and silent inside his head as the flames in the background flickered off everybody's faces.

Muddy's wife was taking turns cussing out her husband and then Aileen. Aileen was fighting with the wife and yelling at Muddy, too. Then there was Leeba — something was going on with her and that guitar player. She was huddled up close against him, her arms around his waist. Walter was draining his flask, pointing to the flames shooting twenty, maybe thirty feet into the air like a goddamn Fourth of July display.

Leonard was watching all this when there was an explosion and he stood back with his brother watching the roof collapse, his heart nearly collapsing with it. Everyone gasped. There were more explosions, walls crumbling, sparks going off in all directions.

Before the sun came up, all that was left of

the Macomba Lounge was a heap of smoldering rubble. And by seven that morning Leonard and Phil had already met with the police and the fire inspector.

They crossed the street and took turns at the pay phone on the corner, calling their wives and then their parents. Letting everyone know they were okay.

After Leonard hung up the phone, he squeezed his eyes shut. "God damn it. Motherfucker. Shit." He banged the handset in the holder, over and over, until Phil reached in and stopped him.

"C'mon," said Phil. "Get a grip. C'mon now."

Leonard was still in a fog. He kicked a bottle across the sidewalk. He looked back at the ruins and shook his head while his younger brother led him down the block and into a diner. All Leonard could think was *What now?* With the club gone he had nothing. He'd never have the money to buy out Evelyn. He'd have to get a job — that was a given. But doing what? Maybe he'd learn a trade, become a mechanic, work with his hands. He didn't know. He'd sell the new car, move Revetta and the kids into a smaller apartment. With each thought the dread and panic escalated. He was sweating, nauseous; his chest felt tight.

They took the booth in the back and Phil ordered a couple of coffees. Kids at a nearby table were screaming. Leonard's head filled with the sound of dishes clacking, the smell of grease in the air. He looked at his hands, black from soot. They were shaking.

"What are we gonna do?" Leonard gazed up at Phil and was taken aback. He could have sworn he saw him smile. He kept looking. God damn it, he was. The motherfucker was smiling. Leonard wanted to clobber him. "What, you think this is fuckin' funny? The club's gone. It's finished."

With that Phil tried but failed to suppress a laugh. He took his hat off, set it on the table and began to laugh, his shoulders shaking.

"Are you trying to tick me off?"

Phil couldn't stop. He laughed so hard he snorted. He planted his elbows on the table and hooted into his hands, his eyes leaking tears. "Oh, thank you, sweet Jesus!"

"I'm gonna fuckin' knock your block off."

"Leonard, do you have any idea what we're insured for?"

"For that piece-of-shit building? Wake up. It couldn't be worth more than a few grand. That's all we paid for it."

"But, Len," Phil said, still laughing, "we have business interruption insurance —"

"What the —"

"Don't you remember? I took out a policy when we first opened the club."

"What the fuck are you talking about?"

"That policy pays for *lost* profits. The building may be worth shit, but that policy covers our lost revenue. You want to buy out Evelyn Aron? You want to buy Aristocrat? You got the insurance money for that now. And then some. That fire is a godsend, Len. This is the answer to our prayers."

Six weeks later Leonard stood on a riser before a three-way mirror. The suit jacket was tugging across the shoulders.

"We'll let this seam out a little," said Avrom, marking the fabric with a square of white tailor's chalk. Avrom was the best tailor on Maxwell Street and, besides, Leonard had heard from someone in the old neighborhood that Shirley was working for Avrom now. It wasn't so much that he had to see her, but rather the other way around. Leonard needed to be seen by Shirley as the man he was today.

He pulled the price tag from the cuff. Fifty-seven dollars. He'd never spent that much on a suit before in his life. Avrom ran the measuring tape from Leonard's shoulder seam down his sleeve. Leonard glanced again in the three-way mirror and caught a glimpse of Shirley standing behind the counter. When he'd first walked into the shop, she was ringing up another customer's order and got so flustered she rang the sale twice and had to void it out and start over. She said a quick, cool "Hello, how are you?" and then busied herself in the back of the store. Even before he saw her come back up front, Leonard felt her presence.

"I'll take the other suit, too," he said, loudly enough for Shirley to hear.

Avrom nodded.

"And I'll need some more shirts and ties, too."

Avrom pulled a pencil from behind his ear and jotted down the measurements on a notepad. "So, *nu,* tell me, how is Leeba?"

Leonard had wondered how long it would take for him to bring her up. She'd taken to calling herself Leah these days, but she'd always be Leeba to him. She was with Red Dupree now and driving Leonard crazy, hounding him about auditioning her boyfriend again. Leonard knew Red's playing; he'd heard his demo and had seen him in Mud's band. But Leeba insisted he had his own songs and swore he had something special. Muddy's harp player, Little Walter, was on Leonard, too, wanting to audition. Christ, he told them to all slow down. He and Phil hadn't even found new office space yet.

"So she's well?" Avrom asked again.

"Who, Leeba? Yeah, she's fine." And she was. She seemed happy with Red, although Leonard couldn't imagine her parents ever accepting a Negro for their daughter.

"Will you tell her I asked about her?"

"Sure," said Leonard, still watching Shirley.

"Yeah. I'll tell her."

When Avrom finished, Leonard went up to the cash register and handed Shirley a brand-new Diners Club credit card. He kept his poker face on as he watched the numbers popping up on the register each time Shirley rang up another item.

"It's good to see you, Lenny. I'm glad things are going so well," she said as she handed him the credit card slip and a pen.

"Business is good. Very good," he said, scanning down the bill. Christ, he'd spent even more than he thought. "I've got no complaints." He should have left it at that, but his ego wouldn't have it. "Don't know if you heard or not, but I'm a record executive now."

"How wonderful. Very impressive."

He had no idea how to interpret her smile. Was she patronizing him or did she really mean it? And why did he still care? It killed Leonard to sign that sales slip. Revetta would have a fit when she saw the credit card bill, but he told himself he needed new suits. He told himself this had nothing to do with showing Shirley he could afford them.

She handed him his receipt and let her eyes linger on his just a beat too long. He could almost see the memories replaying in her mind — wet kisses and groping sessions in the living room while her parents were asleep, making promises and plans for the future.

Leonard wasn't a cruel man, but he did take a ridiculous amount of satisfaction in that look of hers as he folded the receipt and slipped it into his wallet and left the shop.

As he got back into his Cadillac he thought about how it must look to others. The timing couldn't have been more convenient. But he hadn't set the fire. His friends had been in the club that night. Hell, his own brother had been in there. Besides, the authorities had conducted a full investigation and it turned out that faulty wiring was to blame. The electrician had warned them about that months before. Still, it looked suspicious.

But thirty days later when the insurance money arrived, Leonard didn't give a goddamn what anyone thought. He wrote Evelyn Aron a check and he and Phil took over the company. One of the first things the brothers did was change the name from Aristocrat to Chess Records.

■ ■ ■ ■

Two:
1951–1953

■ ■ ■ ■

Twenty-Three:
"Rocket '88' "

LEONARD

The *drip, drip, drip* was driving Leonard crazy. He could hear each droplet hitting the pail under the sink in the kitchen down the hall from his office, but he wasn't about to pay the eight dollars the plumber wanted to fix it. It had been nothing but money going out for almost a year while they got set up. South Cottage Grove was the new home for Chess Records. They took the space after they lost their lease at the old Aristocrat office just a few blocks away. It may not have been perfect, but it was his. His and Phil's.

"Red's here," said Leeba, poking her head inside his office. "He's ready to audition."

Leonard got up, grateful to be getting away from that *plink, plink, plink.* He followed Leeba down the hall to the main room where their makeshift studio was. "Studio" was an exaggeration. All they had were some music stands, a few microphones, a reel-to-reel and the upright piano he'd bought from Evelyn.

275

It wasn't ideal, but at least he could do some recording here without having to shell out for a studio. Bringing an engineer in and renting extra recording equipment was a hell of a lot cheaper than paying Universal by the hour and coughing up the money before they even walked through the door.

Red was standing around making small talk with Phil. That was Phil's job. Leonard couldn't be bothered with niceties. He said a quick hello and a "Let's see what you got." When Red picked up his guitar and began playing, Leonard stood with his arms folded across his chest, cigarette dangling from his mouth, listening. As Leonard watched Red he thought, *Man, that is one tall motherfucker.* Red had a great presence, but his style wasn't unique enough. The music sounded familiar, and not the song — that was something Red had written himself — but the playing. When Red hit the last note, Leonard glanced at Phil, offered a nonapologetic shrug and said, "Sounds too much like Muddy."

There was nothing more to say about it. He turned and went back to his office, knowing that Phil would handle the rest — shake Red's hand, thank him for coming down and walk him out.

Leonard sat at his desk and there it was, *drip, drip, drip, plink, plink, plink.* Driving him goddamn bonkers. He couldn't concentrate. A moment later Phil came into his office to report that Red was gone.

"I think Leeba's more disappointed than he is. You might wanna say something to her."

"You hearing this shit?" Leonard asked, ignoring what Phil had just said.

"What shit?"

"That leak from the kitchen."

Phil shrugged. "It ain't bothering me."

It figured. Knowing Phil, he was probably too busy to have noticed. Leonard could always hear Phil through the wall that separated their offices. He was nonstop on the phone, one call after the other, talking with distributors, record pressers, radio stations. Now, *that* kind of noise didn't bother Leonard. That was the sound of business. The sound of money.

Besides, Phil was good with people, better than Leonard was. Leonard turned on the charm when he had to, but *only* when he had to. He was great when it came to dealing with the disc jockeys and distributors — with the people who mattered — but he was too busy for small talk and pleasantries. He didn't have time to worry about coddling people.

Phil went back to his office as Leeba came and stood in the doorway. "Hey, Len —"

"Don't start in on me about Red."

"I'm not," she said. "Although I think you made a big mistake. Anyway, I was just coming to tell you that Sam Phillips is on hold for you."

Leonard told Leeba to close his door behind her as he grabbed the phone and swept his legs up onto his desk in one fluid motion. "How the hell are ya, motherfucker?"

"Doing A-OK," said Sam, "but I got a question for you."

Sam spoke with a hint of a Southern accent. He was down in Memphis and had recently started doing some recording work. Leonard had been introduced to Sam through a mutual friend during one of his early trips down South. It wasn't often that Leonard met another white man interested in producing race records. He spent a lot of time with Sam whenever he was down in Memphis. The two were convinced that white folks — even in the Deep South — would buy race records if they could find a way to market the music to them.

"I swear they like this kind of music," Sam had said one night. "The problem is, they think Negroes only make music for other Negroes, not for whites. So the question is, how do you get them past that?"

"You find yourself a white boy who can play a guitar as good as Muddy and can sing like a motherfucker."

"Lots of luck there," Sam had said.

Leonard leaned back in his desk chair, crisscrossed his ankles and lit a cigarette. "So what's on your mind, Sammy?"

"What's this bill you sent me for 'Rocket

"88" '?"

"Rocket '88' " was a romping, hard-driving song that a couple young go-getters, Ike Turner and Jackie Brenston, had recorded with Sam. When Sam had played the song for Leonard during a trip to Memphis, Leonard flipped. "Rocket '88' " wasn't like anything he'd heard before. Heavy on piano, a sax solo, fun, upbeat lyrics, snappy as hell. Leonard knew he could turn it into a hit. He had to have that song and convinced Sam to sell him the rights. So while Leonard went about getting the record airplay, Sam sent Ike, Brenston and their band on the road for a promotional tour. It was the right combo at the right time.

"That song's still at the top of the charts," said Leonard.

"That's right. So why the hell did you send me a bill for seventeen dollars?"

"That's for Ike's ticket home."

"You're kidding, right? You don't actually expect me to reimburse you for a seventeen-dollar bus ticket."

"Why not? Ike sent it to me by mistake. I'm just passing it along. It's part of his touring expenses."

"Leonard, for God's sake, I sold you the rights to that song for a pittance. You've made a killing on that record — and in part because *I* shelled out the money to tour them. And now you want to nickel-and-dime me on bus fare for Ike Turner? That's really the way you want to do business?"

"Hey, an expense is an expense." Leonard took a long puff off his cigarette. He couldn't understand why Sam was getting so hot under the collar.

"So you're saying you're not going to pick up the cost of Ike's bus ticket?"

Leonard laughed and planted his feet back on the floor. "Why the hell should I?"

"Because it's the decent thing to do."

Leonard took one last drag and ground out his cigarette. "Look, Sam, Ike made a mistake and sent the bill to me. All I did was send it on to you. If Ike had sent the bill to you in the first place, would you have paid it?"

"Of course I would have paid it. I paid all their touring expenses."

"Exactly."

"Leonard, this isn't about the lousy seventeen dollars. This is the principle of the matter."

They went a few more rounds before Leonard said, "Bottom line is, I ain't paying for that motherfucker's bus ticket."

"All right. Fine — you win, you cheap son of a bitch. I'll pay for Ike's ticket. But from now on, don't you dare send me any more of your petty bills."

Leonard shook his head after Sam slammed down the phone. There was a moment of stillness. Of utter quiet. And then *drip plink, drip plink, drip plink.* It was enough to drive him mad. He pushed himself away from his desk and stormed down the hall to the closet where they kept the toolbox.

Five minutes later Leonard was on the kitchen floor, his legs sticking out from under the sink. Using a wrench, he took apart the P-trap and figured out what the problem was. Twenty minutes later, the leak was fixed. And that goddamn plumber wanted eight dollars.

Twenty-Four:
"Tell Mama"

Leeba

After being with Red for the past two years,
Leeba's family knew she was seeing someone.
But this someone had no name, no face. As
soon as she'd told her parents he wasn't Jewish that was enough to render him invisible
and insignificant in their eyes.

Leeba listened to Red's heart beating
against her ear as she rested her head on his
chest. His eyes were closed, his breathing
rhythmical, musical itself. About a month
back, Leeba had convinced Leonard and Phil
to audition Red, but it hadn't gone well. She
was sure that he'd been crushed, but the
rejection had rattled her more than him.
Hearing no from Leonard only stoked Red's
drive. He began working on new songs, more
determined than ever to get a record deal.
When Leeba said she admired his resolve,
Red told her he had no choice. "Music's all
I've got. It's my whole life. If I don't make it
as a musician what am I gonna do?"

Now Red stirred next to Leeba, tightening his arms about her. Someone was yelling out in the hallway and Leeba looked at the clock then at the spider-cracked walls and ceiling of Red's kitchenette. There was a warm breeze coming through the window, fluttering the blinds. Leeba sat up on the side of the bed, her blue veins that he loved so much visible across her breasts and legs. She reached for her stockings, bunched up on the floor, and he rolled onto his side watching her, but saying nothing. They were always quiet when it came to this point. This was the hard part, leaving him, saying good-bye.

"Don't go yet," he said softly.

"I have to. It's Shabbos, remember?" She buttoned her dress. "One of these days I'm bringing you home with me for dinner."

"C'mon, baby, you can't take me home to meet your mama and daddy."

"Why not?"

"Because they aren't going to let their daughter go with a Negro. You know that."

"But I've heard stories about white men with colored women."

"That's different. That's been happening since the slave days, baby. But this — a white woman with a colored man — that's a whole other matter. Nothing gets white folks riled up like seeing one of their women with a Negro. I told you, if we were in the South

283

they'd lynch me for what I'm doing with you."

"But we're not in the South."

"Yeah, you go tell your mama that." He laughed sadly.

She leaned across the bed and kissed him a long, soft good-bye, murmuring into his lips, "I miss you already."

She left Red's tenement and waited almost fifteen minutes for the 14/16 bus. She was running late and should have already been home by now to help her mother get ready for Shabbos. During the bus ride to Lawndale, Leeba rested her head against the window, wishing Red was coming home with her. She loved this man and wanted everyone to know it, especially those closest to her.

When Leeba keyed into the apartment she was surprised to find her mother sitting on the davenport with Aileen, who was holding an ice pack to her mother's forehead. "It's okay, Mrs. Groski," Aileen was saying. "It's not bleeding. You just got yourself a good bump is all."

"What happened?" Leeba chucked her pocketbook aside and went over to her mother, sitting down next to her.

"Ikh arofakn," her mother said. *"Meyn niz, meyn niz. Meyn niz, meyn niz."*

"Ah, she just took a little spill is all," said Aileen. "I came by to see you before I start my Shabbos rounds and found her on the kitchen floor. She fell, bumped her head on the counter. You'd think she just 'bout died, the way she's been babblin' and pointin' to her knees. I don't know what the hell she's sayin'."

"Watch it," said Leeba with a grin. "I think she understands more than she lets on." The look her mother gave her confirmed this to be true. Leeba inspected the bruise on her forehead, which was already swelling up. "You'll be fine, Mama," she said in Yiddish. "You'll probably have a good headache later. You should take some aspirin."

"Di goy gat aspirin far mir."

Leeba turned to Aileen. "Thanks for giving her aspirin already."

After they made sure her mother was okay, Leeba and Aileen went back to Leeba's bedroom. She barely got the door closed before Aileen launched into her latest tirade about Muddy. She was either madly in love with him or else just plain mad at him. It was the same with him. As a couple they couldn't find their equilibrium.

"I can't trust nothin' that man says. He was supposed to come by later tonight before his gig and now he's sayin' he's gotta stay home with Geneva."

"Well," said Leeba, searching through her closet, "she is his wife."

"Common-law wife."

"Still." Leeba pulled out a green dress with

a satin ribbon around the neckline. "I know you love him, but —"

"I want him to leave that woman and come be with me. Just be happy Red ain't living with some common-law wife."

"If only *that* was our biggest problem." Leeba laughed as she worked her way into her dress. "What would you say if I told you I'm thinking about introducing him to my family?"

Aileen raised her eyebrows. "I'd say you crazier than I am. You see the way your mama treats me. She still calls me her damn Shabbos Goy. I ain't even sure she knows my real name. How you think she's gonna react when you bring your colored boyfriend home?"

Leeba knew it would be a shock at first. But she was sure they would see that Red was more than just some colored man. He was Red Dupree and he was smart, charming, polite and charismatic. She'd seen the way people in the clubs fawned over him after watching him on stage.

"If anyone could win them over," said Leeba, "it's Red."

"I wouldn't be too sure 'bout that."

"Why?"

That was her mother's reaction when Leeba said she wanted to bring her boyfriend home to meet them.

They were sitting at the kitchen table the

next day after Shabbos had ended. The bump on her mother's head was purple and yellow. She wasn't concerned about her forehead, though, just her legs. Her mother's housecoat was bunched up in her lap, exposing her bare freckled kneecaps so that Leeba could rub them with liniment oil. Her father was in the living room watching *The Amos 'n Andy Show*. It was sweltering inside and even with all the windows thrown open the mentholated scent of her mother's ointment was overpowering.

"Why don't you have the doctor look at your knees?" Leeba asked.

"*Auch,* it's arthritis. There's nothing he can do and don't change the subject. I don't see the point in meeting him," her mother said as Leeba slathered more oil onto her knee.

"Hear her out, Freyda." Her father spoke up from the other room during a Pepsodent commercial. "It wouldn't kill you to listen once in a while."

"Why should I hear her out?" her mother called back. "I don't see the point of her bringing him here."

"*Shah —*" The commercial was over and her father couldn't hear his program. Leeba didn't care. She wiped her hands on a dish towel, went out to the living room and turned off the television set.

"What?" Her father looked lost, something vital taken from him. "Leeba? What are you doing?"

"I mean it. I want you both to meet him."
She went back to the kitchen, her father trailing behind her.

"Is it serious with this young man?" he asked, as if the possibility had never occurred to him.

"Auch." Her mother raised her leg up and down, wincing with each movement. "How can it be serious? He's not Jewish. She's not going to marry him. We don't even know his name."

"It's Red. Red Dupree."

"What kind of a name is that?" her father asked.

"It's his stage name," she explained. "He's a musician. Like you, Papa. You'll like him. I know you will."

Her mother grimaced as she took over massaging her own knees. "It's a phase. She's rebelling."

"Please don't talk about me like I'm not here. And what's this rebelling business? I'm not twelve years old. I'm a grown woman and I've met someone special."

"It wouldn't kill us to meet the young man," her father said.

"You're agreeing to this?" Her mother sat up straight and glared at him, slapping her palms down on the table.

"Relax, Freyda. Like you said, she's not going to marry him. And it won't kill us to meet someone our daughter's spending so much time with."

Leeba reached over and hugged her father, knowing what it took for him to stand up to his wife.

"But he doesn't speak Yiddish," her mother said. "We won't be able to talk to him."

"No," said Leeba. "*You* won't be able to talk to him. Everyone else can manage to speak English in this house for one night."

Her mother looked punched down like dough left to rise on the counter. She sighed, resigned, and Leeba didn't know what to do with this victory. She wasn't used to winning when it came to her mother. Suddenly she felt undeserving of getting her way and immediately began second-guessing her stand.

"When?" her mother asked. "When do we have to do this?"

Leeba wrestled with herself, wondering if she should tell her family ahead of time that Red was colored. She feared that if they knew, they'd refuse to meet him. So instead she prepared herself for an awkward introduction and hoped that afterward they'd see him for the man he really was.

The whole family had gathered that Sunday night to meet him: Aunt Sylvie, Uncle Moishe, even Golda, Ber and their two small children were there. When Leeba heard a knock at the door she jumped, but her father got there before she could. Leeba watched everyone huddle behind him, anxious to get a look at her beau. Her father opened the door and there he was, standing on the threshold in a dark suit and tie, a bouquet of flowers in his hand.

Her father turned back around, confused. "Is someone expecting a flower delivery?"

"No, no," Leeba said, breaking through them and reaching for Red's hand. Her own was sweating, her heart pounding. "This is him, everyone. This is Red."

She didn't imagine it — she heard a gasp. A gasp and then silence. She was afraid to look. The walls grew narrow around her, the lights began pulsing and the air turned thick with her mother's cooking. She could not have anticipated just how bad a reception Red would get. You'd think she'd brought home a mass murderer. They did nothing to try to mask their shock and, in the case of her mother and sister, their disgust. Leeba led Red inside the foyer, all six foot four of him towering over her wide-eyed family. One by one she made the introductions. Stiff handshakes, bewildered stares, barely a welcome. It was Aunt Sylvie who eventually invited him to come have a seat and asked if he wanted something to drink.

"Just water. That would be fine, ma'am. Thank you."

"Well, this is certainly a surprise," Leeba's father said, nonplussed. "Leeba didn't tell us much about you."

"He's a musician, Papa. I told you that."

"A musician, huh?"

"Yes, sir. I play guitar. A little piano, too." Red gestured to the upright, flush against the wall.

"Hm." Her father nodded and took a sudden interest in the area rug.

The room fell silent again except for Aunt Sylvie translating for Leeba's mother, who cocked her head to the side. Aunt Sylvie told her what he'd said and added in something else, hushed and private, that made Leeba's mother smile. Not a big smile, but a smile just the same, a crack in her wall. That was what Leeba had been waiting for and in that moment the tension in her shoulders began giving way. Her mother had smiled. *She smiled.* Everything would be okay.

But when it came time for dinner the awkwardness returned. Her family sat at the table, not talking to Red or to one another. Once again, it was Aunt Sylvie who broke the tension.

"What do you do for work?" she asked.

"I work in a brickyard, ma'am."

"Oh."

The others seemed to watch her "oh" floating by like a cloud of dandelion seeds. No one else said a thing.

"But I'm hoping to start making records soon."

Another "oh." And then nothing. It went like this off and on all evening. A burst of filler conversation followed by nothingness. Amazingly enough, her mother's expression hadn't changed. It was calm, tranquil. Leeba couldn't believe it.

But poor Red. He shifted anxiously in his seat, tried to smile and be polite. It was Leeba's fault. She'd done this to him, put him in this predicament.

While they were clearing the table, Leeba pulled Aunt Sylvie aside. "What did you say to Mama before dinner that made her smile?"

Sylvie gave off a chuckle as she stacked a plate on the counter. "I just told her not to worry. It won't last."

Leeba's heart sank. This relationship was not a joke. Why couldn't they see that she was serious about this man?

When there was no more food to distract them and nothing left to say, it was time for Red to go. Leeba walked him out and as they stood beneath a streetlamp on Karlov Avenue, aware of her family watching them through the parting in the curtains, she could find no words to make things better. She wanted to open her arms to him and apologize because this good man had been humiliated and it was her fault.

He stuffed his hands in his pockets and looked back toward the four-flat. "You better get back in there. I don't want to cause any more trouble than I already have."

Her heart ached as she watched him walk away. She listened to the hum of traffic on Thirteenth Street as she braced herself to go back inside. Everyone had moved away from the window and was back in their seats when she closed the door behind her. She'd expected a barrage of disapproval, but everyone was eerily quiet.

After another moment she had to break the silence. "Well, what did you think?"

This was where everyone shifted their attention toward her mother, who sat in her chair, hands folded in her lap, her jaw set. Leeba detected the rage seething beneath the surface, behind her eyes, under her skin. But surprisingly her mother was keeping her temper contained.

"Mama?" She waited. "Mama? Aren't you going to say anything?"

"What would you have me say? As if it wasn't bad enough that he's not Jewish, but now I find out that the boyfriend is a *schwartze,* too." Her mother's voice remained even and calm as she stood up, went to the closet, pulled out her vacuum cleaner. No one else said a word. It was as if it were just the two of them in that room. "Tell me, Leeba, what would you like me to say?"

"I realize he's not what you were expecting, but once you get to know him, you —"

"I'm not going to get to know him because

you're not going to see him again."

"Mama —"

"I mean it." She plugged the vacuum cord into the wall socket. "I forbid you to see him again."

Leeba laughed sarcastically. "You can't forbid me to do anything. I'm not a child. And I'm not going to stop seeing him. The only reason you won't give him a chance is because he's a Negro and that's just as bad as the way people treat Jews."

"*Auch,* it's not the same."

"Yes, it is. And that makes you a hypocrite."

Her mother stared her down cold. She turned on the vacuum switch and everything she'd been holding in all night came rushing out. "A *schwartze,*" her mother screeched, running the sweeper over the same spot. "The boyfriend is *schwartze!*" She rammed it up against the baseboards, nicking up the walls, driving it hard against the bottom of the davenport.

"Mama, quit it." Golda reached for the handle, trying to stop her, but her mother wouldn't ease up. Aunt Sylvie tried, too. No one could stop her from cleaning and when there was nothing left to vacuum she started in on the kitchen, scrubbing the counter and sink.

"I know what I'm doing," her mother said. "Let me just get my house back in order."

It was as if she felt Red had contaminated

everything. And it wasn't that she'd never had a Negro in her home. But her mother only regarded Aileen as their Shabbos Goy. No different from her friends who had *schwartze*s do their housework. Bringing Red home as a suitor was very different. Her mother wasn't about to sit down and socialize with a Negro, let alone have him date her daughter.

Talking to the rabbi had been her mother's idea. Leeba agreed to it only to appease her. One week later she found herself sitting across from the man at his oversize desk, the walls lined with thick leather-bound books. The clock in the corner ticked with a maddening tinny sound.

Hands laced together, the rabbi leaned forward and cleared his throat. "Your parents are concerned about your future. You know this, don't you?"

"Yes." Leeba nodded and fidgeted in her chair. The room was hot, smelled like cedar.

"And why do you think that is?"

"Because I've fallen in love with a man who's not Jewish. Worse than that, he's a Negro." His eyes flickered when she said that. "It's not a crime," she reminded him.

"But it *is* a sin to ignore the Torah's teachings." He wagged his finger. "He is not a Jew. You are disobeying the *mitzvot,* the commandments of our people. You come from different worlds, you and this man. You have no common ground."

"That's not true." Her voice came out strong, purposeful. She and Red had plenty in common. They had music. They had oppression — he a transplant from the South, she a Polish immigrant. He was a Negro — a nigger. She was a Jew — a kike. How many conversations had they had about that very thing? How many times had he played songs for her on his guitar and taught her chords, encouraging her songwriting? How many times had he made her laugh till she cried? How many times had they sat together in silence, both perfectly content?

"You must end it with the young man."

"End it? No. I don't want to end it."

"Leeba" — he leaned forward and pressed his fingers together — "I'm going to be frank with you. You're not a young girl anymore. Most women your age are already married, raising children. Where can it go with this man? He's a Negro. You can't marry him, can't have a child with him. You need to stick with your own kind, Leeba. You're breaking your mother's heart."

"And she's breaking mine."

TWENTY-FIVE:
"CROSS ROAD BLUES"

RED

Eight o'clock in the morning and already it was near ninety degrees. Red had taken the day off, called in sick, because Muddy had finally convinced the Chess brothers to let him record with his band. And Red knew that had taken some arm-twisting.

According to Muddy, Leonard didn't want to pay to bring on a piano player, a harp player, a drummer and a second guitarist when Muddy's records — backed by just a bass — were selling fine. But Muddy threatened to go to another label and Leonard relented. So that day they were recording in Chess's makeshift studio. No glass booth or control room like Red heard about. No, all they had was a reel-to-reel and enough electrical power for their guitars and amps and microphones.

And, man, it was hot inside. The amplifiers alone kicked off enough heat to melt them. Even with the windows and the front door wide open, it was like a steam room. Red's shirt stuck to his skin. He watched Leeba running around trying to keep up with the demands for cold beer and ice for the scotch.

"Let's do this, guys," said Leonard. "From the top."

The drummer, Elgin Evans, together with Big Crawford on bass, was laying down the beat, Otis came in on the piano and Muddy and Red were leaning back in their chairs, wailing on electric guitars. Little Walter was playing his harp, giving it everything he had. Red watched the sweat pouring down the sides of Walter's face and he could tell something was bothering him. Between takes he'd slap his hands to his sides and shake his head.

Leonard stopped the tape and called to him. "What's the problem, Walter?"

Walter reached for his scotch, taking a long pull. "Can't nobody hear me over all them electric guitars."

" 'Cuz this ain't about you, motherfucker," Leonard reminded him. "And go easy on the sauce."

"Yeah, I'll go easy, all right," said Walter, taking another defiant swig.

"Okay, let's do it again." Leonard motioned for Phil to start the reel-to-reel.

Muddy hadn't even gotten the first few lyrics out when Little Walter snapped. He grabbed Muddy's microphone and cupped it around his harp, blowing in a way that could not and would not be ignored. Red had seen Sonny Boy Williamson do something similar with a harp and a microphone, but he'd never heard anything like what Walter was doing just then. He used that mike to blast out a squeal and a series of *wah-wah-waaahs,* changing the whole feel of the instrument. Red didn't even know a harmonica could make that kind of sound. Judging by the looks on everybody's faces, neither did they. Muddy and Red eased up on their guitars. Elgin, Otis and Big Crawford did the same and gave Little Walter space to see where this was going.

The boys kept playing and when Little Walter blew his last howling note Leonard said, "Do it again. Just like that. Somebody get another mike for Muddy." He looked around and called to Leeba, "Where the hell's that mike? C'mon, c'mon, I don't wanna lose this energy."

They laid that song down and went right into Muddy's next one, "She Moves Me."

"And, hey, Elgin," said Leonard, "when you come in with the bass drum I want you to hit it and hit it hard. Hard and steady. Okay" — Leonard motioned to him — "count it off."

"A-one, a-two, a-one, two, three —"

The room filled with music. Red watched Leonard pacing, shaking his head until he spun around and shouted, "Stop. Stop!" He called out to Elgin, "I said to play it hard, motherfucker. Straight on. No turnaround. Just give it to me right between the eyes." He pounded his fist into his open palm. "You got it?"

"Got it," said Elgin.

But evidently he didn't.

"Okay," said Leonard running his hands through his hair, "somebody put a mike on that bass drum. I wanna hear that motherfucker." Leonard stopped them again on the next take. "No — no. You gotta come in strong. Steady. Hard. Right on the beat. Give it to me straight on." They tried it again and that was when Leonard charged over to the drum kit. "Fuck it, man, I'll do it myself. Get out of there."

Elgin sprang up and Leonard sat down and hit the pedal on the bass drum with all his might. It sounded like thunder. He was right, though, thought Red. That was exactly what the song needed.

"Phil, roll tape. Let's lay this down."

And they did. They separated the drum kit and recorded Muddy's latest song with Leonard Chess on the bass drum and Elgin playing the rest of the percussion. Red was amazed. They had struck on something. Afterward Little Walter was happy again and he and Crawford were clowning around while Muddy wiped the sweat off his guitar and put it away. The only person not pleased was

Elgin. Red saw him grab his drumsticks and storm off.

While the others were goofing around, Red picked up his Gibson and eased into a little impromptu jam of his own, fooling around with an old tune called "Cross Road Blues." He kept his eyes closed, his mouth set, with a cigarette trapped between his lips moving up and down in time with each chord, each bend of a note. He was leaning so far back in that chair, the front legs had come up off the floor.

He heard Leonard call to Phil, "We rolling tape on this?"

"Oh, hell yeah," said Phil. "We're rolling."

Red's eyes flashed opened and he saw Leah standing with her hands clasped close to her chest, a big grin on her face. Then he looked over at Leonard and Phil, the two of them smiling, standing next to the rolling reel-to-reel. It had been almost a year since they'd rejected him, accused of sounding too much like Muddy. Red figured he had nothing to lose so he cut loose and began singing. He was just messing around, vamping. He wasn't expecting anything, so he was caught off guard when he finished playing and Leonard turned to Phil and said, "Now, that's a hit record."

They had him record it again and an hour later Red found himself at Deutsch's diner down the street. He knew that was where the brothers liked to do business. Red sat in the booth across from Leonard and Phil, still not sure why he was there.

"I'll tell you what," said Leonard as he doused his eggs with hot sauce, "we can either pay you today for your session or you can have the union cut you a check in a couple of weeks. If we pay you today, it's half of scale, but it's cash. Up to you. Forty-one fifty in a few weeks or twenty dollars and seventy-five cents right now."

Red needed the cash, but he didn't like the idea of giving up half his pay. "I think I'll just wait on my check from the union."

"Suit yourself," said Leonard, shoveling in a mouthful of eggs.

"We're not here to discuss the session fee," said Phil, cracking a smile that made Red feel a little better. The other brother, Leonard, didn't smile much. Not at Red anyway.

"It's because we want to release that recording you just did for us," said Leonard.

Red didn't want to let himself get too excited in case he hadn't heard right.

"When you play like that — like you just did back there at the office," said Phil, "you've got your own sound. It's not Muddy's or Tampa Red's or anyone else's."

"You think you can give us more songs like that?" asked Leonard.

"Yes, sir. Yes, I know I can."

"Good."

Phil opened a folder, pulled out a couple sheets of paper and plunked them down in front of Red, along with a fountain pen. "That's a recording contract," said Phil. "We want you to sign it."

A recording contract? Red sat up straighter, his blood rushing faster through his veins. He'd spent years chasing a record deal and this one had come to him. Red looked over the contract, but all he saw was a lot of legal mumbo jumbo.

Phil pointed out the particulars. "We'll pay you an advance of two thousand dollars against royalties. We're making Walter the same offer. That's what we gave Muddy. And Sunnyland Slim, too. Then after that's earned out, you get a percentage of each record we sell . . ."

Phil was still talking, but all Red heard was that they were paying him two thousand dollars up front. His eyes raced over the contract looking for the signature line. He saw the way Muddy lived and even before he reached for the fountain pen Red was miles down the road, headed toward the big house, fancy cars, tailored suits. A chance to prove to Leah's family that he was good enough for her, as good as any white man could be.

So he signed the contract and the next week Leonard pressed five thousand copies of "Cross Road Blues."

Leah had grabbed one of the finished

records and had surprised Red later that night, showing up on his doorstep with his own copy, a brand-new portable RCA Victor record player and a bottle of champagne.

Red stood in his kitchenette holding his 78 like it was a newborn. He and Leah played it over and over again while they drank the champagne straight from the bottle, dancing and kissing. It was a hot August evening and they were sweating, working off their layers of clothing until they were dancing naked, her pale breasts catching the light each time she swayed her hips back and forth.

That night he made love to his woman to the sounds of his own music playing in the background. That was a powerful moment for him and afterward as they lay side by side, trying to catch their breath, he said, "So what happens now?"

"Now we cuddle and you tell me how much you love me."

"No, I mean what happens now? With the record?"

She laughed. "I knew what you meant." She rolled over onto her back. "So now they try and get your record on the radio and in jukeboxes and record stores. It could take a little time, so you just have to be patient."

And he was. At least he thought he was. But after two weeks it seemed like nothing was happening so Red stopped by Chess to talk to the brothers and see what was going on. The place seemed all but deserted and he found Leah at the piano, working on a song.

"Tell me what you think of this," she said, playing a classic twelve-bar blues intro.

Red wasn't really listening. He looked in on the dark, empty space they used as a studio. The folding chairs were put away and even the ashtrays had gone cold. The place was abandoned. "Where is everybody?" he asked.

Leah got up from the piano and came up behind him, circled her arms about his waist. "They're on the road."

He twisted around to face her. "You mean to tell me Leonard and Phil aren't even here? Where'd they go?"

"Leonard went down South with Muddy and Phil's up North with Walter."

"*That's* who Muddy went down South with? I thought he was just going to see his kin. Why didn't they take me with them? And what's Walter doing with Phil?"

"Relax. Sometimes they take the artists with them to introduce them to deejays. But it doesn't matter. They've got 'Cross Road Blues' with them and they're going to try and get you distributed. You just have to be patient."

Time crept along and Red grew antsy. Couldn't eat, couldn't sleep, couldn't focus on anything but that record. Everything was riding on that song becoming a hit and he couldn't do a thing to help it along. A week passed. Nothing. Another week and another. The Chess brothers were still gone. Red turned the radio knobs up and down the dial, hoping he'd hear his song. He went into every music store he could find, flipping through the rows of 78s, looking for his record. He stopped into diners to search the jukeboxes. There wasn't a trace of "Cross Road Blues" anywhere.

Two more weeks passed. It was a blistering hot September day and Red was working down at the brickyard, shoveling clay into a Dumpster. Sweat dripped off of him, soaking his shirt. When they went on break, Red and the guys headed into the lunchroom, grateful to get out of the hot sun.

Red was getting some water when he first heard it. He stopped, turned around. He couldn't believe it. But there it was — the opening chords of "Cross Road Blues" coming over the radio. He rushed over and turned up the volume. He called to the others, turning it up even higher. They all gathered around, listening, until the boss man came by and snapped the radio off.

"Get back to work."

"But that's my song," Red said, pointing to the radio.

"Don't you go getting uppity with me, nigger. Get your ass back out there and get to work."

Red felt the assault. Everything inside him

bristled and a voice inside his head — the same voice he'd heard as a child that day he went into that store for chocolates — screamed, *You don't have to take this.* He stepped forward, towering a good four inches over his boss. "What did you just say?"

Judging by the shocked look on the man's face, Red knew he wasn't used to a Negro, or maybe any of his workers, talking to him like that. "Let me tell you something." Red leaned over and turned the radio back on. "You hear *that*? That's *me* on the radio. Red Dupree. That's my song, and you know what that means? That means you don't get to tell me what to do ever again."

Red walked off his job that day. He was a different man. He was on his way.

"Five times." Leah smiled and held up her hand, fingers splayed apart. "I heard 'Cross Road Blues' five times on the radio today. And Phil and Leonard want to get you back in the studio."

"Did they say anything about recording more with Mud, too?" He pulled his suitcase from the closet. He was going on the road, heading to a gig in East St. Louis. He was playing at the Manhattan Club, opening for Ike Turner.

"Don't worry about Muddy," she said. "Just forget about him."

But Red couldn't. Critics, deejays, *Billboard*

and *Cash Box* magazine all made the comparison, calling him a Muddy Waters wannabe. Leonard and Phil had been worried about that from the get-go, but with "Cross Road Blues" they thought he had his own sound. And Red did have his own sound. He'd been playing electric guitar, even slide guitar, before he'd met Muddy. Still Red measured himself against his friend. He was in a race with Muddy Waters and he couldn't catch him no matter how he tried. The man was too far out in front with a two-year lead.

"Cross Road Blues" was out there and it was selling okay. It was enough to get people to pay Red some respect. Besides, Red knew he wasn't going to get rich off his record sales anyway, not when he was only making two cents a copy. The brothers said Red's contract was the same as the one Muddy signed, so he felt okay about it. He didn't understand all the fine print, but that didn't matter because he was making good money playing the clubs.

When Red first left Muddy's band and struck out on his own he was playing small, run-down joints, lucky if he could pull in thirty or forty dollars a night. Now he was packing the house, making up to two hundred a gig. He even had some white folks coming into the clubs to hear him and afterward they slapped him on the back, bought him drinks, told him how much they loved his music.

Some invited him to play at their private parties in their big houses up on the North Shore. He'd never had so many people admiring him, treating him like he was something special. His guitar was his ticket. He wasn't just some dumb nigger to them, because he could do something they couldn't. He'd come away from those house parties with three hundred dollars in his pocket and a picture in his mind of what his future could be like in Leah's world. If a house full of rich white folks could accept him, her family could, too.

After Red packed the last of his things he laced his fingers through Leah's and kissed the back of her hand. What he felt for this woman had sneaked up on him. How could he have not immediately noticed her rare beauty, the exquisite brightness of her eyes, the smooth complexion, the natural pink blush to her cheeks, her tall, curvy frame? Now when he looked at her he couldn't get over her loveliness. He could hardly believe that this wondrous creature loved him back.

Leah was different from other girls. And not because she was white. It was who she was. Hard to believe they'd been together for almost three years. It seemed like only yesterday when they'd first tentatively circled each other, wondering how to proceed. In the beginning they couldn't get enough of each other, could barely make it inside his kitchenette. By now the urgency may have faded, but as the passion burned away he had discovered something deeper, richer underneath. He found a friend, a true friend like none other.

Their time together was never enough. He hated when they had to say good-bye, and found himself thinking more and more about waking up to her, growing old with her. His life had been on hold until now, but a record contract changed everything. Made him legit and freed up possibilities he wouldn't have let himself consider before. He had a two-thousand-dollar contract and a record on the radio. He had put together his own band and had booked club dates around town and in nearby cities. If he could do all that, anything was attainable.

"I'm going to miss you," she said.

"It's just for two nights. And when I get back . . ." He snapped his suitcase shut and wrapped his arms around her waist, pulling her close.

"And when you get back *what*?"

This moment, like everything else with Leah, had snuck up on him. He'd thought he'd wait until he came back from the road and do it right, down on one knee, ring in hand, the whole bit. But now was the time. He knew it wouldn't be easy — his mama and kin would be shocked; her parents would oppose it — but he had to let her know he wanted to spend the rest of his life with her. If she'd have him.

"Red?"

"When I get back," he said, kissing her, speaking into her pale lips, "I'm gonna talk to your daddy about us getting married."

Twenty-Six:
"Hideaway Man"

Leeba

Red was back from St. Louis, but Leeba felt it would be better if she told her parents herself. She waited until *Your Show of Shows* was over. Her parents were sitting side by side on the davenport when she stood in front of the television set and said, "There's something I need to tell you." She'd rehearsed this so many times in her head and now she didn't know how to get it out.

"What's the matter?" her mother asked. "What's wrong?"

"Nothing's wrong," she said. "Red asked me to marry him. And I said yes."

Her mother's jaw dropped open. *"Iber meyn toyt gut,"* she said. Over my dead body.

"Mama, you have to give him a chance."

"No, I don't."

"Are you in trouble?" her father asked. "Is that why you're getting married? Because you're in trouble?"

"I'm not in trouble, Papa. I'm in love." She

laughed because it was easier than crying.

He dragged his hands over his face and let his head drop forward as if he were reading something off his chest.

"I'm getting married because I'm in love and I can't live without this man."

Her mother got up, the creak in her knee joints audible from across the room. She went into the kitchen and began slamming cupboards and drawers. Her father stayed seated, his mouth pinched, eyes darting back and forth, torn between hearing his daughter out and consoling his wife.

A crash came from the kitchen. They both sprinted through the alcove. Her mother had gone mad. Shards of porcelain were on the floor at her feet. She reached for a serving platter that she'd borrowed from Aunt Sylvie and held it high above her head ready to smash it, too, until Leeba stepped in and stopped her.

"I want you out of here," her mother said, twisting free from Leeba's hold. "Out of this house."

"Freyda, please." Her father protested, but it made no difference.

Her mother's face was bloodred as she muttered, "Marrying a *schwartze*. Loving a *schwartze*. Can't live without the *schwartze*."

Leeba pulled the platter from her mother's weakening grip and placed it on the counter. She towered over her mother, but still she feared her. For such a tiny woman her mother displayed a kind of superhuman strength that Leeba couldn't match. Hers was that mother who could lift an automobile off her daughter trapped underneath — provided that daughter was Golda.

"I mean it," said her mother. "I want you out of here."

Leeba reached for her mother, but her hand was swatted away.

"You disgust me," she said. "I can't stand the sight of you. Go, go — you're dead to me now."

Leeba felt flushed with heat. Her mother was still hollering while her father covered his ears, shaking his head. He didn't want to hear any more. Leeba couldn't bear the anguish she was causing, and the longer she stood there, the worse it got. Without another word she went to her bedroom and packed her things.

As she emptied her drawers and closet she heard her parents still arguing, but couldn't make out any of it until her father raised his voice, saying, "If this was Golda you wouldn't be acting like this."

"Because Golda would never do such a thing. Golda has some sense, some decency. Leeba has been defiant all her life."

"And whose fault is that?"

"Don't you start with me on that."

Leeba snapped the buckles shut on her

suitcase. She wasn't even sure if she'd packed everything, but she needed to get out of there. She turned off the overhead light and headed down the hallway, her parents still quarreling in the kitchen. Though she adored her father, her mother's moods and presence filled every room, every corner of their home, making Leeba feel like a burden, an outsider. She had never been especially happy in that home, but still it was difficult for her to leave. With one last glance, she drew a deep breath, opened the front door and was gone.

It hit her hard after she walked out of her parents' home and boarded the bus for Maxwell Street. She would have no wedding, not that she'd expected a big affair like the one they threw for Golda and Ber. Something small, private, after her mother had come to accept Red. But no, that would never happen. And there would be no going down South to meet Red's family, either. He'd already told her the Klan would come running if they even suspected a white woman was in his mother's house. There would be no wedding dress, no honeymoon. They were on their own and she'd never felt more alone.

By the time she turned up on Red's doorstep, suitcase in hand, she had tears in her eyes. Red was still living in the same tenement house down on Canal Street, saving his money for a better place. The hallway always smelled of urine and stale beer. People a few doors down were yelling. She stepped into Red's apartment, seeing it through new eyes. Milk crates for tables, splinters and nails sticking out of the floors, naked bulbs overhead, rust stains in the sink. From now on this was home.

"You can't stay here," he said, as if reading her thoughts, cupping her face in his hands. "I'll find us a better place."

"Where? Where are we going to go? Who's going to rent to a white woman and her Negro husband?" She glanced around, thinking how this place wouldn't have fazed her when she first arrived in America. It wasn't any better or worse than how they'd lived back in Poland. But now, having grown used to hot water, a real kitchen, a sturdy roof, a bedroom and a bathroom with a door, she realized how spoiled she'd become.

Later that night she eased onto Red's bed. He'd finally gotten a proper box spring and mattress, but still the bed creaked beneath them each time they moved. He made sad, slow love to her while she held on tight, clinging to him like ivy to a trellis. He was all she had left.

When Red reached over and turned off the night-light she listened in the dark as the room came alive. The mice and rats scratched behind the walls; a couple argued in the apartment down the hall. She pictured the cockroaches coming out of hiding, making their way inside her suitcase, crawling along the countertops, over the dishes and glasses. Before they'd gone to bed she'd taken their toothbrushes and put them in a box, sealing the lid with tape in hopes of keeping them out.

She rolled onto her side and looked at Red. Even in the dark she saw his lashes blinking. "Can't sleep?" she asked.

He shook his head. "You deserve better than this. Better than what I can give you right now. Who knows how many records I'll make, how many club dates I'll book. There's still time to change your mind. Go find yourself some nice rich Jewish boy to give you a proper home —"

"But if I have that, then I won't have you."

Leeba nestled into the crook of his arm like that spot had been created for her. Just then that was all she needed. No matter where they lived or how many people gave them sideways looks, she knew she wanted to be married to this man, and only him, for the rest of her life.

The next day they left city hall as husband and wife. Two thin gold bands pawned by another couple were now on their ring fingers. After the ceremony, Leeba and Red celebrated with their friends at a black-and-tan club in Bronzeville.

Leeba looked around the long table in the back, a centerpiece of overflowing ashtrays and whiskey bottles. No flowers, no wedding cake — although Aileen had bought a day-old unclaimed cake from a bakery that said *Happy Birthday, Brenda* in pink icing. As a young girl this wasn't the wedding reception she'd pictured for herself.

She was pleased, though, that Leonard and Phil stopped by with their wives. They were the closest thing to family she would have there.

"Do you hear that?" Leonard said to Leeba, his hand cupped to his ear.

"Hear what?"

"The sound of young men's hearts breaking back at the J.P.I. dances."

She gave him a playful slug.

"Come here, you motherfucker." He pulled her in for a hug. "Seriously, I know your family ain't too crazy about this, but I'm happy as hell for you."

Revetta stepped in and handed Leeba a gift from the four of them, Phil and Sheva, Leonard and herself. It was a beautifully wrapped box with a silver bow on top. It would be the only wedding present they'd receive.

Aileen, who had already had too much to drink, swayed and slurred as she raised her glass. "To my best friend in the whole wide world — Mrs. Red Dupree." She paused for a round of cheers. "Soon there's gonna be babies and —" She stopped, seeming to have lost her train of thought, and picked things up somewhere else. "I'm gonna miss you, girl. I really am . . ."

Aileen was rambling and Leeba wanted to stop her, but didn't know how.

"So let me just say —" Aileen paused in the middle of her toast to take a sip. She'd been talking for so long that people had set their glasses down, resumed their conversations. "I'm happy for y'all," she said as her eyes turned glassy. Hefting her glass up again, she had tears running down her face. And Leeba knew these were not sentimental ones. "I really am happy," she said, breaking down into full-blown sobs.

She dropped to her chair and tugged on Muddy's arm. He was talking to the woman who had come with Walter. She was stunning and with skin so fair Leeba thought she was white at first. Her name was Mimi Cooke. She was introduced to Leeba as an old, old friend of Red's and Walter's.

When Aileen couldn't get Muddy's attention, she poured herself another drink, dribbling some onto the table. There was another toast, this one by Little Walter, who was almost as drunk as Aileen, and Leeba braced herself for what might come out of his mouth.

With his eyes glued on Mimi, Walter started talking about love. "If you ain't got love, you ain't got nothin'. Now, Red here, he done found his true love . . ." The only time Walter took his eyes off Mimi was to address Muddy. "Now, y'all gotta stick with your own love. Don't be takin' nobody else's . . ."

As the party wore on, Aileen got sloppier and sadder. "I've been with Muddy since before you were with Red," she said, leaning her elbows on the table. "This ain't fair. I was supposed to marry Muddy before you married Red. And look at him — Muddy's been drooling over that woman since we got here. And she's been flirting with Red, too."

Leeba didn't know what to say. She wasn't worried about Red, but it was obvious that Muddy was making a play for Mimi and right in front of Aileen.

Even Walter knew it, because as they were slicing the cake Walter pushed his plate aside, bolted out of his chair and whipped out his gun, pointing it in Muddy's face. "You'd better back off," Walter slurred.

Muddy jumped up and so did Mimi, shaking her head as she reached for the gun. "Every time, Walter," she said, taking it from him like it was a toy, "every damn time, you gotta pull out your gun. Gotta be the big man, huh?"

And that was the end of their wedding celebration.

The following week Leeba and Red got lucky and found an apartment in Hyde Park on

Fifty-seventh Street. Nothing fancy, just a small one-bedroom, but it was clean, or at least cleaner, and it had a real kitchen with an icebox and a stove and a bathroom right in their unit. Hot water, too.

The downside was there was no room for a piano and the walls were so thin they could hear their neighbors' conversations, their radio and TV programs playing, their alarm clocks going off. But it was one of the few places that would tolerate a couple like them. It was close to Bronzeville, so a Negro passing by on the streets wouldn't pique anyone's curiosity or cause concern. Some neighbors knew they were a mixed couple. They gave Leeba looks when she took out the trash, went down to get the mail or ran into them in the laundry room. Others didn't say anything but they were cool to her, kept their distance. Still, the neighborhood had lots of jazz clubs and black and tans, like the Nob-Hill and Club Rodeo on East Forty-seventh Street.

Leeba's father came to see the apartment after they moved in. Red wasn't home and Leeba wasn't sure if she was relieved about that or disappointed. She desperately wanted her father to get to know Red but didn't want to cause any more upset than she already had. When her father arrived, the place was barren, without any real furniture, but he didn't comment on that.

"Now, don't tell your mother I was here," her father said, kissing her hello.

"Don't worry. She hasn't said two words to me since I moved out. She's always in a hurry when I call and hangs up right away."

"Give her time," he said as he inspected the windows, flushed the toilet, told her she needed a new washer for the kitchen faucet. He twisted the knob on the radiator and it made a terrible squeak. "Have your husband oil that."

Her husband. He'd called Red her husband. A small concession that made her eyes mist up.

Eventually Leeba and Red settled in. They got some furniture, some of it found in alleys or Dumpsters. They dragged a chest of drawers up three flights of stairs, maneuvered a table through the hallway, turning it sideways to get it through the door. They sanded, nailed, painted and polished, made do with what they could afford. Leeba sewed pillows for the secondhand davenport they found in a thrift store and the landlord came through with new shades for the windows. It started to be a comfortable place, and feel like home.

When they first got married the simplest things filled Leeba with pleasure: watching Red shave while she perched on the edge of the tub, bringing him coffee in bed and reading the *Defender* over his shoulder. He read that newspaper front to back. She'd never seen it before and certain stories disturbed her, stories about segregated schools, Klan rallies, torched churches, discrimination and violence. It reminded her of the brick thrown through the stained-glass windows of their synagogue, or that day at Marshall Field's when she overheard the salesclerks saying they didn't want to wait on "that Jew lady."

A Jew lady married to a Negro man. It was complicated. She hadn't figured out how to balance their lives, how to bring their worlds together. She wrestled with herself over abandoning her faith for Red, fretting about not keeping a kosher home, not observing Shabbos. She didn't exactly miss any of it, but still feared that God would punish her later on.

And He did. Two months into her marriage the cramps woke her in the middle of the night, the sheets already bloody. They spent the next four hours at the hospital only to discover that she'd lost a baby she didn't even know she'd been carrying.

The next day she lay in bed, drifting in and out of sleep. Red was gone. He had a rehearsal that day and was going on the road at the end of the week for some club dates in St. Louis and Kansas City. He wanted to cancel the trip, but she wouldn't let him. He needed to play in front of as many people as possible to prove that he was his own man and not a Muddy wannabe.

Leeba rolled over, stared at the wall and imagined what might have become of the child she'd started with Red. Would it have been a boy or a girl? Red's rich dark skin, or her paleness? A combination of the two? Height and musical abilities — this child was certain to have had both. She thought about holding their baby and she cried.

When she couldn't lie there anymore, when she was cried out for the moment, she called Aileen; and twenty minutes later her friend was at her front door. Leeba padded across the living room in her bare feet and when she let Aileen inside she practically collapsed into her friend's arms. In between gasping sobs, she told her what had happened. It was one of the only times Leeba had been the one to lean on Aileen for comfort and strength. It felt strange and Aileen's response was to go into the kitchen and get a bottle of whiskey.

"You gonna have more babies," she said as she poured a glass and pushed it toward Leeba.

Leeba ignored it. "What if God's punishing me for marrying outside my religion? Outside my race?" She thought back to what the rabbi had said to her and felt the panic building inside her. *He said she had sinned.* "What if I'm cursed?" She began to cry harder now, on the verge of hysteria. "What if I'm never able to have children?"

Aileen picked up the glass and put it in Leeba's hand. "Drink," she ordered.

And Leeba did this time, letting the whiskey burn the back of her throat, calming her as its heat spread across her chest.

"You're sounding as superstitious as Leonard."

"I can't help it." She took another sip.

Aileen stayed with Leeba until she'd finished off three whiskeys and had to leave for work. The hotel had recently put her on the night shift and she told Leeba she'd gladly call in sick.

"You can't call in sick again," said Leeba, showing her to the door. "You're going to get fired. And make sure you don't breathe on anyone," she added. "You're drunk."

"I don't care. I hate this damn job anyway." Aileen hugged her and said, "Go write me a hit song so I can quit." She laughed, turning just as one of Leeba's neighbors came down the hall. The woman eyed them with suspicion and Aileen snapped at her, "What the hell you looking at? Huh?"

Before Leeba could apologize, her neighbor slipped into her apartment and Leeba heard the dead-bolt lock turn. Aileen laughed some more and disappeared down the hall.

Everything was quiet again and Leeba contemplated crawling back into bed but feared lying there in the dark and thinking too much. Music had always been her salvation so she went over to the Electrohome reel-to-reel recorder that Red had bought for her with some of his advance money from Chess. He knew she was frustrated that Leonard and Phil hadn't recorded any of her songs and thought the Electrohome machine might help, especially since they had no piano at home.

So she sat down on the floor, held the Electrohome microphone in one hand and started the reel-to-reel while she hummed the opening of something brewing inside her head. Despite what Aileen had said, Leeba wasn't thinking about writing a hit. No, she only wanted to distract herself. There were no words yet, but it was usually the melody that came first anyway. And in this case it was coming almost faster than she could keep up.

The next morning, wanting to put the sadness behind her, Leeba got up early and went into the office so she could jump on the piano before anyone else was there. She brought the tape she'd made at home with her and played it back on the office machine while she worked out the chords on the keyboard.

She was in the middle of this when Willie Dixon came in, giving her a start. Her heart was hammering, her face flushed red with embarrassment. Her song wasn't ready for anyone to hear. Especially not Willie. Leonard and Phil had hired him as a full-time songwriter for Muddy and some of the other artists. He was a big, husky man who played an upright bass. When he spoke you could see only his bottom teeth and Leeba didn't think he had any top ones until the first time she saw him smile.

"Now, don't stop," he said, setting his bass down on its side. "Let me hear what you got there."

"Oh" — she swiped her hand through the air, shook her head — "it's nothing."

"Sounded like somethin' to me."

"I'm just fooling around."

"No, you ain't just foolin'. Now let me hear it from the top."

Leeba took a deep breath and started over. "I'm not much of a singer," she warned.

"That don't matter. You writin' the song, you ain't performin' it."

She watched Willie, his arms folded across his big chest. His expression didn't change as she sang. But when she was done he unfolded his arms and said, "You know what your problem is? You ain't got no blues in there."

"What are you talking about? That's a twelve-bar —"

"Oh, you playin' the blues, but you ain't *playin'* the blues. You playin' with your fingers and what you need to be doin' is playin' with your heart, see. I ain't feelin' no pain. No struggle. Nothin' real."

Willie pulled up a chair and sat down. "The blues are the true facts of life. The blues came out of gospel, out of the days when we was slaves. Now, folks'll say you're a white girl and you can't know the blues. But I tell you — you got the blues. Leonard's got the blues. Phil's got the blues. The president of the United States has got the blues. All a man's got to do is have a fight with his woman and he's got the blues. Now, let me ask you — what's heavy in your heart? Whatever it is — that's what you write about."

What was heavy on her heart? The baby she lost. Being torn between her husband and her family. Willie Dixon inspired Leeba, and that night, after everyone was gone, she stayed at the office and sat at the piano, working on a song about a love affair that no one would accept. She did that for the next two nights while Red was still on the road, and on the third day she had a song. A song that was perfect for Aileen. She called it "Hideaway Man."

The following week Aileen and Leeba performed it for Leonard and Phil. Aileen sang powerfully, keeping her fists clenched, her head tilted back, like she did as a child that first time Leeba heard her singing outside the church. She gave Leeba goose bumps and she could see Phil tapping his toe under the desk and Leonard nodding them along.

"God damn it," said Leonard when they finished. "This one I like."

"So you'll record it?" asked Leeba.

"I didn't say that." He wiped a hand across his face. "I'm not sure yet. You got something here, though. I just don't know what the hell it is."

Twenty-Seven:
"I Ain't Superstitious"

LEONARD

Leonard sat on the edge of the bed, clipping his toenails, saving all the cuttings. When he finished he counted them up and scanned the floor to make sure he hadn't missed any. Satisfied that all were accounted for, he put them in an ashtray, pulled out his Zippo and set them on fire, the edges curling up, a ribbon of pungent smoke rising.

Revetta was passing by in the hall and paused in the doorway. "You and your silly superstitions."

"Don't poke fun." Leonard took this seriously. His mother had taught him and Phil to burn their toenails so no one would walk on their graves.

Revetta waved her hand through the smoke. "That stinks." She stepped inside and opened the bedroom window. "Don't forget to leave the rent check for me so I can give it to the landlord this afternoon."

"We'll get him a check over the weekend."

"It's the seventh already," she said. "Rent was due on the first. We're going to get thrown out."

Leonard watched the last of the flames die down. "No one's gonna throw us out."

"I just don't understand how you can have all these hit records and we still can't pay our rent on time."

"I've explained it to you a hundred times. The business doesn't work like that." He went into the bathroom down the hall, emptied the ashes into the toilet and gave it a flush.

"Well, I don't want to end up on the street with my children," she said, following him.

"Nobody's gonna end up on the street. And by the way, they're my children, too."

"Then why don't you try spending a little time with them once in a while? Your brother spends more time with your children than you do."

"Oh, that's right, good old Saint Phil."

"At least he finds time for his children. For his wife. Your children need you, Len." Her voice cracked and the sadness seeped out. "I need you, too."

Leonard dropped the toilet lid with a loud clack. She wasn't going to make him feel guilty again. "You want me to provide for this family? Do you? Then I have to work."

She was crying when he stormed down the hall and out of the apartment, got in his

Cadillac and drove off toward the office. He knew she was right about the kids, about her, but he didn't know how to be any other way. He wanted a better life for his family and the only way he knew how to get it was by working harder, faster, longer. If Muddy hit number two on the charts, what could he do to make him number one? And if he hit number one, how many weeks could he keep him there?

When he walked into the office, Leeba handed him a half dozen phone messages. "Don't forget we're recording with Aileen today."

"I know. I know." He shuffled through the messages: Shelley Stewart, a disc jockey from Birmingham, called. Alan Freed, another deejay, called. Al Benson called. Art Sheridan called.

He looked up. "Nothing from Sam Phillips yet?" Leonard had telephoned him at Sun Records down in Memphis twice already.

"Nope. Sorry."

He went into his office, reached for a cigarette and stared at the telephone. What the hell was taking Sam so long? Sam had a real feel for talent and his latest find was a singer with a deep, haunting voice who played guitar and harp. His name was Chester Arthur Burnett, but he called himself the Wolf. Howlin' Wolf. As soon as Leonard heard the two songs Sam had recorded — "How Many

More Years" and "Moanin' at Midnight" —
Leonard had begged Sam to sell him the
rights. Sam was still thinking it over.

It was the fall of 1952 and Leonard and
Phil were busy with a new batch of songs and
artists. Muddy continued to be their biggest
name, but Leonard needed someone else —
someone new who could be just as big. Red
was great, but he tended to sound too much
like Muddy, and Leonard wanted someone
with a completely different sound and that
was Howlin' Wolf.

Leonard broke down and put another call
in to Sam. Marion, the girl who ran Sun
Records, said he was on another call. "Did
you tell him it's me?" There was a time when
Sam would have dropped everything to take
his calls. He was holding a grudge, still
punishing Leonard over Ike Turner's bus
ticket. When Marion said he couldn't break
free, Leonard slammed the phone down and
stormed into Phil's office.

"That goddamn motherfucker."

"Which motherfucker are we talking
about?" asked Phil.

An hour later Leonard looked at Aileen and
signaled his brother with a finger slice across
his neck. Phil went over to the reel-to-reel
and stopped the tape while Leonard dragged
his hands through his hair and blew out a
deep breath. He listened to the playback,

paced, stopped tape, gave directions, rolled tape and stopped it again.

"Okay," he said eventually. "Let's everybody take five."

The smart thing would have been to re-schedule the session with Aileen. But he was under pressure to get a new sound going. Deep down he knew it wasn't going to be Aileen, but she was right there in front of him, the song was good and he was going to do his goddamn best to squeeze whatever he could out of her. But still, something wasn't clicking. Maybe it was him. He was in a foul mood. He hadn't slept well the night before, and Sam not taking his call was bothering him, not to mention his fight with Revetta that morning.

"Okay," said Leonard, gathering everyone back into the room. "Let's do this." He propped his cigarette in his mouth and clapped his hands. "Let's lay this down."

The musicians took their places and Leonard paced again while they went back to recording "Hideaway Man." It was hot in there. His head was throbbing as he walked back and forth, trying to block the noise inside his head. *Is Sam gonna give me Howlin' Wolf or not? Which account should I move money from to pay the rent?* He couldn't shut out the distractions. He couldn't hear the music.

And the music — hell, the music was all

wrong. Aileen's voice was dripping with honey. She sounded all smooth, polished and perfect. It was wrong.

"Stop — wait." Leonard walked up to Aileen. "What the hell was that? You call that singing?"

"Yeah." She planted her hands on her hips. "I do. What do you call it?"

"I call it shit. Who are you, fuckin' Doris Day now?"

"Hey." Phil stepped in. "Easy."

Leonard saw the hurt on Aileen's face. The shock on Leeba's. Even the engineer looked put off. Leonard knew Phil was right, he was out of line; but he couldn't rein himself in. He was ticked off about a million things that had nothing to do with Aileen; and yet, he wasn't wrong about her singing.

"You wanna make a record? Then you gotta put your whole heart into it," he said. "You gotta reach down and grab that pain and I don't give a shit if it hurts."

"Okay," said Aileen. "I get it. Let's try it again."

The music started up and she got about three bars in and all he heard was fear. He stopped her before she even got to the chorus. "C'mon — quit wasting my time."

"What do you want from me?" She threw her hands out to her sides. "I'm doing the best I can here."

"Well, maybe your best ain't good enough."

Her eyes turned glassy as soon as he'd said that. She was right on the edge, ready to crack. "Well, maybe you're right." She stepped away from the microphone, stormed past him and walked out the door.

"You're an asshole," said Phil.

Leonard went after her and found her just outside the door, bawling like a baby. "Hey — hey, come here." Leonard put his arms around her and held her as she tried to wiggle away from him. "Look, we've known each other since we were kids. You know me. I ain't big on apologizing. I've never recorded a girl singer before. I'm treating you the same way I treat the guys and maybe I shouldn't."

"You talk to Muddy like that? Walter? Red?"

"If I have to. Yeah. This is a tough business. You gotta get a thicker skin if you wanna do this. You got a big, big voice. But you gotta let it out. You're in there trying to sound like somebody else. All polished, with no rough edges. And that ain't you. That ain't this song. I want you to sound like *you.* So we're gonna go back in there and we're gonna do this again. And this time we're gonna do it right."

She dried her eyes and bit down on her lip, nodding.

They went back inside and he leaned forward and whispered in her ear, "Just be *you.* Nobody else. Go up there and sound like *you.*"

She nodded again.

"Okay," he said. "Let's do it."

And this time when she sang even he couldn't believe what was coming out of her. All that mamsy-pamsy bullshit was replaced with guts and growls. He'd never heard that deep of a sound from her before. He couldn't take his eyes off her and right then and there he watched a star coming into focus. She had that fire and the passion and he could see it in her eyes — she wanted it bad enough to make it happen.

When she sang her last note, he went up and hugged her so hard, her feet cleared the floor.

Twenty-Eight:
"Call It Stormy Monday"

Leeba

Leeba would never forget the day their record arrived at the office. She had practically torn the disc out of Leonard's hand and the first time she held the pressed 78 she felt as though she were holding the future. Each groove in that record represented another opportunity for a colored woman and white immigrant to make their way in this world. "Hideaway Man" was the A-side and for the B-side Aileen did another song Leeba had written, called "Baby, You Tangled Up My Heart." Leeba played piano on both songs. Less than a month after its release, Phil invited Leeba and Aileen out for lunch. Leeba assumed he wanted to discuss running ads in *Cash Box* and *Billboard* to promote their record, but Aileen was sure he had big news for them. And in a way he did.

The two of them were sitting across from Phil in a booth at Deutsch's on a rainy Monday afternoon and Aileen was excited,

338

rambling on about how she was going to spend her first royalty check. She was going to buy a mink and fancy luggage to take on the road when she toured with Muddy. She was already a star, sparkling and filled with hope for her future. She was giddy, too giddy to notice the expression on Phil's face. But Leeba caught it.

With his hands splayed on the table, fingers drumming, he said, "This is a tough business, girls. And sometimes a record takes off and sometimes it doesn't. If we knew what worked, we'd do it every time."

"But the record's just getting off to a slow start, right?" Leeba felt the knot forming in her gut. "That's what you're saying, right?"

Aileen's bubble was beginning to burst. Leeba was sitting next to her and could feel Aileen's leg bobbing up and down, going faster and faster. Leeba placed her hand on Aileen's thigh, hoping to steady her. "Maybe if we run some ads," said Leeba. "Then we could —"

"No ads." Phil dragged a hand over his face. "I'm sorry, but we're not putting anything more into the record."

"What do you mean?" Aileen looked at Phil and then Leeba. "What's he talking about?"

"He's saying our record's dead. That's what you're saying, Phil, isn't it?" The knot in Leeba's gut twisted.

"I'm sorry, girls. Like I say, it's a tough

business."

"That's it?" Aileen's mouth was hanging open. Her nerves were coming unhinged. "But how can you just give up on it?" asked Aileen. "How can you give up on us?"

"I don't want you to take this personally," said Phil.

"Oh sure, Phil," Aileen said with a sarcastic sneer. "Nothing personal about my whole future riding on this." She scooted out of the booth, grabbed her pocketbook and umbrella. "You tell Leonard thanks for nothin'. He didn't even have the guts to come tell us himself."

"Wait —" Leeba reached out for her arm, but Aileen yanked it away and headed up front.

Leeba started after her and Aileen paused, her hand on the door already setting off the chimes overhead. "I don't wanna talk about it. Just leave me alone, okay?"

"Where are you going?"

"I'm gonna go find Muddy." She turned and stormed out of the restaurant.

Leeba went back to the booth and propped her head in her hands. So naïve she was. Even though she worked in the business, knew the odds, she had thought they were on their way. It had never occurred to her that their record could flop. But it did. Spectacularly. They never even got it played on the radio.

Part of her, like Aileen, was angry with

Leonard and Phil for not doing more to promote the song, but she understood this was a business decision. Still her heart broke in so many places, for herself and for Aileen, whom she feared would be plunged into darkness once again.

Two days after her friend had stormed out of Deutsch's, Leeba found Aileen sitting on the floor in her kitchenette in her underwear, ankles crossed, her arms looped about her shins. She stared into her potted plant watching the fruit flies. She'd had them for years — they'd breed, die, breed, die, breed some more.

"Are you okay?" Leeba asked foolishly, not knowing what else to say.

Aileen wouldn't answer.

Leeba opened the window shade, letting the sunlight glint off the empty bottles of bourbon cast about the room. And a syringe.

"Aileen?" Leeba held it up, alarmed. "What's this doing here?"

Aileen glanced back over her shoulder. "Oh, that. That's J.J.'s. He must have left it here."

"J.J.'s? What was he doing here? Are you on dope now? You're not getting mixed up with him again, are you?"

"No, I am not on dope and, no, I'm not getting mixed up with him again." A fly landed on the floor near her foot. Aileen leaned over and squished it beneath her index finger. A green inky smudge lingered. "He

341

just stopped by 'cuz he knew I was upset."

Leeba went over and sat down next to her. "I know you're disappointed. I am, too. But look how far we got."

Aileen shook her head. "Why do I let that man do this to me?"

Leeba sighed. "J.J.'s no good."

"I'm not talking about J.J." She looked up at Leeba with tears trundling down her cheeks. "It's Muddy. I don't know where he is or who he's with. I just know he ain't here with me."

So this had nothing to do with their record. This was about Muddy.

"And you wanna know what the really crazy part is? I ain't worried about Muddy's wife. It's all those women at his shows. They're passing him phone numbers and addresses, sending him drinks. They get up on the stage dancing with him, running their fingers through his hair." She paused as a tear ran down her face. "I get so jealous I can't see straight."

Leeba reached over and thumbed away her tears.

"The worst part about havin' a jealous kinda love is that you end up having a relationship with the other woman, not with your man. 'Cuz you're thinking about her when you should be thinking about him. A jealous kinda love is the worst kind of love there is." She covered her face in her hands and cried. "Sometimes I swear I'm going crazy. Just like my mama did before she killed herself."

Leeba held her while Aileen sobbed. "You're not like your mama."

"I swear I just want out. I just wanna die."

Leeba had heard that so many times she no longer flew into a panic. It was just talk. It was just Aileen.

Another twenty minutes or so and she managed to get Aileen off the floor and into bed. Her eyes were swollen to slits from crying so much. Leeba stayed with her, perched on the side of the bed until Aileen had cried herself to sleep. Leeba pulled a blanket up to her chin, turned off the lights and let herself out, locking the door behind her with her spare key.

It was late. Red was on the road, touring in Cleveland and Cincinnati to promote his new record, "Settle Down, Boy," which was climbing the charts. Leeba didn't feel like going home to an empty apartment. Besides, something Aileen had said earlier had been knocking around inside her head, so she went to the office and headed for the piano. With her right hand she tinkered with something, letting the thoughts tumble out:

I got a jealous kinda love for you, baby
A love that burns down in my soul
Yeah, I got a jealous kind of love for you

now, baby
and it's a burnin' in my soul
I got a jealous kinda love
and where my heart was, there's a hole.

The melody was there as more lines came to her, all of it tied up in a neat package. The song "Jealous Kinda Love" was born.

The next night Leeba brought Aileen down to the office and played the song for her. As soon as Aileen heard it, her eyes sparkled wide and bright for the first time since Phil had told them their record was dead. "This is it," she said. "This is my song!"

They stayed at Chess working on "Jealous Kinda Love," the two sitting side by side at the piano, drinking coffee from paper cups and going over and over each line. Sometimes they got stumped by a phrase and it lost all meaning, like a word said too many times in a row. But when the lyrics and the music were working, Leeba felt it melding together inside her. The song was energy — a living, breathing thing. When they'd gotten it to where it needed to be, they both knew it. Leeba had never felt this way about anything they'd ever done together. It had the right melody, the right emotion; and it had a catchy hook.

The next day Leeba went to Phil. "We have a new song," she said. They were in his office and she had just handed him a stack of mail and the new trade magazines.

"A new song, huh?" Phil opened the latest edition of *Billboard,* turning first to the charts. "You saw what happened to your last song."

"I know, but wait till you hear this. You have to hear it. You just have to."

Phil closed the magazine and squared his elbows on his desk. "Will we listen to it? Sure. Will we produce it? Probably not."

"But this is the best thing I've ever written. And it was made for Aileen."

Phil reached for his cigar resting in the ashtray and rolled it between his fingers, stalling, thinking. "Get her in here tomorrow afternoon. I'll make sure Leonard's around."

Aileen came into the office the following afternoon and sang her *kishkes* out. She growled that song out, word by word, note by note. When they were finished, Leeba looked over at Phil and Leonard. Leonard had his eyes shut, his face frozen in a grimace. The first glimmer of doubt came to her. And it multiplied on the spot. She began to panic. Leonard had a gut feeling for what would and wouldn't work. But how could he not see the potential in a song like this?

Leeba looked at Aileen. She wasn't blinking and Leeba knew her sanity balanced on a pinhead, waiting for the verdict.

"What's wrong with it?" Leeba asked finally. "Maybe we can change it. Fix it."

Leonard opened his eyes, pounded his fist

to the console and shook his head. "Don't you dare change a thing. It's goddamn great." He dragged his hand through his hair and turned to Phil. "Shit, now we gotta record this motherfucker."

Leeba and Aileen gasped with relief and jumped up and down, arms circled about each other.

"But" — Leonard stood up — "that don't mean I'm gonna press and release it. I can't make that decision right now. But we gotta record this. We gotta get this one down."

One week later they recorded "Jealous Kinda Love." It was the easiest session Leeba had ever been through with Leonard and Phil. No shouting, no take after take after take. Leeba thought that was a good omen and she knew Leonard, superstitious as he was, believed in signs.

Yet despite all that, Leonard wasn't ready to put their record out. Weeks passed and not a word was said about pressing and releasing the record. It didn't make it any easier knowing that Leonard and Phil were putting out records by Muddy, Little Walter, Jimmy Rogers and Red.

TWENTY-NINE:
"THE WOLF IS AT YOUR DOOR"

RED

There weren't many men who could look Red Dupree in the eye. He had always been the tallest man in the room, until the day Howlin' Wolf showed up at Universal Recording.

Red was filling in for Jimmy Rogers that day, Muddy's second guitarist. Muddy's band had just started recording when Leonard walked in with a menacing-looking man. Red and Wolf were about the same height, but Wolf was huskier all the way around. Big square head, neck as thick as a tree trunk and that voice. Deep and growling, the Wolf spoke with a gurgle, like he was always on the verge of clearing his throat.

Leonard, who barely came up to Wolf's shoulder, made the introductions and invited Wolf to have a seat and listen in while they recorded Muddy's band doing "Who's Gonna Be Your Sweet Man." When the big man sat down, Red noticed his white socks sticking out through a gaping hole in the front of each shoe, his toes pulsing in time with the music.

They got through the first verse and had just reached the guitar solo when Red watched Muddy throw down the most twisty, whining, squealing riffs he'd ever heard from him. He seemed angry and when Red saw the way Muddy eyed Howlin' Wolf he understood that this was his friend's way of marking his territory, letting it be known that he was the top dog around Chess Records.

Red knew that Muddy felt he was losing ground. Just a few months before, Little Walter had hijacked Muddy's band to record his own song. Muddy didn't mind at the time. Hell, he'd even backed Walter on the record, a harmonica instrumental. There wasn't anything like it out there and when "Juke" started climbing the charts, passing up Muddy's "Please Have Mercy," it left Muddy rattled. Since then Walter had been a front man in his own right. He didn't have time for the old band anymore so Muddy brought in Junior Wells on harp. But he told Red he would have done anything to get Walter back.

They were in the middle of recording and Red had a nice, even rhythm going when Muddy reached over and yanked the cord out of his amplifier.

Leonard slapped his hands to his head.

"Why the fuck did you do that? We almost had it."

Muddy ignored Leonard and stormed up to Red. "What you tryin' to do? You play this damn song the way I tell ya to play it, ya hear me?"

Red shot up and glared at Muddy. "I'll play the damn song the way it needs to be played. And you can't hear it 'cuz you're too busy putting on a show."

"Who you think you talkin' to like that?"

"Okay, guys." Leonard rushed over and put himself between Red and Muddy. "Everybody calm down. Take a break. Everybody take five."

Red went outside to clear his head. It was cold and the wind had a bite to it. It was snowing, too, and Red tilted his head back and watched the sky sprinkle down. Even after five winters, snow still fascinated him.

"Sure do get cold up here, don't it."

Red looked over and there was Howlin' Wolf, shivering, his hands stuffed down in his pockets.

"First thing you need to do is get yourself a warmer coat. And the second thing," said Red, pointing to his feet, "is get yourself a pair of shoes that aren't full of holes."

"Those ain't holes," said Wolf, looking down at his socks sticking out. "These are brand-new shoes. Biggest size I could find and I still had to cut 'em open so they'd fit."

Red laughed.

"You play good, man," said the Wolf. "You got something, you know that?"

"So I've been told."

"I mean it. Now, I tell you what, I heard you, so now you come hear me. I'm playing at Silvio's tonight."

That night Red and Leah bundled up and rode the El down to Silvio's. He paid a dollar at the door for the two of them to see Howlin' Wolf. Silvio's was a tiny, smoke-filled room with a long bar, a short bandstand and a few tables. That was all there was to it. It looked like any other blues club, not too different from the old Macomba Lounge. And Silvio, like Leonard, was a white man who owned a nightclub for Negroes. Things got rough down there, too, as rough as they'd ever been at the Macomba. Leah was the only white woman in the place and Red saw the men looking her up and down and the glares coming from the women.

"You sure you want to stay?" he asked.

"I've been in tougher clubs than this," she said with a smile.

When Howlin' Wolf opened up with his first number Red was impressed. He'd never seen another musician take command of a stage like that. Dressed in a white shirt and black necktie, a pair of black trousers and those white socks showing through his cut-up Stacy

350

Adams shoes, he was a showman all the way. And the name Howlin' Wolf fit, especially when he rose up from his chair in the middle of "Dog Me Around," acting like a wild creature on the stage. "Moanin' at Midnight" sent chills through the air when his voice howled on the high notes and then dipped lower than a bass singer's. When he switched from guitar to the harp, that harmonica was the size of a chicken bone in the man's massive hands. All you could see were the two enormous gold rings he wore on either pinky.

Red eased back in his chair and took a pull from his whiskey, enjoying the show. After the first set Wolf came over to their table. Red reintroduced him to Leah. They'd already met back at Chess when Leonard brought Wolf around. The Wolf took a seat and slipped on a pair of horn-rimmed glasses. He looked like a lawyer or a doctor.

"Now that you seen what I can do," said Wolf in that deep, gravelly voice, "how 'bout joining my band? Ain't nobody gonna work you harder, or treat you more fair. I pay you what you're worth and then some. And I pay you every week. Now, how do that sound to you?"

"I've got my own band, Wolf. I can't come with you."

"Well, I had to ask; ya know I had to."

Red laughed. He was flattered.

"Then at least come up on stage tonight

and join me for a set," said Wolf. "Could use you on guitar while I'm blowin' harp."

"You think that stage is big enough for the two of us?"

"There's only one way to find out." Wolf laughed, a deep rumbling coming from his belly.

"Go on, Red," said Leah, gently pushing him. "Do it."

So when it was time for his next set, Red joined Howlin' Wolf on stage. They were doing a bunch of old Charley Patton and Robert Johnson songs from the delta; but the number that really got the crowd going was "Sweet Home Chicago." When Red pulled the pick that was resting between his teeth and played the intro, the audience started clapping, swaying. Wolf came in with the lyrics and Red joined him on the chorus.

It was a fun night and when he and Leah made it back to their apartment she was tipsy, leaning on his shoulder, singing "Sweet Home Chicago." The hallway smelled musty, like wet dog. A pair of salt-stained penny loafers were outside a neighbor's door. Leah was still singing as she gripped the banister while he keyed into their apartment.

He glanced down and noticed that someone had slipped a piece of paper under their door. Leah swooped down, humming now as she picked it up; and as she read it, he saw her eyes open wide as her hand covered her mouth.

"What is it? What's wrong?" He was worried they'd gotten a late notice from the landlord.

Her hand was trembling as she gave him the sheet of paper. There it was, scrawled out in thick dark letters: *Go home, nigger, and take your nigger lover with you.*

THIRTY:
"KEY TO THE HIGHWAY"

LEONARD

It was a meeting of the brothers. Leonard and Phil sat on one side of the booth and Gene and Harry Goodman sat on the other. They were New York City music publishers. Their brother Benny Goodman had told them to come to Chicago and talk to Chess. They were at Deutsch's and the table was covered with kreplach, chopped herring, kishke and kasha.

"Ah, I do miss Chicago," said Harry, taking a bite of his corned beef sandwich. He and Gene had grown up in the old Lawndale neighborhood, and Leonard vaguely remembered them from the old days.

Harry dabbed his lips and folded his napkin. He still had mustard stuck in the hinges of his mouth. "Let's get right to the point. You two have signed some nice artists. That Muddy Waters and Little Walter are gaining in popularity. So is Howlin' Wolf."

"And let me tell ya, it wasn't easy to get

that motherfucker," said Leonard. "I had to beg Sam Phillips for his contract."

"The point is you got him," said Gene. "And some other up-and-comers, too, like John Lee Hooker and Red Dupree. Your catalogue is very promising."

Leonard scooted his plate aside and leaned forward. "So what exactly are you getting at?"

"As you know," said Gene, "Harry and I have our own publishing company in New York. It's time for you to do the same with Chess and we're here to help."

"Think about it," said Harry. "Atlantic has its own publishing arm. So does RPM and all the other independents. Now, I know you boys don't have time to be worrying about copyrights and that's where we come in."

Leonard sat back and listened to their spiel. When he started making records with Evelyn, he didn't give a crap about copyrights and publishing. But the business was changing. Now songwriters were joining associations like BMI — Broadcast Music, Inc. A few also belonged to ASCAP — the American Society of Composers, Authors and Publishers. Those organizations collected royalties on any copyrighted songs for musicians and publishers from radio stations and appearances. Now everyone registered their songs to make sure they'd get what was due them.

Those organizations had already forced Leonard and Phil to rework their arrangements with songwriters like Willie and Leeba. Now songwriters were "work for hire" employees, which meant that after Chess paid them a flat fee for their songs, whatever was recorded became property of Chess Records. Unfortunately there were no loopholes like that for the artists, but at least Leonard and Phil were able to keep the royalty rates low.

Gene Goodman jumped in. "What we're proposing is that the four of us form our own publishing company for Chess Records. We split the pie four ways. Twenty-five percent apiece."

"Listen, guys," said Harry. "We know you don't wanna be screwing around with copyrights and all that other bullshit. We'll make it a standard arrangement. You'll get your share every time a piece of music gets played. That amounts to two cents per drop. The songwriter gets half and the publishing company gets the other half."

"And what about the artists?" asked Phil.

"That's all separate. They get paid just like before, straight royalties."

They talked awhile longer and a week later, Leonard and Phil agreed to the deal. They decided to name the publishing business A Record Company and called it Arc Publishing for short. Leonard didn't give it much thought after the Goodmans went back to New York. He had bigger matters to tend to and told Phil to handle the Goodmans, who were calling nonstop. They were going through the catalogue and registering all the songs. They wanted to put those songs out there and see if any other artists wanted to record them. *Fat chance,* thought Leonard. They wanted to draw up new agreements that made sure they got their cut if anyone bought the sheet music or an instrumental version or if they wanted a song for a motion picture or a play. Leonard threw up his hands. To him it was busywork. He had no more interest in Arc than he did in making out the will that Revetta had been on him about.

Just that morning the two of them had been sitting at the breakfast table when she brought it up. Again. Sunlight was poking through the curtains and Leonard felt rested for once. Finally got a decent night's sleep. Marshall and Elaine had already left for school and he was a bit irked that Revetta hadn't woken him up in time to have breakfast with them. He'd hardly seen the kids all week and Susie was napping. Always napping. His youngest daughter and he didn't even know her.

Revetta poured him a cup of coffee and flung a newspaper at him. "See," she said. She pointed to an obituary of someone named Raymond Cunningham. "He was forty-three years old."

"Who the hell's Raymond Cunningham?" Leonard set the newspaper aside and reached for his coffee.

"You're missing the point." Revetta's cheeks turned pink like they always did when he flustered her. "He was forty-three and he *died.* You need to meet with the lawyers and draw up a will."

"I've told you, I don't need a will. You know who has wills? People who are about to die. And people like that poor schmuck." He pinged the obituary with the back of his hand and grabbed his pack of cigarettes.

"You and your superstitions. And these aren't helping matters." She plucked the cigarette from between his lips and broke it in half, letting the tobacco rain down. "None of our tomorrows are guaranteed. Any normal, responsible human being — especially one with a family — makes out a will."

"I'm not ready to draw up a will. I ain't going nowhere yet, so don't rush me."

He felt guilty when he left the house that day. He wanted to get Revetta something special to make it up to her so he went to Saks Fifth Avenue. He'd been fighting with himself for weeks not to go there. He'd heard that Shirley had gotten a job there, working in the jewelry department.

He saw her right away. She was waiting on another customer when he got up to the jewelry counter. Her auburn hair was pulled back off her neck and she was in a simple black dress with a strand of pearls hanging down. The woman she was waiting on was making a return. He took off his coat and folded it over his arm as he stood to the side watching while Shirley took down some information, placed a telephone call and chewed off her lipstick. She looked tired and all he could think was that if she'd married him instead of that *putz* her father picked out, she wouldn't have had to work at all. Revetta never had to work.

It wasn't until Shirley finished with the return that she looked up and saw Leonard. A hand went to her throat when he smiled, waved.

"Leonard." That was all she said.

"How are you, Shirley?"

"Surprised. I'm very surprised." Her hand was still at her throat.

"I was hoping you could help me pick out a gift."

Shirley coughed softly. "Of course."

Leonard spent the next hour having Shirley show him necklaces and earrings and bracelets and brooches for Revetta. He ended up with a pair of pearl drop earrings set in fourteen-karat white gold. He even went so far as to have Shirley try them on so he could see how they looked. He wasn't trying to be cruel, just trying to make a point, thinking how later that night she'd call her father and say, *You'll never guess who was shopping in Saks today . . .*

"Your wife's a very lucky woman," Shirley

said as she wrapped them up in shiny paper and white satin bows. "I'm sure she'll be very pleased."

Leonard turned and left with the package, but before he made it back out to his car, he thought about how much money he'd just spent and had an urge to return the earrings.

THIRTY-ONE: "JEALOUS KINDA LOVE"

LEEBA

There were more threats, scribbled down on sheets of paper, crumpled and shoved under the door. Each one left Leeba shaking. But nothing terrified her more than the night someone wrapped that hate around a rock and hurled it through their bedroom window. She woke with a start, shards of glass everywhere, the rock lying like a bomb on the floor. She couldn't bring herself to read the note that was attached. Red looked at it and fisted it up in his hand. She never did ask him what it said.

After that Leeba and Red got a dog. A German shepherd with a menacing bark heard all the way down the hall. They named her Sophie and she never left Leeba's side. According to Red, she moped whenever Leeba wasn't home and lay in front of the door waiting for her return. But underneath Sophie's sweet nature was a vicious watchdog that alerted them at the first sounds of a stranger's footsteps in the hallway, who went mad whenever someone rang the buzzer or knocked on their door. Leeba and Red hadn't had any trouble since they got her.

Life had returned to normal and one drizzly June evening, as rain pelted the windows, Leeba made dinner for them: a pork shoulder smothered in mustard and peppered with cloves. Pork, *treyf,* what would her family say! Red opened a bottle of wine and Leeba put on a record, Big Joe Turner's "Honey Hush." They had a stack of 78s waiting their turn in line. Red set the bottle down and grabbed her hand, spinning her to the music. Sophie was on her hind legs trying to get in on the act. Howlin' Wolf was up next with "How Many More Years" and Red pulled her in close. They kissed through most of it even with Sophie yelping, poking her snout in between them.

A few more songs and it was time for dinner. She was asking Red about his upcoming tour with Muddy while she lifted the pork from the roasting pan and set it on a platter. "You'll get yours later," she said to Sophie as she carried it to the table.

While Red carved the roast, the phone rang. It was Leonard calling. "Is everything okay?" she asked, one hand on the receiver, the other holding Sophie by the collar to keep her away from the roast.

"We're gonna do it. We're gonna release 'Jealous.' "

"What?" She let go of Sophie and gripped the phone with both hands.

"As soon as we get the pressed records, you, me and Aileen are leaving. We're heading down South."

"Whoa, wait a minute. I'm going with you?"

"We gotta do this and we gotta do this now. And I need you down there with me to keep Aileen in line. I don't need her mouthing off to anyone or going off the deep end."

It had been at least six months since they recorded "Jealous Kinda Love" and suddenly now Leonard decided the time was right. No one, not even Phil, understood what made Leonard release a record when he did.

She hung up the phone and turned to Red. "He wants me to go down South with him and Aileen. But . . ."

"But what? That's fantastic. That's what you've been working toward."

"But you're going on tour with Muddy next week. What am I gonna do with Sophie? I have to do laundry, pack, pay all the bills. I can't just pick up and leave without any notice."

Red went over and cupped her face in his hands. "Listen to me. Leonard Chess is going down there to distribute *your* record, to sell a song that *you* wrote. Who cares about laundry and paying bills? Baby, you're going down South with Leonard."

Three days later, Leeba dropped Sophie off with Revetta, who had agreed to watch her while they were gone. Leeba, Aileen and Leonard piled into the Cadillac and hit the road, with the girls taking turns riding up front. They listened to the radio and sang along when a good song came on.

Other than their train ride from Ellis Island to Chicago, Leeba had never been outside the city and the idea of exploring new parts of the country seemed daring and adventurous. She'd never imagined herself making such a journey. As they drove through the back roads of Illinois and the southern tip of Missouri, Leeba noticed everything starting to change. Gone were the traffic lights, the billboards touting Burma-Shave and Maxwell House, gone were the buildings and factories with their smokestacks.

When they crossed the Tennessee state line they stopped at a filling station and that was the first time Leeba saw two water fountains side by side and a set of signs, one that said "White" and the other "Colored." It made her recoil and seemed to bother her more than Aileen, who drank from the "Colored" fountain like it was no big deal. Aileen had family down South, she'd been to Georgia, Mississippi and Louisiana before, so maybe she was used to it. But Leeba wasn't.

The deeper they traveled into the South the more disturbed she became. They passed a sign out front of a general store that read: "No Dogs, Negroes or Mexicans." They couldn't go more than half a block without some sign reminding them that *coloreds go here, stay there, don't go here.* And to think she thought she was mistreated as a Jew.

Knowing they'd never find a restaurant that would serve them at the same table, Revetta had packed a cooler with sandwiches and bottles of soda. When they made it to Memphis ten hours later, Hotel Clark, the only colored hotel in town, was full. The three of them couldn't very well waltz into the Peabody, or any other hotel, so Leonard arranged for them to stay with a friend, Morgan.

Morgan was a tall, skinny colored man who'd lost most of his teeth. He had a modest house with broken shutters and a busted-up porch swing. He lived on the outside of town, in the middle of nowhere. His closest neighbor was a quarter mile down the road. Morgan's wife cooked up fresh catfish and corn bread and after dinner they all sat on the front porch and listened to Morgan playing an old beat-up guitar with only three strings that he made sound like six.

That night Leeba and Aileen shared a lumpy mattress in the spare bedroom. Leonard slept out on the couch. They could hear the springs squeaking through the wall each time he moved. Other than that, it was quiet and peaceful. There were no sirens going by, no horns honking like back in the city. It was almost too quiet. Leeba couldn't sleep, and neither could Aileen.

Leeba thought about all the signs she'd seen that day. She reached for Aileen's hand. "How can you put up with this?"

"With what?" Aileen rolled over. "What are you talking about?"

"I had no idea it was like this. When I see the way they treat Negroes down here, it makes me sick."

Aileen squeezed her fingers. "But that's the way it is. Especially down here."

"But it's not fair. It's not right."

"It ain't so great for us back in Chicago, either. And down here, well, that's all these folks know."

"How can you not hate them?"

Aileen turned onto her back. "You gotta remember, we all grew up in the church. God's all about forgiveness. I remember my daddy used to say bitterness and hatred will poison you from the inside out. The best thing you can do for yourself is to forgive."

"You're a bigger person than I would be."

Aileen yawned and mumbled, "You don't do it for them. You do it for yourself."

The next morning they went to Sun Studios to see Sam Phillips. Marion Keisker, Sam's office manager, greeted them when they arrived. She had wavy blond hair resting on her shoulders and a wide mouth painted in the brightest red lipstick Leeba had seen since the days of Evelyn Aron.

They had showed up unannounced and Marion invited them to wait while Sam finished a recording session. Guitar music and a tremulous voice leaked out from the studio. Leeba peered through a small cutout window and saw Sam Phillips through the glass. She'd met him before when he was in Chicago. He was a clean-cut white man with a sprig of hair that rested on his forehead. She couldn't see who he was recording.

"You hear that?" Marion gestured toward the studio. "He sounds nervous now, but I'm telling you, that kid's got a million-dollar voice. I predict he's going to be huge. Nobody else sounds like him."

Leeba closed her eyes and listened. After a few more takes the singer grew bolder, louder, more confident.

"See?" said Marion. "What'd I tell you?"

When they finished their session, Sam came out with a young man with jet-black hair and pasty white skin. Leeba was shocked because he'd sounded like a colored singer.

"That was *you* in there?" Leonard looked at the kid and then back at Sam.

"This here's Elvis. Elvis Presley."

"Motherfucker." Leonard shook both Sam's

and the singer's hand. "And people say *I* sound like a Negro."

Elvis gave him a curious look like he didn't understand.

"Go on," Sam said to the boy, "we'll finish up tomorrow." After Elvis left, Sam turned to Leonard. "So what brings you down here?"

"I'm shopping a new record and I couldn't come to town and not drop by." After Leonard had made the introductions, he said Aileen was the female Howlin' Wolf. "Wait till you hear her. Give this a listen."

He handed Sam the record and they all followed him back into the studio. Sam put the 78 on the record player and Leeba watched him shuffle his weight from leg to leg while "Jealous Kinda Love" spun around and around.

Phillips tapped his foot, nodding. "That came out of you?" He smiled at Aileen. "She's got a new sound," he said to Leonard. "That's for sure. Who's the songwriter?"

"I am," said Leeba.

"You?" Sam half smiled, searching Leonard's face for confirmation.

Leonard nodded.

"Well, I'll be." Sam planted his hands on his hips, shaking his head. "I like it, but —"

"What do you mean, but?" said Leonard.

"*But* you're breaking all the rules here. I don't know if people are ready to accept that kind of a sound coming out of a woman. And

I sure wouldn't let anyone know that a white girl wrote it for her."

Leeba felt dismissed. She'd worked hard on that song. It came from her. Sam didn't seem to have a problem with Elvis being white and singing on a race record. Why did he think people would mind her writing one? It would be the first time that she felt discriminated against for *her* skin color.

"What do you say?" Leonard said to Sam. "You gonna call your buddy Dewey at the station and help me get some airplay for this or what?"

"I'll put a call in to him, but you're on your own after that."

Sam sent them to WHBQ in Memphis, where Daddy-O Dewey was the number one deejay in town. Dewey was in his booth and motioned for them to come inside. The floor was full of broken 78s that he'd smashed on the ground because he didn't like them.

Dewey gave "Jealous Kinda Love" a listen and while he didn't break their record on the floor he didn't play it on the air, either. As he put it, "I've got a respectable white audience — you know that, Leonard. They don't wanna hear a woman growlin' and groanin'. Even if she is colored." He turned to Leeba and Aileen. "Sorry, ladies, this one just ain't gonna fly down here."

From there they went to WDIA, an all-Negro station. But their reaction wasn't all that different from Dewey's. Even after Leonard slipped the deejay a twenty.

"I don't know," said Leroy LaRoy as he pocketed the money. "That's a woman sounding like a three-hundred-pound man. I don't know nobody that's gonna wanna hear that."

Leeba and Aileen were discouraged, but not Leonard.

"That's only two stations," he said. "And LaRoy didn't say he *wouldn't* play it. He just wouldn't commit on the spot. And don't forget, we still got Alabama, Mississippi, Arkansas and Louisiana to hit."

As Leonard talked to the different deejays, Leeba watched him in action. He had a rapport with people, whites and Negroes. He swaggered into radio stations and record stores and he had his spiel down: Aileen Booker, the female Howlin' Wolf.

Leeba stood back, watching the expressions change on people's faces when they heard "Jealous Kinda Love."

"She soundin' kinda rough," said a record store owner in Chattanooga. "I ain't sure I can sell a song like that."

The three of them were moving from town to town so quickly that Leeba had no way of knowing what happened after they left a radio station, a record store or a distributor. Leonard was dropping twenties and fifties along the way, but it didn't seem to matter. The deejays took the money and that appeared to be the end of it. Her heart sank, her hopes fading like the fields in the rearview mirror.

They spent six days traveling, Leonard's Cadillac bouncing along the bumpy dirt roads. Sometimes they had to roll the windows up — even in the heat — just to keep the dust out. They passed a sign for Merrydale and Leeba thought about Red growing up here and how hard it must have been. Now he was up North touring with Muddy. Seeing where he'd started from made her appreciate his journey all the more.

As the miles rolled by, Leeba watched America's portrait pass outside her window. Things she'd only heard or read about were right before her eyes: the mighty Mississippi, the swamplands and plantations, endless fields of cotton, soybeans and sugar cane, dotted with sharecroppers and huge plumes of dust kicking up from the tractors in the distance.

The people in the little towns along the way were poor, all sitting on their front stoops or gliders on their porches, listening to the radio. Leeba noticed that the trees had bottles turned upside down and shoved down onto the branches. Aileen explained that those were there to trap the evil spirits and keep them from getting into the houses. Leeba tilted her head, watching how the blue- and green- and brown-colored glass gleamed in the afternoon sun.

Each time they got out and walked around, stopping at a radio station or record store, Leeba noticed how the townspeople down South were as different as the land. Back home everyone was in a hurry, keeping to themselves, not paying attention to anyone or anything, but here folks ambled down the sidewalks and every single person they passed — without exception, white or Negro — stopped to say, "Hey, how y'all doing?" Leeba did notice, however, that the whites directed their greetings to Leeba and Leonard, not even acknowledging Aileen.

They went from Helena, Arkansas, to Oxford, Mississippi, zigzagging across state lines with no rhyme or reason. Leonard followed his gut and not a map. On a whim they went to a barbershop in Clarksdale and while Leonard got a haircut and shave, the owner played a razor strop. He had a way of dragging that straight edge against the leather belt that filled his little shop with its own kind of rhythm, its own kind of blues. The next day they found themselves at a juke joint in Winona, where an old wrinkly bluesman played a washboard with a pair of spoons. It seemed like there wasn't anything they couldn't turn into music down South.

After stops at radio stations and record stores in Jackson, Natchez, Zachary and Baton Rouge, they arrived in New Orleans. A city had sprung from the fields and swamps of the South and its sophistication was a stark contrast from where they'd been. The streets were crowded, packed with stores, restaurants, saloons and hotels — none of which would accept Aileen as a guest. So Leonard arranged for them to stay with friends in the Garden District. They had a big house with fancy ironwork down the front, their street dressed with colorful beads draped over the tree branches and power lines, the ghosts of Mardi Gras past.

After dropping off their suitcases and freshening up, Leonard took Leeba and Aileen to another station where he went through his sales pitch. The deejay clearly liked the music. He was tapping his toes, snapping his fingers, nodding to the beat.

"You know what you oughta do with that," the deejay said after listening to the rest of the song. "You oughta go back home and have one of your boys rerecord it."

"What the hell's wrong with the recording we got?" asked Aileen. "You're damn lucky we came in here to see you at all."

"Leeba?" Leonard gave her a warning look and she went and placed her hand on Aileen's shoulder to steady her.

"C'mon," said the deejay. "What you expect when you bring me a girl singer?"

"It ain't over yet," Leonard said to the girls the next day as they pulled up to the Court of Two Sisters restaurant in the French Quarter.

"What are we gonna do here?" asked Aileen, her arms folded across her chest in a huff. "Have ourselves a po'boy?"

"We're gonna get this song on the air. That's what we're gonna do." He grabbed a record and Leeba followed him inside. Aileen used the colored entrance and met them in a back room.

"Welcome, ladies, to WMRY." Leonard made a sweeping gesture with his hand. When he introduced them to Vernon "Dr. Daddy-O" Winslow, he said, "This here motherfucker is the first colored deejay in New Orleans and he broadcasts his show from right here in the back of the restaurant."

Dr. Daddy-O shook their hands, welcoming them to New Orleans.

"I want you to listen to this." Leonard held up the 78. "It's a hit. I feel it in my bones. Give it a play on the air. That's all I'm asking. Just give it a chance."

Dr. Daddy-O didn't seem convinced, so Leonard reached in his pocket and slipped a fifty inside the sleeve, hoping it would change his mind. Apparently it didn't.

"I'm gonna try one more place," he said to Leeba and Aileen as they headed for WJMR. There they met with a deejay who called himself Poppa Stoppa. He was white, but he loved race music and he loved Aileen's record, especially when Leonard slipped another couple twenties into the sleeve.

"I don't know if folks are ready for this or not, but there's only one way to find out." He winked, pushed a button and spoke to his listeners: "This is Poppa Stoppa coming to you live from WJMR, and I have something brand spankin' new for y'all. Coming out of Chicago this here is Miss Aileen Booker — you heard right. Not Mister but *Miss* Aileen with 'Jealous Kinda Love.'"

Poppa set the needle down and Aileen's voice filled the station, filled the airways. Leeba had imagined this moment for so long, hearing their song over the radio. She thought about all the people listening at that very moment. She pictured radios and transistors on kitchen counters, on cluttered desks, in speeding cars all blasting "Jealous Kinda Love." It was the moment they'd waited for, prayed for and worked for, and it was over before they knew it. Afterward Leeba looked around the studio — at the records mounted on the walls, at the turntable already spinning with the next song. Afterward nothing had changed.

"Now what happens?" Aileen asked as they got back in the car.

"Now we wait," said Leonard. "We wait and see."

That night Aileen and Leeba stayed close to the radio, running up and down the dial, looking and hoping, but they never heard their song again. The next morning they began making their way back home. It seemed as if it had all been for nothing. Leonard's Cadillac was pulling out of New Orleans and no one was saying a word. No one spoke of the disappointment, but the letdown was palpable. It settled into the car like a fourth passenger. The air was filled with Leonard's cigarette smoke and the Dominoes singing "Sixty Minute Man."

They hadn't eaten anything yet and Leonard knew of a diner that served breakfast all day long and to anyone coming through the door, colored or white. He and Muddy had been there for coffee and flapjacks. Leeba poked at her food. The radio was playing "Rocket '88' " and that lifted Leonard's spirits some. Aileen was nonplussed and Leeba feared her friend was already sinking. She could feel Aileen's sorrow mounting on top of her own.

Leonard paid the bill and they were starting back to the car when the song came on the radio. They all heard the opening chords and sat back down.

Leonard cracked a smile.

Leeba reached out and gripped Aileen's arm. "That's you. That's us."

There it was. "Jealous Kinda Love" coming over the radio on WJMR. Leeba was still clutching Aileen's arm. It was out there like a flash and then it was gone, replaced by John Lee Hooker's "Boogie Chillen'."

"What does this mean?" Aileen asked when they were back in the car, pulling out onto the dusty road.

"Means that at least Poppa Stoppa likes us. It's a start. Beyond that, I don't know."

They were back on the road. The closest town was Baton Rouge and it was just them and open country. Leeba leaned her head back and closed her eyes while Leonard fiddled with the radio, squeaking up and down the dial, until he heard something that sounded familiar.

Leeba's eyes flashed open. At first she thought it was Poppa Stoppa playing their record again, but no, this time it was Dr. Daddy-O — the colored deejay who hadn't been interested just the day before was now talking it up on his show.

"That's a mighty big voice comin' outta a little lady by the name of Aileen Booker and that was her new record, 'Jealous Kinda Love' . . ."

By the time they got to Jackson they'd heard their song six times. Each time it came over the radio, Leeba squealed and Aileen bounced up and down, pounding her hands on the seat.

Leonard went to a pay phone and called Phil. Leeba and Aileen cheered and yelped when they heard him say, "Hey, Phil, get

'Jealous Kinda Love' over to Benson at WGES and don't leave until that motherfucker plays it on the air. We got us a hit."

THIRTY-TWO:
"NOBODY KNOWS YOU WHEN YOU'RE DOWN AND OUT"

RED

Red sat on the side of the bed in a dump of a motel. He heard the bedsprings squeaking and the headboard banging against the thin wall that separated Muddy's room from his. The girl was young. Probably too young. Muddy had spotted her in the front row. The night before, it was a different girl from a different club in a different motel, in a different town. But always it was the same.

The moaning coming from Muddy's room competed with the radio, so Red raised the volume and tried to focus on the newspaper. He was reading an article about the demise of the Communist Party's membership and glanced up at the masthead: the *Pittsburgh Post-Gazette*. For a moment he'd forgotten what city they were in. Tomorrow they'd head for Detroit and after that, Cleveland . . . Or was it Cincinnati? He couldn't keep it straight.

Being on the road was harder than he'd

expected. The venues were getting bigger. The crowds were growing, too. Especially when he went on tour, opening for Howlin' Wolf or, like he was this time, for Muddy. One minute he'd be up on stage surrounded by fans, everybody watching him, clapping for him, wanting a part of him. But after that last song, everyone went away. It was like the match got blown out. He'd walk off the stage with the loneliest feeling sinking down inside him. He was always surprised by how much emptiness was there. Where it came from he couldn't say, but even Leah wasn't enough to fill that void. That part of him was always hungry for more, and never really satisfied.

A loud roar and rounds of giggles came from next door. Red rolled onto his side, lit a cigarette and thought about Leah. With both of them on the road, moving from city to city, there was no way to communicate directly, so they'd call in to Chess and leave messages for each other. According to Phil, who was back at the office, Leah should be getting home any day now. Red missed her and was hoping to get back to Chicago for a few days to see her before heading back out on the road with Little Walter. Twenty cities, twenty dates. Then it was back in the studio to make a new record. It was exhausting, and when he caught himself complaining he reminded himself that this was what he'd prayed for and that he'd better be grateful or else God would take it away.

The racket next door kicked up a notch. Red ground out his cigarette, set the newspaper aside and closed his eyes. He was already drifting a thousand miles away from that motel when he heard something over the radio that pulled him right back to the present. His eyes flashed open, his pulse stepped up.

". . . And this one's a new song coming out of Chicago. A big number by Miss Aileen Booker called 'Jealous Kinda Love' . . ."

He sat up, sprang to his feet and pounded on the wall — "Muddy, Mud, turn on the radio. It's them. Are you listening?" If he couldn't share this moment with Leah, then Mud would have to do. Only, Muddy was too preoccupied to care that his woman had made her dream come true. But Red knew how hard the girls had worked; he remembered how frustrated Leah had been when Leonard wouldn't release the record, how she'd started to doubt herself. And now there they were — Leah and Aileen — on the radio. It felt no less magical than the first time he'd heard himself on the radio, singing "Cross Road Blues." At first it was disbelief — like you were imagining it because you wanted it so bad. But then you realized it was actually happening and the pride bubbled up inside and you could hardly contain it — like it was pressurized — and it made you feel ten feet tall.

Muddy was still going at it with the girl, but after hearing that song, Red didn't care how much noise they were making. He was too excited to sleep anyway.

The next day, after a long bus ride, Red, Muddy and their bands turned up in Detroit. It was getting late and they had just enough time to grab some grub before heading over to the Palms Theater and going on stage. Muddy was flirting with the waitress, telling her to come see his show.

"Good Lord," said Red, pulling the napkin from his collar, "how much pussy can one man handle?"

"Never can get me 'nuff," said Muddy, his eyes on that waitress's ass. "How come I don't see you getting none? There be pretty womens all around."

"You know I got Leah. And you got a wife, too. And Aileen. And a—"

"Yeah, but they all the way back home."

Red shook his head, laughed. "Well, if you're gonna get that girl's number, you best do it now. It's time for us to get going."

An hour later Red opened for Muddy before a packed house. From the stage, silhouetted against the spotlights, he saw a sea of faces, people up in all the balconies, too. He was playing the song that had started it all, "Cross Road Blues." He was playing hard and as he closed his eyes a bead of sweat formed along his lashes. He blinked it away, looking through the glare of the stage lights and the haze of cigarette smoke. He closed his eyes again, letting the music lift him up off that stage, take him someplace far, far away. He was a kid again, practicing in secret with his granddaddy, going over and over the chords. Then he was a young man playing those juke joints. From there it was up to Chicago, where he started from scratch all over again. A burst of applause brought him back to the stage and, just like that, the song was over.

Red and his band finished their set and he stood in the wings toweling off while Muddy took the stage. Red was beat; he felt wrung out and was wondering how he'd find the energy to finish the tour.

But the next day they left for another town, and the last few cities after that blurred together, until they were all back on the bus, heading for Chicago.

It was early evening when they arrived in town. Red caught a ride with some of the guys, who dropped him at Fifty-seventh Street. He didn't mind walking the few blocks, even with his guitar and suitcase. He was anxious to get home. He'd tried calling Leah from the road a few times, but there had been no answer at the apartment. Before they left Cincinnati, Red had put another call in to Chess, and Phil had said that because the record was doing so well Leonard and the girls decided to hit a few more cities on the way back. That was two days ago and Red just hoped Leah would be waiting for him when he got there.

The sun was starting to set, leaving bands of pink and orange in the sky. The air was sticky, humid, and carried the scent of fresh-cut grass. A group of young white guys, maybe a half dozen or so, probably in their late teens, were hanging around on the street corner outside their apartment building. One of them, a tow-haired young man, sat perched on a fire hydrant. They were all smoking cigarettes, drinking from brown paper bags. Red felt their eyes on him as he walked by and climbed the stairs to the apartment.

The hallway was quiet, no barking, a sure sign that Sophie was still with Revetta and that Leah wasn't back in town yet. He keyed into the apartment. It was dark and hot inside. He turned on a light and as he went to open the windows he saw Leah getting out of Leonard's Cadillac with her suitcase. As the taillights on Leonard's car disappeared around the corner, he called down to her from the open window before he raced out of the apartment to meet her.

As he flew out the front door the first thing he saw was Leah's suitcase lying on the grass.

He looked over and those boys who'd been hanging around on the corner had now surrounded her, and Red heard them taunting her.

"You're not a bad-looking woman," the tow-haired guy said. "You could get yourself a white man, you know."

"Leave her alone," said Red, heading toward them. She looked panicked.

The guys turned around and one of them, the biggest and huskiest of them, shoved Red back. "You better shut your mouth, boy," he said.

The towheaded guy stepped closer to Leah. He wasn't much taller than her, and Red saw the spiteful way she eyed him. "I think it's 'bout time we show this nigger lover here what a real man's all about." He placed his hand on Leah's neck.

Her eyes, still defiant, were locked on the kid's. He leaned in to kiss her and a second later he jumped back, his hand pressed to his mouth. "Fuckin' bitch bit me." He drew back his hand to slap her and that was when Red lunged forward.

The others were on him at once. Someone kicked Red in the stomach and he doubled over, gasping for breath, while someone else clobbered him over the back of the head and he collapsed to the ground.

"Red —"

He heard Leah calling to him and when he

looked up he saw the blond kid pull out a switchblade. In a blur he came charging toward Red like a madman. Red pushed himself up off the ground and raised his hand, trying to grab the guy's arm. But his aim was off just enough that the top of the knife sliced Red from his palm to his middle finger.

At first he didn't feel a thing. For a split second he thought he was okay. Maybe the blade had only nicked him. But then he saw the blood. It was everywhere. He grabbed his left hand with his right, a spurt of crimson gushing through his fingertips from a deep gash in his palm. He was still bent over when something sharp came down on the back of his head. He felt himself starting to fall and heard his attackers howling as they tore out of there.

The last thing Red remembered before he passed out was Leah rushing toward him.

The switchblade severed two tendons in Red's left hand. Seventy-nine stitches and three months later Red found himself alone in the apartment one afternoon, sitting on the davenport, clenching and unclenching his hand, wincing from the pain. His joints were stiff and he'd lost the feeling in at least two fingers. The feeling in the third came and went. He opened his fist and stared at the huge scar running across his palm and up to his fingertips.

He reached for his second whiskey of the day and thought about the gigs he'd missed and the tour with Little Walter that had been canceled. He'd lost about fifteen hundred dollars just on club dates alone. Chess had given up on ever getting him back into the studio to cut another record and Red felt guilty about letting the brothers down, especially since Leonard had paid for all his doctor bills. Red glanced at the garbage, which Leah had asked him to take out. *Later,* he said to himself as he thought of ways to salvage his career. He still had his voice, but he couldn't see himself singing without playing. It was the guitar that gave his voice power. The two were connected for him. He thought about doing some songwriting, but he played by ear; he couldn't write or read music or do arrangements like Leah and Willie Dixon could.

In his rising panic, all Red could hear was his granddaddy's warning: *Protect your hands, son. Protect your hands.* But he'd been protecting his wife and that had just cost him his career.

He polished off his drink and slammed the empty glass down on the table. He looked at his guitars lined up along the wall, calling to him. When the stitches had first come out he remembered trying to play the Gibson, thinking electric would be easier. But his fingers wouldn't cooperate and he sounded like shit. He missed the feel of his Stella but hadn't been able to touch her since the accident. But she was eyeing him now, like a neglected lover. He took another swig of whiskey, this time straight from the bottle, and went over and picked her up. He could still strum and pick with his right hand, but his left hand was numb and stiff. He couldn't feel the strings, couldn't work the neck beneath his fingers. He could see exactly where to place his fingers, but he couldn't get them to move there fast enough. After trying for a half hour, he became so disgusted and so discouraged that he threw his Stella across the room, almost busting her up.

The radio was playing and, sure enough, Aileen's song came on. He turned it off. He must have heard "Jealous Kinda Love" a half dozen times already that day. He needed air and went out on the wooden porch with his bottle. He sat there drinking, smoking, watching the world he once felt a part of moving along just fine without him.

The sun was starting to set when Leah came home. He heard her calling for him. "Red? Red?"

He didn't answer at first. He couldn't. He just needed a few more moments before he'd have to pretend he didn't resent his wife. Rationally he knew none of this was her fault. He'd told himself that while she may have cost him his career, he'd cost Leah her family. Other than her aunt and sometimes her father, Leah had hardly spoken to them since he'd married her. But still every time he looked at this woman he loved, he relived *that* night, remembered her eyes filling with fright, the thugs circling around her, her suitcase flung onto the grass. He saw the blade and the clean cut in his flesh — he swore he saw down to the bone just before the blood rushed in. And then his world began falling apart.

"Red?" she called again. "Are you home? Where are you, baby?"

"Out here," he said, blowing out a big sigh, trying to get himself right.

"There you are." She was all smiles when she poked her head out the kitchen door. "What are you doing out there? It's getting cold." She stepped outside and joined him on the porch, sitting beside him like she sometimes did in the summertime. But it was fall now. The leaves were turning; the winds were picking up. Her curls blew into her eyes as she buttoned her sweater, hugging herself to keep warm.

"So on my way home I got this idea for a new song for Aileen," she said. "You know how everybody's surprised to hear that voice coming out of a woman? It just popped into my head: 'Little Woman, Big Voice.' " She sang him a line or two and stopped when she saw him sigh impatiently and reach for the whiskey bottle. "Okay, well," she said with a frown, "I can tell you're not in the mood for this." She got up and went back inside.

He stayed out on the porch watching the lights come up, feeling like a heel. He was proud of her, but she'd never know it, because he was also jealous. He couldn't help but feel that way. He didn't know how to get beyond it.

When he eventually came inside and sat next to her on the davenport she shot up and stood by the window, the neon lights outside flickering, playing off her cheeks.

"Did you look for work today?" she asked.

"No." And it wasn't just that he hadn't looked for work; it was the way he said that "no." It was out there, sinking through the air like it was made of lead.

"Why not?" she said, her own voice taking on an edge this time. "Because you've been too busy drinking?"

He threw his head back and closed his eyes. "You gonna give me grief now, too?"

He saw her glancing at the overflowing garbage that he'd neglected to take out, at the empty bottles lying around, the crumpled-up packs of cigarettes. He saw the disappointment on her face and nothing stung more than knowing he'd let her down. But he couldn't get out of his own way.

"Did you at least remember to feed

Sophie?" she asked. "Did you at least walk her?"

"Nope." There was that tone again. It just came out that way.

She grabbed the dog's bowl and slammed it on the counter. "What are you doing to yourself, Red? You're a mess. You're falling apart."

"Then why don't you just go ahead and quit me." He was pushing her away with both hands, but he couldn't stop. "Go find yourself a white man, some rich Jew boy, and make your mama happy."

"You're drunk. And you're pathetic."

"And you don't get it, woman. I can't play no more."

"So that's the sum of your whole existence — that guitar? Those six strings?" She pointed to his Stella lying on the floor where he'd thrown her earlier. "You can't just give up on everything else."

"I've got no choice."

"Yes, you do. You can fight back. And if you won't fight for yourself then at least fight for me. For us."

"I've got no more fight left in me, baby. I've lost it all."

"Well, you better find it."

He shook his head, looked away.

"I'm sorry about what happened to your hand, Red. It was my fault. I'm the reason you can't play anymore. And that kills me. If

391

I could change what happened, I would. But I can't and I have to learn to live with that and find a way to forgive myself. But you have to forgive me, too, because I can't handle watching you destroy yourself. And destroy us."

"There's the door," he said. "All you got to do is walk on through it."

But she wouldn't budge. With tears running down her pale face, she watched him take another slug of whiskey.

She didn't get it and he couldn't make her understand. He wasn't anything without his guitar. When people had seen him play, they'd looked at him like he was somebody. They showed him respect just because he could do something with that instrument that they couldn't. That was the only way for a Negro to cross out of the South Side of this town — of this world. That was how you blurred the divide. Without his guitar people would think of him as nothing but another dumb nigger and Red Dupree knew it.

He woke up the next morning with his head feeling like it weighed fifty pounds. Red had been so out of it he hadn't even heard Leah leave for work. He stumbled into the kitchen, squinting at the light coming through the window. He got some aspirin and a cup of coffee. Sophie was whimpering at the door, so he walked her, came back and read the newspaper. He halfheartedly looked at the want ads: *Experienced Toolroom Foreman, College Grads, Die Designers, Experienced Sheet Metal Template Makers.* The only thing that seemed remotely promising was an opening at Moore Brothers' Shoe Factory. *No experience needed.* Fuck it. He was a bluesman, not a shoemaker.

He traded up his coffee for something stronger and lazed around till noon, facedown in a puddle of pity. When he'd finished off all the whiskey in the house, he headed to the liquor store around the corner for more.

He knew he shouldn't have been spending money on booze. He hadn't worked in months, hadn't brought in a dime. He was broke, down to his last few dollars. If it weren't for Leah, he would have starved. They were living off her salary and the money Chess paid for her songs. There was a little money in a savings account, but that was hers — the money she'd saved for her Bösendorfer piano, and he wouldn't touch that.

As he was coming down the sidewalk a colored kid, not more than seven years old, stopped him. "Hey, ain't you Red Dupree?"

Red turned around. The kid was standing in a pair of bib overalls and a ratty coat, clutching a one-string diddley bow.

Red was in a foul mood and kept walking.

The kid jogged up alongside him. "You is

Red Dupree, ain't ya? Man, I got all your records. I think you're the greatest bluesman who ever lived."

Red stopped at the crosswalk and glanced at the boy. "Where's your mama at, boy?"

"I ain't got no mama."

"Who's looking after you?"

"I look after myself." The kid mugged with his chin raised.

Red shook his head. He wasn't in the mood for this.

The boy must have sensed that, because he dropped his tough-guy act. "I live with my grandma right over there," he said, pointing down the street.

"What's your name, son?"

"James, but you can call me Curly. That's my blues name." He strummed his diddley bow. "Will you learn me somethin'?"

The kid held the rickety instrument out to Red. It wasn't too different from the one he'd made himself, the one he'd brought to his granddaddy when he wanted to learn the blues all those years ago.

The boy was still holding out the diddley bow. "C'mon, man."

"Nah, I don't play anymore. You go find someone else to teach you. Go over to Jewtown, find someone there to help you." Red brushed past him.

"Jewtown?" the kid called after him indignantly. "Why should I go all the way to Jewtown when you right here? What's the matter, you scared old Curly here's gonna show you up?"

Red ignored him and kept going. He felt bad walking away from that kid. A few months back, Red would have jumped at the chance to help him — the kid had spunk — but Red had nothing to offer him, nothing to offer anyone.

He kept walking and when he passed a bum on the street with his hand out, Red realized that could easily be him if he didn't turn himself around. Used to be he'd ignore those panhandlers, pretending not to see them and not giving them a second thought after they were out of view. He didn't wonder where they'd sleep or what garbage can they'd eat their dinner from. He didn't wonder because he didn't care. And he realized with great shame that he'd treated those poor souls just as heartlessly as many whites down South had treated him. Truth was that each of those broken people had fallen from someplace higher. Everyone had a story. Red was in the middle of his own. And oh, how different the world appeared when you were on the bottom looking up.

He went into the liquor store and got stuck listening to the bored clerk complain about hoodlums in the neighborhood. Red knew all about them. He didn't want to hear it. After those punks had attacked him, Red had gone to the police, but they'd done nothing but file a useless report. Red knew that if he'd been a white man, they would have gone after those thugs. The clerk kept talking for ten or fifteen minutes before Red made his getaway and walked out with a bottle of Old Grand-Dad. He was half tempted to open it and drink it straight out of the paper bag.

He turned the corner on his block and saw that same kid, James or Curly, only now he was sitting right on the stoop in Red's doorway.

"When you gonna learn me to play?" he asked, holding out his diddley bow.

"I've already told you, I don't play anymore. Now go on home."

But the kid didn't budge. Red stepped around him, went up to his apartment and slammed the door. He pulled the bottle from the brown paper bag and guzzled down a few good gulps. He turned on the radio and there was Al Benson, the Old Swingmaster, cuing up Aileen Booker's "Jealous Kinda Love." Red snapped it off and chucked the radio across the counter, watching it hit the wall and explode into fragments. The sight of what he'd done shocked him. He froze, short of breath.

What the hell is wrong with me?

He stared at the pint of Old Grand-Dad, hating how much he needed it. He was shaking with anger and self-loathing, and suddenly knew that if he didn't destroy that bottle, it would destroy him. Before he could take another drink he hurled it against the wall and sank to the floor. He bawled like a baby, his chest heaving as the tears streamed down his face. He was done. Ruined. Exhausted and ashamed. And down there on his knees with no one else to turn to, he turned to God. He talked to Him, begging for His mercy, praying to find some purpose for his life.

Red didn't know how long he was on the floor praying and crying. Could have been five minutes. Could have been an hour. But when the tears subsided, he found that he was surprisingly calm. The fury inside of him had burned itself out and now he saw a clearing in the fog that had eluded him these past few months. Whether the insight had come from God or from somewhere inside him, he couldn't say. But for the first time since his injury he knew what he had to do and had somehow found the wherewithal to do it.

He pushed himself up off the floor, grabbed the newspaper and checked the address in the want ads. Twenty minutes later he found himself outside the Moore Brothers' Shoe Factory, looking at a sign in one of the windows that said "Now Hiring." Red went inside, where he found a white man with a pink pockmarked face and a thick middle. Red told him he was there for the job.

The man looked up from his clipboard and said, "What's your name, boy?"

He hesitated, thinking maybe it was time to go back to calling himself Reggie Smalls.

"I said, what's your name?"

But he couldn't. Reggie Smalls didn't have a woman like Leah Grand. No, he couldn't go backward, erase the person he'd become up North, so he cleared his throat and said, "Red. Red Dupree." Foolishly, he thought the man might recognize him. And he would have if he'd been a Negro. But this guy had no idea who Red was.

"Here's the rules —" The man looked back at his clipboard. "You start at six in the morning. For every minute you're late, we dock your pay. You get fifteen minutes for lunch." He took a sniff. "And no booze, ya hear?"

"Yes, sir." His ego protested at the thought of doing menial labor again, but he needed the work if he was going to save his marriage. And his life. "When can I start?"

"Tomorrow. And don't be late."

Red hesitated for a moment before he said, "Yes, sir. Tomorrow morning. Six o'clock. I'll be here." He left the shoe factory knowing that he'd just taken the first step back toward salvation.

When he made it home the sun was starting to set and that same kid was there on his stoop with his diddley bow. It was like he'd been waiting all this time for Red to return.

The boy looked up but didn't say a word. He just held out his homemade instrument.

"Don't go anywhere," Red said to him. "I'll be right back."

He went inside and grabbed his Stella, then went back down the stairs and out the front door.

"Here —" Red thrust his Stella into the boy's hand. "It's yours."

The boy's eyes grew wide. His mouth dropped open, but nothing came out. He set the diddley bow down and hugged Red's Stella like an old friend. It was too big for him, but that was all right, he'd grow into it.

"You come back here tomorrow around this same time," said Red. "I'll teach you a thing or two."

■ ■ ■ ■

THREE:
1955–1956

■ ■ ■ ■

THIRTY-THREE: "MAYBELLENE"

LEONARD

Leonard sat at his desk twisting the radio knob. Up and down the dial, he heard "Shake, Rattle and Roll" on one station, then "Sh-Boom" on another. The sound was changing. Hell, everything was changing. No one was calling it race music anymore. Now it was R&B — rhythm and blues. Even the market and the audience were changing. Every day Leonard talked to another distributor claiming they couldn't stock R&B records fast enough. And according to them, it wasn't just coloreds listening anymore. It was all those white kids defying their parents by discovering what Leonard and Phil had tapped into years before.

Leonard had no idea how far this R&B music could go. Vee-Jay Records, another independent label, had sprung up in Chicago. Leonard didn't think much of the records the new label was putting out, but he and Phil were working harder than ever to make sure they stayed ahead of the competition. The one edge Vee-Jay had over Chess was that it was owned by a colored couple, not two Jewish Poles.

Phil came into Leonard's office with the latest issue of *Billboard*. "You're not gonna believe this shit." He plunked the magazine down on Leonard's desk. "Look at that. 'Earth Angel' — number three on the pop charts. When the Penguins recorded that song no one gave a damn, and now Mercury puts it out with some white boys who call themselves the Crew-Cuts and it's a hit."

Leonard looked at the chart and closed the magazine, setting it aside. He'd seen the same thing happening with their own artists. "It's like when we recorded 'Sincerely' with the Moonglows. It did okay for us. But when those white McGuire Sisters came along and did the same song, it goes gold."

Phil shook his head. "When we got started did you ever think that white singers would want to record Negro music?"

"It's like what Sam Phillips always said. Whites like race music — always did. But they didn't think it was something they ought to be listening to. And lucky for us they're getting over that."

"You can say that again."

Chess was going like gangbusters at the start of 1955. Aileen's latest record, "Who's A-Foolin' You," had just been released and

Leonard was counting on it climbing the R&B charts. Leeba was writing another set of songs for her and now that they knew there was a market for female singers after all, Leonard and Phil were on the lookout for another one who had the pipes. They'd auditioned a lot of girls, but not a one had anything special.

Chess's other artists, like Muddy, Walter and Wolf, were big names and Willie Dixon was a hit-making machine. Thanks to him they were topping the charts with Muddy's "I'm Your Hoochie Coochie Man" and Little Walter's "My Babe."

Leonard felt bad about Red, especially since he'd been with Leeba just moments before it happened. He'd seen those punks on the corner, but didn't give it a second thought. How many times had he cursed himself for just dropping Leeba off and pulling away like that? But he'd been on the road, driving for two days straight. They had just let Aileen out and he was beat and anxious to get home. He remembered trying to console Leeba after she told him what had happened, insisting it wasn't her fault, but aside from picking up Red's medical bills there was nothing he could do.

Leonard reached again for the *Billboard* he'd set aside and fanned through the pages until he came to the R&B charts. "Look at Muddy" — he pinged the page with the back of his hand — "that motherfucker is still on top of the charts."

"Jukebox charts, too."

Muddy should have been elated, but every time Leonard and Phil brought in a new player, Muddy got bent out of shape, drinking too much, being ornery and swinging his dick around to let the new artists know he was top dog.

Leonard didn't know how to tell him that he had recently signed another new kid with a different kind of sound. Ellas McDaniel had initially auditioned for Vee-Jay Records and after they turned him down the kid walked into Chess. He just came in off the street and asked Phil if he'd listen to a song. Phil liked what he heard and so did Leonard. He'd been in his office when he first heard the guitar music coming from down the hall. He sprang out of his chair and rushed up front to see where and who it was coming from. When they offered Ellas McDaniel a recording deal later that day, the name he signed on the contract was Bo Diddley.

The first song they recorded with Bo was a catchy-as-hell tune with the same name, "Bo Diddley." Leonard wasn't sure what to do with the song so he hadn't pressed the record yet. He and Phil agreed that they should wait until summer to release it and hope it would make some noise.

They still had a few months before then,

and ironically Muddy, in spite of himself, was sending a new guitarist and singer from St. Louis their way for an audition.

Leeba poked her head in the office. "Guys? He's here. Muddy's with him, too. You wanna come give a listen?"

Leonard and Phil followed Leeba down the hallway that led to a little audition room. Muddy was standing there next to a tall, skinny, good-looking, almost pretty boy with a full head of wavy hair and skin the color of milk chocolate.

"You Chuck?"

"Yes, sir, Mr. Chess." He extended his hand and smiled. "I'm Chuck Berry. It's a pleasure to meet you."

He was well-spoken and Leonard wasn't used to a musician coming in so buttoned up and acting so professional.

"Well, Chuck Berry, let's hear what you got."

"The sound quality isn't the best," said Chuck as he took out a tape. "I made it on a quarter-inch machine at home."

"That's okay. Let's give it a listen."

"Yes, sir. This is a song I wrote myself. I'm calling it 'Ida May' since I got the idea for it after listening to a song called 'Ida Red.' " He hit play and stood back, his palms pressed together like he was praying.

Leonard was reaching for a cigarette when out came a sound that caught him so off guard he nearly lit the wrong end of his Lucky Strike. His eyes moved from Phil to Muddy to Chuck Berry. "You're a country singer?"

Phil turned to Muddy. "You didn't say nothing about him singing country-western music."

"Just give him a chance," said Muddy.

Leonard listened with his mouth hanging open; his eyes were glued on this pretty colored boy who sounded like he was from the heart of Nashville. He didn't know what to make of this kid. Or his music. Willie Dixon and Little Walter happened to be in the office and when they heard the music, they stopped by the audition room.

"Sounds like hillbilly music to me," said Walter. "What're you gonna do with that?"

Leonard didn't answer because he didn't know. It sure as hell wasn't the blues. He'd never heard anything like this.

At the end of the tape, Leonard said, "I like it. I do. But I don't know what to do with it."

"Don't you get it?" said Muddy, pulling Leonard aside. "Didn't you tell me how Sam Phillips is recording that white boy 'cause he sounds colored? Well, take a look at what you got here. Close your eyes and tell me if he sounds colored or white."

Leonard let that soak in. Several months before, he had tried to buy out Elvis Presley's contract. He knew Sun Studios was having

408

financial troubles and that Sam needed money. Leonard offered twenty thousand dollars and Sam said he might have considered accepting if only Leonard hadn't been such a cheap son of a bitch about Ike Turner's bus fare. Because of that goddamn bus ticket, Sam insisted on the asking price of thirty-five thousand for Elvis's contract and Leonard told Phillips to go fuck himself.

Muddy was right. Sam had a white boy who sounded colored, but here Leonard had a handsome colored boy who sounded white. And just maybe that would work, too.

Two weeks later they decided to record Chuck Berry's "Ida May." Leonard splurged for studio time at Universal for the session.

"Hey, Willie," Leonard called over to Dixon. "Grab your bass. You're coming with us."

"I don't do no hillbilly music," he said.

"Well, you do now," said Phil.

"C'mon, motherfucker." Leonard jangled his keys in his pocket. "Grab your bass. Let's go."

When they arrived at Studio A at Universal it was a quarter till nine in the morning. Leeba was already there in the control booth and handed Leonard his fifth cup of coffee of the day. Even though she was doing a lot of songwriting these days she still managed the office, kept track of the paperwork and sat in on sessions.

While the engineer was setting microphones and checking levels, Leonard looked out through the control room window. Phil stood off to the side, doing a run-through with Chuck and the band. Willie was plucking his upright like his fingers were in pain, like he was doing Leonard a goddamn favor. Leonard didn't give a shit. It wasn't the first time he and Willie hadn't seen eye to eye. At the end of the day, despite all his moaning and bitching, Willie was a pro. By the time they were ready to roll tape, he'd come alive. Leonard had no doubt.

But when the levels were set, the guys were rehearsed and it was time to lay down the song, Chuck was as stiff as hell. His long, lanky body sat in a chair, the overhead lights beating down on him so that Leonard could see the sweat pooling on his brow, running down the sides of his face. The kid looked scared to death.

Leonard just prayed he'd loosen up after a few takes.

On take thirteen, Leonard got up in Chuck's face, saying, "What happened to the guy I auditioned? Do you wanna make this motherfucker or not? 'Cause we can call it a day right now. You're boring me, man."

After that, something clicked. They rolled tape and Chuck sprang out of his chair and kicked it aside. He started playing all out, jumping around, dancing in front of the mike.

The kid was a force and he got Willie going, too, his head moving back and forth to the beat. He may have said he didn't like the song, but he had a big fat smile on his face now.

Still Leonard wasn't happy. He had something inside his head that he wasn't hearing in the studio. There was something about the lyrics. Leonard loved the backbeat, the energy and the words to this song — except for that "Ida May" part.

After a few more takes, Leonard needed a break and so did the musicians. He grabbed a piece of scrap paper and patted his empty breast pocket, looking for a pen. "Anybody got something to write with?" The console was littered with papers, tapes, dirty ashtrays and coffee cups but not a single goddamn pen.

"I have one," said Leeba, pinching open her pocketbook. She was digging around inside and her lipstick fell out, the tube rolling on the floor. Leonard stopped it with his foot, bent down to pick it up, and there it was, on the side of the lipstick tube. He got that feeling in his gut that he always got when he was right. That was it. *Maybelline.*

"Somebody get Chuck," he said. "Get the guys back in the booth. Forget 'Ida May.' We're gonna call this 'Maybelline.' "

Berry and Dixon and the others went back into the studio and laid it down again, replacing the name Ida May with Maybelline.

"Now we're getting somewhere," said Leonard, talking into the speaker box. "We're gonna do it again and this time you're gonna play this motherfucker like your lives depend on it."

They started rolling and Leonard lit a cigarette and paced inside the control booth until he shook his head and rushed back to the console. "Stop! Let's do it again, damn it. Harder."

They tried again and again. Leonard stopped them on each take, telling them to play it harder. He smoked cigarettes, drank coffee, paced and watched the hands on the clock. Berry was getting hoarse and needed some tea.

At one point Willie put his bass down and came into the control room. "What are you trying to do, kill us in there?"

"I'm trying to make a hit record."

Willie shook his head and went back into the booth and Leonard saw him place his hand on Berry's shoulder in a fatherly way. When Leeba told Leonard they were going into overtime, he didn't care. They were so close and they had to get it right.

At last, on the thirty-fifth take, at ten o'clock that night, Berry pounded it out and they finally had it. They nailed it.

Leonard loosened his necktie, unbuttoned his collar and rolled his shirtsleeves to his elbows. He was so exhausted he almost drank from a cup of coffee with a dead cigarette butt floating in it. But they weren't done yet.

"Now we gotta go through your contract," Leonard said to Chuck.

"Now?" Chuck's hair was matted down with sweat, his shirttails out, eyes heavy lidded.

"Now," said Leonard. He went over to Dixon, who was sacked out in a chair, fingers laced together, propped up on his belly. Leonard gave his shoulder a shake. "We're good here. Go on home. Get some rest. You, too," he said to the other musicians. "Go on. Get the hell out of here."

They headed back to the office and while Leeba ran across the street to get sandwiches from Deutsch's, Leonard and Phil sat down with Chuck and two contracts.

"This one's your contract with us." Phil pointed to the first sheet of paper and scratched his five o'clock shadow. "And this one's your contract with Arc."

"And what's Arc?" asked Chuck.

"That's our publishing company. It's standard. Boilerplate stuff," said Phil, handing him a pen.

"Well, you don't mind if I read it all before I sign, do you?"

"Go ahead. Be my guest." Leonard took out a cigarette, expecting Berry to skim through it like the other musicians did. But

Chuck Berry sat there and carefully read it, line by line, using his finger as a cursor, looking up every now and again with questions. "What's 'mechanical rights'?"

"That's in case someone else wants to record the song."

"I see." He nodded, but Leonard got the sense he didn't fully understand. "And what's a 'publisher's fee'? What's that for?"

"Just standard. Like Phil said, boilerplate stuff. All the labels have the same thing."

Leeba had come back with the sandwiches and Chuck was still on the first page of the contract. It was going on midnight and Chuck Berry was still asking questions. Finally, at a quarter till one, he reached for the pen.

"I'm not even sure exactly what I'm signing," he said, scratching his name across the line. "But I promised my father I'd read every word before I signed anything."

Phil yawned. "We can assure him you didn't miss a single one."

THIRTY-FOUR:
"MANNISH BOY"

LEEBA

Leeba was exhausted from the recording session with Chuck Berry the night before. Plus she had just gotten her monthlies and felt the cramps starting up. They'd been trying for a baby for so long, but here it was, another month, another disappointment.

On her way home she stopped at the bank and cashed a bonus check for twenty dollars from Leonard and Phil for working overtime on the Berry session. She was surprised by Leonard's sudden burst of generosity. Just when she thought he was being cheap and trying to take advantage of her, he'd turn around and do something like this. As the teller counted out the money, Leeba thought about having to tell Red that parenthood had passed them over again. The teller gave her the money and Leeba tucked it in her wallet and headed for home.

As she was coming up the sidewalk, nearing the apartment building, she had visions of soaking in a hot bath and curling up with a hot water bottle. That was her plan, anyway, until she spotted the boy. Actually, she spotted Red's Stella first and then the boy. He was sitting on the front stoop in a pair of torn jeans that let his bony kneecaps show through. The guitar that she'd seen Red play so many times looked enormous in that child's lap.

Red had been giving this boy guitar lessons off and on for the past two years, starting around the time Red took that job at the shoe factory. Their lessons were always at the musicians' union hall, but Red was working late that day and Leeba knew he had asked James to meet him at the apartment instead. She felt guilty about Red occasionally taking on a second shift, knowing how much he hated it at the shoe factory, but they needed the extra money. These days the only things Red looked forward to were getting off work and giving James his guitar lessons.

Having never met the boy before, Leeba went over to introduce herself. "You must be James," she said.

He nodded but didn't say anything. Then, much to her astonishment, he pulled out a crumpled package of Pall Malls from his pocket and a box of matches.

"Aren't you a little young to be smoking?" She figured he couldn't have been more than eight or nine.

"I can smoke if I wanna," he said, striking a match against the pavement.

"Not in my house, you can't."

"I ain't in your house," he said, taking a defiant puff.

"But you will be if you want a guitar lesson today."

The boy looked at her, cocked his head to the side.

"I'm Leah. Red's wife."

Now he really looked puzzled and Leeba realized that Red probably hadn't mentioned that she was white. She imagined James had never known a mixed couple before.

"I mean it," she said, pointing to the cigarette. "Put it out."

He gave her his best version of a snarl and she covered her mouth to hide her smile while he took one final drag and threw it to the ground.

Leeba went over to grind it out beneath her heel. "Now that you've kicked the habit," she said, "you're welcome to come upstairs and wait for Red. He should be home any minute."

James didn't say a thing as he followed her inside the apartment building. Leeba stopped at the mailbox, thinking she wasn't too sure about this kid, and hoped Red would be home soon. As she and the boy approached their apartment door, Sophie started barking and James jumped back, frightened, clutching his Stella like a shield.

"Don't worry," Leeba assured him. "She's friendly. She just gets excited when we come home." Leeba turned the lock and grabbed Sophie by the collar to stop her from trampling the boy. "C'mon in," Leeba said. "It's okay. She won't hurt you."

He sidestepped inside, keeping a watchful eye on the dog. When Sophie had calmed down, she padded over, sniffing the familiar scent of Red's old guitar. That was when Leeba saw James smile for the first time. An infectious, innocent smile. "Can I pet her?" he asked, every bit the little kid he really was.

"Sure."

James tentatively reached out his hand, but when Sophie barked, he pulled back and gripped the guitar again.

"It's okay. She's just playing." Leeba set the mail and her pocketbook down on the kitchen table and reached for James's hand, guiding it over Sophie's fur. "There, see?"

It didn't take long for Sophie and James to warm up to each other. He'd set his guitar down and was petting the dog with both hands when the telephone rang. Leeba stepped into the kitchen to answer it and barely got a hello out before Aileen started in. Muddy had given her a wristwatch and you'd think it was a diamond ring by the way she was going on about it.

". . . and it's fourteen-karat gold . . . with

seventeen jewels . . ."

Leeba shifted the phone to her other ear, smiling as she overheard James playing with Sophie in the other room, going, "You a good girl. Yes, you is, yes, you is . . ."

"Wait till you see this watch," Aileen said. "It's the prettiest thing I —"

"Listen, I hate to cut you off," said Leeba, "but the boy Red's giving lessons to is here. Let me call you back after Red gets home and then you can tell me all about the watch."

After Leeba hung up with Aileen and came back out to the living room she found James rolling around on the floor, giggling and playing with Sophie. Leeba went over to the table, closed the clasp on her pocketbook and shuffled through the mail.

"Word on the street," she said, "is that you're a pretty good bluesman."

James laughed and buried his face in Sophie's fur. "Did Red tell you that?"

"Sure did."

Leeba asked James who his favorite blues musicians were.

"I like Lead Belly, Charley Patton, Tampa Red, Robert Johnson . . ." He was still petting Sophie and rattling off names when Red came through the front door, rousing the dog's excitement all over again.

"Well, I see you've all met," said Red, reaching over to scratch Sophie's ear, patting her loins and making her tail swish back and forth.

"Yeah. James and I had a smoke, a little chitchat." She nodded with a wink. Red smiled and Leeba was pleased to see him in such a good mood. She attributed this to James being there, because normally he came through the front door grumpy and complaining about the glue fumes.

Red patted Sophie again and turned to James. "Have you been practicing, Curly?"

"Wait till you see." James swung the guitar into his lap.

"Well, c'mon now. Show me what you got."

James played the low E and adjusted the tension on the tuning knob and then did the same thing with the A and D strings.

"Now, before we get started," said Red, "tell me again, what's the most important thing to remember about being a bluesman?"

"Protect your hands," said James.

"That's right. And clean those fingernails once in a while while you're at it, too. Now, let's start with some pick work . . ."

James began playing the chromatic scale to warm up. He kept going over it again and again. After that they must have spent twenty minutes practicing the chord changes in one song. It was tedious, but Red told James that was the only way to learn.

Leeba had worried when Red first started giving these lessons that he would feel slighted, being relegated to teaching rather than playing. But watching him with James for the first time put that fear to rest. She hadn't seen that look of satisfaction on her husband's face in so long. Not since he'd last played. It was almost as if James was an extension of Red. That little boy was giving Red a second chance at creating music.

They ended their lesson that day with James playing and singing "I'm a Steady Rollin' Man."

Leeba had a good feeling about James, until the next morning when she reached into her wallet and found that the twenty-dollar bill was gone.

THIRTY-FIVE: "EVERY DAY I HAVE THE BLUES"

RED

The kid had let him down. And it wasn't so much about the money, though Red and Leah could have used that extra twenty bucks. It was more the boy's lack of respect and regard for everything Red had done for him. Giving him his guitar, giving him lessons, encouraging him to stay in school. Red felt betrayed and he was angry about it.

The next day when Red got off the El, beat and irritable from a long day of work, he spotted James across the street, outside the pool hall. He was hanging around out front with a bunch of older boys. Red took a drag off his cigarette, tossed it to the curb and sprinted across the street.

"Hey, man," said James, a broad smile rising up on his face. "Whatchu doin' here? Hey, guys, guys, take a look — this here's Red Du—"

"We need to have a conversation," Red said, interrupting James's introduction. "Come with me."

James dropped the smile, dropped the glib attitude and followed Red. When they turned the corner, out of view from the other boys, Red grabbed hold of James by his collar. "Why'd you do it?"

"I didn't do nothin'." James tried to pull away, but Red held him in place.

"You lie to me and you'll only make it worse." Red tightened his grip. "You think you're such a tough guy, huh? I'm gonna teach you a lesson and it won't be on the guitar." Red crouched down, forcing James to look him in the eye. "I thought we were friends. Why'd you do it? Why'd you go into Leah's wallet and take that money?"

James gave him a defiant, hard glare, his lips set tight, not a shred of remorse visible on his face.

"That wasn't your money. You knew it was wrong. So why'd you do it?"

Still James gave him nothing and Red realized this kid was harder to reach than he'd thought. "So, what, now you're gonna be a liar on top of being a thief?"

James just sneered at Red.

"I'll tell you what, if you're gonna act like that you and me are through. No more lessons. You're on your own." And as he said that, Red felt a stab of guilt because this kid was already on his own and that was part of the problem. No one was looking out for him.

Red was sure that James was going to say something, but instead he stuffed his hands into his pockets, hung his head low, turned and walked away.

"So that's how it's gonna be, huh?" Red tried again, hoping the boy would turn back around. "You're just gonna walk away 'cause you're too much of a coward to admit what you did. You know a man owns up to his mistakes. You're behaving just like a little baby."

James kept walking and when he turned the corner, Red knew he couldn't let him go. This boy needed him. Just an apology, one "I'm sorry," and all would be forgiven; but when Red had just about caught up to him, James saw him coming and took off running.

Red stood helplessly on the sidewalk watching until the boy disappeared in the distance. What was the point in going after him a second time? Obviously James didn't want Red's help, even if he needed it.

Red had just arrived at work, taking his place on the assembly line, waiting for Smitty at the next station to shave the edges off the cork backings and send them down the conveyor belt to Red, whose job it was to glue them to the soles. The hardest part of the job was dealing with the glue fumes. They got up in his sinuses, made his eyes water, his nose run and his head throb. He began gagging as soon as Smitty sent him the first cork.

As Red ran his shirtsleeve across his eyes to clear them, he thought about James. It had been a week since Red had seen him, and even though he had told James they were through, Red had still waited for over an hour at the musicians' union hall the day of their lesson hoping James would show. When he didn't, Red had wandered through the neighborhood looking for him, but James was nowhere to be found. Red didn't know anything about disciplining children and feared he'd come down too hard on the kid. Yes, he wanted to teach him a lesson, but now he regretted how he'd handled the situation.

Red slathered more glue on the next cork and fell into a coughing jag.

"You okay there?" Smitty called over. His skin was as black as coal and sleek with sweat.

Red nodded, recovering. "These fumes are gonna kill us," said Red.

"You know they'd never make a white man do that job."

"Why don't they just lynch us," Red called back. "It'd be a lot faster."

Smitty laughed bitterly and Red gagged a few more times while he brushed glue on the next cork backing and the next and the next. Five more hours of that and it was lunchtime.

Red headed into the cafeteria, took a seat at one of the long tables and pulled a sandwich from a brown paper bag. Billy Moore, the oldest of the Moore brothers who owned the business, was standing around with the supervisors, keeping tabs on the workers, making sure no one took even a minute longer than they were entitled for their break. Billy Moore was one of the meanest sons of bitches Red had ever known. With his pock-marked red face, big wide forehead and pointy chin, he reminded Red of a strawberry.

Red looked at the sandwich Leah had packed for him that day, brisket left over from the night before. He loved her brisket, but the fumes had killed his appetite. Still he knew he had to put something in his stomach if he was going to make it till quitting time.

He had just forced himself to take a bite when Smitty came out of the lavatory swearing and went up to Billy Moore.

"There's no soap in the washroom," said Smitty. "I'd like some soap so I can wash my hands before I eat lunch."

"Why do you need soap, boy? You can't tell if your black hands are dirty or clean anyway." Billy snickered and looked over his shoulder, soliciting laughter from the supervisors.

Smitty tried again, his voice rising above the mocking. "I said, I'd like some hand soap for the washroom."

Red watched in amazement. He had known Smitty for about six months, and he'd never before stood up to the boss man. He'd always been as meek as could be, doing whatever they told him to and never complaining, not even in private to Red.

"Clock's ticking, boy," said Billy. "You want soap or you want to eat your lunch? 'Cuz I'll dock your pay for every second you're late."

Smitty gave up and took the seat next to Red, muttering, "They'd treat a goddamn dog better than they treat us."

Red set his sandwich down. "What's wrong with you? You're gonna get your ass fired if you keep that up."

"I don't care. I might just up and quit on that racist."

"Man, what has gotten into you?"

Smitty peeled back the top slice of bread on his sandwich, gave a look and shoved it aside.

"Seriously, man," said Red, "what has gotten into you?"

"I'm done putting up with their ways."

"And what choice have you got? A man needs to work and it's the same just about every place you go."

"Yeah, well, we're fixing to change all that."

"Who's 'we'?"

Smitty crumpled up his paper bag and gave Red an exasperated look. "Where have you been, man? You got the NAACP, you got CORE — I joined up and I'm glad I did. They're all talking about how it's time to put an end to how our people are being treated

427

in the workplace."

"So what are you saying? That you're prepared to get yourself fired because you joined the NAACP and CORE?"

"I joined the Urban League, too."

Red wasn't surprised. He knew that lately more and more Negroes were joining organizations like that.

"With all those newspapers you read," said Smitty, "I'd expect someone like you would get involved."

"Me?"

Smitty turned and looked him square in the eye. "Why *not* you? I've been to a few meetings now, and I *get* it. Like they explained to me, we're all part of this. You do nothing and you're part of the problem. You stand up and you become part of the solution."

Red didn't respond. He felt ashamed, like he'd been dodging his responsibilities as a colored man.

Smitty wasn't done yet. "You can sit back and take whatever the white man throws at you, or you can make a stand, do something to change things. The choice is yours."

But there was no choice in the matter. From the time he was a young boy, going into that candy shop and being told they wouldn't serve him, Red had known the way he was being treated was wrong. Why was he putting up with it now?

He turned to Smitty. "So when's the next meeting?"

THIRTY-SIX:
"IT HURTS ME TOO"

LEEBA

Leeba had spent her day reviewing dozens of publicity photos they'd taken of Chuck Berry. His wavy black hair had never looked so lush, the devilish twinkle in his eye never more alluring, and yet Leonard didn't like them. He had decided to hire another photographer and redo the photo shoot. It had been two weeks since they'd recorded Chuck's song and Leonard wanted everything perfect and in place before he would release it.

When Leeba got home that night the apartment was dark and Sophie was waiting by the door, her tail thwacking against the wall, her paws stomping as she playfully yelped. Leeba was petting her as she turned on the lamp, calling out for Red. "Red? Red, are you here?" She checked in the bedroom, looked out on the back porch. No sign of him.

That was strange. Red started work at six in the morning and usually got home long before Leeba did. She wondered if maybe he

430

was working a second shift and had forgotten to tell her. Or maybe he purposely hadn't told her because he knew she'd try to talk him out of it. She still felt guilty that he had to work there at all, aware that it was her fault he wasn't performing anymore.

Sophie was circling in front of the door, needing to go out, and Leeba took her for a walk. As they wandered the neighborhood she wondered if Red was over by the schoolyard or if he'd maybe gone down to the musicians' union hall looking for James. She knew Red felt his attempt at discipline had backfired. Leeba tried to make him see that James was a troubled boy, but Red didn't want to let him go.

After Sophie had chased some birds and a squirrel they headed back inside. Still no Red. She fed the dog and watered her houseplants and was about to pour herself a glass of wine when Sophie starting barking a beat before Leeba heard Red keying into the apartment. Leeba was relieved and when she saw the cheerful expression on his face as he walked in she was surprised.

"Are you okay?" she asked after kissing him hello. "I was worried. I didn't know you were working a double."

"I wasn't."

"Oh." She was taken aback. Where had he been? A bar? No, he wasn't drunk. Did he go listen to music? Doubtful. Had he found

James? Perhaps.

Red led her to the couch and sat her down. She felt her stomach drop. She had no idea what was coming.

"My granddaddy used to say, 'You've been in the cellar for so long you forgot what fresh air is like.' And I feel like tonight I was finally getting fresh air. I could breathe."

"I don't understand. What's going on with you?"

He reached out for her hand and looked into her eyes. "I was with a group of people tonight — a group of strangers — and, Leah, I felt like I found a home. A place to take everything I've been holding inside of me."

She'd never heard him speak like this before and it confused her. "What are you talking about?"

"I found a place to bring everything I've been feeling my whole life. I've been wronged, denied, insulted — and why? Because I'm colored. I've always known it was wrong, but I didn't know how to do anything about it. But tonight I was surrounded by people who are willing to stand up for themselves. We don't have to sit here and quietly accept the way we're treated. I've made up my mind — I'm not going to take it anymore."

He couldn't contain his energy. He stood up and began pacing. "I wasn't put on this earth to be treated like I'm inferior. This isn't what God intended for me. Or for any other

Negro." He turned and faced Leeba again. "I joined the NAACP tonight. I'm through sitting on the sidelines. There was a force in that room tonight and if we pull together I know we can start to set things right."

She saw the passion and energy blazing inside him, a light she hadn't seen from him since he'd stopped playing music. She thought about how Jews in Europe had been so passive when the Nazis mistreated and abused them. It struck her that Negroes in this country couldn't afford to make that same mistake. "I think you're doing the right thing," she said. "I'm proud of you."

They stayed up talking late into the night. Mostly he was talking, and she was listening, trying to understand. Some of what he said she easily related to, but still she knew Red's experience as a black man in America was different from what Jews in Europe had been through. There was no one gathering up Negroes and putting them into death camps here. The problem was more insidious than that. And she knew that, as much as anti-Semitism and racism had in common, Red's growing up in the Deep South was very different from her family's experience before immigrating to America. The only way to support Red was to respect that difference.

He was going back to another meeting the next evening and she contemplated joining him. But he didn't invite her, and she sensed that he needed to go alone. Red was rediscovering the self-respect he'd lost as a young child. She had to let him go on that journey by himself.

Another month came and went and so did Leeba's monthlies. "I don't think I'm ever going to have a baby," she said, looking upside down at Aileen, feeling all the blood rushing to her head. She was in her apartment, standing on her head, her legs propped up against the wall.

"Tell me again, how's that supposed to make you have a baby?" asked Aileen.

"I read about it in *Reader's Digest.* Something about standing on your head makes it easier to conceive."

"Is that the same article that told you to eat all them yams?"

"Yeah, well, that didn't work. Obviously."

"How long you gotta do that for?" Aileen asked as she lit a cigarette and blew the smoke toward the ceiling.

"Almost done."

After a few more minutes Leeba lowered her legs and sat up leaning against the wall, faint stars filling her vision.

"Ain't we a pair," said Aileen. "I'm trying not to get pregnant and you're trying everything you can think of to have a baby. You ever think maybe you're trying too hard?"

"I can't help it. I want a baby. I can't

imagine my life without a child in it."

Once she felt steady enough to stand, Leeba patted her hair back in place and reached for her pocketbook and keys. "Well, shall we?"

It was a Monday morning and they were on their way down to Chess to work on a new song. Chess had put out a couple more records with Aileen; one was a song that Willie Dixon had written but the rest were all Leeba's. None of them had performed the way "Jealous Kinda Love" had. They didn't even chart in the R&B top one hundred and Leeba knew Aileen was feeling desperate for another hit.

As they walked toward the El platform, they came to a red light and Leeba noticed a group of boys across the street hanging around outside a pool hall. They were all in their teens except for one. Leeba took a second look at the littlest of the boys, almost comical with his head bent trying to light a cigarette. When he straightened up she saw that it was James.

"That's him," she said, gesturing with her chin. "That's the boy Red was giving guitar lessons to."

"You mean the little thief who lifted that twenty out of your wallet? C'mon, I'm gonna set him straight —"

"Whoa." Leeba stopped her, looping her arm through hers. "Forget it. That money's long gone. It's been a month since he took it.

Besides, Red's done with him."

"Little brat!" Aileen shouted through her cupped hands.

James heard her and his head shot up. He looked in their direction, his eyes locking onto Leeba's. Up until that moment she'd been angry about the money and, despite Red's feelings, glad he was out of their lives. But just then she saw that he was only a child, a misguided, innocent child, lost in this world. She felt strangely protective of him and he seemed to sense this because he kept staring at Leeba until one of the older boys shoved him so hard he was knocked to the ground.

"Ha! Serves him right," said Aileen.

Leeba wanted to go over to him, but feared Aileen would make a scene.

"Ain't he supposed to be in school now anyway?" she asked.

"I think James only does what James wants to do. Nobody's looking after him. I don't know what happened to his parents. I think he lives with his grandmother."

"She sure has her hands full, don't she? C'mon, our train's coming."

Leeba followed Aileen to the El and went about her day. But when she came home from work she found James sitting in the hallway outside their apartment door, his knees propped up, his head cradled in his arms.

"Are you looking for Red?" she asked.

He didn't answer and she heard Sophie on the other side of the door, her nails scratching against the floor and her tail thumping the wall as she whimpered at the sound of Leeba's voice. She asked James again if he was there for Red.

The boy said no and when he lifted his head she saw that he had a black eye, a real shiner.

"Oh my gosh, James, what happened? Who did this to you?" She crouched down beside him and went to touch his face, but he shrugged her away like the tough guy she'd first met. Leeba stood up. Obviously he didn't want her sympathy. She wasn't sure what he wanted. There was an awkward moment of silence and she saw his lower lip tremble. "James?"

"I'm sorry I took that money from your wallet," he said as he began to cry outright. He reached into his pocket and pulled out a crumpled bill and a handful of coins. "All I got is two dollars, but it's yours."

"Keep your money," she said. "But don't ever steal from me or anyone else again. You understand?"

The boy nodded as he shoved his money back in his pocket. She waited, but he didn't say anything. His lip was still trembling. He hadn't moved from his spot on the floor and didn't look like he was going to.

437

"James," she said after another long silence, "is there something else you want?"

He looked up at her and dragged his arm across his eyes to wipe the tears. "Can I come play with your dog?"

That night Leeba set an extra plate at the table so James could join them for dinner. When Red came home from another one of his meetings and saw James playing with Sophie on the floor, his face lit up. Between his meetings and finding the boy there, it was as if someone had shined a light on Red's life. She couldn't remember the last time she'd seen him so happy.

When it was time to eat, Leeba and Red exchanged a look when they saw the way James gobbled down his stew, sopping up the gravy with a heel of bread, gulping down a tall glass of milk.

"Is your grandma a good cook?" Leeba asked, dishing out more stew for him.

"My grandma done passed." James licked the back of his spoon.

"She did?" Leeba was shocked. He said it so matter-of-factly. She fought the urge to take James in her arms.

"When did that happen?" asked Red.

James shrugged and dug into his second bowl of stew. "Um, 'bout six months ago."

"Oh, you poor thing," said Leeba, studying James's ratty clothes, his dirty fingernails.

"Who's looking after you now?"

"A foster family." He took another mouthful of stew. "This sure do taste good. My foster mother don't cook."

"Not at all?" asked Leeba.

"Nope."

"What do you eat, then?" asked Red.

The boy cocked his head to the side, thinking. "Um, potato chips, soda pop, sometimes caramel corn . . ."

Leeba brought her hand to her mouth and looked at Red.

"Do you like it there with your foster family?" Red asked.

James shrugged again, kept on eating.

"Do you have any aunts or uncles? Any cousins? Any kin at all?"

He shook his head.

Leeba set her fork down. She hadn't realized just how alone this kid really was. Without a proper family, he'd end up like those hoodlums he hung around with.

After dinner, Leah packed up some leftovers for him and Red walked James over to his foster home. She stood at the door watching them and wondering if that foster family was more interested in the money they were getting from the state than in looking after James.

Thirty-Seven:
"Rock and Roll Music"

LEONARD

Six weeks after they recorded "Maybelline," Leonard was finally ready to release the record. It was July and hot as hell. They threw open the doors and windows and the office was still a goddamn steam bath.

"I got those records all boxed up for you, Dad."

Leonard looked up at his son. Marshall's eagerness to please stabbed him with guilt. He was thirteen and had his choice of going to summer camp or working down at Chess. He chose Chess.

"What should I do now?" Marshall asked, hovering over his father's shoulder.

"Go to lunch."

"Lunch? It's not even ten o'clock."

"I don't know — go get the shipping labels ready."

"Sure thing." Marshall smiled and sprinted out the door.

Leonard got up from his desk and wiped

the sweat creeping down his neck as he walked into Phil's office. Leeba was already in there; the two of them were discussing Berry's record.

"So what's the latest from the lawyers?" Leonard asked Phil as he slumped down on the couch.

"They want us to change the spelling of Maybelline. So I said fine, we'll replace the *i* with an *e*. And they said okay."

"That's it?" Leonard was surprised.

"That's it. They said if we spell it *e-n-e* the cosmetics company can't say a word."

"And what about the trade ads?" he asked Leeba, moving on to the next subject.

She glanced over her notes, stalling. She seemed distracted, tired. The day before, the two of them had grabbed coffee at Deutsch's. They were reminiscing about ice skating together as kids, playing tetherball and hide-and-seek and how frosted Phil got when he couldn't find them. They were laughing, clowning around, having a good time, until a woman showed up with a baby stroller. Leeba took one look at that infant and burst into tears. Thinking he could lighten the mood he'd told her she could have Marshall, but that had only made her cry harder.

"Leeba?" said Phil. "*Nu?* The trade ads?"

"Well," she said, still leafing through her notes, "we haven't reserved space yet for the release of 'Maybellene,' and" — she flipped through the pages some more — "we said we wanted to promote Muddy's 'Mannish Boy.' We have a full-page advertisement set for that — two columns."

"Okay," said Leonard, "so what we'll do is divide it up. Half will promote Muddy and half will introduce Chuck."

"But you can't do that to Muddy," said Leeba. "He'll be furious."

"Mud's a big boy," said Leonard.

"Oh, that reminds me," said Leeba. "I noticed a mistake on the copyright application for 'Maybellene.' I don't know what happened, but it came back with Alan Freed as the co-songwriter along with Chuck."

Leonard looked at Phil, as if to say, *Do you want to explain this or should I?*

Leeba leaned forward, her brows hiked up. "What's going on, Lenny? I know when you're up to something. What are you doing?"

"Look," said Phil, "it's very simple. Freed's the biggest deejay in New York and with his name on the copyright we're guaranteed the song will get more attention."

"It's business, okay?" said Leonard.

"And Freed is going to get paid for Chuck's work? That's not right."

"It's right if it gets us airplay on the station with the highest ratings in the country."

"But what about Chuck? Does he even know about this?"

"Don't you worry about Chuck," said Leonard. "Chuck Berry's gonna make out just fine."

It had been a hell of a lot easier when Alan Freed was in Cleveland. New York in August was no picnic. Leonard was sweating through his shirt as he jostled through Times Square making his way to East Fifty-eighth Street to the WINS radio station.

Leonard had known Alan Freed since his days as a deejay at WAKR in Akron. Freed liked race music and jazz and had started gaining a following of white kids who defied their parents and listened in. The son of a bitch thought he'd invented the wheel when he started calling race music "rock 'n' roll." But Leonard had heard that phrase long before Freed said it on the air. His musicians had been singing about rocking and rolling since before the Aristocrat days and now Freed was taking curtain bows, hailed as a genius for coming up with it.

Through the years Leonard had brought a lot of songs to Alan and had paid him well in exchange for airplay. Of course, now that he was in New York the price of entry had gone way, way up.

Leonard went into Freed's corner office. He had gold records on one wall and a credenza lined with crystal decanters of liquor. Freed was in a leather wingback chair with a view of Manhattan visible through the window over his shoulder. Leonard sat opposite him in a chair he wasn't sure he'd ever be able to get back out of.

After they shot the breeze for a few minutes, Leonard put "Maybellene" on the turntable. As soon as he dropped the needle, Leonard saw the look come over Freed's face. It was love, and Leonard knew it wasn't just because he was sharing the writing credit for the song.

From the very first time Freed played "Maybellene" on his all-white station, listeners were calling up requesting it. Even Leonard didn't realize the torrent that had been unleashed. Chuck may have been a good ole Midwestern boy, but he had that hillbilly twang going for him and Leonard knew "Maybellene" would get some attention down South, but what he hadn't counted on was the rest of the country going nuts for the song, too. Deejays could barely keep up with the requests, playing it ten or more times in an hour.

Two days later when Leonard returned to Chicago, Leeba handed him a stack of papers. "Orders," she said. "Everybody wants the Chuck Berry record."

Leonard called every record presser from Memphis to Los Angeles, trying to fill all the orders coming in. They were working fourteen-hour days just to keep up with the demand. Even Marshall came down to help.

They ordered in pizzas and sandwiches and packed up boxes, cranked up the addressograph machine and slapped each one with a shipping slip and a label.

They were in the middle of all this chaos when Muddy came into the office one afternoon. He flipped up the grease-spotted pizza box lid, checking under the hood. "Thought we had us an appointment today, Leonard. I'm here to talk about my new record." Muddy examined a cold slice of pizza before dropping it back in the box.

"Gonna have to wait, buddy." Leonard had a cigarette dangling from his mouth, one eye squinted. Even through the smoke he saw that Muddy was offended, especially when he picked up one of the 78 discs.

"Chuck Berry, huh? You mean to tell me y'all ain't got time for me on account of this?" Muddy tossed the record back on the pile and left without saying good-bye.

Leonard knew Muddy was sore and apparently so was Revetta. He got home that night and after Marshall went to bed, she stormed into the kitchen and stood at the sink, her back toward Leonard, counting off all his fatherly failures. He'd missed Elaine's ballet recital the day before, forgotten to leave something under Susie's pillow from the tooth fairy, hadn't gotten Marshall home on time like he'd promised. And most of all she got on him about not taking better care of himself.

"You don't eat right. You don't sleep. All you do is drink coffee and smoke cigarettes. You're working yourself to death, Len."

He took it for about five minutes before he snapped. "You want me to buy that big house in Glencoe? You want to move to the suburbs, get the kids in better schools? Well, it ain't cheap. This is what I gotta do. I'm doing this for you — for the kids."

"That's a load of crap." She spun around, her fingers twisting up a dish towel. "This isn't for me. It's not for the kids. It's for Shirley and you know it. Everything you've *ever* done has been for Shirley."

He was shocked, suddenly warm and light-headed. He felt behind him for the counter, needing to grip something to steady himself. Of course Revetta knew Shirley from the old neighborhood, but she had never mentioned her before.

"You think I don't know?" she said. "I see the credit card statements. I see all the bills from Saks for your suits and your ties, your shoes and your hats. And I know there's only one reason why you go there to shop."

"I've never laid a hand on her."

"I didn't say you did." She bunched up the dish towel and threw it on the countertop. "But you can't stand there and tell me you're not still trying to prove something to her —

or to her father."

Leonard hung his head. He had no defense.

"I've always known I was second best," she said. "I knew that when I married you. But don't insult me now by lying to my face. I'm not stupid, Leonard."

The next morning when Leonard got in his car the radio was playing "Maybellene." Everywhere he went he heard that song: in the stores, on kids' transistors. He'd play a game with himself, going up and down the dial on his car radio to see how many times he'd hear the song between his house and the office. The record so far was seven times.

By September "Maybellene" had hit the top of the *Billboard* charts. The day Leonard saw it in the trade magazine, Muddy came to him with a big chip on his shoulder. He had his own copy of *Billboard* in his hand. He'd seen the charts, too. Through the years he'd learned how to read enough to be able to decipher what he saw in the trade magazines.

"Looks like your man Freed is a big fan of Mr. Berry's. Lookee here." He eyed the chart. "Looks like he's playing a lot of crap, too. Pat Boone's number nine with 'Ain't That a Shame.' And if you ask me, ain't that a shame that they'd let Pat Boone record Fats Domino's song."

Leonard laughed until Muddy turned the next page and there was the full-page ad they were running for Chuck Berry with a little photo of Muddy and a mention touting his new record, "Trouble, No More."

"Now, Mud" — Leonard got up from his desk and walked over to him — "you gotta under—"

"When we goin' back in the studio to record my new songs?"

"We'll get to it, buddy. I promise. I haven't forgotten about you."

"You been sayin' that for the past month now."

"Hey, c'mon, Chuck's tapped into something and it's good for all of us. You. Me. Everybody. This is business. It ain't personal." And it wasn't. Muddy's sales were sliding. His audience was shrinking month by month, week by week. Same thing was happening to Wolf, to Walter, to Sunnyland Slim — all the blues guys.

"Yeah," said Muddy, "well, just don't be forgettin' who brung you Chuck Berry in the first place." Muddy flung his magazine down on the desk, turned and walked out of Leonard's office.

THIRTY-EIGHT:
"EVIL IS GOING ON"

LEEBA

Leeba looked around the smoky lounge and counted up the people: three at the bar, a table of four in the back, five seated at a center table, another table for two off to the side. With her and Red there was a total of sixteen. Sixteen people there to see Aileen Booker, who just a few years before would have packed the house.

Aileen stood on the bandstand in a blue sequined dress. She'd had her hair done earlier and wore it swept up on one side, held in place with a rhinestone comb. A glass of whiskey on the rocks beading with condensation was parked on a stool next to her.

The band, some session players Leonard had put together for her, sounded good. They were tight, but it was wasted on this handful of people, there for the drinks more than the music. Leeba saw Aileen struggling up there. Not with her singing. No, Aileen's voice was as strong as ever. It was the people who were talking, their backs toward the stage. It was the woman who got up and went to the washroom in the middle of "Jealous Kinda Love." It was the fact that she was into her second set and Muddy still wasn't there. Leeba noticed Aileen kept looking toward the door, no doubt hoping he'd appear. The hour grew late. Red was tired and had to get up at five to make it to the shoe factory by six.

"We can't leave yet," she whispered to him. "I can't do that to her."

Aileen was in the middle of a new song that Leeba had written, "The Heart Goes Thump," when one of the drunks at the bar started getting loud, arguing over his tab.

"Hey —" Aileen stopped singing and called out to him. "Y'all wanna shut the fuck up?" She turned her gaze toward the others sitting there. "All y'all, just shut the fuck up — I'm singin' here."

The band stopped playing. Leeba looked at Red and grimaced. There was an instant of shock in the room, followed by a burst of laughter before everyone turned back to their conversations. The band started up again, but Aileen didn't make it through the rest of the song before she ran off the stage in tears.

Leeba told Red to go on home and she went after Aileen.

"I can't do this no more," Aileen told her when Leeba caught up with her outside the side door. It was a warm autumn night and

Aileen was sitting on the ground, leaning against the building, her shimmering sequined dress bunched up around her knees. She was holding a bottle of whiskey, sobbing.

"The other night the club owner turned up the houselights on me in the middle of my set. He told me they were closing early because the place was so dead." She yanked the rhinestone comb out of her hair. "This is how I make my money. It's how I survive. Now I'm gonna have to go back to cleaning hotel rooms and waiting tables." She took a long pull from her bottle and started fidgeting, scratching at her legs and then her arms. "And where the hell's Muddy? He said he'd be here. That man is killing me."

"Something must have come up." Leeba couldn't meet her eye.

"Yeah, and I wonder if that 'something' has a name. I feel like I'm losing him. Like he's slipping away. What am I gonna do if he quits me?"

Leeba wanted to say it would be the best thing that ever happened to her; she couldn't stand how Muddy came and went from Aileen's life. But she knew her friend didn't want to hear that. Aileen wept and started fidgeting and scratching at her arms again. As one of her sleeves hiked up, Leeba's mouth dropped open. She saw the marks on Aileen's arm, a series of bruises and pinpricks. Aileen caught Leeba staring and quickly pulled down her sleeve.

"What is that?" asked Leeba, reaching for Aileen's arm. "What are you doing to yourself?"

"I ain't doin' nothin'." She jerked her arm away. "I got a rash or somethin'."

"That's no rash. Did J.J. get you started on this?"

"I ain't doin' nothin'."

"C'mon, I know J.J. does dope. I'm not stupid. Are you going to look me in the eye and tell me that's not from a needle?"

Aileen looked up and fixed her gaze on Leeba. "It's. *Not.* From. A. Needle."

Leeba slapped her hands to her sides and shook her head. "I give up. I'm going home."

"Oh, great. That's just great. You go on and leave me, too."

Leeba looked at Aileen. "There was a time when the only secrets we kept were each other's."

Two weeks later, on the last Friday in September, Chess was cutting royalty checks. Leeba walked into work that day and found a full house. Everybody was already there — Muddy, Aileen, Wolf, Walter, Bo, Sunnyland, Willie, the Moonglows and on and on. Everybody was there waiting for their money. The place was so crowded she had to sidestep her way around the artists to get to her desk. Chess was growing fast and they'd hired on so many new people — bookkeepers and an entire payroll and royalty department — that they were about to bust out of their Cottage Grove building.

Idell, the new receptionist, was taking coffee orders. Most of the performers had probably come straight from their gigs the night before. Leeba could smell the booze and cigarette smoke clinging to them. She gazed about the room. This was Chicago's blues royalty.

Bo Diddley and Chuck Berry were laughing about something and she looked up. They were the next generation of artists. With their new sound they had become the favored sons of Chess. Their records were outselling Muddy's, Wolf's, Walter's, and some of the others combined. They were still laughing and Leeba overheard them talking about Bo's recent appearance on *The Ed Sullivan Show*.

"Sullivan had no idea who I was," said Bo. "I showed up at the studio and his people started telling me to do 'Sixteen Tons.' And I'm thinking, *That ain't even my song. I ain't going on television to perform someone else's song.* So when the curtain came up I started playing 'Bo Diddley.'"

Chuck laughed.

"That ticked Sullivan off. Phil told me, 'Fuck Sullivan. You don't ever have to be on that motherfucker's show again because your record's gonna go through the roof now.'"

Both of them were still laughing and Leeba wanted them to keep quiet. Couldn't they see what their success meant for the bluesmen who had come before them? Couldn't they understand that the more records they sold, the fewer these men who inspired them would sell? But Chuck and Bo — despite having idolized Muddy and Wolf and the others — couldn't contain their glee.

Leeba finally went over and said under her breath, "You might want to tone it down a bit." They looked at her as if they had no idea what she was talking about.

Wolf was in the back wearing his horn-rimmed glasses, reading about the American Revolution. He had gone back to school and was studying for a quiz later that day. Walter was slumped down next to him, taking pulls from his flask and blowing cigarette smoke at the ceiling. Aileen stood off to the side with Muddy.

At last Leonard emerged from his office and gave Phil a stack of checks to hand out before he disappeared again down the hall. With his cigar propped in his mouth Phil shuffled through the envelopes, going up to each musician and handing them out. With each one, he offered either congratulations or a commiserating nod that said, *Tough pay period, buddy.*

"Here you go, sweetheart," Phil said to Aileen. "Don't worry. Next one'll be better."

Leeba watched the disappointment on her friend's face, remembering the first royalty check Aileen got for "Jealous Kinda Love." Leeba would never forget how Aileen's mouth dropped down when she'd opened that envelope. "This is all I made?" she'd said to Leeba. "I had a hit record."

Aileen showed Leeba the check and her jaw about hit the floor. Seventy-three dollars and eighteen cents. Leeba had made more than that when she wrote it. As a work for hire, they'd paid her a flat fee of a hundred and seventy-five dollars in lieu of future royalties. She sometimes wondered if she'd made a bad deal with Leonard and Phil, but compared to Aileen she was coming out ahead.

"Well," said Leeba, "there's obviously been some mistake."

But when she'd gone to Leonard on Aileen's behalf he'd just said, "Nope. No mistake. The performers only get paid on the number of records sold. That's how the business works. Artists make their money off their club dates. And don't look at me like that. I didn't invent this system. It's the same at every label. That's even how the majors do it. She can go to RCA or Capitol and it's the same thing."

Leeba was remembering all this when she heard Aileen hollering at one of the secretaries. "You tell Leonard I wanna talk to him now." Leeba looked over just as Aileen hurled a coffee cup across the room, smashing it against the wall.

"What's wrong?" Leeba rushed over to her side. "What happened?"

"What's that singer doing in there with him?" Aileen shrieked and pointed across the room.

Leeba turned just as Leonard stepped out of the audition room with a gorgeous woman with very fair skin. It took a moment before Leeba realized it was Mimi Cooke. She hadn't seen her since the reception after her wedding.

"Did she audition for Leonard?" asked Aileen.

"You know he's been looking for another female singer." Leeba placed her hand on Aileen's shoulder and felt her shaking she was so mad.

"So you knew about this?" Aileen shrugged her off.

"I knew he was auditioning *someone,* but I didn't know it was her."

"What's y'all fussin' 'bout?" asked Walter. He was sitting along the back wall, looking over his check. "I brung her down here. Ain't no big deal."

Aileen rushed over to Walter, screaming, her fists raised. "Why'd you do that?" She was swinging and punching now. "Why?"

Walter was on his feet, hands shielding his face. "You crazy, woman."

Aileen pounded on him, beating up on Little Walter, until the Wolf stepped in and pulled her back. Aileen had tears streaming down her face as she sank to her knees, keening into her hands, mumbling, "What am I gonna do? What am I gonna do?"

Everyone stood around, watching. Muddy grabbed a box of Kleenex and crouched down beside her, plucking a tissue and handing it to her. "C'mon now," he said. "You can't be doin' this here. Have yourself some dignity, woman."

That only made her cry harder. Leeba knew Aileen was ashamed of her behavior, but she couldn't control herself and that made it worse. "You don't understand, Muddy. Don't nobody understand? I got nothing. I'm already a has-been. Leonard's gonna replace me with that Mimi Cooke just like he replaced you and Wolf with Chuck and Bo."

Aileen pulled herself together and fifteen minutes after her outburst at Chess she announced that she had to go meet someone. She was being cryptic and Leeba had a feeling she was on her way to see J.J. Leeba tried calling Aileen's apartment several times throughout the day, but there was no answer.

When Leeba got home that day she found a note on the table from Red. Now instead of gigging every night he was attending meetings. That evening he was at one for the

Urban League. Red still hadn't asked her to join him, and she was still respecting that he needed to go to the meetings alone.

Sophie scratched at the door so Leeba took her out for a walk. It was a crisp fall night and Leeba heard the crunch of dried leaves beneath her footsteps. The streetlights generated a nice glow over the neighborhood as the murmur of traffic from Fifty-seventh Street filtered through the air. A squirrel caught Sophie's eye and she took off after it around the side of the building.

While Sophie hunted down her squirrel Leeba thought about Aileen, wondering how she could do that to herself — stick a needle in her arm. Were the effects of dope *so* good that they justified the means? Or was it that her life was so miserable that only heroin could make it tolerable? She didn't know what to think anymore and Leeba had to admit that aside from the music, she no longer had anything in common with Aileen. It was getting harder to hold on for the sake of the history they shared and she didn't want to admit that if she'd met Aileen today she probably wouldn't have liked her.

Leeba looked around for Sophie but didn't see her anywhere. She called for her, picturing her sitting at the base of a tree, eyes trained on her squirrel. She'd eventually get bored and come back. She always did.

Leeba's mind began to drift again, thinking

about the royalty checks handed out that day and how difficult the music industry was. She thought she heard Sophie coming, but when she looked over, Leeba froze. A rush of adrenaline raced through her. Out of the darkness, with the streetlights illuminating them from behind, she saw that blond-haired boy who'd cut Red's hand. He was walking with one of his accomplices. Her heart quickened. *Where was Sophie?*

The guys were laughing, oblivious to her presence, until one of them chucked an empty beer bottle into the street. It landed with a sharp *crack* that startled her. She let out a yelp and the boys turned her way.

"Well, well, well." The blond headed over with his friend close behind. "Look who we have here. It's that little nigger lover."

As he came closer Leeba saw the marred skin on his lip from where she'd bitten him. She hadn't realized she'd wounded him so badly. He must have sensed her staring at his scar because he said, "That's right. Take a good look at what you did." He reached in his pocket. "I've been waiting for this chance. So now it's your turn." Out came the switch-blade.

Leeba screamed as he grabbed her and pressed the knife to her throat. "You shut your mouth or I swear I'll do it, you little nigger-loving bitch."

She glared at him and through clenched

teeth she screamed again. As she did, she saw Sophie come tearing toward them from behind the back of the building. The friend saw the dog coming and took off as Sophie lunged for the blond guy, ripping into his leg.

He cried out and tried to free himself, but Sophie had him. Leeba could see the blood through the tear in his trousers. He yelled out again and started waving his knife around almost blindly. Sophie growled, her teeth sinking in deeper until, in horror, Leeba watched the guy drive his switchblade into Sophie's neck, sending up a spurt of blood. The dog's jaws went slack as the boy grasped his leg, wincing and cursing.

Leeba shrieked while Sophie let out a few helpless whimpers, her body going stiff with shock just before her legs buckled. The boy limped away as Leeba rushed to Sophie, reaching for her just as she collapsed. Leeba sobbed, cradling her dog in her arms, crying out for help. It all happened so fast. Within minutes the boy was gone. And so was Sophie.

THIRTY-NINE:
"SHAKE YOUR MONEYMAKER"

LEONARD

Leonard skirted his way around his desk. It was a tight squeeze. His office was cluttered with demo tapes, piles of contracts, file cabinets. The whole place was like that: boxes everywhere, recording equipment stacked up in the hallways. Chess had outgrown the offices at Cottage Grove and Phil was looking into finding a bigger space for them.

One of the girls from accounting brought in a stack of royalty statements. He looked at Chuck Berry's first. That guy was a cash cow. His new single, "Roll Over Beethoven," was climbing the charts and "Maybellene" was still selling strong. Bo Diddley's statement was next. "I'm a Man" and "Pretty Thing" were bringing in big money, too. Then he came to Howlin' Wolf's statement. Leonard looked at the total on the bottom and dragged a hand over his face.

"Hey, Phil," he called out. "Get in here."

Phil came in, the button at his collar

undone, cigar jammed in the corner of his mouth.

"Take a look at this, will you?"

Phil went over and sat in the chair opposite Leonard's desk. He glanced at the statement and looked up. "Crap. I was hoping things would turn around."

"And Muddy's ain't no better. Sunnyland Slim's is in the shitter, too. So's Aileen's."

"Did you see Walter's? What about Jimmy Rogers?"

Leonard frowned, leaned forward and rubbed his eyes. "What's happening? Those guys used to sell twenty, thirty — fifty thousand records. Now this? Muddy's new record sold less than ten thousand copies. He said he can't fill a club anymore. Said he's close to broke. You know how much bread I've given him lately just to float him?"

"We gotta face it," said Phil. "The market's drying up."

"When are we cutting checks?"

"End of the week."

Leonard rubbed his temples. "I say we move some money around. Give a little more to Mud, Wolf, Walter and some of the others. They gotta eat, right?"

"And where's this money coming from?"

Leonard cocked his head and shrugged. "The new kids are doing great. Chuck and Bo got no worries and the way I see it, if it weren't for guys like Mud and Wolf and the others, we wouldn't even have a label. Hell, Muddy's the one who brought Chuck Berry to us in the first place. I think Chuck can part with a few bucks."

"Leonard, we can't do that."

"Why the hell not? It's the company's money."

"It's *their* money."

"Yeah, well, I'm not gonna tell them their records are tanking."

"They *know* their records are tanking. They see the charts. What are you gonna say when they ask where the money's coming from?"

"I'll tell them it's from us."

"So, what, we're gonna rob Peter to pay Paul?" Phil scoffed as he leaned back in his chair.

"If that's what it takes."

"I don't like this," said Phil. "I say we pay 'em out of our own pockets — just take it out of the business."

"It's still money coming out of our business."

Phil didn't respond.

"Okay, then it's settled. We'll move some money around, spread it out and everyone'll be taken care of."

The day after the royalty checks were handed out Leonard and Phil went to see an office building that Phil had found. They parked on a side street and walked up South Michigan

Avenue, passing by Vee-Jay and King and a half dozen other independent record labels that had recently moved to that area. The *Tribune* and other newspapers had already started referring to this stretch of the avenue as Record Row.

Toward the end of the block they came to 2120, a shoddy-looking building, long and narrow. The windows were soaped up and a handwritten sign hung on the front door: "For Sale — Mr. Griffin — BElmont 7310."

"Jesus, Phil, you said you found a great space."

"What, you think the Macamba Lounge was any better when *you* found that?"

Leonard peered through the window soap, his hands cupped about his eyes. "How old is this place?"

"Turn of the century or thereabouts. It needs work, I know," Phil said, adjusting his hat, "but the price is right. We could have it for a steal."

"And then what?"

"We gut it and build it out the way we want. No more paying for studio time. We'll have our own recording facility. A real one this time."

"You know I've always wanted everything under one roof. Offices, a studio, pressing plant. Everything. This isn't gonna be big enough for that."

"We're not ready for that yet and you know

464

it. You gotta be realistic. This space is good. And it's right here on Record Row and that's where we belong."

Leonard planted his hands on his hips and eyed the building. He liked the sound of being on Record Row. The whole industry had moved down here: record pressers, distributors, promoters, studios and just about every record company in the city. Yeah, he'd be surrounded by the competition, but that way he could keep an eye on them, too. And he'd be the biggest label down there, so he wasn't worried about his artists jumping ship. If anything, the other guys would be worried about losing their stars to Chess. Plus, they needed to have their own studio. It was time.

So they went to the pay phone on the corner and dialed Mr. Griffin's number. It was a chilly fall day, and the winds coming off the lake were beating against the phone booth. Twenty minutes later an elderly man with a cane, used more as a pointer than for support, walked them through the building. It was three stories with lots of little rooms, but that could all be reworked. The place was growing on Leonard. He was beginning to see possibilities.

The next day they came back for a second look and this time they brought Jack Wiener with them. Jack was a sound engineer from Universal Recording.

"Well?" Leonard turned to him after they'd

finished the walkthrough and found themselves in the open space he was envisioning as the studio. "What do you think?"

"This isn't suitable for a studio." An ambulance went by and Jack winced. "You hear that? You can't record with that kind of noise going on all day. You'd have to soundproof the living daylights out of the place. You'd have to block all the outside noise — without killing the natural reverberation in the studio. These parallel walls are gonna cause a problem with low frequencies; and with the acoustics in this room and the way sound waves move you'd have to —"

"I don't give a shit about this technical crap," Leonard said. "Just tell me if it's doable. If you can turn this place into a recording studio."

"I suppose it's *possible.*"

"Good."

Even though Jack Wiener insisted it wasn't ideal, Griffin wanted to sell and was coming down on the price. The business was doing well. Sales from "Maybellene" alone would cover the costs of renovating the place. Before they got back to Cottage Grove, Leonard and Phil had made up their minds.

The next step was telling Revetta that he'd just bought a building.

He had recently moved his family to Glencoe. It was a milestone for Leonard, to be a suburbanite and give Revetta the home of her dreams. They had a swimming pool in the back and the kids all had their own bedrooms. It did something for him each time he made the drive from the city and pulled into their long driveway.

Revetta's thirty-fifth birthday was in two days, but he figured now was the time to give her the jewelry. He'd bought it for her after he'd put in the offer on the new space. Gifts first and then he'd tell her about the 2120 building.

He walked her into the living room, which was bigger than their first apartment. He sat her down and handed her three gift-wrapped boxes.

"Leonard" — her face lit up — "what did you do?"

"I couldn't wait till your birthday. Go on. Open 'em. This one first." He tapped the long flat box on top.

She worked her way through the wrapping paper and looked at the lid. Leonard could be dense at times and he didn't realize he'd made a mistake until her expression sagged when she saw that it came from Saks Fifth Avenue.

"So, I see you've been shopping again." She raised an eyebrow as she lifted the lid. She didn't say anything more as she fingered back the tissue paper and lifted up the necklace, letting the diamonds and gold chain shimmer, catching the light.

"Well," he said, "what do you think?"

"It's lovely." But she wasn't smiling as she set the necklace back inside the box.

"What's the matter? Don't you like it?"

"You shouldn't have done that."

"What are you talking about? It's your birthday."

"I meant you shouldn't have done *that*." She pointed to the top of the box.

Leonard sighed, planted his elbows on his knees.

"Besides, this is the last thing you should be spending money on. Especially right now. I talked to Sheva. I know about the building."

He looked up. "Fuckin' Phil. He tells her everything."

"She's his *wife*. He's supposed to tell her everything. How could you have gone and bought that building without even discussing it with me first?"

"Why — so you could tell me not to do it, tell me it's too much money, that we just bought this house and now's not the right time?"

"You know, you could learn a thing or two from your kid brother."

"Yeah, like what?"

"Like how to be a father, for one. He works plenty hard, but he's still there for his family."

"And I'm not?"

"Lenny, when was the last time you went on vacation with us? Phil takes us with his family down to Miami because you're always working. When was the last time you spent any time with Susie? She's starved for your attention. So is Elaine. And the only reason Marshall wants to work at the label is so he can be near you. And now you're buying this new building and I can hear it already, you're gonna have to work longer, harder because of your overhead. When does it stop, Leonard? When is enough *enough*?"

He dropped his head, his hands clasped behind his neck. "I wanted to do something nice for you," he said.

"You want to do something for me? Take these back to Saks. I don't want them." She got up and left the room. She didn't even bother to unwrap the other two boxes.

Leonard would never return the jewelry. He couldn't. What would Shirley think? He left them in the bottom drawer of his dresser and over time forgot they were even there.

FORTY:
"THE SKY IS CRYING"

LEEBA

Leeba and Leonard walked through the new building at 2120 South Michigan Avenue. The workers were gone for the day and it was just the two of them inside. He showed her the first floor and took her up one of the two staircases that led to a bigger space on the second floor.

"Watch your step," he said as they traversed the sawhorses and ladders, the toolboxes and piles of drywall stacked up in the middle of the floor. "And this is where the studio's gonna go," he said. "Well? What do you think?"

Nothing had been built out yet, but still Leeba could see the possibilities. "This is going to be wonderful."

He walked over and put his arm around her. "Can you believe it?"

"You've come a long way, Leonard." She rested her head on his shoulder and together they stood amidst the dust and the exposed

470

wires and took it all in. Sometimes they got so caught up in the day-to-day of the business that their friendship got pushed to the side, but he was still the closest thing she'd ever had to a big brother. "I'm proud of you," she said. "I really am."

"Remember that day on Maxwell Street when I told you I bought a record company?"

"I thought you were crazy." She laughed. "But look at you now."

"Not too shabby for a little Jew boy *putz* from Poland, huh?"

"Not too shabby at all."

They both grew quiet for a moment. Leeba was remembering the early days when it was just Leonard, Evelyn and herself. To think he didn't even know what he was doing back then, and yet, along with Phil, they'd built this company by taking the sound of the Mississippi delta and electrifying it. Music would never be the same and in large part it was because of them.

"So let me ask you," she said, "after all that you've accomplished, are you happy?"

"I'm tired is what I am." He laughed. "C'mon, let's get a cup of coffee."

He locked up the building and they went across the street to Blatt's Restaurant in the New Michigan Hotel. A big sign outside read "Next to Home It's Blatt's."

"I have a feeling we're gonna be spending a lot of time in here," Leonard said as he slipped into a booth toward the back.

They each ordered a coffee and talked about Revetta and his parents. They talked about her family and she said how much she missed them.

"They'll come around," said Leonard. "Red's a good man." He shook a Lucky Strike from his pack and lit it. "He was a real talent, too. I still feel like shit about what happened."

"You? What about me? It was my fault." Leeba circled her hands around her coffee cup. "He's still giving James guitar lessons and he never says a word — not one single word — about not being able to play anymore." She thought about the two of them, her boys, and she smiled. "Red's really great with James. And you should hear that boy play. I hope he gets a chance to do something with his music someday. Poor kid."

She paused and took a long drink of coffee. "They just put him in a new foster home and I think it's worse than the one before. Oh, and get this — he was complaining about a toothache so finally I took him to the dentist. Ten years old and he'd never been to a dentist. He had five cavities." She shook her head. "He's just getting bounced around the system and no one's looking out for him. Red finally got him going to school every day. I've been helping him with his math homework and last week he got his first A." She sighed happily, remembering how he'd rushed over to the apartment, waving his test paper.

A pained expression rose up on Leonard's face.

"What is it? What's wrong?"

He shook his head and lit another cigarette. "I was just thinking, I've never helped any of my kids with their homework. I hear you talk about this kid and I realize I don't know my children at all."

By the time Leeba and Leonard parted ways outside of Blatt's, it had started drizzling and the temperature had dropped. She was wearing a heavy coat for the first time that fall and found a pair of gloves she'd thought she'd lost stuffed inside the pockets.

She rode the El home and before she reached the apartment the drizzle turned to rain. Out of habit she grimaced at the thought of walking Sophie in such weather. Then she remembered there was no Sophie anymore. She hated coming home to a quiet apartment, painfully aware each time she fit the key in the lock that Sophie wasn't on the other side of the door, scratching, yelping, tail thwacking against the wall.

Red had another NAACP meeting that night and Leeba didn't want to be alone. She called Aileen, but there was no answer. They used to talk every day; now it was more like once a week, if she was lucky.

She got herself a glass of wine and turned on the television set. *The Jack Benny Program* was rolling on a screen of static snow until she adjusted the rabbit ears and stabilized the picture. She curled up on the davenport and tucked her feet up beneath her.

It was pouring out now. Streaks of lightning lit up the sky outside the window as sheets of rain came down sideways. Leeba heard someone out in the hallway and her heart clenched. With Sophie gone she feared another threatening note would be slipped under the door, another rock would be thrown through their window. She rushed to the door and looked through the peephole. There was Golda, a puddle of rainwater collecting at her feet.

Golda! Leeba pulled open the door. "Are you all right? What are you doing here?"

Golda stepped inside, shaking off her umbrella and bringing the cold dampness in with her. It was the first time her sister had been to her place and Leeba watched her looking around, as if to say, *So this is where you live, huh?*

"What are you doing here?" Leeba asked again.

"It's Mama," she said and, with irritating nonchalance, added, "We thought you should know she's in the hospital."

"What?" A jolt shot through Leeba's body. "What's wrong with her?"

"It's her knees."

"Oh." It was just her knees. Leeba relaxed some.

"She finally went to the doctor."

"I told her he could give her something for the arthritis."

Golda's beautiful face turned brittle and suddenly the detached, blasé air she'd come in with was replaced with genuine anguish. "It's not arthritis."

"Bursitis? A pinched nerve?"

Golda shook her head and glanced up, her eyes now wet. She began to cry into her hands.

Leeba rubbed her sister's back awkwardly. "It's okay. Calm down."

"It's not okay. It's cancer. Bone cancer. It's metastasized. It's spread everywhere."

Leeba wasn't sure she heard right. The lights began to pulse and her stomach dropped. She didn't feel grounded to anything. "Is she dying?" Leeba heard her voice crack.

"She was getting better," said Golda. "We thought she was improving, but —" She paused and shook her head. "She's taken a turn. Aunt Sylvie thought you ought to at least know what's going on."

"How long have *you* all known about this?"

Golda shrugged, produced a handkerchief from her pocketbook. "About a month or so."

Leeba's eyes flashed wide. She'd spoken to

her father and Aunt Sylvie several times and neither one had said a word. "And you're just *now* telling me?"

"Mama didn't want us to say anything to you."

"And why is that?" Leeba felt kicked in the gut. "I'm still her daughter."

Golda looked at her, cold and spiteful. "Why do you think? Mama wants nothing to do with you and your *schwartze.*"

"His name is Red. And he's my husband."

Golda dismissed that, waving it off. "Just tell me one thing — when did you become such a nigger lover?"

Leeba's hand went up so fast she didn't realize she'd slapped her sister until she felt the stinging in her palm.

Golda glared at her, stunned, a red print rising up on her cheek. "You have no idea what you did to Mama when you married that man. She's sick over it. You're the reason she got cancer."

Now Leeba felt as if she were the one smacked across the face.

Her sister's eyes narrowed with spite. "There — I said it. No one wanted to say it to your face, but it's the truth. We all think so." Golda grabbed her umbrella and yanked open the door. "And don't bother going to the hospital. Mama doesn't want you there."

Before Leeba could even respond, Golda stormed out.

■ ■ ■ ■

The next morning despite what Golda had said, Leeba went to Mount Sinai Hospital. The smell of antiseptic hit her as she stepped inside. Walking down the corridor searching for her mother's room she caught glimpses of other patients in their beds, their ill-fitting hospital gowns exposing a shoulder, a buttocks, a thigh.

When she finally entered her mother's room she had to stifle a gasp. There she was, the once fierce and mighty looking tiny and defenseless, eyes shut, sleeping in a railed bed, hooked up to tubes and machines that beeped, compressed, flashed.

Her family was there, looking just as shocked to see her. Her aunt and uncle were there, too. Aunt Sylvie was sitting up close to the bed; her father was seated on the opposite side. His chair screeched against the floor as he got up and came over to Leeba. She was numb and would later remember the tears in his eyes, the feel of his embrace.

Aunt Sylvie came to her side, too. "I'm sorry, honey," was all she said as she squeezed Leeba's hand.

Uncle Moishe barely glanced up from his newspaper and Ber said hello, but Golda wouldn't even give her that much. Leeba could feel the judgment coming off them and she knew that they really did blame her for her mother's cancer.

No one spoke to her, or to each other. Instead they watched her mother sleep. Leeba didn't know what to do. She stood awkwardly off to the side. Nurses came and went. Doctors were paged over the intercom system. The sounds of the monitors and other machines beeping and buzzing were maddening. Before long Leeba had figured out which one was her mother's blood pressure, her heart rate, her oxygen level. From time to time the smell of antiseptic became overpowering and Leeba felt like she couldn't breathe.

At one point, without warning, her mother stirred and Leeba rushed to her side, leaned over the railing and reached for her hand. "It's Leeba, Mama. I'm here," she said, with a gentle squeeze. The skin on the back of her mother's hand was paper-thin and badly bruised from IVs and where they'd drawn blood.

Her mother opened her eyes, looked at Leeba and said one word: "Golda."

But Golda, her perfect daughter, was out in the hallway, arguing with Ber. Leeba overheard snippets: Ber was spending too much time at work. Golda was spending too much money. Golda said she knew Ber was having an affair. Ber denied it. Leeba's father sat in the corner, pretending not to hear, reading the newspaper and fiddling with the venetian blinds.

"Mama," she tried again. "It's me, Leeba. Mama, I'm —" She wasn't sure what she was going to say and it didn't matter because her mother pulled her hand away with surprising strength and winced, calling out for Golda.

Golda must have heard her and came rushing back into the room. "Look at what you've done," she said to Leeba. "You've got her all agitated. This is exactly why we didn't want you here. I told you not to come. Go," she ordered. "Leave. Just go already."

Leeba felt like a monster watching Golda trying to calm her mother down, saying, "It's okay, Mama. She's leaving. It's okay."

Her father came and stood by her side. "Maybe it is best for you to go," he said with tears misting up his eyes.

"We'll let you know if there's any change," Aunt Sylvie promised, her hand on Leeba's back as she coaxed her to the door.

Leeba felt so dismissed. So excluded. She couldn't keep from crying on the El. Other passengers looked on; one even asked if she was okay. Leeba nodded, trying to compose herself. A moment later another burst of tears flowed down her cheeks. Her family was never going to accept her, let alone Red. And if her own family wouldn't, who would?

When Red came home that night she was sitting on the davenport in the dark. He turned on the lamp and she looked at him through a veil of tears. "I can't do this anymore," she said. "It's too hard."

"Do what?" He hadn't even taken off his coat yet. He sat down next to her, thumbing away her tears. "Tell me. What's too hard?"

"This," she said, indicating him and her. "I love you, I do, but it's just too hard." She told him what had happened at the hospital with her family. "I feel like the whole world is against us."

"We knew this was gonna be tough," he said, trying to soothe her.

"We get threatening notes under our door, rocks thrown through our window. They killed our dog. They stabbed you. What's next?"

"So we'll move to a different neighborhood."

"Oh, Red, there is no neighborhood for people like us. And after what happened today with my family — I can't take it anymore. I love you, but maybe we don't belong together."

"Don't say that." He cupped her face in his hands and made her look him in the eye. "We can fight this. We have to. Why do you think I'm going to all those meetings? This is about our future. It's one of the reasons why I'm getting so involved, and it's time you did, too."

■ ■ ■ ■

The following night Leeba went with Red to a meeting of a group called CORE, the Congress of Racial Equality. It was held in the basement of Hutchinson Commons at the University of Chicago, a small room set up with rows of folding chairs to accommodate the fifty or so men and women who attended, most of them college students. Leeba was surprised to see so many whites there. She'd been expecting mostly Negroes. And she was even more surprised to see so many other mixed couples.

A man with dark brown skin and a full, round face that defied his slender build stood in front of the room and welcomed everyone. He was well-dressed, in a handsome suit and tie. He set a leather briefcase down on the table at his side.

After Red and Leeba took their seats in the back of the room he began to speak. He chose his words thoughtfully and was charismatic. Leeba noticed how everyone, including herself, had inched forward in their chairs as if to get closer.

"Everybody thinks that segregation and discrimination are just problems down South," said the man. "But we know for a fact that our brothers and sisters face that kind of racism and hatred every single day right here in Chicago."

Leeba's eyes grew wide as she soaked it all in. Though Red had told her about the meetings she hadn't expected the speaker's words to resonate so clearly with her own situation.

"We see it in the school system. We see it in the job market. In the housing market. This is no way for a civil society to exist and we are here to put an end to segregation and discrimination. And I'll tell you something else. Everyone's saying that it's Chicago — not Atlanta, not Jackson, not Memphis — it's Chicago that is the most important city when it comes to effecting change in race relations . . . We can't afford to waste time complaining about how we've been wronged," said the man. "We need to focus on the future, on what is to come. What we together can make happen."

With that, the speech was over and everyone began to clap and cheer. Looking around at the room of white and black faces, Leeba was overcome with a visceral sense of belonging and being part of something greater than herself, greater than the rejection of her family, greater than the injustice she and Red had suffered ever since they'd been together.

After the CORE meeting another mixed couple, Wendell and Yolanda, invited Leeba and Red to join them and some others for coffee. There they were, four couples, and instead of boy, girl, boy, girl, it was colored, white, colored, white, up and down the table.

Wendell and Yolanda had been married a little over a year. He said the first time he brought Yolanda home to meet his family was the last time. "They were an embarrassment," he said. "I haven't spoken to any of them since."

Another woman, Janice, told them her parents had had her institutionalized for six months because of her Negro boyfriend. Another couple said their car tires had been slashed and that they'd found *Go back to Africa* spray-painted across their front door.

The more stories they shared, the more Leeba realized that everyone in a mixed relationship had at least one relative who wasn't speaking to them and all of them had been victims of vandalism or more violent crimes. It struck her that their struggles were not unique. She and Red were no longer alone and she was grateful that she'd found people to commiserate with. But it was bittersweet to think that she felt more at home with them than with her own family.

Forty-One:
"Dust My Broom"

RED

Red looked out the front window at the snow coming down. No sign of James. Red was concerned. They had a lesson that day and it wasn't like him to be late.

Red overheard Leah talking on the phone with her aunt about her mother. It sounded like she was home from the hospital and Red could sense the hope in Leah's voice when she asked if she could come see her mother. She asked her aunt that same question every time they spoke.

"But I just want to see her," Leah said. "I won't stay long."

Red looked at his wife, sitting at the kitchen table, feet curled beneath her, clutching the phone, her eyes squeezed shut, as if to keep from crying. Her tears fell anyway as she hung up the phone and a rush of guilt flooded him. He was the reason she couldn't go see her mama.

He couldn't look at her; it was killing him.

He turned back to the window and finally there was James, coming up the walkway with Stella in his hand. It was bitter cold that day and snowing and the kid was wearing nothing but a flimsy coat with half the buttons missing. No scarf, no hat.

"Where have you been?" asked Red when he opened the door.

James looked at him glassy eyed, his teeth chattering. "My head hurts." James set Stella aside, leaning her up against the wall, and rubbed his temples. "My throat's all scratchy, too."

Leah came over and felt his forehead, first with her hand and then with her cheek. "You're burning up." She rushed into the bathroom and Red heard the squeak of her opening the medicine cabinet. She came back with a thermometer and a bottle of aspirin. "Get him a glass of water," she said to Red and she shook down the thermometer, checked the reading and placed it under James's tongue. He tried to say something but she stopped him. "Just sit still."

When she removed the thermometer James said, "I gotta get on with my lesson."

"You, young man, are getting straight into this bed. You've got a hundred and two fever."

Red brought him the glass of water and Leah took over. She gave James aspirin and bundled him up under the covers, but even so, James was still shivering. She instructed

Red to get an extra blanket from the hall closet and when he came back into the bedroom, James was already drifting off to sleep. Leah sat beside him, stroking his forehead.

She met Red's gaze as he stood in the doorway, a blanket in his hands. She got up and took it from him and returned to James's side, smoothing the quilt over him. "We don't have a phone number for his foster parents," she whispered. "All we have is the street address. We need to let them know he's here with us. Will you go and tell them? I don't trust them to take care of him right now."

Red bundled up and walked over to the Macks', James's foster family's house. He hadn't been there before and he noticed the shutters were barely hanging on and the gutters weren't in much better shape. The walkway was snow covered and he saw a single set of footsteps leading from the sidewalk to the door. There was mail stuffed in the box that looked like it had been accumulating for a while.

He tried the buzzer, but it didn't work so he knocked instead, looking through the windows alongside the door. The lights were out, but he could see there were dishes lying around, shoes kicked off, an empty whiskey bottle on a table.

Red knocked again and finally a porch light came on and an elderly woman in a housecoat came to the door. Red explained that James was sick and would be staying with them tonight. The woman just nodded. He couldn't tell if she understood him or not. She had a small box with some knobs hanging off a strap about her neck, attached to her hearing aids.

"Are the Macks home?" asked Red. "Can I speak with them?"

The woman nodded, closed the door and turned off the porch light.

As he walked along, Red thought about that poor boy living with those people and how Leeba had been more of a mama to him than any of his foster mothers, probably more than his own grandmother had been.

When Red came back to the apartment he found James still asleep and a rich aroma coming from the kitchen. Leah was in there making chicken soup for James, cooking chopped onions, celery and carrots. Something about walking into that apartment and knowing James was there with her, safe and being cared for, was exactly the way it should be. It was what that boy needed — what they needed, too.

Without giving it much more thought than that, Red turned to Leah and said, "Let's adopt him."

"What?" She turned, her spoon paused in midair.

"I mean it. James needs a home. He needs

love and we can give him that. Maybe since we can't have a child of our own, God brought us James."

Leah looked at him, barely blinking.

"Well? Aren't you going to say anything?"

She set the spoon down and went to him, burying her face in his chest.

"Is that a yes?" he asked.

She couldn't speak. All she could do was nod.

The next day Red was on the assembly line, gluing cork to soles. He'd slept on the floor the night before and Leah had taken the davenport so they could give James the bed. He kept wondering why they hadn't thought about adopting him a long time ago. The idea of being a father was nothing new to Red. He'd been a father figure for James from the start, but this would make it official. Besides, it was better for the boy, too.

Red was lost in thought and accidentally glued two corks to the same sole. He'd been at the Moore Brothers' Shoe Factory for three years and hated every single day. It was a miserable place. Between the glue fumes and the noise from the stitching machines, the conveyor belts and the giant fans, not to mention the racists that ran the place, Red left every day not wanting to go back. It wasn't hard work, but it was exhausting just the same. The plain nothingness of it was what wore him out. Red felt as if he were wasting away there, one day bleeding into the next. He was always on the lookout for something else, but all the jobs available to Negroes were the same: factory jobs, kitchen help, janitors, drivers. All his life he'd been a musician. That was all he knew and that had been taken away from him. If he couldn't use his talent anymore, then at least let him use his mind to make his way. He didn't want to grow old on that assembly line, but he couldn't see a way out for himself.

When it was break time, Red got the newspaper from his locker and found a quiet place to read. He sat right down on the cement floor and leaned up against the cool brick wall. It was December but felt hotter than August inside that factory. He started reading the *Tribune*. He preferred the *Defender,* but the boss man didn't appreciate seeing a Negro paper with headlines like: "NAACP Say Jim Crow Laws Must Go."

Red was reading an article when he felt the jolt of someone kicking his foot. "Back to work, boy." Red looked up. Billy Moore was standing over him, red faced, gut hanging over his belt, hands planted on his hips. Just the very sight of this man agitated Red. Since he'd started getting involved with things like CORE and the Urban League it was getting harder to take the kind of abuse this guy loved dishing out. Something bigger than this man's bigotry was under way. Red could feel it. Somewhere out there was a man demanding to be served at a lunch counter, another daring to drink from a "White" water fountain, a woman refusing to give up her seat on a bus, a young boy determined to get a better education at a white school. It was like thunder building in the distance, growing louder and bolder by the day.

"I said get back to work."

Red glanced at the clock above the lockers. "I still got five minutes." He picked up his newspaper again.

"Back to work or I'll dock your pay. You hear?"

Red drew a deep breath, trying to hold his temper.

"I said, you hear?"

"I hear you just fine," Red said in a measured tone.

"Then speak up." Billy Moore kicked Red's foot again. "I won't have no uppity Negroes workin' here."

Red shot up, towering over the man, and he saw that Moore was scared. He should have been, too, because Red wanted to deck him. He was shaking to control himself, knowing the last thing he needed was an arrest for assaulting a white man. "Well, then," said Red with full restraint, "I guess you'll have one less Negro to put up with."

He turned and walked out of the factory

and in a way it reminded him of the day he quit his job at the brickyard. Only then he'd had a record on the radio, and this time he had nothing. But maybe that wasn't really the case. Back then, he'd walked out because of pride at having heard his record. Maybe today he walked out based on pride in himself.

It felt good, even as the winds were howling and the full force of winter's cold chill was all around. He realized that in his haste to leave Moore's, he'd forgotten his gloves in his locker. Snow was blowing and whipping around as he turned up the collar on his coat and stuffed his hands inside his pockets. He was making his way to the El platform and while waiting for the light to change he looked over and saw Al Benson. The Old Swingmaster was dressed in a cashmere overcoat, a black fedora and spit-shined Stacy Adams shoes. Red was painfully aware of his shabby coat, his workman's boots. He started back the other way, hoping to go unnoticed.

"Red Dupree! Is that you?"

Red froze, shoulders to his ears, as he turned around.

"Where you been, man?" asked Benson. "Haven't seen you around in ages. How's that hand of yours?"

"Not so good." He held it up so that the scars showed.

"Damn shame is what that is." Benson

shook his head. "So what are you doing with yourself these days?"

"Right now, I suppose I'm trying to find work. Believe it or not, I just walked off my job. Couldn't take it anymore."

"I know how that goes. Yep, I sure do." Benson rocked back on his heels. "So you're looking for work now, huh? You need a job?" He reached into his pocket and handed Red his business card. "C'mon down to the station. I'll put you to work."

"I don't know anything about radio."

"You don't need to know nothing to sweep floors and make deliveries, do you?"

Red forced a small smile. "I've been *on* the radio, man. I can't go from that to sweeping floors."

"Pride won't feed a man. Remember that. You got yourself a wife now, don't you?"

Red nodded.

"Probably be planning on starting a family soon. Gonna need a job to provide for them and I need the help."

The light changed and Benson held out his hand and gave Red a strong shake. As he crossed the street Red thought about what the Swingmaster had just said and he realized that without a job he'd probably ruined their chances of adopting James. Benson was now about a half block away and Red took off after him. He caught up with him at the next light.

"I'll take it," he said, puffing, trying to catch his breath. "I'll take the job. And thank you."

On Red's first day he arrived at the radio station remembering the last time he'd been at WGES. That was when he was Red Dupree the bluesman. The Swingmaster had had him on his show to talk about his records and fans had lined up outside the station hoping to meet him and get his autograph.

Now he was just another man reporting for work. Benson showed him where to hang his coat and walked him into John Dyer's office. Dyer was the general manager and Red had met him before, but the man didn't seem to remember. Or if he did, he didn't care who Red Dupree once was. He just looked at Red through the smudges on his thick bifocals, handed him a broom and told him to sweep the floors.

"And when you finish that you can start cleaning the john."

Red thought about all the forms he and Leah had been given in order to start the adoption process. Seemed like every other page he was asked to write down his employer and salary. He needed this job and so he did as he was told.

Later that morning as he was coming out of the men's room with a mop and bucket he heard a familiar voice in the lobby. His heart quickened. It was Leonard Chess. He was talking with Benson, the two of them discussing Bo Diddley's new record, "Who Do You Love?"

Red darted into the storage room, ashamed of how far he'd fallen. He couldn't bear to have Leonard see him working there, cleaning out toilets.

Even from inside the room, he could hear Leonard's booming voice. "We gotta get Bo on your show," Leonard was saying now. "And I'm counting on you, motherfucker, for heavy rotation."

Red heard Benson laughing in response just as Dyer walked into the storage room. Red quickly busied himself, stacking a couple boxes of paper clips. Dyer looked at the shelves and removed his eyeglasses, squinting at Red.

Don't fire me. Please don't fire me.

Dyer began wiping his bifocals on his necktie.

Red held his breath.

"That's good," said Dyer, gesturing to the shelf. "This place could use some organizing. I think you're gonna work out fine here, Red."

FORTY-TWO:
"I FEEL LIKE GOING HOME"

LEEBA

The day after Christmas, Leonard and Phil took advantage of a slow business week to organize the move from Cottage Grove to 2120 South Michigan. Leeba had been putting in fourteen-hour days packing up files and master tapes, sorting through old contracts and royalty statements. Phil had told her to take the day off and she'd protested, but he'd insisted.

Schools were closed for Christmas vacation and James was at the apartment with her that day. He was in the living room, restringing Red's old Stella, sitting next to the Christmas tree. The tree was puny, a runt, as Red called it. Though Leeba loved the colorful bulbs and sparkling tinsel and lights, she was conflicted about having a Christmas tree — even a tiny one — in her home. She had put a Star of David on the top and hoped that God wouldn't strike her dead for it. She hadn't even bothered with a menorah that year. The ritual of lighting the candles held no meaning for Red or James. She wasn't sure it held any significance for her, either, anymore.

She was admiring the tree as James plucked the low E string. It was sharp and he was tuning it when the phone rang. She was hoping it would be Aileen. They hadn't talked at all over Christmas. She and Red had invited her for dinner, but she never showed. Leeba didn't know what was going on with her these days.

Leeba picked up the phone mounted to the wall in the kitchen and as soon as she heard Aunt Sylvie's voice, her heart stopped. Her aunt always called once a week with an update on her mother. They'd just spoken the day before. Everything had been fine. Why was she calling back so soon?

"Oh God," Leeba said. "What's wrong? What's happened?" She braced herself, leaning against the kitchen counter, her legs already turning to rubber.

"Relax. Everything's fine," said Aunt Sylvie. "I'm only calling because I thought you'd like to know that your mother was asking about you."

"She was?"

"And don't you dare tell her I said so. But yes, she was asking."

Leeba felt a flicker of disbelief followed by a flood of gratitude. God had heard her prayers; He'd been listening all those nights when she'd cried, begging for her mother's forgiveness.

"I think now would be a good time to go see her."

The next morning Leeba was there. She was nervous, not knowing what she'd say or where to begin. As she entered the apartment she took a moment to look around: the photographs on the walls, an umbrella leaning in the corner, her father's slippers just inside the doorway. It was all as she remembered it. Nothing there had changed and yet Leeba's entire world was different.

She inched inside and found her mother in the living room, sitting in her favorite chair watching TV. She'd lost weight — her housecoat was huge on her — but aside from that she looked far better than she had when Leeba had visited her at the hospital six weeks before.

Her mother's face lit up when she saw Leeba standing in the doorway, but she quickly caught herself and fixed her eyes on the *Today* show. She was crazy about Dave Garroway.

"Gutn morgn, Mama," Leeba said tentatively, taking another step closer.

Nothing.

"Gutn morgn," she said again, louder this time. *"Mama. Hela?"*

Still nothing. She'd come here to make peace, but her mother's disregard incensed her. Leeba cut in front of the TV. "*Mama, ikh —*"

"*Shah —*" Her mother held up her hands.

"What do you mean, *shah* — you can't understand what they're saying anyway. How long are you going to punish me? I haven't done anything wrong."

Her mother's eyes flashed wide. "You go and marry a *schwartze* and you don't think you've done anything —"

"Enough!" Leeba cried. "What do you know about my husband? You've never even given Red a chance."

"And why should I? Where did I fail with you? Your sister would never have done something like that."

Leeba slapped her hands to her sides. "Quit comparing me to Golda. You've been doing that to me my whole life. Do you even know who I am? Do you even care?" Leeba was shaking she was so angry. "I know you hated that I was Papa's favorite. I didn't need to be *your* favorite, too. I just wanted you to love me."

Her mother's mouth dropped open and Leeba saw the color leave her face, saw the lines around her eyes and mouth deepen. And then her mother did something she almost never did. She cried. Leeba was shocked. She had broken something in her mother and she instantly regretted it.

She was sobbing now. "You were my first-born. My first. There's something in a mother's heart for her first. When I carried you, I had such hopes for you. The first time I held you, I saw myself in your eyes. How can you think I didn't love you?"

Leeba swallowed hard. Her mother had never spoken to her like this.

"I know I may not have always been a perfect mother. I know I was hard on you — harder than I should have been. But the one thing I know for certain is that this isn't the life I wanted for you." Her mother squeezed her eyes shut, as if trying to stop the tears.

"But it's the life *I* want. I *chose* it." Leeba went to her side and reached for her mother's hand, but the fingers went stiff as she formed a fist, pulling away.

"Oh, Mama —"

She shook her head. "I can't accept him. I just can't."

"Then at least accept me. Please, Mama?" By now Leeba was crying, too. She reached over and hugged her, but her mother didn't respond. "I didn't do this to hurt you. I love you. But I love him, too. Just tell me you'll forgive me. Please, Mama? I need that much."

Her mother couldn't say the words. Leeba knew she couldn't, but she felt her mother's arms open and pull her in. And that was enough. That had to be enough because she knew it was all she'd get.

Leeba stared into her compact and dabbed her eyes. It still looked like she'd been crying an hour later as her El car approached her stop. She touched up her mascara, snapped the mirror shut and walked from the train to the offices on Cottage Grove one last time. She went inside, stepping around the boxes in the hallway.

After months of remodeling the new space, 2120 South Michigan Avenue was ready for Chess. The guys — Muddy, Wolf, Walter, Chuck, Bo and some of the others — were all hanging around the office while they packed things up. Mimi Cooke was there. So was Aileen, who was in a bad way. Her lipstick was smeared on her front teeth, her hair was matted down and her dress looked like she'd slept in it.

"We missed you at Christmastime," said Leeba, giving her a hug.

"Yeah, sorry I didn't make it over." Her eyes were locked on Muddy, who was chatting with Mimi.

"I just saw my mama," said Leeba. "I think she might actually be coming around." When Aileen didn't react to that at all, she gave up trying to have a conversation with her. Aileen knew how miserable Leeba had been about her mother's rejection. But Aileen was so focused on Muddy she didn't hear a word Leeba said.

Aileen was clearly there only to keep an eye on him and Mimi, unlike the other guys who had come to pay one last visit to the place where they'd gotten their start. Some of these guys had recorded their first demos in that makeshift studio. Some had heard their voices over a set of speakers for the first time inside those very walls. Leeba thought about Red and the day he first sang "Cross Road Blues." His records used to be on the wall next to Muddy's and Wolf's and Little Walter's. Now his weren't even up and the others were on the bottom below the Chuck Berry and Bo Diddley records that were framed with little gold plaques next to them.

Phil went to a storage closet and pulled out some old Aristocrat records from Tom Archia and Andrew Tibbs. "Remember this?" he'd say, holding up a 78, or a copy of *Billboard* that mentioned them, or some old dusty photographs of Leonard and Evelyn, smiling. *Smiling!* Leeba never remembered the two of them doing anything other than arguing.

While Phil pulled plaques and photographs off the walls, Leonard stayed hunkered down in his office. Phil said he was finalizing numbers for the move, trying to straighten out a mix-up with the telephone company.

Leeba stuck her head inside his doorway. Leonard was at his desk, the phone cradled between his ear and shoulder. "Are you on hold?" she asked.

"Motherfuckers. They say they don't have the order for the additional lines."

"Why don't you have your secretary do that?"

He shook his head. He looked pale and washed out, with gray circles under his eyes.

"Are you hungry?" she asked.

"No." He switched the phone to the other ear.

"Well, you need to eat something. You drink any more coffee, you're going to burn a hole in your stomach. What do you want? A bagel? A Danish?"

"I don't want anything. I'm not hungry."

"You're such a grouch."

"Can't you see I'm busy?" He held the receiver away from his ear, looking at it like that would shorten the wait.

"How about some juice?"

"Out." He pointed toward the door.

"Okay, I'm going, I'm going. Jeez." Leeba held up her hands in surrender and backed out of his office. She went up front and took food orders from the rest of the guys and headed across the street to Deutsch's one last time. It was snowing outside, typical of Chicago in December. She bundled up for the short walk.

She placed the order and looked around at all the holiday decorations. She saw where someone had stuck a finger in the artificial snow on the window and spelled out *Noel*. She supposed it didn't matter. In another couple of days, right after New Year's, all the garland and bows would be coming down anyway. Her only wish for the New Year was to be awarded custody of James. It had been a month since they'd filed all the paperwork with the Illinois Department of Public Health — the division that handled all adoptions. She was told it was a lengthy process and the wait was agony for them.

The order came up fast and fifteen minutes later she was back with bags of food, buttered Kaiser rolls, egg sandwiches, bagels and Danishes. After she'd handed out everyone's orders she took a sandwich back to Leonard's office.

"Okay, whether you want it or not . . ." She pushed his office door open. He wasn't there. She went back out to the others. "Hey, where'd he go? Where's Leonard?"

"What do you mean, where's Leonard?" Phil unwrapped the waxed paper from his egg sandwich. "He's in his office."

Leeba went back and stepped inside. No, he wasn't there. She heard the others out front reminiscing. As she looked at the photos on Leonard's wall, the records stacked on the credenza, a strange sensation crept up on her, starting at the crown of her head and settling into the pit of her stomach.

"Leonard? Lenny?" She inched farther inside his office and that was when she noticed the coffee running off the lip of the desk, dripping steadily onto the floor. His cup was overturned. A cigarette was resting in the ashtray with two inches of unbroken ash.

"Leonard? Leonard!"

She rushed forward and gasped, letting out a shriek. His wingtips were sticking out from under the desk. She sprinted around to the other side and there he was, lying on the floor, his face covered in perspiration, his hair plastered to his scalp. He wasn't breathing.

"Phil — come here. Quick. Somebody call an ambulance!"

■ ■ ■ ■

FOUR:
1957–1964

■ ■ ■ ■

FORTY-THREE:
"BLUES BEFORE SUNRISE"

LEEBA

Leeba watched the pallbearers lower the casket into the ground. The dirt they shoveled on top rained down the sides and into the grave. As clouds overtook the sun, casting long shadows, she glanced up. Muddy, Walter, all five members of the Moonglows, Howlin' Wolf, Willie Dixon, Jimmy Rogers, Chuck Berry, Sunnyland Slim and Otis Spann kept their heads bowed, their yamulkes in place. Each was there for her, to pay their respects to a woman they didn't even know. What would her mother say if she knew there were almost as many Negroes at her funeral as there were Jews?

Leonard was still in the hospital recovering from his heart attack, but Phil was there along with Sheva and Revetta. Leeba stood clutching her father's hand, noticing that he'd put his wristwatch on upside down. That was the sort of thing her mother would have caught and corrected. The face of his Timex upside down broke her heart. She turned away and there was Red standing on her other side. Golda was incensed that he was there, but Red was her husband and he belonged there.

As they lowered the casket into the grave she heard Aunt Sylvie and Uncle Moishe crying. She herself still hadn't cried for her mother. Anger, frustration, sadness, yes, but tears? They just would not come.

Her mother had been improving and Leeba was certain — they all were — that she had beaten the cancer. And then, out of the blue, just one week after Leonard suffered his heart attack, Leeba got the call from Golda.

Her mother was already gone by the time Leeba made it back to Lawndale. And by then the mechanics of funeral planning had already been set in motion. Burial arrangements, meeting with the rabbi, deciding who should give the eulogy, did they have enough pallbearers — Uncle Moishe couldn't do it. Eli would, and of course Ber was there. What about Avrom. *Avrom? Was Golda out of her mind?* Next there was the matter of where to sit shiva. Why, Golda's big house, of course.

As they were leaving the cemetery, Aileen came up to Leeba and put her arm about her waist. "What's your sister gonna do now when all these Negroes end up in her living room?"

They found out later that afternoon, when

Golda relegated the Negro mourners to the basement. Leeba, along with Phil, Sheva and Revetta, were the only whites in the room.

Red smiled and said, "Unbelievable. Golda managed to segregate her house today, didn't she?"

Leeba held up a flimsy paper plate. "God forbid she should let a Negro eat off her good china."

"Did y'all try this gel-fight fish?" asked Walter.

"It's 'gefilte,' " said Sheva. She was pregnant again, expecting her third child, and Leeba tried not to let her envy show for she did truly appreciate Sheva being there that day.

"Ga-fill-tah, huh?" Walter took another bite. "Sure is good."

"You should try the lox and creamed herring," said Willie.

"That's Jewish soul food, motherfuckers," said Phil with a laugh.

Leeba heard herself laugh, or maybe she only thought she did. She was in a fog even when her father and Aunt Sylvie came downstairs. They were the only members of her family who dared to venture to the basement where the *schwartze*s were.

Her father, in his thick Yiddish accent, addressed them all with his hands clasped, his eyes filled with sincerity. "I want to thank you for coming today. I know how much your being here means to Leeba. She's blessed to have such good friends."

When her father finished, Red went over and shook his hand. "I'm sorry about Mrs. Groski."

Her father's eyes misted over as he nodded, still shaking Red's hand. "I wish things had ended differently," Leeba heard him telling Red. "For all of us. She wasn't a bad woman. Just set in her ways."

"I know that. I know how hard this has been on your family," said Red. "I'm sorry about that."

The look on her father's face was one Leeba knew well. It was that thin smile and that tilt of his head that said, *All is forgiven, all is understood.*

Leeba watched as Red turned to her aunt next, offering his condolences. When he extended his hand to her, Aunt Sylvie didn't accept his gesture. Instead she reached up on her tiptoes and hugged him. Leeba's chest rose up as her heart opened wide. This was something she'd never expected to see. It was as if now that her mother was gone her father and aunt could finally let Red into their lives.

"Take care of our Leeba," she heard her aunt say. "She loves you so."

Her father and aunt stayed downstairs and visited with everyone until one by one people said their good-byes and left. It had been a long day. Leeba was drained. It was quiet now with just her and Red left in the basement.

"Thank you," she said.

"For what?"

"For talking to my father and my aunt. I know, after everything they've said and done, that couldn't have been easy."

He put his arms around her and said, "I don't have a problem with them. After all, we're — what's the Yiddish word for family again — *mishpokhe*?"

He'd pronounced it flawlessly. Leeba bit down on her lip and nodded. Then she began to laugh, until the laughter unexpectedly changed over to tears, like snow turning to rain. Red held her while she cried. Ever since her mother had passed she'd been pushing the sadness down, realizing that she'd been waiting for the right moment to break in Red's arms.

It was the end of January and they'd just finished moving into 2120. Leeba was exhausted. Her back hurt and her arms and legs ached from lifting boxes and pushing furniture around.

As she made her way up the sidewalk heading for home she thought about her mother, something she'd been doing a lot lately. She still couldn't believe she was gone. She had spent the past three weeks saying to herself, *A week ago at this time my mother was still alive . . . Two weeks ago at this time . . . Three weeks ago* . . . Sometimes when she least expected it, the grief walloped her and without warning her chest would squeeze tight as the tears escaped down her cheeks.

When Leeba arrived home that day, the mail had already been delivered, stuffed inside their mailbox. She shuffled through the envelopes: the telephone bill, the gas bill, a direct mail advertisement and . . . a letter from the Illinois Department of Public Health. Her heart began to race. She ripped open the envelope, read the first line and sank to the floor.

We regret to inform you that your request for adoption does not meet the requirements . . .

What requirements? No, they weren't rich, but they both had jobs. Red was working at WGES. She was at Chess. They could provide a stable environment for James. But the Department of Public Health didn't see it that way.

If they'd been a white couple adopting a white child or a Negro couple adopting a Negro child it would not have been an issue. Leeba crumpled up the letter and remained on the floor, shaking with anger until she felt her legs could hold her up.

One month later, at the end of February, she and Red found a bigger apartment in

Hyde Park that they could afford. It wasn't anything grand, but it was a definite step up from where they'd been living and it gave them more space. Finally an apartment big enough for a piano, and a second bedroom for James.

Maybe he couldn't officially live with them, but Leeba and Red decided that even if the state wouldn't let them adopt him, the court couldn't stop them from opening their home to him whenever he wanted to be there, and it couldn't order Leeba and Red not to love James as their own.

It was the middle of March and snowing. Leeba got off the El and walked the few blocks from Cermack to Michigan Avenue, trudging through the slush, negotiating her way around patches of ice. It wasn't even eight o'clock when Leeba stopped into Blatt's and ordered three coffees, which she took across the street to 2120.

Little Walter's Cadillac was parked right out front, smoke puttering from the exhaust. Always the first to arrive, he sat inside, smoking a cigarette, fiddling with the radio. She knocked on the window and motioned for him to follow her.

She knew Walter was still drunk from the night before and had probably just finished at some club a few hours ago. Leonard and Phil had learned the hard way that if they wanted to record with Walter they had to do it first thing in the morning. He might still be tanked, but if they didn't catch him then, he'd be passed out until it was time to get up and go to his club gig again.

"Rough night?" she asked, handing Walter his coffee.

He shook his head. "Somebody took a shot at me. You believe that shit?"

"Coming from you, yes." She handed the coffees to Walter and reached in her pocketbook for the keys. "Walter, wherever you go, someone's getting shot at."

"Yeah, but they never get me," he said, grinning.

"Thank God." She unlocked the door and flipped on the lights. The new space was a palace compared to the place on Cottage Grove. There was an impressive lobby and just beyond that were Leonard's and Phil's offices, with smaller offices down the hall from them, one of which belonged to Leeba.

Walter slumped into a chair in the lobby and drank his coffee while Leeba went down to the basement to wake Chuck Berry. A hit record on his hands and his new song "School Day" rocketing up the charts and he was sleeping on the floor at the studio. The Fairview, a roominghouse, was right next door, but Chuck didn't want to pay the ten dollars to stay there. Instead when he was in town he stayed at Chess or at Phil's house in

Highland Park, sharing a room with his son, Terry.

Chuck was curled up on a mattress, his long, lush hair tucked inside a hairnet. She doubted Elvis Presley was sleeping at Sun Records. The two of them, Chuck and Elvis, had been taking turns at the top of the R&B charts. Elvis Presley had the edge on the pop charts and Leeba wondered if that was only because he was white. Elvis's contract had recently sold to RCA for thirty-five thousand dollars. Chuck's contract could never have commanded that kind of money and all on account of the color of his skin.

"Chuck? Chuck?" She gently shook him and he rolled over onto his back. "Time to get up. Everybody'll be here soon."

"Why, thank you very kindly for the wake-up."

He was the cheeriest person in the morning. And always sober. Never touched a drop of liquor. "Here's your coffee. Just the way you like it."

"You're good to me, Miss Leah. You are good to me."

She went back upstairs to find that Idell, the receptionist, and Carri, the new secretary, were already there, the two of them hovering over a birthday cake.

"I'd get rid of that if I were you," said Leeba.

It was March 12, Leonard's fortieth birthday. And if ever there was a reason to celebrate, it would have been then, but Leonard wouldn't hear of it. He had made everyone promise: no cake, no gifts, no cards, no nothing. He didn't want to give himself a *kenahora* and tempt the gods.

And yet he tempted them every day. Despite his doctor's orders, he was back at work full-time and back to his cigarettes and coffee. He was behaving as if the heart attack had never happened. Revetta screamed at him about it. So did Leeba and Phil. It did no good.

"I mean it," said Leeba. "He'll pitch a fit if he comes in here and sees that."

After they'd served Leonard's cake to Walter, Chuck and the other office workers disposed of all the evidence, Leeba went upstairs to the second floor and turned on the lights. It was a beautiful studio with a control room that had a big picture window that looked out onto everything. She went into the separate rehearsal space just beyond the studio and sat down at the piano and began working out some glitches in a new song. She was halfway through the first verse when Aileen showed up, surprisingly on time.

"Look at you," Aileen said, dumping her pocketbook on top of the piano. "You cut your hair."

Did I? Leeba reached up and touched her curls, remembering. "About a month ago."

"You mean to tell me it's been that long since I've seen you?"

"Actually, it's been longer." She hadn't seen much of her friend since her mother's funeral.

"How's the new apartment? Keep waitin' for y'all to invite me over."

Leeba held her tongue. She had lost count of how many times she'd asked Aileen over.

"Y'all been so busy lately with the adoption and all. How's that going, anyway?"

"It's not, remember? It didn't go through. I called and told you about it."

Aileen looked confused and then put on like she was searching, trying to jog her memory. "Oh, that's right, you did tell me. But you got James living at your new place now, right?"

"We have a room for him. But no, he's not living with us. We're not his foster family." She didn't even know why she was bothering to explain. She could already see Aileen's attention drifting away.

"Do you believe it's snowing out?" Aileen reached into her pocketbook for her cigarettes. "It's supposed to be springtime." She picked a fleck of tobacco off her tongue. "You seen Muddy around here lately? I'm worried about him," she said, lighting her cigarette, hopping from subject to subject. "He's been acting all strange lately. Like he don't wanna be bothered by no one. If he don't get another hit record soon I don't know what he's gonna do."

"Well, why don't we focus on getting *you* another hit record," said Leeba, playing the opening chords of a new song she'd written, called "The One That Got Away." She'd convinced Leonard and Phil to let Aileen record it instead of Mimi Cooke. And not only because she wanted to help her friend out, but because she sincerely thought the song was better suited for Aileen's voice. "They want to record you next week."

So the two spent a couple hours rehearsing and when they emerged from the back room they found all the other artists had gathered in the office for another day at Chess Records. The musicians enjoyed hanging out there. It was like a fraternity house. They sat around playing cards or shooting the breeze through-out the day, gradually replacing their coffee with whiskey and bourbon. When they got hungry they went across the street to Blatt's and came right back and played music and waited for the numbers to post for the latest R&B charts. It seemed that the only time they left was to go to their gigs around town.

There were so many new musicians and new producers hanging around, too. On the weekends, Phil and Leonard brought their sons, Terry and Marshall, down to the studio. Sometimes Phil brought his daughter, Pam, with him before he took her to her ballet class and for lunch at the Pickle Barrel in Old

Town. There was a sense of family there, and now with her mother gone, Leeba needed that feeling of belonging more than ever. But as in any family everyone didn't always get along.

The following week they were getting ready to record Aileen's new song. Leeba was in the control booth with Leonard and Phil. The tiny room was thick with smoke from all the cigarettes going. The musicians were in the studio, tuned up and ready to record "The One That Got Away." All they needed now was Aileen. She was late and when she did finally show up she had that boozy, haven't-been-to-bed-yet look in her eyes.

"Sorry, sorry, sorry," she mumbled, popping her head into the control booth. "Couldn't be helped. Could *not* be helped. I tell y'all it just could not —"

"Just get in there and do the damn song." Leonard shook his head, disgusted.

Leeba walked her out to the studio and adjusted the mike stand for her. Aileen was teetering and at one point Leeba thought she might fall. Once she got her balance, they got started, but the session was a disaster. On the first take Aileen slurred the words. On the second take she forgot them altogether.

"Fuck." Leonard slammed his fist to the console. "She's a mess."

"Let me talk to her," said Leeba.

"You can't talk to her. She's a goddamn

junkie." He turned to Phil. "Let's get Mimi down here. We'll rehearse her this morning and lay it down this afternoon."

Everyone but Aileen cleared the room and Leeba was apologizing to the musicians as she stepped inside the studio.

Aileen lumbered over to a folding chair and practically fell into it. Her chin was on her chest, her eyes barely open. Leeba saw the fresh markings on her arm.

"Just let me rest — just for a minute," said Aileen. "And then we'll do this song. We'll do it real good."

"The session's over."

"Already?" Aileen lifted her head, tried to smile, but it seemed too much to manage. "How'd it go? How'd we do?"

Leeba slapped her hands to her thighs. Leonard was right. There was no talking to her when she was like this.

An hour later Mimi Cooke arrived at Chess and that afternoon they recorded the song that Leeba had written for Aileen.

After the session with Mimi was over, Leeba went into her office and called the Department of Public Health. Their adoption request had already been denied so she and Red had applied instead to be James's foster parents. They'd filed all the paperwork and now Leeba was getting the runaround. Finally the switchboard operator put her call through to a caseworker.

"I'm sorry, Mrs. Dupree, but it looks like they're going to reassign James to another foster home."

"But why?" Leeba heard the rustling of papers over the phone.

"Hm, let's see . . . It just says 'unsuitable.' I am sorry, Mrs. Dupree."

Leeba slammed down the phone just as Leonard came into her office.

"Easy does it there," he said.

Leeba was staring at her hand still resting on the telephone receiver. She was shaking she was so angry.

"You better do something about Aileen. She's always been off her rocker, but this new crap with the dope" — he shook his head — "it's gotta stop. She's gotta dry out."

"I know," she said, her eyes tearing up.

"Hey, c'mon now. It's okay. We'll find a way to get her off the booze and the dope."

"That's not it." She broke down and sobbed.

Leonard pulled up a chair. "Then what's with the waterworks?"

"I'm sorry." She caught the tears on the backs of her hands. "It's this whole foster parent business. They just turned us down. I don't know what more they wanted. They sent a social worker to our apartment and it was like being interrogated. They grilled us about how Red and I met, how long we'd been together, about our families, our incomes. It was like we were on a witness stand. And after all that they still denied us. I don't know what to do."

"Get yourself a lawyer and fight it."

She laughed sadly. "Easier said than done. We can't afford a lawyer."

"Maybe you can't, but I can."

"Leonard, no. I couldn't let you do that."

"Why not? You didn't get a Cadillac, did you? Consider this your Cadillac."

FORTY-FOUR:
"SEE YOU LATER, ALLIGATOR"

RED

Red stood before the shelves of records, organized by blues, jazz, country, classical, Polish, Irish and on and on. He'd been working at WGES for about a year and a half and had gone from sweeping floors and cleaning bathrooms to overseeing the record library, pulling music for the disc jockeys and helping them inside the studio.

At the moment he was having a hard time concentrating on the records he was searching for. They'd just come from meeting with that fancy lawyer that Leonard had hired for them and found out that their appeal to become foster parents had been denied. They were at the end of the road and Leah was devastated. So was Red. He felt like he'd been kicked in the gut.

He heard someone coming down the hall and looked at the clock. Ten minutes till showtime. He forced himself to focus.

Steve Daniels, the morning deejay, was

finishing up his show, playing his last song of the day, "See You Later, Alligator" by Bill Haley and His Comets. Al Benson had five minutes till airtime when Red came into the studio with a couple dozen records, all the songs the Old Swingmaster wanted to play on his R&B show: Jimmy Reed's "Honest I Do," Fats Domino's "Valley of Tears," Clarence "Frogman" Henry's "Ain't Got No Home," a few Chuck Berry and Bo Diddley hits, too. Nothing from the Wolf or Little Walter or even Muddy was in the lineup.

The last time Red saw Muddy play was almost six months ago at the Flame. It was a Saturday night, not more than a handful of folks there to see the guy that once packed theaters and concert halls. Before he went up on stage Muddy was flirting with some girl, Lucille, who looked barely old enough to be in there. Aileen stood by, watching the whole thing. She was a mess, pounding whiskey, drunk out of her mind. Muddy went up on stage, but he looked like he didn't want to be there. He hardly played that night. He sang, but aside from a lick here and there he let his sidemen carry the show, giving all the leads to Jimmy Rogers. Not long after that, Wolf — who was playing small gigs now, too — told Red that Muddy had quit playing guitar altogether. Red wondered what would have happened to his career by now if he hadn't hurt his hand. Would his music be fading like it was for his friends?

Steve Daniels grabbed his hat off the coat tree in the corner of the studio. He gave Benson a pat on the shoulder and waved goodbye to Red, who was cuing up the first record on the turntable, Bill Doggett's "Honky Tonk."

It was hot inside the studio, the August heat seeping in, penetrating the brick and outer rooms of the station. The clock was ticking down to airtime when an urgent telephone call came through for Benson. He was shaking when he hung up the phone. "I gotta get to the hospital. My wife's sick. You gotta cover the show for me," he said to Red.

"I can't do —"

"Oh yes, you can."

"Dyer won't —"

"I'll handle Dyer. I'll tell him you're covering for me. You gotta do this. Now, there's the records — you know 'em all. So you just play 'em. You talk about 'em. Read a few announcements from the sponsors. Read the news. That's all you gotta do."

Al was gone and Red was alone in the booth with three minutes till airtime. It was hotter than hell in there even with the fans going. Red's head was still reeling from the news about James. He was in no position to do this, but he had no choice. After everything Benson had done for him, Red had to at least try. He sat down in Al's chair and when the

On Air sign started blinking he froze. He was sweating, overwhelmed by the mixing board, the different buttons and that flashing sign. All he could think was, *Five thousand watts.* He was sitting before a microphone that had a reach of 5,000 watts. That was a lot of power that would carry a radio signal to a whole lot of listeners. John Dyer stood outside the booth, pounding on the glass and motioning for Red to start talking and play the record.

Red leaned forward and his first words over the air were: "Uh. Um . . ."

Dyer was going crazy on the other side of the glass, making Red more nervous than he already was. He tried to get hold of himself. All he was thinking was he didn't want to get fired. He couldn't afford to lose this job. He'd seen and listened to enough Swingmaster broadcasts. Hell, he knew what to do. He could do this. He could. He'd been on stage thousands of times. He told himself this was no different. And so, with Dyer still pounding on the glass, Red pulled the mike closer, opened his mouth and started to talk.

"This is Red Dupree sitting in today for the Old Swingmaster, who had to step away. But don't y'all worry, we've got some fine listening ahead. Kicking things off we got Bill Doggett, so sit back and enjoy . . ." He dropped the needle, turned off the mike and wiped the sweat off his brow. He was breathing heavy. Dyer had his hands on his hips, watching.

Red cued up the next record, "Over the Mountain, Across the Sea." He remembered Leah telling him what a hard time Leonard had had getting the right sound out of the singers. It was right there on his mind, so when it was time for the second record Red pulled up to the mike and said, "This is Red Dupree, sitting in for the Old Swingmaster today. Next up from Chess Records right here in Chicago we got 'Over the Mountain, Across the Sea.' And I bet you didn't know it took Johnnie and Joe over twenty-three takes in the studio to lay this song down right. So you listen and when we come back, I'll tell y'all some more stories . . ."

Red adjusted his headset and waited for the red light to start flashing. For the next record, "Long Tall Sally," Red set it up with a little story about the first time he met Little Richard. "He was touring with his band the Upsetters. Shy as can be back then. Yes, sir, shy as can be . . ." He dropped the needle and let the song play.

Turned out people liked hearing Red's behind-the-scenes tales. Some listeners, most of them women, called in asking about the new deejay with the big deep voice; others recognized the name and wanted to know if it was the same Red Dupree who'd made "Cross Road Blues." There were questions for Red about what Chuck Berry was really like and did he know the Platters. Red was just getting started and the show was over. Four hours just like that. The telephone lines were still ringing.

Red couldn't remember the last time he felt so alive. He was actually connecting with people. It was the same feeling he once had being on stage only now he had the power of radio behind him.

"You sure surprised the hell out of me," said Dyer, shaking Red's hand.

After that day, Dyer let Red sit in for other deejays now and then. It was especially challenging, though, when he filled in for the Irish or Polish deejays. He didn't know anything about that kind of music so he just played the records, kept his mouth shut.

When he wasn't on the air, or maintaining the record library, they let him read some advertising messages and deliver the news with his deep voice. The only problem was that Red thought some of the news wasn't telling the whole story. He remembered being in the booth, reading about the establishment of the Civil Rights Commission coming over the wire. He read the copy as written, but instead of turning the mike back over to the deejay, Red spoke up.

"Now, this is very interesting. It says right here that President Eisenhower has nominated six men to sit on the board of this commission. One of these six gentlemen is the former governor of Virginia — Mr. John S. Battle. And let me tell y'all something about Mr. Battle. He's a good ole Southern boy representing the segregationists, so I ask y'all, is this the kind of man we want investigating the violations of the Civil Rights Act? Y'all think a man like that isn't gonna stand in the way of a Negro's right to vote . . ."

Dyer was inside the booth slashing his finger across his throat. Red got the message and turned the mike back over to the deejay. The switchboard lit up — callers who liked what he'd said, callers who were outraged.

"You ever pull a stunt like that again and you're out, you hear me?"

Red heard him all right, but he had 5,000 watts of power behind him and he wasn't one bit sorry for what he'd said.

FORTY-FIVE:
"I'M YOUR HOOCHIE COOCHIE MAN"

LEONARD

Leonard reached over and turned up the radio on his desk. Red was on the air again that day, filling in for one of the regular jocks on WGES. He was good. Had the voice for radio, that was for sure. He was criticizing the authorities in Little Rock, Arkansas, who were fighting to stop the desegregation of a high school there. Leonard found himself agreeing with what Red was saying, but that was nothing new. Leonard usually found himself siding with Negro causes.

Phil stuck his head in Leonard's office. "*Nu?* Today already. I'm starving."

Leonard turned off the radio and followed Phil across the street to Blatt's. They always sat at the same booth, the second to the last one in the way back. All the record companies on Record Row had a booth at Blatt's. Vee-Jay had theirs, so did King Records and Brunswick. A young colored man came in right after they arrived and was going up and down the booths, dropping off demos. The day before, another kid came in and started singing, like one of the record men would stop eating and offer him a contract on the spot. It got so that Leonard and Phil couldn't have a goddamn conversation without someone interrupting them, hawking their wares.

"So I was just on the phone with a distributor," said Phil, pulling a fresh cigar from his pocket. "He's telling me the 78 is dead. Now it's all about LPs — long-playing records."

"You know how many songs go onto one LP?" said Leonard.

"It's a big change." He paused and lit his cigar. "So what do you think about this Aileen business? Leeba says she wants to do a jazz record now."

"She's gotta get off the dope before I'll let her record anything." Leonard fished a cigarette from the pack in his pocket.

"What did you decide to do about the Moonglows?" asked Phil as he leafed through a folder.

"I adjusted their royalties."

"You take it from Chuck?"

Leonard nodded. "Did the same thing with Muddy's and Walter's, too."

Phil nodded, made some notes in the margins of his papers. The waitress came over with their orders: two Blatt's specials. Phil set his cigar aside, grabbed the pickle off his plate and took a big bite. They were still discussing shuffling royalties around when John Lewis came up to their booth with a white fellow. John was a bluesman and jazzman from way back, played piano as good as the best of them. He had a long, oval face and a stubbly goatee.

"Say hello to the brothers Chess," said Lewis, sliding in next to Leonard.

"Don't mind us, John," said Phil, shaking his head, laughing. "Why don't you have a seat?"

Lewis made the introductions. "This is Chris Barber. All the way from London, England." Barber sat next to Phil. "And you're not going to believe this," said John, "but this cat right here plays a trombone that sounds like the Mud's slide guitar."

"You're right," said Leonard. "I don't believe it."

"I have a band," said the Brit. "The Barber Band back in England. We play a good deal of jazz."

Lewis laughed. "They call it jazz over there. It sounds more like Dixieland to me. But they're good. They're damn good."

"We've been quite influenced by your artist Muddy Waters," said Barber. "His music is rather popular, you see, and, well, we'd like to bring Mr. Waters over to England."

"For what?" Phil chomped on his sandwich.

"We'd like to tour with him. In England."

"Let me get this straight." Leonard squared

his elbows on the table. "You want to tour in England. With Muddy. And a trombone." Leonard turned to Phil as if to say, *Do you believe this shit?* "How'd you even hear Muddy's music over there?"

"We have some of his early recordings."

"Real early stuff," said Lewis. "I'm talking the stuff you did with him back at Aristocrat."

"His music is unlike anything we've heard before," said Barber. "We think it's brilliant."

All Leonard could think was, *Muddy with a trombone player!* No way in hell would he go for it.

He and Phil finished eating, said good-bye to Lewis and the Brit and went back to 2120. Later that afternoon, sitting in his office, Leonard sorted through a stack of royalty statements. He dropped his pen on the pile and rubbed his eyes. His chest felt tight and he refused to think about his weak heart. The pain was because it was killing him to see what was happening to some of his artists. Especially Muddy. His records weren't selling anymore. He was dying, getting left behind by the whole rock 'n' roll craze, and he was depressed. Used to be Muddy made his money gigging, but he had stopped playing guitar. Leonard was giving him money to live on, was even paying his mortgage. It was like he had another child to support.

That conversation with Chris Barber

nagged at Leonard throughout the day. He'd never considered Europe before, even though he knew Big Bill Broonzy had some gigs over there, said he did all right by the Brits, too. Leonard glanced again at the balance on Muddy's royalty statement. At this point what did they have to lose?

The next day he sat down with Muddy. He wasn't surprised that his initial reaction was the same as his own and Phil's. After Muddy stopped laughing, Leonard said, "It's time to get you playing your guitar again. Think of this as a new market."

"I ain't never been to Europe." Then Muddy bit down on his lip, trying to hide his smirk, his curiosity. "You think they'd pay me all right money?"

"One way to find out. Let me set up a meeting with you and this guy Barber. See what you think."

The next day the three of them — Leonard, Muddy and Chris Barber — sat at the Chess booth over at Blatt's and talked business.

"I've been looking high and low for you, Mr. Waters," said Barber.

Muddy just wrinkled his brow and said, "What?"

Leonard wasn't sure if Muddy was puzzled by this man seeking him out or if it was just that he couldn't understand Barber's thick English accent.

"I'm dead serious, mate," said Barber. "I want to bring you back to England to tour with my band. We have ten dates set up so far. More are likely to come on board."

Again Muddy scrunched up his face. "What?"

Barber was so excited he didn't stop to explain. "We'll cover all your expenses. Your hotel, meals, airfare. And I can guarantee you at least three hundred pounds a night. More if we add on larger venues."

"What?"

A few more "whats" and the meeting was over, and as Leonard and Muddy were heading back across the street Leonard said, "Take the gig. It's more bread than you're gonna make back here."

Muddy followed Leonard into his office and closed the door. He sat down in the chair and drummed his fingers on the edge of Leonard's desk. The Champs' "Tequila" was playing on the radio.

"Why don't you come with me?" Muddy said.

"Me? Why me?"

" 'Cuz I can't understand a word that man's sayin'. Everything he say come out sounding all funny-like. And you know they all gonna sound that way over there. Besides" — Muddy looked down at his hands — "I ain't never been on no airplane before."

Leonard turned off the radio. When he and

his family left Poland he was eleven. He wanted to go back to Europe — Western or Eastern — like he wanted to have another heart attack. But his friend was scared, even if he hadn't come right out and said it. Muddy needed Leonard with him, so he decided he would pack up and cross the pond.

They landed at the London Airport and after clearing customs they found a funny-looking cab, all black and boxy. From the backseat Leonard watched Muddy looking out the window, taking it all in. Bridges and double-decker buses everywhere, remnants of bombed-out buildings left from the Blitz and cranes sweeping the sky where new construction was going up. He could only imagine what was running through Muddy's mind. Did McKinley Morganfield ever think in his wildest dreams that he could have gone from being a sharecropper in Mississippi to a performer in London?

As soon as they got to their hotel at King's Cross they found an entourage of photographers and reporters waiting for Muddy in the lobby. Flashbulbs went off and questions came at them. Leonard hadn't been expecting this and neither had Muddy. But even if Muddy couldn't understand their accents, he got that this was all about him and he stood proud, smiling.

The next day, even before Muddy started his official tour with the Barber Band, someone from the royal palace came calling. The queen's people were hosting the Leeds Music Festival and they'd gotten ahold of Leonard saying they wanted Muddy to perform there.

"I thought we was going on tour with Chris Barber," said Muddy, standing in the doorway in an undershirt and boxers. "I thought that's the whole reason why we here."

"We are. But this just came up." Leonard stepped inside Muddy's room and closed the door. "It'll be good exposure for you. Get your sea legs with these people before you head out on tour."

Muddy agreed but he was nervous. The next day, after a four-hour drive, they arrived in Leeds. The driver told them it was a major city in the north of England and a textile hub.

When they got to the hall and Leonard looked at the audience, he became alarmed. People dressed in all their proper finery, musicians backstage walking around in coat and tails. The guys on stage were playing Beethoven and Bach. *What the hell? I can't put Muddy on stage with a motherfucking string quartet.*

But it was too late to cancel so Muddy went on stage with his white Fender electric and cut loose with "Got My Mojo Working." Halfway through the song, Leonard saw people getting up and leaving. They hated

537

the music. Leonard was watching Muddy. He saw what was happening, too. He was dying out there and cut his set short.

When Muddy got off stage he wanted to back out of the tour.

"You need the money, man," said Leonard, who frankly was getting tired of supporting Muddy. "Just do the tour and when we get back home, we'll go into the studio and record some new songs. We'll put all this behind us."

Muddy agreed, but he wasn't happy about it.

The next day they were on the road at dawn and made a six-hour drive up to Newcastle-upon-Tyne, where they were performing the first night. It was a working-class, industrial town, occupied mostly by shipbuilders.

Leonard was backstage with Muddy, sitting in the wings on some wooden chairs, smoking cigarettes and waiting for Chris Barber to call Muddy on stage.

"You're looking sharp, motherfucker," said Leonard, trying to lighten the tension backstage.

"Yeah," said Muddy. "They better not throw no tomatoes at my new suit here."

Chris Barber and his band were still playing. Leonard didn't think they sounded bad, but they sure as hell didn't sound anything like blues or jazz. *Lewis was right — this is fuckin' Dixieland music.*

After three more cigarettes they finally invited Muddy on stage and Leonard braced himself. He got up and inched closer to the curtains, watching like a nervous father at the school play. Muddy looked small and stiff on that big stage. He and Leonard had agreed earlier that he was gonna at least give those English motherfuckers a real authentic blues song before they booed him off.

He got through the opening riff of "I'm Your Hoochie Coochie Man" and Leonard wasn't sure, but he sensed that something shifted in the theater. Muddy played the next riff. He was right — something was different. This wasn't the queen's audience. Leonard saw the change in their faces — people were smiling; the girls were leaning forward in their seats; everyone was swaying to the music. And when Muddy got to the line about having seven hundred dollars they went wild, cheering, calling out, clapping.

"Baby, Please Don't Go" was the next song, followed by "Got My Mojo Working," and Muddy was pouring it on. With each move of his head, Leonard saw the sweat coming off his hair like a dog shaking off the rain. But, man, that crowd was eating it up. Leonard had a father's pride like when Marshall learned to ride his bike, Leonard running alongside him until he let go and let his son soar. Muddy was soaring.

When they got back to the hotel that night

a strobe of flashbulbs went off as soon as they came through the front door. The lobby was packed with reporters, photographers and people standing shoulder to shoulder, cheering. It took a moment for Leonard to realize that they were all there for Muddy. Leonard stepped in and took the guitar case from his hand and watched that crowd circle around Muddy like they couldn't get close enough.

Almost an hour into it and those reporters were still asking questions. Nobody paid any attention to Leonard and that was fine by him. He was just another white man and this crowd was clearly fascinated with Muddy. Negroes were ultrahip and cool over here and those Brits thought Muddy was one exotic motherfucker.

The girls were posing with their arms around him, their fingers touching his pompadour, their white cheeks pressed to his, all of them wanting to kiss him. That was the one thing Leonard did appreciate about Europe. Chicago may have been light-years ahead of the Deep South in terms of segregation, but Europe was even more progressive than Chicago. Leonard thought about Leeba and Red. They would have been better off in England. It would have been easier for them in a place like London, where skin color didn't determine a person's worth.

Leonard went up to his room and left Muddy in the lobby. He was beat and plopped down on the side of the bed, unlaced his shoes, loosened his tie and almost fell asleep sitting up.

The next morning as Leonard was locking his door, he saw the service tray on the floor outside Muddy's room, along with a Do Not Disturb sign hanging off the door. Just then, he saw a pretty blonde slip out of Muddy's room, still buttoning her blouse. Leonard didn't judge, even though he knew Muddy had a wife and a mistress and another girl in Chicago, a new one named Lucille. Aileen didn't know about Lucille, and Leonard wasn't about to tell her Muddy was serious about her. Crazy about her was more like it, but still, for a dog like Muddy, knowing that his skin color was an asset here and that he could have his pick of women was too much to resist. It must have put him in a state of ecstasy.

Leonard knew this was what Muddy needed. Fuck Elvis and Chuck Berry. Muddy Waters was back. At least in England he was.

FORTY-SIX:
"RAMBLIN' ON MY MIND"

RED

"This is your Inside Man coming to you live from Chicago and before I sign off we're going to 'Kansas City' with Wilbert Harrison. Yes, sir, hang on because I'm taking you straight to Kansas City." Red dropped the tonearm on the turntable and slid the headphones off, setting them on the console for the next deejay coming on.

About six months back, one of the deejays quit and John Dyer, the general manager, gave Red his time slot. Every day he was on the air from one till four. Since then listeners had started calling Red "the Inside Man" because he shared so many inside stories about the musicians and what went into their recording sessions.

Red loved hosting the show. It gave him back that part of himself he'd lost along with his music. Despite the decision about not letting them be James's foster parents, Red and Leah were still looking for a way — any kind of way — to fight the court's decision. And in the meantime, knowing the odds were against them, they focused on their careers. Leah was doing more songwriting for Mimi and Aileen.

Red finished his show for the day and when he stepped out of the studio Jerry Wexler, the head of Atlantic Records, was there waiting for him. The guy had a white beard and was wearing baggy trousers and a cardigan along with a chauffeur's cap. He didn't look like a record executive.

"I like what I'm hearing, Red," he said with a handshake.

"Just doing my job," said Red.

Wexler smiled and handed him an envelope. "And there's plenty more where that came from," he said. "You keep playing 'What'd I Say' and keep Ray Charles on top of the charts and I'll make you a rich man, Red Dupree."

After Red left the station he peeked inside the envelope: two crisp twenties and a ten. That was the third envelope he'd been handed by a record man that week. As a deejay with an afternoon show on WGES, Red had the power to help make or break a record. Promoters and record men from Atlantic and Mercury, Capitol, Vee-Jay and RCA Victor were all knocking on his door with envelopes and gifts and invitations to fancy restaurants. Even Phil Chess came to see him with cash and a handshake.

As a disc jockey Red was coming alive again, finding a purpose for himself and finding his voice. And he was determined to use that voice. So even though the radio station wasn't crazy about it, he'd come across something — another church bombing in Alabama, a Klan rally in Kentucky, Reverend King planning a trip to India — and he'd speak his mind about it. On the air.

One afternoon about a week after his visit from Wexler, it was a quarter to four and the Inside Man was finishing up his show. Red had a stack of newspapers on the console next to the turntables with a bunch of clippings from articles he'd made some noise about. He'd spoken out earlier in the show that day about housing violations in Chicago's Negro neighborhoods and more trouble in the schools down in Arkansas. After Ray Charles's "What'd I Say" finished playing, Red came back on the air to talk about something that had happened to his buddy, another disc jockey down in Birmingham who went by the name Shelley "the Playboy" Stewart.

"Now, before your Inside Man signs off today I want to tell y'all about an incident that took place last week down in Birmingham, Alabama. You see, my fellow deejay, Shelley the Playboy on WEDR, ran into some trouble on the radio. Seems that he had a thing or two to say about those Jim Crow laws and while he was still on the air, guess who showed up? Yes, sir, the Ku Klux Klan in their white robes and hoods. They blocked the doors, broke the windows and messed with the broadcast signal until the station went dead. The Ku Klux Klan shut down WEDR."

Red paused for ten seconds to let his words sink in. He knew how powerful that kind of silence was on the radio. "But they don't know my man Shelley the Playboy. Here we are, just five days later, and he's back on the air and back to speaking his mind. So I want to say a big welcome back to Shelley. And I wanna send a message loud and clear to Bull Connor, the commissioner of public safety down there in Birmingham. Bull, it's gonna take a whole lot more than that to silence us. This is just the beginning and you can't keep us down. And now, my friends, I'll leave y'all with this one by James Brown and the Famous Flames." "Try Me" was cued up on the turntable. He lowered the needle and set his headset on the console for the next deejay.

Red didn't even make it to the lobby before Dyer came over to him. "What the hell was that?"

"What was *what*?"

"You know damn well what I'm talking about. You got the switchboard lit up like a Christmas tree. This isn't talk radio. You're here to play records, not spout off about your political views. I've warned you about this too many times before. I'm sorry, Red." He planted his hands on his hips and shook his head. "I'm letting you go."

"Because of what I just said? Listen, I got a Negro audience and they're entitled to hear the truth —"

"They're not going to hear it from you. Not on this station."

And just like that, Red was off the air and out of a job. The Inside Man was back on the outside, looking in.

FORTY-SEVEN:
"AIN'T NOBODY'S BUSINESS
IF I DO"

LEONARD

Leonard was in his office, finishing up year-end crap. There was a mound of paperwork to get through, and cases of booze and a couple Rolex watches going to deejays and distributors, not to mention checks going to the NAACP and the United Jewish Appeal.

Revetta wanted to take the kids down to Miami for the holidays along with Phil's family. He told Revetta it all depended on him getting his work done. But his work was never done and they both knew that. Bo and Chuck were putting out LPs in the beginning of January and he was putting out a new record for Muddy. Besides, the thought of sitting around the Thunderbird Hotel for two weeks made his skin crawl. Phil was content resting under an umbrella reading a book, finding sand between his toes and in his swimming trunks at the end of the day. Not Leonard. He didn't know how to do nothing. There was something inside him that wouldn't let him stop. Not even for sleep. He couldn't remember the last time he got a solid eight hours in. Four was more like it. If it wasn't his mind keeping him awake, it was heartburn. Sometimes he feared he was having another heart attack. He was eating Rolaids like candy.

Carri, his secretary, stopped into his office. "Alan Freed's on the line," she said, handing him a half dozen pink message slips. "He says it's urgent."

What now? Leonard felt a burning in his gut. He got up, closed the door and picked up the phone. As soon as he heard Freed's voice he knew something was wrong. Freed was talking so fast Leonard couldn't grasp what he was saying. But then he got it. Did he ever.

He sat up straight. "What do you mean you've been fired?"

"The station fired me. Canceled my show. And *The Big Beat* is gonna be next. The IRS, the FTC and the FCC are breathing down my neck. They're looking through my books. Saying I've been taking bribes in exchange for airplay."

Leonard thought about all the money they'd paid Freed, not to mention giving him the writing credit on "Maybellene." "Well," said Leonard, "that *is* what you've been doing."

"*Of course* that's what I've been doing.

They wanted me to sign a statement saying that I never accepted any gifts or money. I couldn't do that. Shit, I'm gonna end up in jail."

"Slow down."

But Freed was panicked. Leonard chewed on a Rolaid and listened to the recap of all the gifts and the money Freed had taken from Chess alone. Leonard wasn't concerned. He and Phil reported those payments and perks as legitimate business expenses.

"My career's finished," said Freed. "I'm gonna go to jail over this. I'm not kidding. And they're going after other deejays, too. They've been talking to Joe Finan in Cleveland and Dick Clark, too. God knows what the hell Dick's telling them."

Leonard reached for a coffee cup. Cold and probably sitting there from the day before. He pushed it aside and grabbed another Rolaid. As soon as he hung up with Freed, Leeba stepped into his office.

"I need you to stay calm," she said.

"I know. I just spoke to Freed."

"It's not about Alan Freed."

"What's wrong? What happened?"

"Just promise me you're not going to react."

"For Christ's sake, what is it?"

"I've got Chuck on the phone. He needs to talk to you. He's in jail."

"Motherfucker —" Leonard punched the flashing light and yanked the receiver off the hook. "Jesus, Chuck —" He motioned for Leeba to leave and close his door behind her. "What the hell is going on?"

"You gotta get me out of here." Chuck sounded more annoyed than scared.

"What the hell did you do?"

"I didn't do a thing. I got pulled over in Topeka and I had a girl in the car with me. And you know it's all because she's white."

"A white *girl*. How young, Chuck?"

"I don't know."

"Chuck."

He heard Chuck sigh. "Fourteen."

"Aw, shit." Leonard thumped his fist against his desk.

"She doesn't look fourteen, I can tell you that much. They got me locked up. And they're saying I violated some Mann Act by 'transporting a minor across state lines.' You have to get me out of here."

"Don't worry. Just sit tight. I'll get you out."

"They're telling me to get a lawyer."

"I'll get you a lawyer, too." Leonard hung up and squeezed the bridge of his nose; the stomach acids were churning.

"Did you see this?" Phil came into Leonard's office holding a newspaper. "The FTC is getting in on the act now, too."

"I know. I just spoke to Freed."

Phil chomped on his cigar and handed the paper to Leonard. "Now they're pointing the finger at RCA." He began counting off his fingers. "London, Cameo Records and a bunch of distributors, too."

Leonard scanned through the article. "Motherfuckers."

"They're calling it payola, saying they 'intentionally misled the listening public.' " Phil pulled his cigar from his mouth. "That's bullshit."

"Christ. This thing's turning into a goddamn witch hunt."

"We need to cancel the trip to Miami. We gotta be here in case this blows up."

"No, no." Leonard shooed Phil away with his hand. "You go. Take the girls, take the kids. Go down, relax. I'll stay up here and handle it."

Phil probably knew Leonard didn't want to go to Florida anyway, because he just nodded and walked out. Leonard let him go without saying anything about the whole Chuck's-in-jail fiasco. After Phil closed the door behind him, Leonard planted his elbows on his desk and rubbed his eyes. He was off the hook with the family but now he had to deal with Chuck and the FTC. What kind of a motherfucker would rather do that than go on vacation with his family?

FORTY-EIGHT:
"MESSING WITH THE KID"

RED

Red left an interview for a job at a rinky-dink 750-watt radio station on the west side of town. It was snowing and cold, the wind whipping through him as wet flakes landed on his face, in his eyes.

He didn't know how the interview had gone. They said they'd *think* about it. Told him to check back after the New Year. It was the third week of December and he'd already spent months knocking on the door of every radio station in town, offering to write sponsor copy and news stories. He'd been doing small jobs — carpentry and maintenance — here and there just to make ends meet. He couldn't believe he was back in this position again. Two steps forward, three steps back. The story of his life. He'd *almost* made it as a musician, then he'd *almost* made it as a deejay.

And yet as 1959 was coming to a close Red saw his radio friends fall, one by one. Either they were canned or they resigned. Even Leah said the atmosphere around Chess was tense because of the payola scandal. She said Leonard was snapping at everyone more than usual. So in a way Dyer had done Red a favor by firing him. At least he wasn't being served with papers and didn't have the FTC, the FCC or the IRS coming after him.

Red hopped on the El and took the train down to Maxwell Street. He jogged down the platform stairs, trudging over the frozen ground, heading deeper into Jewtown. Even after years of living in Hyde Park he still gravitated to his old neighborhood. With all its poverty and dilapidation, he still fit in better down in Jewtown than he did anywhere else. He could walk down the sidewalk and see familiar faces. It was comforting to be back there, predictable and dependable. The weather didn't change the atmosphere in Jewtown. Those folks they called schleppers were still in the doorways, pulling people into their stores. The hustle was still going on, deals, deals and more deals, and the music still poured out of every pocket and from every street corner. Steam was rising off the food stands, the vendors grilling sausages and red hots.

Red passed by a few folks who knew him from his performing days or else from his short time on the radio. It felt good to be recognized, and it made him wonder if he'd ever get another shot at being on the air.

As he was turning the corner he spotted James sitting on a crate next to a fire going in an old garbage can, playing Red's old Stella. He had cut off the fingertips on his gloves so he could feel the strings. They were pale from the cold. It was a weekday and bitter cold, but James had drawn a crowd. People were gathered around listening to him play, tossing some coins in his bucket. James looked up from his crate, a glow from the flames in the garbage can surrounding him as he played "I'm a Steady Rollin' Man."

Red and Leah had been worried about him lately. He'd been acting moody. He was thirteen now and Leah hoped that it was just typical adolescence. All Red knew was that James had skipped his last two guitar lessons and he hadn't stopped by the apartment in almost a week. Normally he was there for dinner almost every night.

Red stayed and listened, waiting until James took a break. James was blowing into his hands to warm them as the crowd began to break up. He still hadn't seen Red standing there and when James took a Lucky Strike from his coat pocket, Red darted over and yanked the cigarette from his mouth.

"What do you think you're doing with that?" said Red.

"Hey." James tried to push his hand away. "You smoke. Why can't I?"

"Because I'm an adult. And I shouldn't be smoking, either." Red saw James shivering. "It's freezing out here. C'mon, let's go to Lyon's and get something to eat. Get out of this cold."

James went with him, but Red watched the way he dragged his feet, keeping his head low, acting as if Stella weighed a hundred pounds.

Lyon's Deli was crowded and while James grabbed a table for them Red ordered a couple corned beef sandwiches from Nate, a tall brown Negro standing behind the counter. Red had been coming into Lyon's for years and he'd known Nate since he was just a kid busing tables. Since Lyon's Deli served as many Jewish customers as it did Negroes, over the years Nate had picked up enough Yiddish so that he was able to talk with the merchants. Leah once told Red that Nate was practically fluent.

Red made his way over to James with a tray of sandwiches piled high with corned beef and two bottles of cream soda. Red was starving and dug in, but James only picked at his food.

"What's the matter? You feeling okay?" he asked.

James shrugged.

"You gonna come over tomorrow night and help us trim the Christmas tree?"

Again James shrugged and Red found himself struggling to make conversation.

"Leah's cooking your favorite dinner and I wouldn't be surprised if you had a Christmas present or two waiting for you."

James didn't say a word. His face was blank.

"C'mon, boy — what the hell's wrong with you?" Red set his sandwich down. "Why haven't you been coming by the apartment?"

"It don't make no sense to keep coming to your place."

Red stopped himself from correcting James's grammar. "And why not?"

"It ain't real. It ain't my home." James pushed his plate away and looked at Red, his young eyes filled with sadness.

"We don't care what the courts say. You belong with us."

"Tell that to the Walkers. They're my new foster parents." His lips started to tremble and tears rimmed his eyes. "I'm sick of being moved around. I don't wanna be with the Walkers. I wanna be with you and Leah."

"That's what we want, too," said Red, trying not to choke up himself. "And you know Leah — she's never gonna stop fighting for you. I won't, either." But as he said that, it felt like a lie. Their lawyer had tried everything. They had nothing left to fight with.

FORTY-NINE:
"I'D RATHER GO BLIND"

LEEBA

On a sloppy December morning after Leeba stopped into Blatt's for coffee she knocked on Little Walter's car window. Drunk and reeking like the bottom of a bottle, he followed her up to Chess and held the coffees while she fished the keys from her pocketbook and unlocked the door. She stomped the slush off her boots and turned on the lights. Walter trudged upstairs to the studio while she went back to the offices on the first floor.

Chuck wasn't staying in the basement anymore. He preferred Phil's house now when he was in town recording. He enjoyed spending time with Phil's kids. Plus, knowing Chuck, he loved that he stayed there for free. Even after all his hit records and his big royalty checks, he still didn't want to shell out the money for a hotel room.

Later that day, Leeba was in the rehearsal space working on a song that she'd written for Aileen called "See Him with Another One."

Leonard walked by and stopped, cigarette in one hand, coffee cup in the other. He listened to the song one time through. "Sounds good," he said. "I like it. Let's give this one to Etta."

"Etta?"

Etta James, the newest addition to the Chess roster. Leonard had wanted a new girl singer to capitalize on the growing jazz market and in the winter of 1959 he found her, buying out her contract from the Bihari brothers at RPM in Los Angeles.

"This song ain't right for Aileen," said Leonard. "It's perfect for Etta. We've got a session with her later today. You can play it for her afterward."

"But I told Aileen this song was for her. What's she going to say when she finds out this is going to Etta?"

"I guess you'll find out when you tell her." He gave her a wink.

"Thanks a lot. You're a *nudnik* sometimes, you know that?"

"So I've been told." He laughed as she shook her head, exasperated. "Ah, c'mon, Leeba. You don't think Willie has the same problem when he tells Muddy he's giving Wolf a song?"

Later that day she joined Leonard and Phil in the studio with Etta James. Leeba had never seen another singer like Etta. She didn't even know a colored girl could have blond hair, and then there was the makeup. Etta looked like a movie star.

Phil was rehearsing one of her songs before they rolled tape. Etta's singing was so powerful Leeba felt the vibration inside her chest. Etta was singing, "All I Could Do Was Cry" and that was all Leonard could do, too. Leeba watched him lean against the doorjamb and pull a handkerchief from his back pocket to catch the tears. She'd never seen another singer move him like that.

When Etta finished recording they went on to rehearse the song Leeba had written for Aileen. Leeba went over to the piano, sat down at the bench and began going through the lyric sheet with Etta, pointing out the chord changes. That was when Aileen barged into the studio, unhinged and raging mad.

"What the hell is she doing here?" Aileen cut in front of Etta. "That's *my* song. *Mine!*" She pounded her chest.

Leeba was speechless. She hadn't said anything to Aileen yet. How had she even found out they were recording with Etta that day?

Etta surprised them all by shoving Aileen out of the way, sending her stumbling, falling onto a stack of chairs.

Phil tried to get Aileen on her feet, but she twisted away from him like a wild animal and lunged toward Etta. That was when Leonard stepped in, guarding his new star, glaring at Leeba. "Get her out of here. Now."

Leeba tugged at Aileen's arm, pulling her into the adjacent rehearsal room. Aileen kicked one chair and dropped down into another one. She let out a scream and then broke down in sobs. Through the window looking out onto the studio Leeba saw Leonard and Phil consoling Etta.

"You need to pull yourself together," Leeba said, scolding her for perhaps the first time in the course of their friendship. She didn't care if Aileen didn't want to hear it and got mad. Leeba was disgusted. "You're blowing it." She handed Aileen tissues while she wailed. "You can't come in here drunk and doped up."

"I ain't drunk. I ain't doped up." She looked up and Leeba realized she was telling the truth. Her eyes were clear but filled with a bottomless sorrow. "Muddy left me. This time for good. It's really over." Aileen sobbed. "He told me he loves that new girl, Lucille — she's not even a woman. She's a damn child. It's been going on behind my back forever." Aileen slumped forward, her shoulders shaking, and gasped for air as more tears streamed down her face. "I don't wanna be here no more. I can't live without Muddy. I'm going crazy — losing my mind. I'm scared. I don't know what's happening to me."

Leeba sat down and rubbed her hand along Aileen's back. "It's gonna be okay. You're gonna be all right. I'm here." A soft tender spot opened up in her heart. All the hurt between them, the disappointments, the conversations that had left Leeba cold no longer mattered. This was the Aileen she knew, the one who needed her, the friend she would forgive a million sins.

"I know what I gotta do," said Aileen, sniveling, rapidly cycling her way to the next level. "And I know how to do it, too." She nodded, talking more to herself than to Leeba. "I can't keep on like this. I can't."

"No," said Leeba, still rubbing her hand along Aileen's back, "you can't."

"I'm gonna change my ways. I'm quitting the booze. I am. And I'm done with J.J. Done with the dope, too."

Leeba's hand stopped, resting on Aileen's shoulder. This was the first time her friend had ever admitted to using dope. "I'm glad to hear you say that."

"I'm scared, you know?"

"I know. But it's gonna be okay." Leeba went back to rubbing circles along Aileen's shoulders.

Aileen sat up a little straighter; her eyes sparkled from a mixture of tears and hope. It was as if some new inspiration had just come to her. "I'm done with all that junk," she said. "I'm gonna beat it. I tried to quit before, but

I'm ready this time. Drugs was the problem, you know. Muddy don't go for drugs. He's always on me about that. So I'm gonna get myself clean. Get myself clean." She nodded with conviction. "And then I'm gonna get him back."

FIFTY:
"SWEET LITTLE SIXTEEN"

LEONARD

"Happy New Year to us." Phil walked into Leonard's office and shoved his cigar in the corner of his mouth as he handed Leonard a certified letter from the Federal Trade Commission.

Leonard read the letter and slammed an opened hand on his desk. "Motherfuckers. Cease and desist." The FTC was ordering Chess to stop paying off deejays.

"Oh, and get this," said Phil. "The Old Swingmaster gave the *American* an interview."

"What'd he say?"

"He told 'em everything, which of course is *nothing.*"

Leonard folded up the FTC letter and shoved it back in the envelope. "Did he name us?"

Phil nodded. "Said we gave him a hundred a month and a new Lincoln. But he swore it wasn't payola. Said no one was paying him to play records."

"Damn straight. And that car was a birthday present."

"Exactly."

Carri popped her head inside Leonard's office. "There's a reporter from the *Daily News* on the phone. He wants to speak with you, Leonard."

Leonard shook his head. "Tell him I'm not here." He looked up at Phil. "This is turning into a goddamn nightmare. What are we supposed to tell all the other deejays?"

"We tell them they ain't getting paid this month — not until we get this cleared up."

Leonard opened the morning edition of the *Chicago Tribune*. "Did you see this?" He turned the paper around to show Phil. "Now they're after Atlantic, too. That's thirty-some labels that the feds are looking into."

"I know that the D.A. is doing an audit on Atlantic. I spoke to Jerry Wexler. He's sweating. Waiting to see if they're gonna slap him with a fine or haul him off to jail. He says he's going to sign a consent decree just to get them off his ass."

"I talked to Joe Bihari yesterday," said Leonard. "Modern had their books looked at, too."

"You think we'll have to go to D.C. and testify?"

"I sure as hell hope not," said Leonard.

"Did you see in that letter from the feds? They want us to sign a consent decree, too. I guess RCA already signed."

"Well, the feds can kiss my motherfucking ass before we'll do that. Let me ask you something, Phil. Do you think we did anything wrong?"

"We conducted business."

"Better fuckin' believe it." Leonard pushed himself back from his desk and grabbed his pack of cigarettes. "Don't we have a session now with Mimi?"

"Change of plans. She called in and canceled."

"What the —"

"Says she's got female problems. I know better than to argue with that. But we got a backup."

"I don't want Etta on this." Leonard lit a cigarette. He was getting ready to do a big production with Etta — full orchestra, strings, the whole bit — for an old Glenn Miller song she found. "I don't want Etta thinking about anything other than recording 'At Last.' "

"I'm not talking about Etta. I'm talking about Aileen."

"Oh no. No way."

"Hold on, wait. I saw her this morning. She's in good shape. Leeba says she been clean. And I say we give the song to her and see what she can do with it. We got nothing to lose. The musicians are already here in the studio."

Leonard was skeptical. Not about the song.

"Lovah, Lovah, Lover" was great. Leeba had written it — a snappy number with a strong backbeat and catchy lyrics.

"I'm telling you," Phil insisted, "Aileen can do this song. I just talked to her — she's clean."

Leonard finally gave in and followed Phil into the studio. He was surprised to find Aileen clear-eyed and sober. It was the first time since she and Muddy split up that she didn't appear to be on something. Still he wasn't convinced. Aileen was a handful even on a good day. She was unstable, always had been, and the booze and dope just made her that much worse.

"Okay, everybody," he called out. "Let's do this."

He went into the booth and joined Phil and the engineer. They did a run-through. Leonard was stunned. He smiled and turned to Phil.

"I told you so. She sounds great, doesn't she?"

Leonard pushed the talk button. "Okay, let's lay one down."

Aileen was nailing it. Line for line she had it. They were getting into a groove when Leonard stopped them.

"Why'd you do that?" asked Phil. "That sounded great."

"It needs something."

"Like what? The piano's —"

"No, Leeba's fine on the piano. It's the bass drum or something — I don't know. Give me a minute here. Let me think." Leonard stood up and leaned into the console, cigarette propped in his mouth. "It needs a *doosh, doosh, doosh.*"

"A *doosh, doosh, doosh*?" asked Phil.

"Yeah, you know . . ." He stomped on the telephone book lying on the floor at his feet. *"Doosh, doosh, doosh."* He did it again. Stomped on the phone book. That was it. That was the sound. "Phil, round up every telephone book you can get."

"What?"

"You heard me. I need every goddamn telephone book we got."

Fifteen minutes later, they were all in the studio stomping on telephone books, creating a thunder of *doosh, doosh, doosh* while the musicians played and Aileen sang. Leonard loved it even if everyone else thought he was nuts.

Six weeks after they released "Lovah, Lovah, Lover" that song started making noise, doing better than expected. Leonard's little *doosh, doosh, doosh* phone book trick had people talking, asking, speculating about "that sound." They didn't know what it was, but they liked it, and now "Lovah, Lovah, Lover" was climbing the pop charts. Aileen Booker was making a comeback.

■ ■ ■ ■

In the spring of 1960 everyone was going to jail. Or so Leonard thought.

First Alan Freed cracked and pled guilty to payola charges. Other deejays, including Dick Clark, followed suit. Leonard knew this was going to change the way they did business with Benson and all the other deejays across the country. Chess had a slew of new records ready to release but no way to ensure a hit.

Leonard was tired. Exhausted really. The business was changing and lately he wondered if it was time to get out. Revetta was always saying the record business was killing him, but still he couldn't let go. He was a record man. That was all he knew.

Alan Freed was supposed to sit in the can for six months, but the judge suspended the sentence and gave him a five-hundred-dollar fine. *Lucky motherfucker,* thought Leonard. Too bad Chuck Berry wasn't getting off that easily. Chuck's case was getting ready to go to trial and it was all over the news. That morning Leonard opened the New York Times and saw the headline: "Sweet Little Sixteen Turns Out to Be Fourteen."

"Did you see this?" He went into Phil's office to show him.

"Saw it." Phil folded the newspaper.

"We gotta get Chuck back in the studio."

"Now?"

"We gotta make sure we got records to put out if he goes to jail."

"You're crazy. He's getting ready for the fight of his life. You can't drag him into the studio now."

"You wanna bet?" said Leonard.

"You're not doing it."

"What do you mean I'm not doing it?"

"I'm telling you it ain't gonna happen." Phil got up and came around from behind his desk.

"Since when do you call the shots around here?"

"I own half of this company, remember? And for once, God damn it, you're gonna put business aside and do the right thing."

"I'm paying his goddamn legal fees. I bailed his ass out of jail. I think I'm entitled to have a few new songs in the can before *he's* in the can."

"What the hell is wrong with you? When did you get so greedy? How much more money do you need? Why don't you worry a little less about making money and start worrying more about your wife and your children?"

"Don't you start with me on my family."

"Your kids don't even know you. They come to me." Phil thumped his chest. "Who took Susie to her dance recital? Me. Who used to go to Marshall's Little League games?

Me. Do you even know what's going on with Elaine at school? Your little girl is growing up. She's becoming a woman — You know what the kids at school call her? Elaine *Chest*. She came crying about it to me, not you. Your own wife needs something and *she* comes to me, too, 'cause you're too damn busy. All you care about, all you ever care about, is making money so you can prove you're a big man. Frankly I'd respect you more if you went ahead and fucked Shirley and got it out of your system."

Leonard didn't think twice; he took a swing. But Phil blocked it, gripping Leonard's arm and twisting it behind his back. Leonard was struggling, cussing, still trying to get a punch in.

"We both know I could put you through a wall," said Phil. "So don't tempt me."

Leonard pulled his arm away and stormed out of Phil's office. The two of them didn't speak for the rest of the day.

Leonard called Chuck the next day. "I need you to get your ass back to Chicago," Leonard said. He was sitting at his desk, crumpling up an empty pack of cigarettes. "You gotta write me a dozen or so songs and we're gonna go into the studio and record them."

"You think they're gonna find me guilty, don't you?" Chuck said over the phone. "You think I'm going to jail."

"I think you're the hottest thing on the

570

charts right now. I don't know what's gonna happen in court. But I know that I'm gonna do whatever I can to save your career and keep your name out there in case you do go off to prison."

The line went silent.

"Chuck? You there?"

"Yeah. I'm here." It sounded like he was crying. "Thank you, Leonard. Thank you."

"All right, then. Get your ass back to Chicago and start writing some songs."

Leonard hung up with Chuck and rifled through his drawers until he found another pack of Lucky Strikes and went into Phil's office. He stood in the doorway waiting for his brother to acknowledge him. Phil had his eyeglasses propped up on his forehead while he reviewed some contracts. He didn't look up the whole time Leonard was talking, recapping his conversation with Chuck.

With his eyes still on the paperwork, Phil said, "Have Chuck stay with us out in Highland Park." He looked up at Leonard and added, "He likes Sheva's cooking and at least we can give him some peace and quiet to write before you try and kill him in the studio." Phil pushed away from his desk and stood up.

"I'm doing this for him," said Leonard.

Phil walked over to Leonard and cracked a crooked smile. "No, you're not."

The two never made up after their argument. But they were brothers. They didn't need to.

Three weeks later, Leonard got Chuck into the studio and in two days they laid down eleven tracks. The lawyers were all there, sitting in the back of the studio, briefcases on their laps. In between songs they pulled Chuck aside and prepped him for his trial. Chuck was a goddamn mess. He couldn't sit still, his leg bouncing up and down, fingers raking back through his hair. He couldn't afford to lose any weight and yet he had. His chiseled face was gaunt, the outline of every bone visible along his jaw and forehead.

Everyone hated Leonard for doing this — Leeba told him he was heartless. Phil wasn't that kind. But Leonard knew what he was doing and, whether anyone else got it or not, he was doing this to protect Chuck. Leonard was doing more than just paying the legal fees; he was going to keep Chuck's music alive. Chuck got it — why didn't anyone else?

Less than a week after they wrapped the session Chuck's trial began. Two weeks was all it took. Guilty of screwing around with an underage white girl. They slapped him with a ten-thousand-dollar fine and a three-year prison sentence.

FIFTY-ONE:
"A CHANGE IS GONNA COME"

LEEBA

It had rained earlier, a spring rain, but now the sun was out and the sidewalk was peppered with earthworms looking for salvation. Leeba and Red were on their way to a CORE meeting at the University of Chicago.

When they arrived they found that a large group had turned out that night. Word had gotten out that CORE's director, James Farmer, was going to introduce a new initiative and everyone was curious. All the seats were already taken so Leeba and Red stood in the back. Latecomers crowded into the doorway.

Farmer was at the front of the room, addressing the group. "We're looking for volunteers — Negroes *and* whites — to attempt something that's never been done before." He paused to emphasize his point. "We're going to challenge the Jim Crow laws of the Deep South. And you might ask, 'How are we going to do that?' We're going to travel by bus. We'll start in D.C. and head south, stopping in as many towns as we can until we reach New Orleans. And in every town we're going to get off those buses and demand that we be served at their lunch counters, be allowed to use their washrooms, drink from their water fountains."

The room swelled with encouragement. Leeba and Red joined the cheers and applause.

"We're calling this a Freedom Ride. We're going to penetrate the Deep South and stand up to the segregationists."

More applause. More hope. Leeba looked at Red, her heart racing. This was the boldest move she'd heard of yet that could bring about change.

"But" — Farmer raised his voice — "we will do it by means of *peaceful* protest. Our goal is to make it to New Orleans by May seventeenth, in time to commemorate the anniversary of Brown versus the Board of Education. And by then we will have broken the Deep South."

Everyone was clapping, yelping. Red raised his fist in the air. Leeba had tears in her eyes. They were united. No one felt alone in this fight anymore.

"But before anyone volunteers," said Farmer, "you should know what we're asking of you. We'll be on the road for two weeks — that means you'll have to take time off from your classes, your jobs, it will be time away from your families, too. We'll provide training in the technique of peaceful disobedience and we'll prepare you as best we can; but it won't be easy. You can and should expect resistance." Farmer steepled his fingers, resting them on his chin, his eyes cast down toward the floor. "I wish I could tell you what lies ahead. The hardest part about all this is that I can't promise you'll be safe. Some of you could be arrested. There could be violence along the way." He paused and lifted his gaze, his voice tight. "I hate to be so blunt, but before you volunteer you need to ask yourself if you're willing to die for this cause."

When the meeting broke up, Leeba pulled Red into a stairwell, the echo of footsteps heard all around as they huddled together. "You know what I'm going to say, don't you?" She squeezed his hand, her conviction strong.

"You want to do it," he said. "You want to volunteer."

"Don't you?"

He reached over and brushed the curls from her eyes. "You heard what he said. This is dangerous."

"It's no more dangerous than having thugs come after you with a knife. It's not more dangerous than having rocks thrown through our windows. We have to do this, Red. We just have to."

Before they left that night, they signed up to be Freedom Riders.

The next day Leeba went into Chess and talked to Leonard and Phil about taking time off. They were in Leonard's office. Phil was sacked out on the couch, his fedora riding low on his brow, shielding his eyes. Leonard was at his desk, sitting behind a mound of folders, records and tapes. The room smelled of tobacco and burned coffee. Leeba was still standing in the doorway, telling them what she was planning to do.

"I know I've already used most of my vacation days," she said, "but they need me to go down to Washington for training and then I'll be gone for two weeks after that. I'm not expecting to be paid while I'm gone."

Phil sat up and adjusted his hat. Leeba watched the brothers exchanging glances and, as well as she knew them, this time she couldn't read their expressions.

"Yeah, well," Phil said, rolling his cigar between his fingers, "I don't think that's gonna work, do you, Len?"

"Nah, I agree," said Leonard. "That's not gonna work at all."

"Oh, c'mon, guys. You have to let me go. You have no idea how important this is to Red and to me. This is something I have to do. You have to let me go."

"I'm sorry," said Leonard, "but I'm not going to let you take time off without pay." He got up from his desk, smiled and pulled her in for a hug. "Go. Do what you have to do. Take as much time as you need. We'll keep you on salary. Just be careful."

At the end of April Leeba and Red met with their fellow Freedom Riders in D.C. for training. They were placed in a stark room furnished with little more than a few chairs and a long table, a first-aid poster on the wall: "Emergency Care for Choking." It was hot and stuffy, even with the windows thrown open. They spent hours acting out seemingly every foreseeable confrontation. They role-played being denied service at a lunch counter, access to a bathroom; being yelled at, pushed, slapped and spit on.

During one exercise the trainer, a white man in his early forties, got up in Leeba's face. He was so close she could see the pores along his cheeks, could smell the last cigarette on his breath. "You nigger lover," he said, shoving her so hard she nearly lost her balance. She'd heard it before from strangers, even from her own sister. And while she knew it was just for practice, it still hurt, still stung. She was offended, but she took it.

Red didn't fight back, either, when another trainer knocked him out of a chair while pretending to be at a "Whites Only" waiting room. Red hit the floor, his chair overturned. He stood up and she saw the rage in his eyes, but he didn't retaliate. It was drilled into them that no matter what, they would conduct themselves with dignity. Leeba wasn't afraid. She was ready to take on the Deep South.

In the first week of May, Leeba, Red and eleven other Freedom Riders — altogether, six of them white, seven colored — began their mission in D.C. Half of them boarded a Trailways bus while the other half, including Leeba and Red, boarded a Greyhound. As Leeba climbed on board she felt lighter with each step. She was proud, defiant and determined. So was Red; so were the others except for the regular passengers on board who had no idea that anything out of the ordinary was under way.

Leeba watched the miles pass outside her window. They were headed into Virginia with all its lush greenness and made their first stop at a bus station to drop off some passengers, pick up others. The Freedom Riders got off to stretch their legs, use the washrooms, get something to eat. It was a warm mild day and the fresh air and sunshine felt good on Leeba's face as she stepped down off the Greyhound. She and Red walked into the station, where they saw the signs that said "Coloreds Waiting Room" and "Whites Only Waiting Room." Seeing that, she recoiled, just as she had the first time she'd gone down South with Aileen and Leonard.

"Ready?" asked Red.

"Ready." She gave a tight smile and nodded as they entered the "Whites Only" room. There were a handful of passengers on long wooden benches, waiting for their buses. Leeba's heart pounded. She wanted to reach for Red's hand, but she knew that would be pushing things. A man reading a newspaper glanced up, pursed his lips and moved to the far end of the room, raising his paper so as not to have to look at Red. A woman stopped her knitting, her mouth agape. Another man in a suit and tie kept his eye on Red, but he didn't say anything, didn't make a move. Similar reactions happened when James Farmer and the others used the "Whites Only" restrooms or went to the counter for a Coca-Cola. Sneers, harsh looks, shock. That was it.

Soon they were back on the bus, each of them puffed up even higher than before. *We showed them,* thought Leeba. They were really doing it. They were integrating the races. She could feel the excitement in the air. It was pure jubilation as they headed for North Carolina.

But when they arrived they got their first taste of what was to come. Leeba and Red were among the group of Freedom Riders who went into the bus station and entered the "Whites Only" waiting room.

An older man with Einstein-like hair and

bow tie set his newspaper down and crossed the room. "What do y'all niggers think you're doin' in here? Y'all ain't allowed in here."

"We're waiting for our bus to depart," said Red.

"Well, y'all niggers sure as hell ain't gonna wait in here." He kicked Red so hard it nearly knocked him from his chair.

That was all it took. Other white men, even the men who worked at the station, were on Red, James and the others. They threw punches, they kicked, they shoved. Leeba winced. It killed her to watch. Not one of the Freedom Riders struck back. They did exactly as they'd been trained to do. They would not meet violence with violence. By the time they got back on the bus the first-aid kit was out and Leeba and the others were sopping up blood, bandaging gashes, grateful that none of them needed stitches.

The next few stops were more peaceful and their sense of confidence returned. Each time they got off the bus and got back on, Leeba needed a few minutes to adjust to the closed-in feeling, the overpowering smells of feet and body odor, stale cigarette smoke and all that comes with living on a bus. Even sleeping on the bus when they couldn't find any hotels or motels that would let them stay. But once on board she got used to it, and all that mattered was that they were closer and closer to New Orleans. They saw passengers come and go; they passed the time reading newspapers, singing freedom songs, sleeping on one another's shoulders until the sun came up and it was time to watch more scenery go by. Leeba wondered how such beautiful country could harbor such ugliness.

The following day they arrived in Atlanta, where Reverend King and members of the movement greeted them. When Leeba shook Reverend King's hand her eyes welled up with tears. There was something in his touch that confirmed her purpose for being there. She had never believed in anything as much as she did this. The pride was overwhelming.

That night Reverend King hosted a dinner in honor of the Freedom Riders. It was held in the back of a church with card tables full of chitterlings and ribs, fried chicken and bowls of collard greens, black-eyed peas, platters heaped with corn bread. Leeba balanced her plate on her knees while Reverend King tucked a napkin down in his collar and informally addressed them all.

"You've taken on a noble mission," he said. "But now is the time to ask if it's wise to continue."

Leeba dropped her fork to her plate and looked first at Red, then at the others. They had all stopped eating, stopped chewing, waiting to hear more.

"I've gotten word that the Alabama Klan knows you're coming." Reverend King pulled the napkin from his collar, wiped his hands clean. "What you experienced in North Carolina is nothing compared to what's ahead. You're about to enter the Deep South and I'm frightened for you. I was told that the police are giving the Klan a fifteen-minute pass to do what they want to you before they'll step in to stop it. You realize what an angry mob can do to you in fifteen minutes? You could all be killed. There's no shame in turning back."

But the Freedom Riders didn't even discuss it. There was no turning back. To do nothing was to condone the Jim Crow laws and the hatred. The next day they were back on the bus. It was Mother's Day and Leeba was melancholy, thinking about her own mother and what she would have thought of Leeba being a Freedom Rider. She thought about the baby she'd lost and she thought about James, her last chance for motherhood. That, too, had been denied her.

"You okay?" Red asked after they got situated in their seats.

She blinked back the heat building up behind her eyes. "It's just another day. I'll be fine."

The others were jovial, anxious to get that much closer to New Orleans, and soon their enthusiasm seeped into her, lifting her spirits, reminding her of what she was doing and why she was there. She eased down in her seat and watched the green fields rushing by outside her window. They were one mile, two miles, three miles closer to New Orleans. They cheered when they passed the Welcome to Alabama sign. They were entering the Deep South.

They traveled through many small towns and as they pulled into Anniston they passed a store, Forsythe & Son Grocers. They had a sign out front for S&H Green Stamps and another for Mello ice cream. The bus station was just up the road and Leeba thought she and Red could walk back and get some ice cream while they waited for the bus to load up the new passengers.

But when they pulled up to the station Leeba looked out the window and swallowed hard. She reached for Red's hand. There must have been two hundred men and women waiting for them, shouting, "Die, you niggers. We's gonna kill you and your nigger lovers, too." Leeba looked at Red and at the others. It was the first time since they'd left Washington that she saw genuine fear on their faces. And that fueled her own fear. She realized she was digging her nails into Red's hand. She saw one of the men pull out a switchblade and she knew he was going for the tires. Others were pounding on the windows, throwing rocks, trying to break the glass. Leeba felt them rocking the bus from side to side. At one point she was sure they

583

would tip over.

Their driver blasted the horn and began to creep the bus through the hordes of people until at last they were back on their way. Leeba was still squeezing Red's hand, her heart palpitating. Less than a quarter mile from the bus station the ride got bumpy like they were traveling over a road of potholes and she realized it wasn't the road. It was their tires. They'd been slashed and had now gone flat. When they couldn't go any farther, the driver got out to inspect the damage. Leeba watched him through the window as the angry crowd from the station came over the hill, heading toward them. In horror she saw the driver take off his cap and run as fast as he could to get away. He was leaving them. They were on their own, trapped inside a bus with four flat tires and hundreds of angry Southern whites coming after them, wanting to kill them.

Leeba held on to Red and another woman who was just a regular passenger on her way to see relatives in Birmingham. She wasn't even a Freedom Rider. It was terror. *This is it. We're going to die.* That was Leeba's thought as a crowbar smashed in the back window. Shards of glass came flying inside and Leeba heard them chanting, "Watch 'em sizzle. Torch 'em niggers. Burn that white trash alive."

Then came the firebomb. Leeba saw it

coming through a broken window and everything inside her went still, silent. She wanted to scream but her voice wouldn't come. The flames soared past her as the back of the bus ignited in a burst of white heat and black smoke. The angry crowd was still shouting, "Kill 'em. Watch 'em burn." Another violent explosion blew out the windows. Leeba couldn't see in front of her. She was on the floor, gasping for air, when someone grabbed her and dragged her off the bus.

She clawed at the earth, gagging, her throat as dry as brittle wood. Blades of grass brushed against her cheek, fluttering against her eyelashes. The other passengers were off the bus now, too, clamoring for air, crying that they couldn't breathe. Black smoke was pouring from the bus and she could hear that crackling fire, the bus's metal frame buckling from the heat. She was vaguely aware of the townspeople standing there, some gawking, others looking horrified. Leeba watched helplessly as one of her fellow Freedom Riders got beaten with an iron pipe. She heard the *thwack* as he was struck over and over again.

She searched and searched through the smoke and the crowd, finally spotting Red doubled over, coughing violently. A man was coming at him with a pitchfork. He was going to kill him. She knew it. Leeba strained, calling to Red, when she heard the sound of gunshots. Everyone froze.

The highway patrolman still had his gun aimed toward the sky. "Enough," he said. "You've made your point. Now it's over. Leave these people alone."

As the mob backed off, Leeba collapsed onto the grass, coughing, hot tears sliding down the sides of her face. She didn't remember much after that other than the crowd dispersing and the fire engines and ambulances arriving. They were all taken to the hospital and emerged the next day covered in bruises and bandages. Leeba was stunned by the number of reporters and photographers waiting for them as they clung to one another, making their way through the hospital lobby. She felt defeated until she realized that they were finally calling national attention to the situation. Their story would appear in newspapers, on radios, on televisions across the country. Surely people would side with the Freedom Riders. Maybe they hadn't made it to their final destination, but they were exposing the crimes of the Deep South, showing the rest of the world the injustice.

It was the end of the road for them. Their bus was destroyed and Greyhound refused to sacrifice another vehicle. Besides, there wasn't a driver in all of Alabama willing to take them any farther. They thought it was over, until another crop of warriors and a brave driver took up the cause. The Freedom

Ride would continue, just not with Leeba, Red and the original Riders on board.

FIFTY-TWO: "RESCUE ME"

LEEBA

There was no leaving it behind and picking up where she'd left off. Leeba had returned to Chicago scarred inside and out. The gash along her arm and the scar on her chin were nothing compared to the wounds and heartaches lodged beneath the surface.

The day after she and Red arrived back in Chicago Aileen was in a bad way. She had just found out that Etta James was going to be on *American Bandstand* and Muddy had told her they were finished, once and for all. Leeba hadn't heard that kind of despair in Aileen's voice in a long time and it frightened her. Her friend had been clean for well over a year — no dope, not even a drink — and Leeba was afraid she might revert to her old ways.

It was a Sunday afternoon and though Leeba was exhausted she dropped everything and went to Aileen's apartment. She found her sitting on the floor in her kitchenette, hugging her knees to her chest. The potatoes in a bag on the counter were growing eyes, watching the whole thing.

"It's too much," Aileen said, wailing. "I can't go on without him."

"C'mon now," said Leeba, sitting down beside her. "You'll be okay. You can handle this."

"When does it get to be my turn, huh?" She raised her head; her eyes were bloodshot. "Muddy's got that new girl, Lucille."

"Well, she doesn't really *have* him, either," said Leeba. "Don't forget he's still a married man."

"Not anymore. He's leaving Geneva. He's moving in with Lucille." Aileen broke down just saying that out loud. "Do you know how many times I begged him to come live with me? But the truth is, he didn't love me. Not enough. He never loved me the way he loves Lucille." Aileen cried some more, dropped her legs out in front of her like a ragamuffin. "I just wanna die."

"No, you don't. C'mon now." Leeba put her arm around Aileen and pulled her close. "Don't say things like that. You've been doing so good."

"What am I gonna do without Muddy?"

"Maybe stop torturing yourself, for one thing."

Aileen cracked a half smile and then burst into more tears as she rested her head on

Leeba's shoulder.

"C'mon now, you've got so much to look forward to."

"Like what?"

"We're going back in the studio soon. We're gonna put out a new record. And you wait and see, I bet it's gonna be even bigger than 'Lovah, Lovah, Lover.' "

Aileen sniffed, wiped her nose with the back of her hand. "You think maybe someday they'd put me on TV?"

Leeba smiled. The fact that she even asked that, that she was looking toward the future, told Leeba that Aileen was coming out of it. "Sure," she said. "I think someday they'll put you on *Bandstand, Sullivan,* all of them. You've got just as much talent as Etta James."

"You used to say I had *more* talent than her." Aileen laughed and so did Leeba.

After that they fell into their usual routine where Leeba told Aileen how talented she was, how beautiful and bright and funny she was. Each accolade seemed to prop her up more. And by the time the light inside the kitchenette had changed, so had Aileen's mood. She smiled, even laughed, and began laying the groundwork for her climb back up.

"Walter told me about a new club, Linda's Place, that's opening up. I'm thinkin' maybe I'll try and get a gig there."

"You should. I think that would be great."

"You think maybe someday I'll meet someone new? Someone better for me than Muddy . . ."

"Oh, I have no doubt about that." Leeba looked at her watch. It was getting late and she was supposed to have met Red and James back at the apartment over an hour ago. "Tell you what," said Leeba, standing up, reaching for her pocketbook, "why don't you come back with me. Pack a bag and come stay with us until you're feeling better."

Aileen smiled and shook her head as she stood up. "No, you go on." She dusted off her backside. "I'll be all right."

"You sure?" Leeba asked as she hoisted the strap of her pocketbook on her shoulder.

Aileen nodded and thanked her and hugged her with such ferocity it stunned Leeba. She had the strongest urge to say *I love you,* but something stopped her. Aileen knew, though. Leeba didn't need to say it.

The next day Leeba drove to the suburbs to pick up her father, who had been visiting with Sylvie and Moishe. She hadn't seen her father since she'd gotten back and on the drive home she tried to explain what she'd been through on the Freedom Ride down South.

"So the whole bus was on fire?" he asked, futzing with the window knob. "And this happened while you were still on it?"

She nodded, gripping the steering wheel tighter, wanting something to hold on to. "It was terrifying." Talking about it had placed her back there in Anniston. "I think the Ku Klux Klan wanted to kill us whites more than the coloreds on board. They saw us as traitors and a disgrace." Those angry faces came rushing back to her, all of them shouting *Torch 'em niggers. Kill that white trash.* "We couldn't go on after that. I've never seen such hatred before. Such ugliness."

Her father said something, or she thought he did. She glanced over. His eyes were closed, his head bobbing, his breathing heavy. Like a newborn, the motion of the car had put him to sleep.

Driving back into the city and back into Lawndale she remembered what it was like growing up there and was struck by the passage of time. They said the neighborhood had "turned," as if they were talking about a bottle of milk. Yes, things had changed. Beth El Synagogue on the corner of Independence Boulevard and Lexington Street was now a Missionary Baptist church. Almost all the synagogues were churches now. The kosher butchers were gone, replaced by shops selling pork ribs and chitterlings. Having so many colored families in the neighborhood didn't bother Leeba. She welcomed them, relieved to see them out of the slums. She didn't think twice when a Negro family moved into Aunt Sylvie and Uncle Moishe's old apartment across the hall. But her father worried.

"Lock the door. Did you lock the door?" That was always the first thing he'd say to her whenever she came by to visit, even before he'd say hello. Sylvie and Moishe wanted him to move to the suburbs, but he didn't want to be that far away from Leeba and Golda.

When they got home that day, Leeba watched her father hobble across the room. With her mother gone he'd become an old man at the age of sixty-four. He went over and sat in the chair her mother used to sit in. He had adopted it after she passed away. Considering all that had changed outside the walls of their apartment, it made sense that her father found comfort in her mother's remnants. There was her Maxwell House coffee can on the kitchen counter still holding her spare change, the needlepoint pillow she used for her lower back. But Golda, newly divorced and in need of a project, wanted to redecorate. Each time Leeba came to see her father there was a new brushstroke — a paint sample — on the living room wall. Golda, the maven when it came to these things, couldn't make a decision.

Even that day Leeba saw that Golda must have been there. Her father slapped his hand to his forehead. "Oy, she's driving me *meshuge,* crazy. What's the difference between *that* beige" — he pointed to one sample on the wall — "and *that* beige? Beige is beige."

Leeba laughed. "How could Golda have been Mama's favorite?"

"*Auch,* your mother didn't have favorites."

Leeba turned toward him, eyebrows raised.

"Okay, so maybe she favored Golda. A little."

"A little?" Leeba was laughing when someone knocked on the door. "It's okay," she said to her father, who gripped the arms of his chair, a worried look on his face.

"See who it is first," he said. "Don't let anyone in."

"Don't worry." She peered out through the peephole and her heart about stopped. A prickly feeling rushed through her. She opened the door and her father let out a gasp. All he saw was a Negro standing there. But Leeba saw Muddy and his face was filled with dread.

"Red told me I'd find you here," he said. "I think somethin's wrong with Aileen. She called me a couple hours ago cryin'."

Leeba couldn't speak. All she could think was, Why? Why of all people would Aileen have called Muddy? What was it about this guy? What kind of hold did he have over her and why couldn't she let go?

"She was in a bad way," said Muddy. "Kept sayin' she's a failure, sayin' nobody loves her, nobody cares if she lives or dies, you know — all that shit she say when she get down on herself."

594

"I know she's down. I saw her yesterday. But she was okay by the time I left."

"I can tell ya she ain't okay," said Muddy. "She sounded messed up. Like she was on that dope again. And now she ain't answering her phone. Won't answer the door, either. And I gave her back her key, so I can't get in."

Leeba swallowed hard. "I've got a key. Let's go."

They left Leeba's father and drove to Aileen's in Muddy's new Cadillac. Muddy was talking the whole way, saying he was sorry for the way he'd treated Aileen. "Especially lately."

"Don't apologize to me," said Leeba. "She's the one you should be saying all this to."

"Can't explain it," he said after they'd parked and were walking up the front steps of Aileen's building. "There's something inside me that can't be satisfied with one woman. It's my weakness. Like how hers is them drugs, mine be womens."

The hallway was narrow and smelled like sulfur and cigars. They came to Aileen's apartment. They heard her song "Jealous Kinda Love" skipping over and over again on the same line: *I got a jealous kinda love and where my heart was, there's a hole.*"

Leeba knocked on the door. "Aileen? Open up. It's me."

Muddy was still rambling. "I ain't proud of

being this way and I know I caused her pain, but I do love her."

The record was still skipping. Leeba pounded on the door again as she reached in her pocket for the key. Muddy continued with his confession, but she'd stopped listening. The song kept skipping, repeating that same line. Leeba had a bad feeling even before she turned the key. Even before she saw the overturned chair; even before she saw Aileen.

As soon as they opened the door Leeba slid down against the wall, her legs unable to carry her. Muddy ran to Aileen, her body suspended from a beam, lifeless legs dangling above the capsized chair she must have been standing on. And all the while her record was skipping: *". . . where my heart was, there's a hole."*

In the days that followed, sometimes Leeba forgot. She would reach for the telephone, thinking, *I have to call Aileen.* She sat in the living room listening to Aileen's records, shuffling through photographs of the two of them from the time they were kids to one more recently taken of Aileen and Muddy with Leeba and Red. Aileen had her face pressed to Muddy's cheek. She looked so happy, not a hint of the demons lurking inside.

After Aileen's funeral Leeba went to her kitchenette to start packing up her things. It was dark and musty inside. It smelled like death. After all those years of threatening to do herself in, Leeba shouldn't have been surprised that Aileen would have taken her own life. She thought it would have been drugs that did her in, but instead Aileen had ended her life the same way her mother had. But still Leeba was shocked and struggled with one nagging regret: Why hadn't she told Aileen she loved her that one last time? The words had been right there, but she'd pushed them down, thinking the gesture unnecessary. It shouldn't have mattered how many times she'd told Aileen before. She wished she'd said it one last time and vowed to never again hold back — she would tell Red and James and her father, Aunt Sylvie and Uncle Moishe and even her sister that she loved them because that chance could be taken away without warning.

She opened the shades and the windows to air out the place. She bagged up some garbage and that sack of potatoes on the counter growing more eyes. When she came back from the trash chute, she noticed the houseplant. Aileen had had that plant since her first kitchenette. For the longest time it just stayed the same, never grew, never died. It was just there. But now it looked like it had new leaves and shoots coming up. And no fruit flies. They were gone. It was like they'd left along with Aileen. Leeba sank down on the floor and cried.

When there were no more tears she managed to stand up. Her heart was heavy as she turned off the lights. She'd started to lock the door when she stopped, went back inside, picked up the houseplant and took it home with her.

FIFTY-THREE:
"Boom, Boom Out Goes the Lights"

LEONARD

Leonard got a call in the middle of the night. The alarm was going off down at 2120. He eased out from under the covers and told Revetta he had to go downtown, turn it off, make sure everything was okay. He'd be back before it was time to get the kids up for school.

He got in his Cadillac and made the drive from Glencoe into the city. Pain in the goddamn ass was what it was. When he got downtown the streets were almost empty, just a few other cars on the road, a couple of late-night bars where folks were still staggering in and out. Leonard pulled up in front on Michigan Avenue. There was no alarm going off. It was quiet. He'd come all the way down here for nothing. Did the security company have the wrong address?

As he turned back toward his car he felt something hard clobber him on the back of the head. He fell to the ground, landing on his knees, and when he looked up he saw a group of thugs. They started in on him, punching, kicking, ransacking his pockets, grabbing his money, car keys, whatever they could get. They kicked gravel in his face; some landed in his mouth as it filled with blood. They shouted at him, "Leonard fuckin' Chess. Jew man. Rich kike record man." They ran the tread on their boots over his knuckles, making them bleed. They left him on the sidewalk, curled up and holding his ribs, a piercing pain gripping him each time he breathed.

Leonard didn't know how long he'd been down before someone spotted him and called an ambulance. He must have passed out at some point because the next thing he knew, he was in the hospital. Revetta, Phil and Leeba were standing around his bed. He was dizzy and stared at the brim on his brother's hat to stop the spinning. When he tried to move, a surge of pain shot through him, making him wince.

"Easy does it. You've got three broken ribs," said Phil.

Phil eventually asked Leeba to take Revetta home while he stayed with Leonard.

"I was set up," said Leonard after they left. "The guys who jumped me knew me. They called the house, said the alarm was going off, and they were waiting for me." He paused for a minute. "And they were Negroes. I

600

never had a problem with Negroes in my whole life."

"Why would a bunch of Negroes jump you? Of all people. You've given more money to the NAACP than anyone I know."

"Because nobody but you knows I do that." A sharp pain gripped him when he breathed too deeply and he had to pause for a moment. "Times are changing," he said after the spasm subsided. "When we got started in this business we all needed each other — they needed us as much as we needed them. There were no Negro record men back then. Now you got Vee-Jay and Motown and other labels — they're all run by coloreds. They've got coloreds in management and coloreds in sales and distribution."

"So what are you saying? Negroes don't need us anymore?"

"We're just in the way," said Leonard. "Maybe it's time to get out of this business. I'm tired, man. I'm tired of it all."

"First things first. You get better and then we'll talk about getting out of the business."

They kept Leonard in the hospital for five days. Five days of lying on his back thinking. Thinking and thinking some more. He and Phil had skated through the payola scandal. The FTC eventually dropped their charges and the IRS had nothing on Chess since they'd declared every penny spent on deejays as a write-off, a legitimate business expense.

But on the other side of payola it was a different ball game. There was no way to influence a record's chances of success. Now when he and Phil went on the road to see disc jockeys, they kept their hands in their pockets. They took 'em out for a nice dinner, but that wasn't enough to guarantee they'd get additional airplay. Plus, Chuck Berry was still in jail. He was writing songs while he was away, but they couldn't do any recording. Etta was taking off and, yeah, maybe Muddy, Wolf and Walter were doing fine in Europe, but back home their sales were still sliding. And now Aileen was gone. That stung. He'd known her from the time they were kids, back in the old neighborhood. He remembered the day her father died and six months later, he was there when she buried her mother. The kid had one tough break after another. She had the guts, though, and she'd gotten herself off the dope and everyone thought she'd beaten her demons. She was starting to make a comeback, too, but in the end the pain in her life was just too great.

Leonard attempted to roll onto his side and shake off the tears collecting in his eyes. He hated being in the hospital. People died in hospitals. Lying there made him depressed and ornery. He was giving his nurses a hard time, snapping at them when they took his temperature, checked his blood pressure, changed his dressings. To pacify him one of his nurses turned on the radio. Moms Mabley was doing a comedy bit about the good ole days and she made Leonard laugh in spite of himself. It shot daggers to his ribs, but he couldn't stop, and it was in the midst of laughing and crying that the light came on.

Phil stopped by the hospital later that day and Leonard couldn't wait to tell him.

"Radio. Negro radio."

"What?"

"You and me. We're gonna buy a radio station for Negroes."

"That's your big idea? You sure those thugs didn't give you brain damage? WGES and WOPA already have Negro programming."

"I'm not talking about *programming*. I'm talking about a station — a whole station — devoted to Negro music, Negro comics, Negro programming all day long, every day of the week."

Where Happy Folks Congregate. That was what the call letters, WHFC, stood for. *That'll be the first thing to go,* thought Leonard as he and Phil walked through the station with the current owner, Richard Hoffman. It was an AM station over on the 3300 block of South Kedzie. It was just 1,000 watts strong, even weaker at night, bringing its power and reach down to just 250 watts. Hoffman had an FM station as well, WEHS — *Elizabeth Hoffman*

603

station — named after his wife. They would change that, too.

Hoffman walked them from room to room as if it were a grand tour. "We do a variety of programming," he said. "We have a Spanish hour, a Lithuanian hour, a Polish hour. Our Sunday morning gospel programming is especially popular."

There was one main room with speakers mounted on the walls, a bunch of microphone and music stands and amplifiers pushed to the side. Part of a drum kit was stacked up, along with a broken accordion and a ukulele missing all its strings.

"What's with all this equipment?" asked Leonard, leaning against a piano in the corner.

"Oh, we used to do live performances down here. We'd broadcast right from this room. But we haven't done that in years." He did a *tsk tsk tsk.* "Most of it's junk now, I'm afraid, but that's still a good piano. I'd be willing to throw it in along with the sale."

"And the FM station, too?" asked Phil.

"And the FM station, too," he said.

Hoffman wanted out. That was clear. Leonard told him they needed some time to think it over and they still had to get clearance and a license from the FCC. He and Phil spent the rest of the day over at Blatt's crunching the numbers, plotting a lineup of deejays they thought they could lure over.

604

"I want this station to be for the Negroes," said Leonard, slurping his coffee. "I want it to be the voice of the Negro."

"Well, there's your call letters right there," said Phil. "VON — Voice of the Negro."

"Bingo." Leonard clapped his hands. "That's it. WVON."

"Don't you think we're getting a little ahead of ourselves? Hoffman's asking a million-five for the station," said Phil. "That's a lot of bread."

"Hell, he's ready to sell and I'm not offering more than a million. And he better throw in the FM station along with the piano."

Fifty-Four:
"Green Onions"

Red

"Well, good morning, Chicago. Hello, hello, hello. This is your Inside Man, Red Dupree, and this may be April Fool's Day but this here is no joke. Your Inside Man is coming to y'all live from the all-new Voice of the Negro on WVON AM 1450. We're gonna kick off our very first broadcast ever with Ray Charles doing 'You Are My Sunshine.' So sit back, relax and enjoy the Voice of the Negro coming your way every day, all day." Red dropped the needle on the turntable and eased back in his chair.

Back in March, one month before he went on the air with WVON, Phil had come to see him at the radio station in Gary where he was working, writing sponsor copy and maintaining the music library. But he wasn't on the air and he missed that part of the business. Red had just finished up for the day and Phil took him to a bar around the corner with a dartboard and pinball machines in the back. There was nobody in there and they sat side by side at the bar. Phil wasn't big on booze and it was a little early in the day for Red to start drinking so they both ordered soda pops. Leah had already told Red that the brothers had bought a radio station just for coloreds. They were going to broadcast twenty-four hours a day and they were having a hard time recruiting deejays.

"So what do you say?" Phil asked as he pulled his cigar from his mouth and set his hat down on the bar, his hair flat against his forehead. "How would you feel about coming with us and doing a show?"

Phil didn't have to ask twice. That night Red celebrated with Leah and James, and a few weeks later the Inside Man was back on the air, taking requests and telling his inside stories. He'd been corresponding regularly with Chuck Berry while he was in prison and read portions of his letters over the air. Red's listeners loved it. He told them how Jackie Wilson had gotten the nickname "Mr. Excitement" from a sixty-three-year-old fan. He invited his friends the Chiffons into the studio — all five of them cramped in the booth, hovered around two microphones. Red asked listeners to call in with questions. The switchboard could barely keep up. For such a small station, only 1,000 watts, word of the Inside Man and WVON caught on. It didn't take long for other deejays to come on board, too. The Old Swingmaster, Al Benson, and Pervis Spann, the Blues Man, came over, along with Herb Kent, the Cool Gent, and others.

Less than a month after WVON went on the air it was Good Friday and Red was in the booth. He'd just started playing Booker T. and the M.G.s' "Green Onions" when he got a call from his deejay friend Shelley the Playboy in Birmingham.

"There's trouble brewing down here," said Shelley. He gave Red a quick recap, telling him that Reverend King had been arrested for demonstrating in Birmingham. Shelley's words took Red back to that Greyhound in Anniston. He could hear those Klansmen calling for his death and Birmingham was even worse than Anniston.

"This thing is ready to break wide open," said Shelley. "Mark my words, I don't know what's going to happen, but I know Birmingham is never gonna be the same when this is done. I'm calling on my friends like you — you who have a voice on the radio — to let people know what's going on."

"I only have a thousand watts, but you know I'll give you all I got," said Red.

He hung up with Shelley Stewart and cut into Booker T. and the M.G.s. "This is Red Dupree, your Inside Man, with news coming out of Birmingham, Alabama. Now, y'all know that Birmingham is the most segregated city in this nation. That's why Reverend King has taken the movement there with the goal of desegregating that city. Because if we can integrate Birmingham, we can desegregate the Deep South.

"And y'all know the movement is committed to peaceful demonstration. I'm talking *nonviolent* boycotts of the stores in town, *nonviolent* sit-ins at lunch counters that refuse to serve our brothers and sisters. We are committed to fighting with dignity, not our fists. That's the strategy behind our struggle. And to think that our white brothers in Birmingham are accusing us of provoking their violent retaliations. This is how they justify responding to our peaceful protests not only by arresting hundreds of peaceful demonstrators but now they've also arrested Reverend King."

Red looked up and saw Phil and Leonard on the other side of the glass booth, watching him. And smirking. *Smirking!* It infuriated Red. He finally played another record and when the On Air sign flashed off, Leonard and Phil came into the booth to have a word with him.

Red was furious. They thought this was a joke. He chucked his headphones on the console and grabbed a cigarette. He'd been down this path before and had been fired from WGES for speaking his mind.

"I know, I know," said Red, his hands raised. "I know what you're gonna say. But let me just remind you that you're calling this station the Voice of the Negro for a reason and I think the colored community has a right to know what's really going on. Not every place is like Chicago — and this city is plenty segregated, too. Now if you want to fire me, then go right ahead, but if I stay on the air, don't expect me to back down on what I'm saying."

Phil and Leonard were laughing now.

"You think this is a joke? People are getting hurt down there. They're getting thrown in jail and for no good reason."

"Whoa, Red." Phil came over and placed his hand on his shoulder. "We're not laughing at you. I promise."

"Look," said Leonard, "Phil and I just came in here to tell you to keep going. We're loving what you're doing, motherfucker."

FIFTY-FIVE:
"WE SHALL OVERCOME"

LEEBA

Leeba and James were in the living room writing a song together. They were calling it "Windy City Blues." James played Red's old Stella while Leeba accompanied him on the piano. They didn't have all the lyrics down yet, but the melody was coming together.

"Okay," said Leeba, "let's modulate right here, like this —" She demonstrated and James smiled and followed on guitar. Creating this song with James reminded her of how her father had once played violin with her. It also reminded her of all the songwriting she'd done with Aileen.

After a few more minutes, Leeba said, "Okay, time for you to do your schoolwork." She gestured toward his books in the dining room.

He set his guitar down and went over to the table, but before he opened his math book James paused and said, "What was Red talking about on the radio today, Leah?"

"What in particular?"

"All that stuff about the movement and peaceful nonviolence. I don't get why they don't want anybody to fight back."

"They are fighting back, just not with their fists. With their words, with their dignity. And believe it or not, that's more powerful."

"I don't get it."

"You will one day."

"I wanna get it now."

Leeba went to his side. "Come sit with me." She led him to the davenport and put her arms around him, pulling him close. He was sixteen, soon to turn seventeen, already becoming a young man; and normally he'd fight her on that, but just then he let her hold him and even leaned into her, to be closer still. "There's a lot of ugliness in this world, James. You know how you're not always treated fairly just because of your race?"

He nodded.

"Well, it may be bad up here, but down South, especially in the Deep South, it's even worse for Negroes."

"But what has that got to do with what Red was talking about on the radio today about Birmingham?"

She rested her chin on his head. "People have had enough. They're sick and tired of being treated unfairly so they're starting to push back and take a stand for what's right."

"Is that what that Children's Crusade is all

about? I heard Red saying on the radio that they're telling kids to leave school and go down there and march."

"That's right." She stroked his hair. "Even here in Chicago you know you don't always get the same opportunities as white kids. But a lot of people are trying to change all that. We want you to be ready for that change. That's why Red and I are always on you about your schoolwork. We want you to go to college and fill your mind with all the knowledge you need so you can become whatever you want to be. We want you to have the same opportunities as any white child. That's why people are down in Birmingham protesting and marching. They're doing it for you. For your future."

"Then why aren't we down there with them?"

As soon as he said that it was like ice water on the face. So obvious and yet she'd missed it, until now. Yes, being a Freedom Rider had left her scarred, but in that instant Leeba knew what she had to do. She was going to Birmingham to march.

"I wanna go," said James. "I wanna stand up for myself."

Leeba wiped a tear running down her face. "You are so brave." She kissed his forehead. Now she would have to explain why she couldn't take him with her. "I'll go down," she said. "I'll go down and fight for you. I promise."

When Red got home that night, Leeba told him she was going to Birmingham. "I already checked the bus schedule. There's a Greyhound leaving here tonight. I'll be in Birmingham by noon tomorrow."

"I'm coming with you."

"No." She shook her head. "You need to stay up here — stay on the air and keep people informed. That's just as important. Where else are they going to hear the truth? You stay here and do your part on the radio and I'll go down to Birmingham and do mine."

Leeba packed a change of clothes and not much else. Red took her to the bus station just as the Greyhound was boarding. It was a calm spring night in early May. She hugged Red fiercely and kissed him hard on the mouth, not giving a damn who saw them. She told him she loved him and before she started to cry she climbed on board that bus.

There weren't many passengers and walking down the aisle reminded her of the day they boarded that Greyhound in Washington. Now as the bus was pulling away from the station she grew frightened and regretted not having Red with her. But as the miles rolled on, her courage and resolve came together.

They drove all night and the next day Leeba arrived in Birmingham. She checked into a motel and reported to the Sixteenth Street Baptist Church. Reporters were clustered outside the church and cameramen were everywhere: on the street corners, up in the trees, on the rooftops. Even before she told members of the movement who she was and said that she'd been a Freedom Rider on that Greyhound in Anniston, they welcomed her, offering her lemonade and sandwiches. Some squeezed her hands, others hugged her and thanked her for coming. She wept at their graciousness.

Groups of people were gathered around transistor radios, listening to Shelley the Playboy on WJLD and Paul White on WENN, waiting for instructions. A woman named Thelma explained that they had to be careful about what was said on the air because of Bull Connor, the commissioner of public safety. He was monitoring them, so everything was said in code.

"Now listen here, baby," said Shelley. "Some folk may not give y'all the time of day, but I sure will. And I do believe it's two thirty."

Thelma explained that Shelley meant they would start marching at two thirty.

"And don't y'all forget to pack your toothbrushes today."

"He's warning us that there's going to be arrests," said Thelma. "The idea is bring your toothbrushes since you're gonna be in jail."

By two o'clock the church was filled to capacity. Children of all ages — some much younger than James — congregated there, and in an orderly fashion they began making their way over to Kelly Ingram Park. Someone handed Leeba a sign — "We Shall Overcome" — and she entered the park carrying it, splinters in her hands from gripping the wooden stick so tight. She joined the others in singing "Lift Every Voice and Sing" and other freedom songs. As a Jew, Leeba had never knelt in prayer, but that day she got down on her knees with the others and prayed, prayed with all she had, until they heard the signal.

"We got the weather report," said Thelma. "Shelley just announced on the radio that it was 'cold outside' and in ninety-degree weather that means it's time to head toward city hall."

There were thousands of children marching along with Leeba and the other adults. In the heat of the South she got a chill when she passed by Bull Connor and his army of policemen, their clubs poised, itching to strike, holding back their attack dogs. Some of the police were attaching fire hoses to the hydrants, getting ready to turn them on.

Leeba was standing so close to Bull Connor, she could see his pink sweaty face and the broken capillaries across his cheeks as he shouted at the crowd, "I'm banning all demonstrations. Break it up. Now."

The marchers didn't budge. Bull shouted louder. "I said break it up. Now!"

The crowd kept marching and Leeba heard Bull say to his men, "That's it. Go on now, round 'em up and put 'em under arrest."

The police moved in fast, colliding with the crowd, their clubs swinging as people began to scream and flee. Leeba took off while the cops grabbed men, women and children and stuffed them inside paddy wagons. She saw the police laughing, calling the demonstrators names as they shoved them into the wagons, like it was a game to them.

Leeba made it safely back to her motel room that day and the first thing she did was turn on the TV and telephone Red. She was still panting while she told him everything. "It's all over the TV stations down here."

"Up here, too," he said. "They're saying the jails are full. And mostly with children. I've got James with me and we're watching the news right now."

"Let me talk to him." When James got on the phone he said he still wished he was down there fighting. "Let me fight this one for you," she said. "Believe me, I'm afraid you'll have plenty of opportunities to fight for yourself when you're a little older."

They talked a bit longer and before he put Red back on the phone James said, "Leah?"

"Yes?"

The line was silent. She almost thought he'd hung up until she heard him say, "Be careful, okay?"

She nodded into the receiver, too choked up to speak.

Early the next morning Leeba was back at the Sixteenth Street Church, gathered with others around the radio to hear Shelley the Playboy reporting the weather. "So okay now, babies, better wear your raincoats today . . ."

Leeba knew the code by now and that meant Bull Connor was going to use those fire hoses on them. As they left the church Leeba fell into line with the others, inching their way toward city hall. The sun was beating down, glaring in her eyes. Step by step, she was clapping, singing and marching with the other demonstrators.

About a quarter of a mile up the road they came to an impasse, standing face-to-face with swarms of riot police, dozens and dozens of white shirts standing two and three rows deep. Their dogs were pulling their leashes taut, waiting for the command to attack. She saw officers rapping their clubs to their open palms, anticipating Bull Connor giving the signal so they could start clobbering people.

They were singing "We Shall Overcome," drowning out Bull Connor's voice coming over a loudspeaker. "I'm warning you niggers to go on home. You have no license to be here parading. Now break it up."

The singing continued, their voices so loud that Leeba didn't even hear Bull Connor give the order. But all it took was a split second for the fire hoses to be turned on. She didn't know what hit her. It felt like a million knives stabbing her, sinking into her skin. The force caught her off guard. She swallowed a mouthful of water, making her gag. That water was still blasting. It went up her nose and in her eyes. She heard the screams but couldn't see through the rush of water pounding her face. Her feet had no traction; the water pushed her around like a dry leaf on a windy day. She slipped and fell, bit her tongue, a metallic taste filling her mouth. As soon as she got back up she was sprayed down again and rolled along the street. She managed to get back up and crouched down alongside a building, trying to shield a young boy with her body.

Finally the force of water moved off her and an eerie calm surrounded her. That was when she felt the sting of her injuries. She checked to make sure the people around her were okay and as she turned back around she saw the attack dogs charging toward them. Vicious barking. All teeth. The incisors sank in through her pants, clamping down to her bones. A riot policeman grabbed her by the arm and dragged her, pulling her along before he shoved her into the back of a paddy wagon.

They were plastered up against one another, some bleeding, everyone soaked from the fire hoses. When it wasn't possible to fit another demonstrator inside they slammed the paddy wagon door shut. It was dark, hot, hard to breathe, and Leeba began a claustrophobic panic until she heard a child's voice cutting through the commotion, singing, "Ain't Nobody Gonna Turn Me Around." Another voice joined in and another and another until everyone was singing and suddenly it wasn't so bad. They let the music get them through it.

When they arrived at the jail Leeba and the others were ushered past the reporters and cameramen and guards. If she thought the paddy wagon was crowded that was nothing compared to the cell she was crammed into. It was hot and packed, cockroaches crawling down the wall and over her feet. People were lined up in the back, taking turns using the one toilet, clogged and overflowing. They had every reason to be miserable and frightened. And yet, there was not one tear, not even from the youngest among them. Everyone was together, defiant, proud. They sang more freedom songs. They knew their purpose. They showed no fear. Leeba had never seen such a display of courage. They'd been blasted with water hoses, bitten by dogs, beaten with clubs, and whatever blood and torn clothing they had, whatever bruises and pains, they were worn like a badge of honor.

Leeba grew to admire and love those children, their spirit and the spirit of the other adults in the cell, too. She lost track of how long she'd been locked up. She had no idea what time it was. What day it was. She was too invigorated to sleep, too caught up in the movement, so that when one of the guards came and undid the lock and threw open the door she wasn't sure what to do. No one else knew, either.

"Go on. Move on out. Clear out. Your bail's been posted. Go on home."

Leeba inched her way out of the cell, watching the children become children again, running, scampering, scattering out of the jail. Leeba moved slower, more cautiously. She had no idea who had posted their bail until she turned the corner.

"You motherfucker you." Leonard smiled. He was standing there with Phil. They both held their arms out to her.

FIFTY-SIX:
"ROLL OVER BEETHOVEN"

LEONARD

Leonard sat at his desk at WVON fighting to stay awake. He was tired as all fuck. He wanted to stop or at least slow down, but he didn't know how. He had no shutoff valve. Even though they'd signed some new artists, like Buddy Guy and Koko Taylor, he was losing interest in the record business and now his obsession was the radio station.

It was June and the ratings had just come out. WVON was the number one station in the Chicago market, beating out WGN, WLS and stations with fifty times the power and reach. He never could have predicted this for his little 1,000-watt station. And now with all the commotion down South, the station's role in the civil rights movement was getting bigger. Leonard had watched the news coming out of Birmingham with tears in his eyes. He knew people on the front lines. Not just Leeba, but people like Ralph Abernathy and Reverend King. Sure, he and Phil had given money to the NAACP and CORE and they'd bailed hundreds of kids out of those Birmingham jails, but as far as Leonard was concerned, WVON was his most powerful weapon in the civil rights struggle.

He got up to get more coffee, sidestepping his way down the hall. The station was growing and they were packed in like sardines. The previous owner had left so much crap behind that was just eating up space — old office equipment, old reel-to-reels, the piano. He decided to make arrangements to move it all over to 2120. They'd store it there until he figured out what to do with it all.

In the meantime, he still had a record company to run, and later that afternoon Leonard and Phil were across the street at Blatt's sitting in their booth with Chuck Berry. He was finally out of prison and looking a little rough around the edges. He'd lost weight, his face showing every angle, but even so, Chuck was still one pretty-looking motherfucker.

Leonard and Phil were going back in the studio with Chuck to record the songs he'd written while he was in jail. Leonard especially liked "No Particular Place to Go" and "Nadine." But so much had changed in the music scene since Chuck had been away and Leonard worried if his sound would still be able to compete.

"What's happening with the Beach Boys?"

asked Chuck. "What did the lawyers say?"

"They're working on it," said Phil.

"Well, I sure hope so," said Chuck. "They stole my song. All you have to do is listen to those two songs side by side and you'll see. 'Surfin' U.S.A.' is 'Sweet Little Sixteen.' Note for note. It's my song and they stole it."

Phil placed a calming hand on Chuck's arm. "We know it is. Our lawyers know it is. They're working on it. It's just gonna take a little time."

"Right now we got a bigger problem," said Leonard. "It's called the Beatles."

"Vee-Jay's gotta be kicking themselves for letting those mop-tops get away," said Phil.

Chuck's brow furrowed. "What happened with Vee-Jay and the Beatles?"

"You ain't been keeping up with the business?" said Leonard. "Same thing that happened with Elvis." Leonard sympathized with Vee-Jay Records. They blew it with the Beatles just like he'd blown it with Elvis. And in his case it was all because of that fight he had with Sam Phillips over Ike Turner's bus fare.

"What happened," said Leonard, "was a few years ago the guys from Vee-Jay went to England and EMI over there sold them the rights for Frank Ifield. And to sweeten the deal, EMI threw in a new group called the Beatles."

Phil shook his head. "They were given the

golden goose and didn't even know it."

"So Vee-Jay releases the Beatles' first single — 'Please Please Me' and the motherfucker tanks. So did the single after that — 'Ask Me Why.' Vee-Jay still had another dozen or so songs from these guys sitting in the can, but they couldn't afford to release any more losers so the songs just sat there, collecting dust. Eventually the Beatles wanted out of their contract and Vee-Jay said, 'Hell yes. Go. Take your lousy music and go.' So they did and a year later they get snapped up by Capitol."

"And the rest," said Phil, "is history. Here we are, it's 1964, and we've got this thing called Beatlemania."

"And that's what we're up against," said Leonard.

"I'm ready," said Chuck. "I'm ready."

As they were leaving Blatt's, Leonard eyed Chuck head to toe. He didn't look ready. Chuck had always prided himself on being a sharp dresser, but styles had changed since he'd been locked up. Leonard's number one star was still walking around like it was 1958. All those checkered and plaid shirts were passé. Now the look was longer collars, wider ties, and men wore sports jackets with a pair of slacks instead of suits.

"Come with me, motherfucker." Leonard put his arm around Chuck's shoulder. "You and me are going on a little shopping spree."

Chuck needed a new wardrobe, all new threads, but he didn't need to get them at Saks Fifth Avenue. Leonard knew it was foolish, but he couldn't help himself. Even after all these years.

Shirley was still working there, still in the jewelry department. Leonard was glad she hadn't seen him walking in with Chuck looking so raggedy. First thing Leonard did was whisk Chuck off to the men's department.

The salesclerk knew Leonard from his previous spending sprees and recognized Chuck Berry right away. He brought out all the latest fashions. Chuck was a flashy guy on and off the stage and Leonard knew that. Chuck was looking for red suits, purple suits, loud shirts and shiny Stacy Adams shoes. He didn't go for the kind of classic, conservative clothes they sold at Saks.

Chuck looked at a price tag and balked. "You gotta be kidding me."

"Don't worry about the money," said Leonard. "I'm paying for all this."

When they got Chuck suited up in clothes that were all wrong for him, Leonard wanted to parade him over to the jewelry department and have Shirley show them Rolex watches.

"You're buying me a Rolex?" said Chuck, giddy with disbelief.

"Nothing but the best for you. Consider it your welcome home present."

They went to the jewelry department, all those sparkling cases, not a fingerprint on the glass. Shirley was behind the counter, ringing up another sale. Leonard stood off to the side and waited until she was finished before he and Chuck went over. He said hello and introduced her to Chuck.

"I'm a big fan of your music," she said before turning her focus back on Leonard. "You've done so well for yourself, Lenny. You must be very proud."

"What would your father think now, huh?" He laughed. "Give him my regards, will ya?"

"Leonard," she said with a pinched expression, "my father's dead. He died over seven years ago."

Leonard slapped his forehead. He felt like a clod and apologized, wishing he could dart out the door, forget this moment ever took place. But Shirley had already let it go and kept talking, chattering on while Leonard wrestled with his embarrassment.

"Do you remember the first time I brought you home to meet my father?" she asked with a smile.

He remembered. The problem was that he never forgot. Shirley was smiling at him now, leaning forward on the counter, reminiscent of the girl he'd once dated. Once loved. In many ways she looked the same and it wasn't that she was such a beauty. She wasn't nearly as attractive as Revetta. But Shirley had come to represent something to him. Something unobtainable. Through the years, he knew he could have had an affair with Shirley. The spark was still there in her eyes, but Leonard never pursued it. That wasn't what this was about.

Just then he wasn't sure *what* this was about anymore. He hadn't realized it until that moment standing there with Chuck, but after all this time he finally got it. Something had just shifted inside him; at long last he saw the absurdity of it all. *What the hell was he doing?* He'd just dropped almost a grand on clothes that Chuck would never wear and now he was going to drop another grand on a watch, and for what — to impress Shirley? Her father had died seven years before and he was still doing this shit. Still trying to show her and her dead father that he'd made it. Before her old man died he *knew* Leonard had made it. *Everyone* knew he'd made it. Leonard Chess, poor Polish immigrant, little Jew boy, dirty kike, had made more money than he ever could have imagined and he wasn't finished yet.

The whole shopping spree hadn't been for Chuck. It had all been for Shirley and a dead man. Suddenly Leonard understood that none of it mattered. He was good enough for Shirley. In fact, he was too good for her and not good enough for Revetta. He had a wife who loved him and put up with his nonsense. He had three kids who had grown up when he wasn't looking. Revetta always knew, always said that he was killing himself, missing out on his own life, and for what? For *this*? He realized how far off his aim had been. A wave of utterly depleting exhaustion came over him. It was as if all the long hours, the miles on the road and the sleepless nights had caught up to him. He was tired, man. It was time to go home. All the way home.

"C'mon, Chuck," he said, "let's get the hell out of here."

"Hey, wait. Wait a minute — what about my Rolex?"

FIFTY-SEVEN: "ROLLIN' STONE"

LEEBA

The radio was on in the bedroom. Leeba was listening to WVON as she stepped into a pair of Capri pants and zipped them up the back. She pulled on a black top and went to the mirror, where she slipped a white headband over her hair, which she'd recently had straightened. Twenty-three dollars to end a lifetime of longing. Now that she had that fine, silky hair she realized she preferred her natural curls. *It'll grow out,* she told herself while she clipped on her white hoop earrings and applied a thin sheen of pale pink lipstick.

The current show was wrapping up and then Red would come on. The Inside Man had one of the largest listening audiences. Red and the other deejays on WVON kept black Chicago informed on the issues. Red called for prayer vigils and peaceful demonstrations. His listeners trusted him and his was one of the opinions that weighed most heavily with them. He had civil rights leaders on his show, like Reverend James Bevel, James Farmer of CORE and Reverend King. And when he wasn't talking about the movement he was playing records and taking requests over the air. Red Dupree truly had become the Voice of the Negro.

Leeba was about to leave for work when she heard a commotion outside. Looking out the window she saw a moving van idling out front of their apartment. The doorbell rang a few moments later and a man standing at her threshold in a green uniform and cap said, "You Leah?"

"Yes."

"We got a delivery. Mr. Chess said to bring it to you."

"What?"

"I got a delivery. Mr. Chess wants it over here."

Leeba gazed out at the van, puzzled and annoyed. Leonard hadn't said a word about a delivery. What did he think — that she was his storage locker just because she and Red had a bigger place now?

"Where do you want it?" asked the deliveryman as the telephone rang.

"Oh, I don't know." She ran toward the kitchen to answer the phone and called back to him, "Just put it anywhere."

She caught the telephone on the seventh ring and as soon as she heard the lawyer's voice her pulse jumped. For a long time she and Red had accepted that they couldn't adopt James or be his foster parents, but out of the blue, two months back the lawyer Leonard had hired for them years before had contacted Leeba. He said there was a new organization handling adoptions for the state now: DCFS, the Department of Children and Family Services. He thought DCFS would be more lenient than the Department of Public Health in their fight to adopt James. Overnight their hope was reignited, their dream given a second chance.

"I'm calling," said the lawyer, "because I just spoke with the caseworker from DCFS."

Leeba cleared her throat and sat down at the kitchen table. A cool sweat had broken out along the back of her neck. "Well?" she asked, twisting the telephone cord about her wrist, pulling it tight.

"I'm sorry, Leah. They still feel that James would be better off being raised by two parents of the same race, meaning the Negro race."

Leeba released the tension on the phone cord and squeezed her eyes shut. Her mouth went dry.

"I know you don't want to hear this, but the court thinks James would benefit from being adopted by a couple that can provide an environment that will promote his culture, his heritage, his —"

"Do they know that I've been an active

member of CORE, that I marched in Birmingham? Do they know that I was a Freedom Rider? My husband and I were just down in Washington marching with Dr. King. I've *met* Dr. King. I've shaken his hand, I've —"

"Of course they know all that, Leah, but they've made their decision."

"Can we appeal it?"

He gave a long heavy sigh. "As your lawyer, I have to say that I don't see this turning in your favor. James is seventeen already. By the time we get this through the system again, it's going to cost more money, more time. He'll be eighteen soon and this'll be a moot point. He'll be an adult and can decide for himself."

After Leeba hung up with the lawyer she tried not to cry. She had cared for James as her son from the time he was eight. When he got sick, she was there. When he came home from school with his first A she was there. She had held his hand the first time he went to a dentist and had five cavities filled. She'd been there. Through birthdays and holidays she and Red had been there. And now the courts were denying them custody just because she was white. It was so unjust, and if her lawyer hadn't discouraged her from doing so, she would have gone to DCFS and talked to them, made them see how unfair this was. She and Red couldn't be the only couple trapped in this predicament.

Leeba heard the deliverymen out in the living room and went to see what was going on. The coffee table and sofa had been pushed out of the way and Aileen's plant, now full and thriving, was scooted to the side. Three moving men, in matching green uniforms, rolled in something big and bulky covered in a blue quilted blanket, secured on a dolly, held in place with ropes and buckles.

"What is this thing anyway?" she asked.

"A piano."

A piano? What was Leonard thinking? She already had a piano. Where was she going to put a second one?

The movers unbuckled the ropes and she was trying to hide her annoyance as they unwrapped the piano, piece by piece. When they unveiled the main section Leeba's eyes grew wide. This was not just a piano. This was a baby grand. They unwrapped the next section and the next. The whole time Leeba stood with her hand covering her mouth, thinking, *Oh my God, it can't be.* It wasn't just any baby grand but a Bösendorfer. She inched closer and let out an audible gasp. She couldn't believe it. There it was on the fallboard — the scratch, the thunderbolt. This was her piano — from the Maxwell Street Radio and Record Store, the one she'd been saving for that Bernard Abrams had sold out from under her. But like a lost cat that finds its way back home, her baby grand had come back to her.

"You okay, miss?" asked the driver. "Mr. Chess said to deliver it to this address. He said, 'Take it to Leah. She'll know what to do with it.' "

Leeba nodded, wiping the tears from her eyes as she signed the delivery form.

Days later Leeba was still stunned over the piano. She found out that Red had spotted it at the radio station, saw the scratch on the fallboard and realized that it was her Bösendorfer. He'd talked to Leonard about it and Leonard said he wanted Leeba to have it. Red coordinated the whole thing with Leonard. Even measured the room to make sure it would fit and made arrangements to have the old upright removed.

Leeba was thinking about all this as she was heading toward the studio. Coming up the sidewalk she saw a cluster of guys in mod-looking vests and jackets. Even before she heard their accents she knew that these boys with the long, long hair — even longer than the Beatles' — had to be the British musicians who were coming to record at Chess. They had pulled up along the curb outside of 2120 and were unloading a van packed with a drum kit, guitars, amps and a case of Jack Daniel's.

She remembered the day she and Marshall

went into Leonard's office to tell him and Phil about this band. Marshall had grown up around the studio and now he was working there full-time. He and Leeba understood why this band wanted to record in their studio, but Leonard wasn't in favor of it.

"Why the hell do they want to come all this way to make a record?" Leonard said. "We don't rent out the studio to bands. We record our own artists and that's it. They're not booking the studio for two solid days."

"They're huge blues fans," Leeba said. "Remember when the Beatles first came to America? All they wanted to do was meet Muddy and Bo Diddley."

"They're gonna tie up my whole operation here for two days," Leonard said.

"I spoke with their manager," said Marshall. "These guys are big in England. And Leeba's right. They're huge blues fans. They know all of Willie Dixon's and Howlin' Wolf's music and Little Walter's and Sunnyboy Slim's, too. They said their favorite bluesman is Muddy and they want to come record in the very same studio that their idol recorded in — and yeah, they called him their idol. These guys even named their band after one of Muddy's songs."

"No kidding, huh," said Leonard. Leeba could tell that he was beginning to soften.

"And don't forget," said Marshall, "if these guys record one of Mud's songs and it takes off like their other songs have, can you imagine the kind of money we're talking about?"

"He's got a point," Phil said, starting to come around to their side of the argument. "Those songs weren't worth shit when Muddy and Willie and the others first wrote them. Now think about the royalties that could come in for the songwriters."

"Not to mention the royalties for Arc," said Marshall.

"Okay, okay." Leonard held up his hands. "You can stop selling. Go ahead and book them. But you" — he pointed at Leeba — "keep an eye on them while they're here."

Leeba was remembering all this when one of the Brits called to her. "Excuse me, miss? Is this the location of Chess Records?"

"It is. And you must be the Rolling Stones."

"Yes. Yes, we are."

"Welcome."

Leeba looked up the sidewalk and there was Muddy, right on time. She'd called him earlier and told him that his biggest fans were coming to record with Chess and invited him to the studio to meet them. "Hey, Muddy." She waved to him.

"That's him?" said one of the band members, visibly giddy and awestruck. "That's Muddy Waters?"

Leeba smiled. "That's him, all right. Hey, Muddy, I do believe these fellows have come quite a long way just for you."

Muddy said hello and shook their hands and the Brits gushed like schoolgirls meeting their crush. The one guy named Mick just smiled — all teeth, cheeks puffed up high. The band members had their guitars, drums and equipment stacked up on the sidewalk next to their van, the June sunlight glinting off the cymbals.

"Let me give y'all a hand here," said Muddy, grabbing hold of an amp. "We'll go up the back way. Closer to the studio."

The band members were nudging each other, grinning — they couldn't believe it.

When they got inside, Leonard and Phil came into the studio. Leeba made the introductions and again the Rolling Stones gushed over meeting the brothers.

Leonard shook their hands and said, "Just don't make a mess." He turned around and walked back into his office.

Phil, being Phil, stood around and made small talk with the guys, asked about their flight over, their hotel and when the hell they were going to get haircuts.

When it was time to start recording, Leonard and Phil were both out of the office, over at WVON. Leeba hung around the studio in case the band needed anything. She watched the Rolling Stones guzzle whiskey, each band member pulling from his own bottle and firing up cigarettes between takes. There was a giant cloud of smoke hovering above them. The studio always took on a certain scent during recording sessions: a combination of sweat, smoke and booze. But this time, the smell was more acrid. The studio reeked of them. It was like they hadn't bathed in a week and the stench grew more pungent over the next two days. They were working hard and fast, laying down a slew of tracks. They recorded Muddy's "I Can't Be Satisfied" and Chuck Berry's "Around and Around." They did some old Willie Dixon numbers and Big Bill Broonzy songs, too. Each time someone came into the studio Brian Jones or Keith Richards would stop playing and say, "Is that him? Is that Willie Dixon? Was that Little Walter?"

After they'd recorded their last track the engineer marked up the master tapes and stepped out of the booth. Leeba took a seat in the control room and through the glass window she looked out onto the studio, watching the Rolling Stones coil up power cords, tuck guitars in their cases. They were just about done packing up when Muddy stopped by. They seemed just as starstruck around him then as they had been the first day they met him.

"Where y'all rushin' off to?" Muddy asked, picking up his white Fender electric. "Thought we'd have us a little fun before y'all leaves town."

That was all it took for the guitars to come back out, and within minutes all of them joined in on a jam session. They were playing Muddy's "Baby Please Don't Go." Muddy was sitting down, dressed in a beautiful silk suit and tie. Mick, Keith and Brian stood around him in their sweat-soaked shirts with sleeves rolled to their elbows, top buttons and vests undone and ties loosened about their necks. Charlie Watts was back on the drums and Bill Wyman was laying down the bass line. Mick and Muddy traded off, taking turns with the lyrics, Muddy calling out a line and Mick answering back. Muddy and Keith did the same with the guitar solos.

Leeba wished they'd been recording this because she recognized that she was witnessing a powerful moment. Back in 1947 when she went to work with Leonard and Evelyn at Aristocrat, who would have imagined, who could have possibly predicted, that what they once called race music would become all this? Who knew that the music could have crossed an ocean and erased the line that separated white from black?

She watched Muddy singing and laughing with his new friends and she just knew that something historic was going to come out of this day.

EPILOGUE:
"WINDY CITY BLUES"

1969

Phil sobbed the whole way back to Glencoe. How he made the drive he'd never know. The police had telephoned earlier. He'd been at the office, on another call with a distributor, which he'd put on hold. He never went back to that call. The officer said he needed Phil to come down and identify the body.

It had started to drizzle and as Phil turned on the windshield wipers it cleared away the present and took him back. All the changes from the last few years flashed before him. There were young boys going off to fight in Vietnam, Martin Luther King had been fatally shot, some crazy cult in California had gone on a killing spree, Elvis was playing Vegas and outdoor concerts were lasting three whole days.

Closer to home the Chess family had lost Little Walter, his antics finally catching up to him in February 1968. Walter opened his mouth to the wrong guy and got beaten to death. Record Row was dying, too. Vee-Jay Records had fallen on hard times. Some of the other labels had also gone under.

Chess, on the other hand, had expanded. They'd outgrown 2120 and moved to a bigger building at 320 East Twenty-first Street. Leonard had always dreamed of having a one-stop shop with a studio, a pressing plant and all their offices — the whole operation — under one roof. And he finally got it.

But the biggest change came when, after all that, Leonard and Phil decided to sell the label. It was time. It was everybody's music now, not just music for blacks. And they were blacks now. Not coloreds, not Negroes. It was the age of Black Power and Leonard and Phil had had a good run. So they sold Chess Records to GRT, General Recorded Tape. GRT made reel-to-reels, and those new eight-tracks and cassettes. They wanted to get into the record business and Leonard and Phil wanted out.

Leeba was smart. She'd seen what was happening and even before they sold the company she had one foot out the door. She was still doing a little songwriting here and there, but now her real work was for the Department of Children and Family Services. She'd found her calling in finding homes for orphaned and abandoned children. It made sense. She and Red had fought their own battle trying to adopt James. So now she was helping other couples do the same and by the time they sold the label, Leeba had already resigned and accepted a job with DCFS.

When the artists found out they were selling Chess, they took it hard.

"I've done for you all that I can," Phil remembered Leonard saying to Muddy and Wolf. "You've got major rock bands covering your songs now. I put you motherfuckers on the map — you don't need me anymore."

Phil blinked away fresh tears and thought about the last time he saw Leonard. It was just that morning. October 16, 1969. Leonard had gotten into a screaming match with the guys at GRT over some outstanding bills and Phil recalled walking him out to his car trying to calm him down.

"You gotta watch your temper, motherfucker," he'd said, waving a finger in Leonard's face.

Leonard had cracked a smile as he got into his Cadillac and drove off toward WVON. Phil was supposed to meet him at the station after lunch that day for a meeting that would never take place. Because fifteen minutes after Leonard left Phil, he suffered a massive heart attack while he was driving. It happened just a few blocks away from WVON. Leonard was found slumped over his steering wheel. His Cadillac hit two parked cars.

Phil dried his eyes as he pulled up to Leonard's house in Glencoe. He recognized the cars out front. Marshall, Susie and Elaine were there. So were Revetta, Sheva and Phil's kids. They all knew there'd been an accident; they heard it had been Leonard's car, too. Now Phil was confirming what they already knew, though they didn't want to accept it: the body inside was that of fifty-two-year-old Leonard Chess.

After the funeral, after the family had sat shiva and everyone had gone back to their lives, Revetta found herself alone. No one there to coddle the grieving widow. What was there to do but wander through the big house that had meant so much to Leonard, even though he was hardly ever there. Now it seemed too big. It was so empty, so quiet. She could hear the water lapping against the sides of the swimming pool out back. She should have already drained the water for winter, but that was something Leonard always handled. If the pool remained filled it seemed like he was still around, just waiting to get to it. But that game only worked for so long. Truth was he had left her with all *this* and now she didn't know what to do with it. She sat down on the staircase and sobbed.

Weeks went by and it was time to pack up Leonard's things. He never did make out a will. Phil had already taken the few things he wanted, mostly old photographs. Marshall had his father's watch and Elaine had his ring resized for her. Susie got the diamond from his stickpin. Even in death he was still giving them *things* when what they wanted was him. Now it was too late.

She sealed up a box of his sweaters and vests, and tried to picture life without him, forecasting five, ten, fifteen years into the future. She stacked the box on top of the others she'd already packed. Goodwill would be by in the morning to pick them up. There was still the chest of drawers in their bedroom that she needed to go through. Socks and boxer shorts, undershirts and pajamas. She scooped them up and dropped them into a box. When Revetta opened the bottom drawer she found handkerchiefs and a couple old sweaters he never wore. And under those she saw the Saks Fifth Avenue boxes. She knew immediately what they were. Her thirty-fifth birthday presents. He was supposed to have taken them back to the store, but obviously he never did. Two of the boxes were still gift-wrapped, the tape and bows yellowing with age. She looked at the necklace, remembering how furious she'd been with him when he gave it to her. She still had no idea what was in the other boxes that she had refused to open.

As promised, Goodwill came the next day and carted everything away. After they left, Revetta fixed her hair and makeup. It was the first time in weeks that she put her face on and dressed up, changing into a brown tweed skirt and jacket that was one of Leonard's favorites. She'd never liked driving into the city and rode the train downtown instead. It was chilly; the November winds were already picking up steam, coming off the lake. Some of the stores along Michigan Avenue already had their Christmas decorations up.

As she pushed through the revolving door at Saks Fifth Avenue, the store was playing the Muzak version of "Johnny B. Goode." Leonard had always liked that Chuck Berry song. She took it as a sign.

As she made her way to the jewelry counter she tried to recall the last time she'd seen Shirley. It was back in the old neighborhood. Shirley was at the butcher's buying skirt steaks. She remembered thinking at the time that Shirley had heavy legs.

When Shirley turned around at the cash register, Revetta double-checked her name tag to make sure it was her. It had been that long, and Shirley's hair was more gray than brown now. She had a ribbon on her tag, some sort of award for excellence. By now Shirley noticed Revetta and both women looked at each other for a moment before either one spoke.

"Revetta," she said finally, "I'm sorry about Leonard. Really I am."

"I know you are." Revetta smiled and they

lapsed into another silence.

"Is there something I can do for you?" Shirley asked eventually.

Revetta shook her head as she reached into her pocketbook and pulled out the gift-wrapped boxes she'd found in the bottom drawer. She handed them to Shirley along with the necklace.

"I think Leonard really bought these for you. I think he'd want you to have them."

He was nervous, standing backstage, too afraid to steal a glance at the audience. He'd never played in front of so many people before. This wasn't like the little neighborhood gigs and joints he was used to. No, this was the big time. This was the Chicago Theatre.

He finally peered around the stage curtain. Every seat in the house was filled and almost every face was white, except for Red's. You couldn't miss him and that Afro of his. He was sitting right in the front row with Leah. She had a 'fro, too — modest, though, kept short and close to her head. It was because of the two of them that he was there at all and he knew that.

Muddy was in the middle of "I'm Your Hoochie Coochie Man" and he was groovin'. The man was the definition of cool, leaning against a stool in his tailored suit, his slide guitar squealing and twisting. And that voice.

No one sounded like the Mud. The crowd was going nuts, singing along, swaying back and forth. When Muddy played that last note, the applause seemed to go on forever. It sounded like thunder and that kicked his nerves up another notch because any second now he'd be out there, in front of them all.

Muddy grabbed hold of the microphone and thanked the audience while their applause died down. ". . . And now I wanna introduce y'all to a fine young musician . . ."

This is it. Here we go.

". . . Let's bring him on out here. Ladies and gentlemen, get ready for Ja-a-mes Du-pr-e-e-e!"

James's legs were shaking as he took his place center stage. Muddy shook his hand, whispered in his ear, "Go get 'em," and made his exit. James was on his own now with Muddy's band backing him. He couldn't make out any faces in the audience; the stage lights were blinding. He closed his eyes and took a deep breath. He clutched his guitar, his father's secondhand Stella, and played the opening chords of "Windy City Blues." He opened his eyes, opened his mouth, and the song began to happen, coming out of him like it'd been sitting there, waiting on him all this time, all his life. He was on his way, the next generation, there to carry on the tradition of the blues.

AUTHOR'S NOTE

The subject of the blues is vast and impossible to cover fully in one book, let alone a novel. The Chess Records story is at the heart of the blues and therefore at the heart of this book. Chess and its iconic artists not only created a new sound for Chicago and the country, but they took their Chicago sound around the world. By recording electrified blues this music laid the foundation for rock 'n' roll and helped to blur the racial color line for a new generation.

My intention was to let the Chess Records story stand as the cornerstone of this novel while weaving in the fictional lives of characters Leeba Groski, Red Dupree, Aileen Booker, J.J. Johnson, Mimi Cooke, Smitty and the Groski family.

As much as I've tried to tell the story of how the blues got started in Chicago, I have taken some literary license with certain events, details and embellishments that grew out of my imagination. For instance, Chuck

Berry indeed had his run-ins with the law. In fact, he had two trials and ultimately went to jail for violating the Mann Act. For the purpose of this book, I combined those two incidents and moved up his jail time.

Similarly, Aristocrat Records was founded in 1947 by Evelyn and Charles Aron along with their partners, Mildred and Fred Brount and Art Spiegel. For the purpose of this novel I chose to focus on the partnership between Evelyn and Leonard (who soon joined Aristocrat to help with distribution). Together, Evelyn and Leonard were equally instrumental in launching Muddy Waters's career.

The original second guitarist in Muddy Waters's first electric band was Jimmy Rogers, but for the purpose of this book, I've substituted the fictional Red Dupree. I mean no disrespect to the talented Jimmy Rogers, who is later identified as Muddy's second guitarist in these pages.

The Five Blazes changed their name to the Four Blazes in 1949 when a member dropped out of the group in 1948.

Please note that I have also compressed the following timelines in order to help the flow of the narrative: Tom Archia's "Fishin' Pole" was recorded in July 1947 rather than April 1947. Al Morgan's "Jealous Heart" was released in 1947 rather than 1949. Sunnyland Slim's "Johnson Machine Gun" was recorded in September 1947 rather than February

1948. The Rendezvous in Memphis opened in 1948 and here Leonard pays his first visit to the restaurant in 1947. Theresa's Lounge opened in December of 1949 rather than November 1949 as I have suggested here. The Macomba Lounge fire occurred in the fall of 1950 rather than January of 1950. Bo Diddley appeared on *The Ed Sullivan Show* on November 20, 1955, rather than in September 1955.

Over the years Chess Records created several subsidiary labels, including Checker, Argo and Cadet. For simplicity's sake I put all the artists and their records under the Chess label.

Also please note that while "Bilbo Is Dead" met with controversy at white radio stations in the South, it did not generate a boycott or create the kind of backlash depicted here. That was the fiction writer in me, embellishing the premise for the sake of the story.

I did a great deal of research for this book and was fortunate enough to talk with several members of the Chess family, including Pam, Terry and Roberta Chess. I also had several meetings with Keith Dixon, Willie Dixon's grandson, and spoke with blues musicians Sly Johnson and Chuck Crane. Many of the details from the Children's March in Birmingham were relayed to me by Shelley Stewart during our interview as well as through his book *Mattie C.'s Boy.*

I would also like to acknowledge the work of authors and filmmakers who provided me with excellent source material. I've listed them all here and highly recommend them for further exploration of the blues, Chess Records and the civil rights movement.

BOOKS

The Record Men: The Chess Brothers and the Birth of Rock and Roll by Rich Cohen (New York: W. W. Norton, 2005)

Spinning Blues into Gold: The Chess Brothers and the Legendary Chess Records by Nadine Cohodas (New York: St. Martin's Press, 2000)

Deep Blues by Robert Palmer (New York: Viking, 1981)

When I Left Home: My Story by Buddy Guy (Boston: Da Capo Press, 2012)

Can't Be Satisfied: The Life and Times of Muddy Waters by Robert Gordon (Boston: Little, Brown, 2002)

Chicago Blues: The City and the Music by Mike Rowe (New York: Da Capo Press, 1981)

A Natural Woman: A Memoir by Carole King (New York: Grand Central, 2012)

Chuck Berry: The Autobiography by Chuck Berry (New York: Harmony Books, 1989)

Mattie C.'s Boy: The Shelley Stewart Story by Don Keith (Montgomery, AL: NewSouth

Books, 2013)

Race Mixing: Black-White Marriage in Postwar America by Renee Christine Romano (Cambridge, MA: Harvard University Press, 2003)

The Jews of Chicago: From Shtetl to Suburb by Irving Cutler (Urbana: University of Illinois Press, 1996)

Chicago's Jewish West Side by Irving Cutler (Chicago: Arcadia, 2009)

Chicago's Maxwell Street by Lori Grove and Laura Kamedulski (Chicago: Arcadia, 2002)

DOCUMENTARIES AND FILMS

The Howlin' Wolf Story: The Secret History of Rock and Roll directed by Don McGlynn

Deep Blues: A Musical Pilgrimage to the Crossroads directed by Robert Mugge

Martin Scorsese Presents the Blues: Godfathers and Sons directed by Marc Levin

Maxwell Street Blues directed by Linda Williams and Raul Zaritsky

Record Row: Cradle of Rhythm and Blues written by Geoffrey Baer and Michael McAlpin

Cheat You Fair: The Story of Maxwell Street directed by Phil Ranstrom

Cadillac Records directed by Darnell Martin

Who Do You Love directed by Jerry Zaks

Freedom Riders directed by Stanley Nelson

King (miniseries) directed by Abby Mann
Born in Chicago directed by John Anderson

■ ■ ■ ■

READERS GUIDE:
WINDY CITY BLUES

RENÉE ROSEN

■ ■ ■ ■

QUESTIONS FOR DISCUSSION

1. *Windy City Blues* is set in the 1940s, 50s and 60s and deals with themes of racism and segregation. Given today's rise in racial tensions, do you think as a nation we've made progress in terms of racial discrimination or do you see us going backward?

2. Leonard Chess was a complex man. What did you think about his motivations for wanting to be successful? How did you think he treated his artists? And Leeba? In the end, did you think he was a savvy businessman or someone who exploited his musicians? Or perhaps something in between?

3. As *Windy City Blues* points out, there were many similarities between Jewish immigrants coming from Eastern Europe and black migrants come up from the South. Did this parallel surprise you? What did you think about the way the two groups helped each other? Do you think that same alliance still exists today?

4. It was a fact that Leonard and Phil Chess did not possess any musical abilities of their own and yet they were two of the most celebrated record producers of all time and were inducted into the Blues Hall of Fame and the Rock & Roll Hall of Fame. What was it about them that you think made them so successful? What do you consider to be their biggest contributions to the blues and rock 'n' roll?

5. The payola scandal truly shook up the radio and record industries, and yet in the end the "pay to play" practice was not found to be illegal. The only crime involved was not reporting and paying taxes on the money the deejays and stations received. Do you still think it was wrong for record companies to pay in exchange for airplay? Do you think they misled and manipulated the listening public? And if so, how is that different from today's manufacturers — of everything from soda pop to shampoo — paying retailers for display space and product placement in movies and videos?

6. As an interracial couple, Leeba and Red faced many obstacles. What stood out to you as their most difficult struggles? In 2017 do you think an interracial couple would experience any of the same challenges? Or do you think it's a nonissue in today's environment?

7. When Red and Leeba become involved in the civil rights movement they basically put their lives on the line for their cause, as did the real-life Freedom Riders and civil rights activists. Is there a cause in your life now that you feel just as passionately about? What social movements under way now are just as important as the civil rights movement?

8. Leeba's mother strongly disapproved of her friendship with Aileen and her marriage to Red. How did you feel about Mrs. Groski? Did you think she was a hypocrite? Why do you think Leeba never shared her mother's racist views?

9. Despite coming from such different backgrounds, Leeba and Aileen share a very tight and special friendship. Obviously Aileen has some demons and emotional problems, but still Leeba stood by her side. Did you think Leeba's devotion to Aileen was admirable or unhealthy?

10. Many music critics and music historians have stated that if Chuck Berry had been white, he would have surpassed Elvis in popularity. Do you think that's true? What did you think about Berry's run-in with the law?

11. It's often been stated that popular music,

especially rock 'n' roll, can be traced back to the days of gospel, jazz and the blues. The Rolling Stones are mentioned in *Windy City Blues,* but can you think of other examples of artists and bands that were heavily influenced by the blues?

ABOUT THE AUTHOR

Renée Rosen is the bestselling author of *White Collar Girl, What the Lady Wants, Doll-face* and the young adult novel *Every Crooked Pot.* She lives in Chicago. Visit her online at reneerosen.com, facebook.com/ReneeRosen Author and twitter.com/ReneeRosen1.

The employees of Thorndike Press hope you have enjoyed this Large Print book. All our Thorndike, Wheeler, and Kennebec Large Print titles are designed for easy reading, and all our books are made to last. Other Thorndike Press Large Print books are available at your library, through selected bookstores, or directly from us.

For information about titles, please call:
(800) 223-1244

or visit our website at:
gale.com/thorndike

To share your comments, please write:
Publisher
Thorndike Press
10 Water St., Suite 310
Waterville, ME 04901